# CRAITOR'SDAUGHTER

## LILY DEWARUILE

# TRAITOR'SDAUGHTER

*Lily Dewaruile*

o o o o o

# Eres

EresBooks.com

o o o o o

o o o o o

Also by Lily Dewaruile

*Invasion (Pendyffryn: The Conquerors #1)* November 2012
*Salvation (Pendyffryn: The Conquerors #2)* January 2013
*Betrayal (Pendyffryn: The Conquerors #3)* March 2013
*Revival (Pendyffryn: The Conquerors #4)* June 2013

Forthcoming in the *Pendyffryn: The Conquerors* Series
*Reconciliation (Pendyffryn: The Conquerors #5* Summer 2013

Forthcoming in *The Tywi* Series
*Vengeance's Son* Fall 2013 (The Tywi: Book Two)

A Glossary of Welsh words, as well as further information, is
provided at the end of this book for your convenience.

o o o o o

ISBN: 0-6158440-5-7
ISBN-13: 978-0-6158440-5-3

# ΟΕΟΙCΑΤΙΟΝ

I'm cyfeillion, am ddarllen, holi a mwynhau'r
stori hon.

*To my friends, for reading, questioning and enjoying this
story.*

# CONTENTS

# ACKNOWLEDGEMENTS

Hoffwn ddiolch i Judith Chilcote a'i staff a rhoddodd y hyder i fi i barhau ysgrifennu.

*I would like to thank Judith Chilcote and her staff who gave me the confidence to continue writing.*

# ONE

*The woman's hand grew cold as the child pressed it to her cheek. Color drained first from the manicured tips of the woman's fingers and a red necklace the child had never seen before spilled its beads over her linen tunic. The soldier dragged his hand over the child's hair, crushing her small head, forcing her to watch as the woman crumpled to the ground. Beads trickled from his sword, splashed into her eyes, dripped from her hair onto her cheeks.*

Heledd shook the dream from her head, the dream she had when she was too tired to resist her fascination for the beads cascading to the stone floor of the round house. Nothing else of the day, fifteen years before, remained in her memory. She never saw the face of the soldier who killed her mother, but the memory of blood, its hideous metallic taste filling her mouth, remained.

The steaming heat in the valley where the River Tywi began its rush to the sea whipped into her face the moment she emerged from the *beudy*. Her work in the milking shed was finished for the day and she had a few moments before she had to go into the oven the kitchen became at that time of day. The top of her linen tunic hung over the strings at the back of her milking apron and her bare arms absorbed the sun and browned as though she was the bread in the oven. As she walked across the yard, she imagined the brown dappling on her skin spread from her pale shoulders down her arms to her already darkened wrists. One of the other milkmaids nudged her in the ribs. Heledd turned her head with an inward groan to see her cousin, Alys Llew, on the wide stone wall and her cousin's ten year old

3

maidservant, Betsan, coming toward her.

Rolling her head slowly from side to side to relieve the ache in her shoulders, Heledd changed her direction and climbed the steps to stand on the wall of her uncle's hill *caer*. Staring at the crest of the mountain towering over her, she took her place beside Alys to comply with the younger girl's demand for company. Though she had never traveled more than an hour's walk in any direction, Heledd did not share her cousin's craving to study every new face appearing among the soldiers in her uncle's war band.

"I'm sure Dada is preparing for war," Alys said, dragging Heledd to the edge of the wall. "These men fight like wolves. Look at that one, Heledd." Her cousin pointed through the field toward two men striking at each other with short swords, defending against blows with the round shields strapped to their arms.

"Which one?" Heledd asked without looking. One shouted. The other hissed. The metal of one's sword struck the edge of the other's shield and Heledd's throat seemed to fill with the taste of her own blood. She lifted her chin, clenched her body but imagined the blade – hot with the fury of the soldier's rage – slice through her belly. With each strike they took against one another, she felt their grunts and shouts pierce her skin. They trained on a patch of ground that, until a few days before, had been a wheat field in which Heledd and the other servants had toiled to bring in the harvest. Toil had been her life since she was old enough to stand. "May I go?"

"Look at the tall one, with dark hair," Alys said. "He's magnificent and so strong." Since the harvesting had finished, the visit to the wall had become a customary respite in the daily drudgery of the small amount of work Alys did on the estate. She had an avid interest in every new man who wore her father's colors. Her only useful occupation was weaving and she excused herself from the task as often as possible to educate herself to the ways of men. She turned her blue eyes on her cousin. "Why are you always so reluctant to watch them? You could easily do battle with any one of these warriors, Heledd."

"Why do you say that?" Heledd asked, knowing she gave Alys another opportunity to wound her. In the same year Hywel had celebrated ten years on his throne, Meilor Gwesyn had descended from among the high mountains to the north to murder her family and avenge her father's betrayal. From the age of three, Heledd Bannawg had lived as a prisoner of war and bondservant to her uncle. Though she was a member of his household, Heledd had none of the privileges her cousins enjoyed. She was now old enough to have a husband, but she had been denied the right to wed. Her claim to her father's property was lost when Ieuan Bannawg betrayed his brother and his friends.

"Look at your arms. You are so muscular. Are your legs the same? Let me see," Alys demanded, gesturing for Heledd to lift the skirt of her plain frock. Heledd pulled the back of the ragged skirt up to her knee and dropped it at once. "Take off that awful scarf. You look like an old woman." Heledd raised her hands, untied the knot at the back of her neck and drew the white scarf clear of her blood red hair. The severe plait tumbled down her back and she twisted it up again into a tight knot at the back of her head. "You do look like a man, you know. A young one, of course, but that soldier – the handsome one training with Urien Macsen – has been watching you ever since you joined me here. He must be wondering what you are."

Against all her strongest instincts, Heledd looked in the direction her cousin indicated and saw Urien, the commander of her uncle's war band, with the dark-haired soldier. Both men were looking in her direction and she lifted her chin, turning her gaze again toward the mountain in the west. "They are soldiers. I don't care what they think. There are always too many."

"What do you expect?" Alys laughed. "We are here to watch them train."

"You are here to watch them. You have called me here to keep you company," Heledd replied, steadfastly gazing at the Gurnos but it hid the sun from her.

"My father needs these men – to protect us. Would you rather have no one to lift a sword to defend you when our enemies come – as my father did when he was betrayed by his own brother? Not one of our enemies would distinguish between me and the daughter of a traitor. You would be at their mercy as much as I, perhaps more so … if they knew who you were."

In the moment the tall woman on the wall removed her scarf, Garmon's sword was raised at arm's length at his shoulder, ready to strike his opponent. He saw her hair tumble from its constraint, as red as the rowan berry, gilded by the blaze of the lowering sun behind her. Urien's blade struck him, flat-edge, on his upper arm.

"Do you like that one?" Urien laughed.

"Who is she?"

"One of the dairy women, a bondservant. Alys Llew is her mistress."

"Her name?"

"Heledd."

Garmon considered the sound. His education painted the picture that felled Troy, the same beauty worked its poison to fell him. "Does she have a favorite?"

"Not that one. Llew has wanted to breed her since she came to womanhood but none of my men will have her. Talk is she will go to Meilor Gwesyn."

Garmon glanced over his shoulder at his friend and commanding officer. "He's—. Meilor Gwesyn won't …"

"He'll tame her," Urien said, "or break her. Llew would rather his soldiers have the pleasure." Urien's laugh struck Garmon between his shoulder blades, just as the woman lifted her face toward the west. "If no one else, though she's not to my liking," Urien continued, "I'll have her. Better an even older man than you, Garmon, than chained alive in Meilor's cromlech." He dropped his hand on his friend's neck. "She isn't to your taste. A man with your schooling—."

"Is she always so arrogant?"

"Not always, but often. Some say her smile, when she offers

one, can break a man, even one as hard as you."

Garmon's jaw set and his granite-hued eyes narrowed. "You know me well."

"Well enough, Northerner. It's a rare man can bring a smile to that one's lips. I'll stake a month's drink on your determination, Garmon, against her pride."

"I do not wager for women, Southerner."

"Whatever you do, she is destined for Meilor's bed unless she's taken."

"You know my reason, Urien. There is only one way I will take any woman," Garmon said, flexing his arm and striking his commander's shield. "Let us finish this."

"That can be arranged, brother," Urien grinned, throwing his weight into the blow, driving the northerner back a step. "You know the law. Make your choice. She will be for the next man to speak. I will not standby for Meilor to leave his mark."

"You are too old, Southerner. Neither you nor Meilor Gwesyn will have her." His blows thundered on Urien's defenses, greeted by laughter and equal force as they crushed the grain stocks with their studded boots.

Llew's warriors were the same men who cut the wheat, working alongside the other inhabitants to bring in the harvest. The warrior staring at her had come since the harvest or Heledd would have worked beside him while he reaped, she had grown so much taller than the other women.

"Your pride will not deter that one," Alys said, tilting her head to the side to study the newest recruit. "I think he must be wondering what he would have to do to you to bring you down. I think he wants—."

"How can you know what he wants?" Heledd asked, turning on her heel, her chin rising with each insult her cousin flung at her. "You know even less of men than I do."

"I think that one will teach you soon enough, more than you want to know, Heledd—. Oh, why are you so angry? I'm only teasing you. You're in no danger of ever knowing anything about that – except in the way of all Bannawg women." She glanced at Urien Macsen and his comrade. "I wonder where he was before he came here." Alys leaned forward for a closer look at the men in the harvested field.

"He is only a soldier," Heledd said, her gaze traveling across the horizon toward the setting sun. If ever her uncle decided to trade her for land or loyalty, she had only one favor to beg of him: that the man was not a soldier.

"My brothers are soldiers," Alys said. "You like them well enough."

She did not like her cousins any more than she liked soldiers or the endless toil of her life. She did not like she was a prisoner of war or that she could not read or write. She did not like that all of her days began at daybreak and ended with the darkness, without beauty or song or any other thing to lift her heart. When Alys, at seven, was sent to the cloister school to learn reading as well as other skills, Heledd had already worked for six years with the house servants and the stewards in menial tasks. She was not allowed to learn the precious skill of cheese-making. Alys was betrothed to Meilor Gwesyn's son – an allegiance forged in the blood of Heledd's family. *What will be my worth to anyone, if my uncle has no need of loyalty or influence?*

"I wonder what he is called, from what district?" Alys asked, following the movements of the dark-haired newcomer.

"He is hired and will be dead before anyone here knows anything about him."

"That was unkind, Heledd. Knowing their names is the least we can do to show our respect and gratitude for their sacrifice."

"They fight because they are paid. That is all they know – brutality and killing."

"You are hard-hearted. You, of all people, should know what they are forced to do. Look, how bold he is," the blonde girl exclaimed. "He's staring at us." Alys smiled, bowing her head to the man who gazed back in the girls' direction. "He cannot take his eyes off you."

Heledd turned her head to look in the same direction as her cousin. She met the gaze of the tall, lean man among the other soldiers and raised her chin higher, but not before she noticed he wore his dark brown hair to his shoulders, in waves sweeping back from his brow. Her back and shoulders ached but she remained still, assured that he saw as Alys saw – a tall, boyish girl.

"I do not think it is hard-hearted to speak the truth," Heledd said. "I did not say I do not respect them or fail to appreciate their work anymore than I fail to value the work of the stewards and the farmers, but you should not forget their true nature."

"Still," Alys insisted, "this one is special. I wonder where his home is and why he has come here. Perhaps he is one of Meilor Gwesyn's soldiers."

"Ask him," Heledd said, blushing under the warrior's scrutiny. She wished she had not succumbed to the heat. She wished she had a shift that fit her and was not straining at the seams to contain a bigger girl than the child she had been when it was passed down to her years before.

"Oh, I could not. I would die of embarrassment. You will ask him for me."

Heledd's green eyes darted to Alys's sweet, smiling face. She could not refuse the command. For a moment, her chin sank but the tilt was severe when she met her cousin's cold glare.

"You need not be so frightened, Heledd. I'm sure he is not old enough to have fought against your father, although *his* father may have been one of those who took revenge when Ieuan Bannawg betrayed them."

In the following few days, Alys made no further request to learn the soldier's name, neither did she insist Heledd accompany her to the wall, though she went herself and sometimes with her two brothers. Heledd was left to her tasks in the *beudy*. The work was heavy that time of year as the household prepared the provisions they needed for the winter months.

At the end of the week, when her work was done for the day, Heledd took her meal of bread, new cheese and ale to her small cell, to enjoy one evening and the Sabbath apart from the family. She balanced the wooden bowl on her knees, dipping chunks of bread in the wet cheese, washing both down her throat with the ale. Before she had finished the meal, one of the stewards pushed aside the tattered length of homespun separated her from the passageway to the kitchen.

"You are wanted," he told her and walked ahead of her through the doorway, not toward the family hall as she expected but into the kitchen yard.

"What am I to do?" Heledd asked, as they crossed toward the barracks.

"I was told you knew," the steward replied, knocking hard at the planked door of the soldiers' barracks. Heledd took a sudden breath. Through the gaps in the planks, she could see a wall of men's bodies as the soldiers rested from their day's work. Among the soldiers, she could see women, some younger than herself. "There is a woman here to see one of the warriors."

A few of the soldiers covered themselves at the steward's announcement; most did not bother until they saw the woman was not one of their usual visitors. Heledd averted her glance from the coupling, her chin jutting upward. She followed the steward through the bodies stretched at ease on their cots.

"What are you doing here?" a man demanded, grabbing her arm. He yanked her aside and propelled her back in the direction she had come. "You should know better than to bring a girl here," the man hissed at the steward.

"She will have to grow up one day," the steward replied, taking a seat among the soldiers waiting their turns with the women.

"Are you mad?" the newcomer demanded once they were in the yard. "Barracks are no place for a girl. Why did you come, *merch?*"

He called her a child, a maiden, a daughter. She was only one of these. Through the open door, some of the soldiers and their women watched her. The dark-haired warrior stared at her with such intensity she was compelled to meet his gaze. When he bowed to her, Heledd clenched her body at the civility of his greeting. He was tall but she could look into his eyes without tilting her head. His face was clean-shaven, sun-browned and smooth. He was as old as Urien Macsen and high-ranking, judging from his dress and manner.

"I have been ordered to speak to you," she said, reeling to the side and taking a step away. The warrior followed. She held herself erect, but nothing masked her trembling.

"Have you?"

"What is your name?"

"My name is Garmon." He smiled.

"And from what district do you come?" Heledd asked, taking a slow, deep breath to quell the rising fear. Alys's questions came from her mouth too fast.

"I have traveled here from the mountains of Dolwyddlan."

"I do not know it." Heledd bit her lips together to keep from asking more, though many questions had tumbled through her thoughts during the long days of drudgery.

"I did not expect you would. My district is many miles to the north."

"I have also been told to ask what brought you here," she said, blushing again. She remembered too many of the questions Alys wanted answered. Any moment one of her own threatened to escape. She stared back at him, defying his scrutiny with a toss of her head.

"If I were able to answer that, we would both be more knowledgeable," he said, moving so he stood between her and the barracks, "though I am beginning to understand something of the mystery."

Heledd was immobile, as though chained to the spot by a force that strangled her. "You must know what caused you to travel so many miles to be here." She had no sense of these directions except to know moss grew on one side of the tree and the sun descended beyond the Gurnos. North was the cold and dark side. She did not want him to think she was ignorant so she said, "So many miles to the south." She had proved the opposite but he smiled at her feeble effort.

"And many miles to the east, Heledd."

"Yes," she faltered. He said her name as though he was accustomed to the intimacy of speaking to her. Her neck was so hot her throat was choking dry. "But you still have no reason to travel here."

"I could answer in many ways, but I am compelled to be honest with one so beautiful, lest you think badly of me from the start of our friendship."

Heledd's chin shot up as if she had been slapped. "I do not want your friendship."

"I came here on the strength of Talgarth's reputation," Garmon answered, narrowing his eyes. "A warrior does well to train with men who have survived betrayal and slaughter."

Heledd drew her breath, knowing her resentment meant nothing to him. "Why do you stare at me?" She stepped back, raising her hands. Her mind showed her the bodies of little girls, stripped and bloodied. She heard the growl of a dog and its yelp at the end of life.

"I would like to see you laugh, *merch*. Those freckles on your cheeks do not belong on the face of one so sour. They belong to a pretty girl, one who is happy to be admired by a man."

Heledd remained silent, fury scorched her face. She heard boys screaming. *He's a soldier.* Terror quickened in her body.

"You have no cause to respond in that way, *merch*," Garmon laughed. "I do not bite, though your lips are tempting. I am honest. I am not your only admirer among my friends. One of us will win you. You have given me reason to believe I will be the man you choose."

"You— you should not speak to me in that way." Her throat thickened with the smell of blood and she gagged.

"In what way? How else should I speak to you?"

"You are too free." *He will kill me.* Her hands made a feeble wall.

"I am a free man," he laughed again.

"You are a soldier." Her voice was no more than a breath.

"True." He leaned forward, bowing his head near her throat. As his eyes closed, he drew her scent into his body. "And you are a bondservant, Heledd. A pretty, sweet-smelling one. Why else do you come here, if not to be admired?" His arm encircled her waist and he pressed his large hand on the small of her back, tugging her against him.

Though he told her she was sweet-smelling, she knew she was not and strained to be freed. "I was told— commanded." The whisper fought her blind horror for reason. *I can escape. I can. I have before.*

"You could have called me to you," Garmon murmured, searching her eyes. He had seen the change, felt the barrier of her strong hands holding him back. "Or, if you wished to be more discreet, sent the steward to ask your questions. The message is the same. The answer as well. I accept your invitation."

"I—," Heledd gasped. "I was commanded to speak to you, in Alys Llew's name."

"Talgarth's daughter has an interest in hired men?"

"No."

He raised an eyebrow, clenched his arm harder so she felt the ridges of his muscles wherever their bodies met. This was not as Urien had led him to expect. This girl was not for him, at least, she did not know she was for him and every muscle in her body was coiled to fight him. He couldn't hold her without hurting and that was the last thing he wanted that night, or any other. "Then it must be you who has the interest."

*If I die for this, I will not be a coward. I am not like my father.* "I despise soldiers."

"You do not show it by coming to me at the end of a long day, *merch*, when a man is hungry for refreshment. I can be forgiven for thinking I have won your regard," he said, releasing his grip a sinew at a time. "There are better places than the barracks to conduct this interview, Heledd." His breath whispered against her temple. His body and clothes were scented, his skin was still moist from bathing. "A beautiful girl has nothing to fear from her bondmaster's hirelings, even one as bold as Heledd *merch*—."

"They are — you are all savages, murderers." She heard the laughter in the barracks, the cheers when he grasped the back of her head.

"I can understand why you believe that, Heledd, but I would not say such things so near men who are expected to sacrifice their lives to protect you," Garmon Dolwyddlan said, his mouth close to hers. "One or two of these murderers would not hesitate to prove you right. The rest may decide to let them. And as you have seen, their brutality extends to willing women as well as haughty ones."

His threats, the laughter of his friends, riveted through every bone and muscle in her spine. Heledd glared at the barracks door, still crowded with the faces of soldiers and some of their women. She turned her fury on Garmon's face. "Never speak to me in this way again or I will have you whipped," she growled, spinning away from him.

"You won't," Garmon replied, catching her arm and pulling her to face him, "but you can be certain I will speak and often, Heledd, as I please. My friends," he murmured, studying her face, "have told me much about you." Urien Macsen had not told his younger foster brother much – only enough to stoke his interest. The girl told him plenty to warn him but her resistant hands were strong on his body and what he knew, however scant, made her a welcome possibility. The challenge was worthy of his best. "You do not disappoint me."

Heledd hesitated, raising her clenched fist but let it fall as she ran from his laughter. "That one is rude. He's a northerner," she muttered as she reached the kitchen. "They are all heathens."

When she repeated the same to Alys, her outrage was met with giggling, growing in vibrancy when her brothers joined in Heledd's humiliation. "Poor Heledd. One would think you know nothing of life in a *caer*. Warriors have even more rights than either of us. He, Garmon," Alys said his name again for what Heledd thought must be the eighth time since learning it just two minutes before. "Garmon may speak to you in any way he likes. His skills are of great value to my father. You are only another mouth to feed and another helpless woman to protect … or use. You are much less important than even the lowest char. Garmon Dolwyddlan is a commander, a high ranking warrior in his district. He commands—."

"How do you know that?"

"I have done my own investigation," Alys said, "and I did not have to go to the barracks like any whore would do."

"Where else was I to find him? That is where the steward led me," Heledd protested. "I am lower than the lowest char."

"And so easily led to shameful places. Did you see the whores my father provides? All the Bannawg women are there. If you are not more obedient, he may send you to Garmon – at least you will be the slave of a high-ranking warrior ... Think of how it will be to be owned by such a man. I almost envy you," Alys whispered.

"I am not helpless. Let one of them try to come near me." Heledd exclaimed, drawing back her fist. Alys's eldest brother caught it and twisted her arm behind her. The younger brother held her by the elbow. "Let that one come near me. I will show him—."

"You are funny. I was only joking about your battle skills. Do you think your anger will save you?" Alys asked. "Your private thoughts are quite stupid, Heledd."

"It is only this one—."

"Garmon?"

"Yes," Heledd sighed. "That one. He frightens me. He means to frighten me. He laughs at me."

"You are laughable." Alys pouted when Heledd's chin rose a fraction. "But perhaps he senses your dislike, or he likes women to fear him ... that must be it, Heledd."

"Why do you tease me?" Heledd demanded. "He has no more interest in me than to taunt me. I am more amusing than the woman he abandoned when I entered the barracks."

"Which one was that?" her cousin demanded. "Which of the whores dares—? She will be beaten for interfering."

"I did not see her ... clearly," Heledd said. She had not looked at the women. She had not seen the northerner at all until he dragged her from the barracks. She felt the pressure of his hand on her back and straightened as if to pull away. Alys's brothers tightened their grips on her.

"He must find you more than amusing to answer a few silly questions."

"They were your questions." Heledd's embarrassment seared her cheeks.

"You asked them," Alys replied, smiling prettily. "You are Bannawg to the bone. A natural whore. We will see soon enough what Garmon Dolwyddlan does with you. Be careful, Heledd. He is a stranger, but he has heard enough about you to infuriate him."

At the end of another sweltering, heavy afternoon, Heledd was milking for the second time, her head pressed against the haunches of the newly calved heifer. The animal was restless and dry from suckling but what the calf left could be enough for a meal for Talgarth's table during the winter. When she could get no more from the heifer, Heledd dried the animal's teats with her apron. She carried the molded leather bucket to the inner *beudy*, scooped the cream from the top and poured the rest into the vat with the milk from the other women's buckets. The cream folded into the churner and Heledd took her place to turn the crank paddle for another hour of toil.

When Goewin, the *beudy* mistress, judged the butter was ready for the molds, all of the women joined in the lighter work of spreading the thickened, salted butter into the wooden molds and carrying them to the vault in the mead-cellar. When the work was done, the light had faded to mark the end of the day and the women put away their tools. In groups of twos and threes, they wandered back to the main house or to their own homes to prepare meals for their families. Several turned toward the barracks.

"Where are they going?" Heledd asked Goewin and felt her cheeks redden. She had seen the women part company before. She knew the answer and the shame of her curiosity deepened the stain on her dappled cheeks.

"They have work tonight."

"But Heulwen is pregnant. What about her child?"

"She will have some rest in the soldiers' barracks—."

"With soldiers?" Heledd demanded, staring after her friend, fists ready.

"— Until the child is born," Goewin continued, wrapping her graying hair beneath the white scarf she used in the kitchen, "but, unless she is fortunate, no one will claim the child she carries."

*Whose child?* Heledd walked into the kitchen with her head bowed. None of the women who worked beside her in the milking shed were like the women she had seen in the barracks, but she knew them to be the same. She had helped Heulwen cut a length of fine cloth for her unborn child. She had pulled the wash-baskets from the river with another. Neither had admitted they had laughed at her when the northerner dragged her into the yard for all to witness. She had never considered a soldier was the father of Heulwen's child.

Alys grinned when she found Heledd in the inner kitchen and grasped her hand. "I know how you can make this up to me. You can serve my evening meal." Though Heledd served the family often, she had hoped to have another evening to herself. The meal was served in the hall and the family went to their beds late. She would be at work by dawn and begin the Sabbath, reeking of animal sweat and dung, like the rest of the servants.

"There is no time for me to bathe before I serve the meal. If I promise to come tomorrow, Alys?" Allowing her to live as a family member was Talgarth's duty after the death of her parents but her position as bondservant was clear. Heledd's debt to her uncle and his three children was never far from the surface of their dealings with her and small payments were exacted as suited them. If a soldier was encouraged to treat her without respect and the other bondservants were allowed to laugh when she was humiliated, Heledd had no one other than her father to blame.

"There's no need for that. I have something I want to share with you." Alys's smile was warm and there was no question of refusing the demand although she was too tired to be as civil as the hall required. Heledd rinsed away the grime of her day's toil from her face and hands before Alys pulled her through the door to await Llew Talgarth and his sons.

# TWO

"What is he doing here?" Heledd lifted her chin and straightened her weary spine when Garmon Dolwyddlan entered from the courtyard with her male cousins.

Deion, the younger of the brothers, looked from one to the other of his companions, nodding his sandy head in agreement with every word the northerner spoke, imitating his emphatic gestures and his confident stance.

Bold, at ease, Garmon used his long fingers in open gestures, closing his fist with a snap made both Deion and Heledd, on the other side of the wide room, jump.

"He has come to dine, like the rest of us," Alys answered, swaying her round hips.

"Here?"

Alys peered at Heledd in amusement. "He has been invited – my father is fond of him, and, since you asked his name—."

"Because you commanded me."

The newcomer had lowered his gaze for a moment to listen to something Deion was saying but when he looked up again, he found Heledd in the room and, without deference to his companions, turned to answer her stare with a grin. He met her anger with a bow of his head and continued his conversation with Elis, the elder brother.

"Urien Macsen," Alys told her, "has recommended him to my father and he came one evening after you visited him. He is very amusing and so well educated, a scholar as well as a powerful commander. I believe he is even more beautiful than the first time we saw him, don't you agree? So well-dressed and obviously from good family." Alys swung her blue skirts away from Heledd's ragged work tunic. "Garmon has come to have his meal with us many times, but tonight is a special occasion."

Llew Talgarth called Alys to her place by him and, to Heledd's dismay, Garmon crossed the room toward her. His gait, though proud and forthright, was uneven. She fixed her eyes on his face and he smiled at her as if they were friends, as if he believed she was glad to see him. Her frown deepened and her gaze dropped to his injured leg. Though he hesitated for a moment, he continued toward her. Heledd raised her eyes when he was near, stunned by the warmth in his smile as he lifted her stained fingers to his lips, studying her dappled face.

"Thank you for accepting the invitation to share this meal with me," he said against her fingertips. The touch of his hand made her conscious her skin was red and roughened. His grip was strong, his palm was smooth. He had bathed and wore clothing was of better quality than Heledd had seen among any of the *pennaeth* – whether highborn or wealthy chieftains – who had visited Talgarth-y-Bannawg. The stitching on the cuffs of his tailored linen shirt was delicate and expert. His slate-colored woolen tunic was embroidered with black silk and his *trwsus* were of the softest leather, made to sheath his thighs as the scabbard on his belt had been made to sheathe his hunting knife. "The company here is dull in comparison to yours, Heledd."

Speechless, Heledd's eyes darted from his face to the family across the room. Their avid interest in the warrior's behavior crushed her protest. Garmon drew her hand through his arm and held her near him. Everything about him – from his damp hair to his polished black boots – told her he had taken care to dress well. She studied her uncle and his children. They too had seen fit to dress well. She had come to the hall in her work clothes, barely washed, disheveled and tattered. The cuffs of her frock were frayed and discolored. Her shapeless tunic was work-stained. When she met the northerner's gaze again, he was laughing at her. They were all laughing at her. Heledd fought to deny them the knowledge of how they hurt her.

"With you?"

"Yes, if you agree." He studied her, his granite-hued eyes widening. "Do you object?"

"Yes, I object——. No one asked me. I will not stay."

"Now I am surprised, Heledd. I thought you would welcome——."

"What do you mean?"

"Only that you are very beautiful," Garmon replied, a frown crossing his brow. "There are many who wish to be here in my place."

"Soldiers?"

"Yes. I do not intend to insult you. I am no more accustomed to offering invitations than you to receive them. We should start again."

"Again?"

"My name is Garmon, Heledd. I am a soldier from the north."

"I know that. Why have you asked me here?"

"I wanted to be with you, to enjoy your company," Garmon replied. "Despite the generous hospitality of Llew Talgarth and his sons, your smile, when you offer one, is far more welcome than the best fare and the most charming conversation. In this place, you are a blessing, a gift from God."

"I do not smile at you." Heledd stared at him. "I would not do such a thing." She realized he still held her hand, now pressed to his heart. She could feel its beat, strong and steady, against her palm. Her fingertips still felt the warmth of his kiss.

"I know you have not, but I think you will," Garmon murmured. "Soon."

"Do I have a choice?"

"Your wishes will always matter to me, Heledd," Garmon replied, in a low voice. "I can guess what they are as we speak."

"I do not want to know what you think. And I do not want to know you."

"I will change that."

"I do not want to know you," she repeated, lifting her chin and turning her face away.

"That cannot be helped and is my misfortune. Nevertheless,

I will persuade you otherwise, in time."

"Do you think I am so ignorant I do not know what—." Heledd stopped herself and glared back into his dark, gray eyes. "You have power and influence. I have neither. I know what happens to girls who anger soldiers. I do not care. I would rather—."

"Do not say you would rather die," Garmon warned her, kissing the palm of her hand. Out of the corner of her eye, Heledd saw Alys swirl the skirt of her gown so it shimmered in the glow of the fire as she beckoned Garmon Dolwyddlan to come to her father's table.

"I would," she hissed. Despite her outrage, Heledd felt a sense of relief when, after he acknowledged Alys, he returned to his study of her. The fire in the open hearth spit embers across the floor, snapping at her feet, but Heledd did not take her eyes off his face, conveying her defiance in the tense line of her fine-boned chin. The warrior stared at her as though he had never seen anything of her like before.

"You would not and you will not," Garmon told her, catching her proud chin between his thumb and fore-finger. "This pretense will not deter me, Heledd. I have met more arrogant girls. I have known more tempting women."

Her captor led her to the long table, taking a seat on the bench between her and the Talgarth family. Garmon spoke freely with his host, her male cousins, shared flirting jokes with Alys. Rage seethed through Heledd's body as she came to a confused understanding her uncle and his children had abandoned her. Each time Heledd moved or tried to pull away from the northerner, he seemed to awaken to her, turning his attention on her as if he were surprised she was still seated beside him.

"I see," he murmured, tearing the bread she had helped to bake and laying it at the side of her plate, "no expense has been spared to present you to me as the beauty you are."

Heledd shrank from his sarcasm into her ragged clothing. She watched in dismay as her uncle clasped his guest's hand, laughed with him and saluted him with drink. Alys was as eager to show her approval of the northerner as her father, glancing at Heledd with a sneer. As the meal came to an end, Llew Talgarth called for the storyteller to entertain them. Heledd turned her face away as the storyteller took a stool to sit before Talgarth's table.

"In days long ago, when there were two brothers in this valley," Catwg began as he had begun countless autumn nights before, "they were threatened by greed and jealousy."

Catwg the Teller sang of how Llew Talgarth had earned his name as a young man when he built a fortress, a vast *caer*, high above and further north of his brother on the slopes of Carn Bannawg. "Though they were brothers, an animosity grew between them when the elder, Ieuan Bannawg, resentful of his brother's success, attacked. Llew Talgarth's position on the highest part of the slope was strong. He withstood the harassment of his brother for loyalty to their father but, despite his kind nature, with the riches of the Tywi to defend for his household, he was harried by his brother until there was no choice but war. In the weaker position, Ieuan Bannawg, led his war band against his brother but when his cause was lost, he abandoned his friends and ran.

"The great *pennaeth* of the region, Meilor Gwesyn hunted the betrayer. Ieuan Bannawg and his wife, Anwen, were killed along with his warriors and all, save one, of his seven children. The people who survived returned to Bannawg and Llew Talgarth accepted his brother's people as his own and took the traitor's daughter into his household as his own child. And from that day to this," Catwg said as he concluded his story, "Llew Talgarth has peacefully extended his land and influence to the south and west, climbing the slopes of the valley toward the Gurnos, securing peace for all in his estate through treaty and the marriage of his daughter to the son of Meilor Gwesyn."

Heledd could not lift her chin to defy her uncle. She had heard the story from her earliest recollection. The tale of her father's betrayal was for her benefit, to remind her of the reason for her bondage.

"I do not ask to hear this story often," Llew said to his

handsome guest. "I do not do so to cause grief but to remind all present of the precarious peace now gracing our lives since my brother's betrayal."

Even so, Heledd could not contain the sorrow the story recalled and struggled to suppress a mournful cry. Somewhere in her head she heard little girls' cries for mercy and boys' wails of horror. *Why do I live?* The answer was always the same. *To pay my father's debt.*

"What is wrong?" Garmon demanded, turning toward her with a furrowed brow. Knowing the answer did not change his part in that night's conspiracy. He was as guilty as any other; he could not claim ignorance as his defense – he had known enough and had plummeted into the trap because the bait was sweeter than any that had tempted him before. There was no escape for him and there was no other end than this moment – her life and her honor stolen on a friend's lie and a brother's dare. Heledd Bannawg was not for him, could never be.

Heledd shook her head. Garmon gazed at her pale, sun-dappled cheek and his gray eyes revealed a frown but he said nothing more to her. When he returned his attention to the others, he held Heledd's upturned, clenched hands. Any tremble passing through her body brought his scrutiny throughout the remainder of the evening. Heledd struggled to stay motionless. Every time the muscles in her fingers betrayed her, Garmon stared at her and she was compelled to meet his gaze, as though he willed her to communicate everything in her heart.

"You are tired," he said at last. Heledd made no answer but the quick contraction of her hands brought a scowl to his face. He made an effort to settle his expression before he turned once again to look at her. "Go to your bed, *merch*." He released her hands slowly, as though with each muscle relaxing its grip, he savored and caressed her. "This girl asks to be excused, sir," Garmon said. Talgarth dismissed her with a wave of his hand and a wide grin for his hired man.

Heledd pulled herself to her full height, lifted her chin and walked from the hall. She lit the wick of her tiny oil pot from the brazier in the kitchen and slipped into her cell. She sat on the edge of the low, narrow cot that had been her bed almost her whole her life. Her throat ached with the effort to hold back tears of rage. Heledd held herself rigid, her hands clasped together in her lap and her green eyes fixed on the rectangle of homespun covering the opening to her cell – her flimsy defense against intrusion. She heard the laughter and gaming in the hall, the raucous singing in the barracks and sobbed aloud.

Although she had only been asleep for a moment, the eastern sky was pale gray. Heledd's heart thrashed against the wall of her chest and her eyes shot open. She had heard no footsteps approaching along the corridor from the hall but felt a breath on her cheek. Gasping for enough air to scream, she struggled to escape as the warrior leaned closer, peering into her eyes.

"You will wake the household." He crouched beside her. "I am not here to harm you."

Heledd bolted away from him. "No. I will scream."

"If you want more witnesses, scream," Garmon said, "but you will bring all the dishonor and shame Talgarth intends for you. Sleep, Heledd. No harm will come to you, on my honor."

"I will not help you do this to me."

"I have no time to explain," he said, unfastening the bone toggles on his tunic. "Do as I tell you, *gwraig*," Garmon murmured, opening his shirt. "Move over." He dragged the shirt over his head and removed his leather *trwsus*. His thighs glistened in the faint light of the oil lamp. The fabric of his linen was taut over his muscular hips and, as he laid down beside her, she felt him harden.

"Let me go," Heledd cried, dragging her arms free, doubling her fists. He had called her *gwraig* – woman, wife – she was neither, determined to be neither if she could fight him.

"You are too angry, *gwraig*, and I am too drunk, for love to be any good for either of us," he whispered, stroking her cheek. Heledd lashed out, sinking her teeth into the heel of his palm. "I see you know how to inflict pain, Heledd. I will remember that." The warrior captured her hands and held them behind her back, running the tips of his fingers along the shoulder of her frock. "This is a rag, not fit to be worn."

"Don't do this." His hand slid to the neck opening. "Don't tear it."

"You defend this rag with more passion than you defend your family's honor."

"This is all I have."

"Is it?" He traced his long fingers over her cheek and laid his wounded hand on her hip. "I did not come here to hurt you, or to fight. I know Hywel's law, Heledd. I will not break it. Go back to sleep, *gwraig*."

"Does the king's law give you right to do this to me?"

"With your uncle's consent, yes."

"Then I can have neither king nor uncle," she said under her breath.

"You have both," he replied with a laugh in his voice, "and you know which you can trust, Heledd Bannawg. I have done what had to be. For now, sleep. You have my word, Heledd. You are in no danger."

His assurances meant nothing. His fingers explored and his eyes studied. Her breath stopped when he loosened her hair and brought handfuls into her view, allowing it to cascade over their bodies. The sickness of her terror overwhelmed her, closing her throat. "I have known beautiful women, Heledd," he said, weaving his long fingers into the hideous web that clung to her shoulders and gagged her. After a long silence, he turned onto his back. "A thing that seems the simplest ..."

She stared at the warrior's sleeping face, not daring to breathe for fear of waking him, frozen under the weight of his hand. The northerner woke at dawn and left her bed, keeping his eyes on her as he dressed. When he crouched by the bed, dragging the ragged woolen *carthen* to her chin, he traced the curve of her breast with a trembling hand. Heledd lowered her eyes, crimson shame obscuring her dappled skin to the top of her brow.

"One day you may understand but I doubt you will ever be glad of this, *gwraig*. As yet, I cannot know what will be the end but I am still hopeful I will see you smile. When I know more of this riddle, I may even hear you laugh."

With a sob, she turned her back as he left. She did not lift her head again until the morning was gone. Her dark red hair was spread around her like a pool of blood and she scraped it back, out of sight, grabbing at the flax strip that had fallen to the floor. With hands shaking with rage, she wrapped it twice around her mass of hair and tied a knot with such violence she cried out. She swallowed hard on the wave of sickness threatening to weaken her and forced herself to sit up, tossing the threadbare *carthen* away.

With a long breath, she took stock of every sensation. Apart from the lingering scent of his clean body, there were no other signs the northerner had been near her. Confident he had done nothing worse than sleep beside her and loosen her hair, Heledd peeled away her clothing to wash his scent from her skin. *I have done nothing for which I need be ashamed.*

The moment she cleared herself of blame, Alys flung aside the homespun rag, a grin on her pretty face as she flounced onto the cot, staring at Heledd.

"How are you?" she asked, raising her voice high on an excited whisper. "What— oh, Heledd, what is it like? I must hear. Tell me everything," she demanded, breathless. "Were you frightened? What did he do?"

Heledd's green eyes widened and her breath choked the rage swelling inside her. She felt her eyes stinging, narrowing.

"Don't be shy," Alys cajoled. "We are still friends. That will never change."

"Everything has changed," Heledd said. "Everything."

"You must tell me what happened," Alys said, her brow knitting over her blue eyes.

"Nothing happened," Heledd replied. "I fell asleep and I awoke this morning."

"Why are you angry? Why won't you tell me? I would tell you everything, from the first kiss to—. Everything."

"If I had anything to tell you," Heledd said, rising from the cot and tying the white scarf over her hair, "I would not."

"Ach, I do not believe you. The whole of Talgarth knows what has happened. They know that northerner has paid for you and they will know this," Alys answered, throwing aside the *carthen* from the bare mattress. Heledd stared at the drops of blood. "And that," Alys said, pointing at a smear of blood on Heledd's thigh. "You are not a maid now, Heledd. There is nothing to stop any of the soldiers from taking you. If you are not careful, Garmon will break his promise to protect you. He has paid a good price to have you. He will want its full worth."

"How can you say these things to me? Why has my uncle done this?"

"Why do you complain?" Alys asked, tilting her head to one side. "You knew this would come one day. He is not so old and still handsome." Alys reached her hand toward her cousin but withdrew when Heledd refused any contact. "Did you expect my father to find you a lawful husband when you have nothing to bring to the contract but what he has given? Be grateful you will have someone to feed you this winter," Alys said and lowered her eyes. When Alys again looked at Heledd, her eyes revealed her fury. "There is no reason for *you* to be angry with *me*. My father has done the best he could for you. Garmon will find you amusing for a while. Considering what you have … *had* to offer, you are a fool to be ungrateful … and, when you have told me everything," Alys offered as she left the small room, "you will see, Heledd, nothing will change between us."

Heledd walked alone behind the women of the kitchen and *beudy* at the end of the day. Her cousin's servant, Betsan, passed the group and trotted beside her, slapping her knees and waggling her tongue. "Barracks whore," she laughed, grabbing Heledd's scarf away. When her hair tumbled down her back, she caught her breath, clutching at the scarf but it was too late to cover her head. Goewin whisked the scarf out of Betsan's hands and thrust it back at Heledd.

"When it is your turn to provide comfort for the soldiers," Heulwen said to Betsan, "you will be sorry you were spiteful today. You will be sorry none of us will help you heal your injuries. We will be glad to see you crippled."

"Heulwen, you know she was sent to torment," Goewin said, tying Heledd's scarf at the nape of her neck. "Betsan is a slave like the rest of us."

"That is no excuse for enjoying what she is made to do," Heulwen said, walking closer to Heledd.

Before she reached the safety of the kitchen to begin her work there, Garmon Dolwyddlan rode through the yard, followed by his command of eight soldiers. He halted the chestnut warhorse and his command, stroking the stallion's shoulder as the women passed. He kept his eyes fixed on Heledd's face, bowing his head to her in greeting. Behind him, the soldiers stared at her, grinning, making gestures toward their bodies, pursing their lips at her.

In the kitchen, two of the boys ogled her as she went about her work until Goewin struck at their heads with a ladle. The steward who had taken her to the barracks blocked her path from the pantry, demanding she kiss him. Heledd drew back and doubled her fist. The steward laughed until she made his nose redder than it already was. "You will pay for that, Heledd Bannawg."

"I have already paid and you will pay again if you come near me."

That night, she slept alone and, at the end of the following day, Garmon Dolwyddlan greeted her with a smile. She ignored his salutation, but the eight soldiers who followed on patrol kept their eyes fixed on their commander's back. Heledd glanced once over her shoulder as she entered the kitchen but none of them turned, not even the one whose cheek bore a fresh bruise.

The steward who had demanded a kiss lowered his gaze when he walked past her as she worked, mumbling. Heledd lifted her chin with a sniff, concentrating all of her energy on the smooth bread dough but the meal put in her hand came from him and he grinned as he rubbed his belly. The two boys tore the rag over her cell door, shaking it in her face and laughing when she couldn't catch them to take it back. She wrapped the threadbare *carthen* around her to undress and stared at the doorway until she couldn't resist sleep.

Hours were long in the *beudy* and the days were shorter. A cold wind whipped through the upper Tywi valley on its journey from the mountains to the sea. Gray skies and grayer hills replaced the bright golden air at harvest time. Woolen shawls covered the linen frock and light flannel tunic were the summer costume of every woman and girl. Wooden clogs replaced their deerskin sandals.

The men covered their tunics with thick, hooded coats. The fields were hardening, lying fallow until the spring, there was no training and the soldiers spent their days rebuilding walls and repairing the roof thatches on her uncle's house. The northerner was among the few still patrolling the borders of the Talgarth estate to keep raiders at bay during the early days of winter. Bands of wandering folk, the 'dusty-footed,' tested the preparations of all of the landowners, searching for a weakness to exploit for their winter shelter.

Fear for their own survival over winter did not stop some of the Talgarth-y-Bannawg inhabitants from offering meager comfort to the wanderers as the days grew wilder. Among the bits of stale bread, hardened cheese, worn out shoes, tattered clothing, and kindling the women hid in the gorse as they returned from gathering fire wood and winter berries, Heledd left her outgrown shift and a pair of over-darned stockings.

In darkness, Heledd returned to her cell, unable to be grateful even for a few hours of rest. A woman stood with her back to the doorway, bent over the cot and Heledd lurched at her, her fists clenched and raised. "What are you doing in my room?"

The woman swung around and put her hands on her hips. "I work here, the same as you. If I am told to come to this room or any other, I do so. If I am told to take something or to leave something, I do so."

"What have you taken?"

"Do you think you have any more of value than any of the

rest of us?" The woman shoved Heledd out of her way. "You can be grateful you have nothing worth taking, Heledd."

Heledd searched the meager contents. The mattress was still shabby, the room bare. She still had no cushion for her head but the black and red *carthen* the woman left folded on her cot was thick and so soft she wrapped it around her and held it close until she felt warm again. When she lay down on the bed, she put it under the other, to have it next to her skin. After she smothered the flame of the oil pot, Heledd turned to face the door of her cell. Except for the gusting visits of the north wind, no one came to trouble her.

On a sodden morning, from the door of the *beudy*, before she started work, Heledd caught sight of wanderers at the top of the Carn Bannawg, coming from the estate to the north. She watched them searching for shelter among the overhanging rocks until her interest in the towering carn brought attention to them. Within moments, Garmon Dolwyddlan led his patrol toward the crest of the Bannawg. They rode the brow of the carn into the valley beyond but she heard no sounds of battle or the terror of women. At the end of her work in the *beudy*, Heledd walked with Heulwen and another woman through the yard when the patrol returned.

Garmon dismounted and ordered the eight soldiers to the barracks. "Are you well?" Heledd lifted her chin to answer but the northerner had not spoken to her.

"Very well, thank you."

"How long before this little one is born?"

"Another season. Soon enough," Heulwen answered, laying her hand on the crown of her belly. "Thank you for the cloth, Garmon."

"The length was sufficient for the child?" As he asked, he glanced at Heledd, acknowledging her with a nod. She folded her arms across her waist and stared at the ground, waiting for the women to finish their conversation, glancing once at the kitchen door, but Goewin was not there to scold her. "Have you been waiting for me?" Heledd did not hear Heulwen's response and, when no one else spoke, she raised her eyes. "Did you want to say something to me? A question?"

"No." Heulwen and the other woman had resumed their walk toward the barracks. "How can you do this?"

"What is it I have done, Heledd?"

"A bit of cloth. A bright trinket. A soft *carthen* – do you think any of that can make good what you have done?"

"Soft?" he asked. "Was it soft, Heledd?" When she refused to answer, he laughed. "Can anything be soft enough for you?"

"Why do you bother asking such a question?"

"I want to know," he said, catching her hand, "because, when I see you, my mind turns to softer thoughts, the softest I have ever known."

"I am not one of *them*. I will never be like them."

"*They* are women, Heledd, like you."

"I am not like them." She pulled against his grip.

"You are like them." He raised her hand to his lips and brought her close to him, encircling her waist. "You are as kind, as generous, as sweet."

"Why are you doing this? There are plenty of women in the barracks. Heulwen and … and…"

"I have no interest in Heulwen or Elain or Catrin or—."

"You know their names."

"Of course, I know their names, *gwraig*. What manner of man do you think I am that I would not know their names? I know your name. And you know mine. We are acquainted. I am also acquainted with Heulwen. She laughs more often and Elain's smile can fill a man's heart with joy. But they are not Heledd Bannawg, '*ngwraig*." he finished in a low voice.

She gasped at the realization of his meaning. "I am not your woman." Her chin lifted. "They are whores."

"Do you think you are better?"

"I have not …" She knew as well as he there was no substance to her claim. She was what people believed her to be – because of him. "I am not. I will never be, no matter what you do to me."

"Some women are tricked. Some are forced. Some, like you, are willing."

"I am not. How can you think I am willing?"

"To know love?"

"That is not love."

"You will know love, Heledd Bannawg. You will know what it is to tempt a man beyond endurance. And you will know the depth of his love."

He was laughing at her and every word lashed across her hard-worked, aching back even the warmth of his hand could not ease. And she was leaning into his embrace, absorbing his scent into her body as though she couldn't breathe without him. "As often as I remember your soft hands and the silk of your sun-kissed skin, as much as I dream of your delicate body yielding to mine—."

"Don't come near me." She struck at him with her fists. "Never ever come near me." Heledd wrenched out of his grasp, stumbling back into the mud. She did not have to see the faces of those she ran past to know who had laughed with him.

Goewin met her at the door of the kitchen, a scowl dark enough to frighten the stars from the sky. Heledd grabbed the apron from her hand and went to her place at the board. "You give them all they want, *merch*."

"How? How do I do that?"

Goewin brought the mallet down on the slab of mutton so hard Heledd felt the impact through her hands as she shaped the loaves. The steward stood on the opposite side of the board, shaking his fists in the air like a madman and popping his eyes at her.

"Like that," Goewin said.

The steward's chin jutted into the air, bowing to the laughter of the boys.

"Should I let him talk to me like that? Do I have to listen to a soldier's insults?"

"How else should a man talk to his—."

"I am not his whore."

"Garmon does not want you," Goewin hissed at her, "but if you are not more careful others will. Remember who you are, *merch*."

"How can I forget? How can I ever forget?"

# ChREE

As the last month of the year crept to its end, everywhere she turned, Heledd saw nothing but gray and drizzling grayness. There were no distractions from the drudgery of work, no moments of wonder or joy to make the dark days fly, nor any nights when fear kept her from much needed sleep in her hoar-frosted cell. Against all her best wishes and better judgment, Heledd looked for Garmon Dolwyddlan among the blanketed soldiers who came to the house on the final day of the Holy Season to hear Catwg the Teller repeat the Nativity story and to drink the hot wassail. It was the only night of the year all of the Talgarth inhabitants were in one place for the celebration and the comfort of a gift-filled night.

She sat among the women, wrapped in a shawl as colorless as her tunic, clasping her cup close to her chest to warm her hands and face. The northerner was not among the soldiers nor with the family. Heledd watched Urien Macsen when he entered, taking his place among his command, accepting their toasts and offers to fill his cup, his perpetual scowl marring his strong, sure features. Some of the men stood to make room, leaning their backs against the wall next to the hearth where the stones radiated some heat. The commander returned her gaze and smiled, raising his cup in salute to her and his soldiers stared across the hall at the northerner's whore. Heledd dropped her gaze to her chill-whitened fingers.

In the tradition of the district, Llew Talgarth bestowed gifts on each of his household and the men of his war band – lengths of cloth for the women, a bronze clasp or buckle for his stewards, an extra jug of mead for the soldiers. Heledd did not expect to see Garmon go to Talgarth's table to receive his jug – all of the soldiers sat together at the far corner of the hall while the stewards set the jugs on the benches and tables near them. She had no sense of his presence in the room. When her turn came to receive her gift, Heledd walked the short distance with her chin tilted, extending her hands with a curtsy. She received a folded square of cloth, no larger than her hand, and a cold dismissal as other women came behind her.

"Thank you, Uncle." She bowed her head and resumed her place among the servant women. Her parcel was too small for cloth to make a new shift or flannel yarn for stockings, as the other women of the household had received. Her lips trembled when she peered at the token gift. She was no longer Talgarth's responsibility. If she received any gift, it would come from her new master.

*Garmon does not want you.*

She could not remember the number of times Goewin's words repeated in her head. More often now than *Why do I live?* More often than she felt the cold. More often than her spirit was crushed when they called her 'traitor's daughter.' So often, she felt she could never hold her head high again though her chin was at a sharper angle with each recurrence.

Between the time for gifts and the long walk to the *Plygain* service to sing carols at dawn, in the meager privacy of her cell, she untied the string and unfolded the square of cloth wrapping her gift. In the dim light of her oil pot, Heledd was surprised by the elegance of the purse. The cloth was like nothing she had ever seen before. Though it was black, patterns shown like silver and others were as black as a night without moonlight.

She hung the purse from her belt but she had nothing of value to put into it. Before dawn, she joined the others of the household to walk down the valley to the chapel. When she returned to her work in the kitchen, her heart was lighter. Although, like the women with husbands, she had received no other gift, not even a strip of flax for her hair from Alys,

Heledd's one gift was finer than any Alys or the others had received. Even if she was wrong, that morning, she wanted to believe it came from someone who valued her. All the *Plygain* carols ran through her head as she worked the dough for the meal later in the day.

"What do you have to sing about?" Goewin demanded, leaning her back into her kneading on the opposite side of the board.

"Was I?" Heledd asked, quelling the flicker of a smile.

"Don't stop on my account," Goewin said. "Your voice is pleasant and we could all use a little cheer. Here, I will keep you company," she volunteered, picking up the tune.

"Your proud bird sings," Elis called to his companion as the two rode past the kitchen to patrol the circuit of the estate. Heledd's hands froze as she peered through the narrow window, her heart shuddering at her cousin's familiar voice, biting her lip as she strained to see to whom he had spoken. Elis's companion turned his back to the east wind and spurred his chestnut horse toward the river at the foot of the mountains.

"What do you see?" Goewin asked, standing by Heledd and gazing through the window. Though the soldier was still visible, Heledd shook her head and looked away. "He has made many friends here," Goewin told her. "You can be proud—." Heledd stared at the *beudy* mistress.

"How can I be proud I am owned, like a cow, but am worth so much less?"

"I see you are not so haughty you cannot appreciate his gift."

"How did you know?" Her cheeks flared like pitch-wood.

"There is not much I do not know." Goewin returned to her bread making.

"How do you know ... about him?"

"I ask him," the mistress laughed. "Do you not?"

"I have never— I have only spoken to him once ... twice," Heledd admitted. "What do you know?"

Goewin gazed at Heledd for a moment, then shrugged, "Since you have asked me—."

"I am not asking about him," Heledd replied.

"Urien Macsen can tell you more than I as they have come to be good friends, but I know he comes from a long way to the north. He is here to train as a commander."

"I know that. What about—?" Heledd bit her lips so hard she felt the bruise before it was made.

"You? What about you? Garmon Dolwyddlan did not come here for you. When he returns to his home, Urien will—." Another woman entered the kitchen and Goewin turned her attention to telling the new arrival what to do.


Meat was scarce and there was little bread on the tables by the time the gales began to lose their bitter sting. Heledd rubbed her chapped hands together over the brazier. Her cheeks were still red from the hours she had spent in the milking shed. The *beudy*'s narrow windows channeled the harsh winds into the faces of the milkmaids and the only shelter was to press their cheeks against the cows' muddy haunches. That her face was as dirty as all the other girls was a small comfort. That they were all laughing and jolly was no comfort at all. *You have only yourself to blame, if you were not so hard-hearted…*

All of the questions she had wanted to ask Goewin were locked in her heart. There was no opportunity to talk over bread making or in the evenings as the days lengthened. Even if she had wanted to talk to Urien Macsen, she did not want her cousins to believe she sought the northerner's company. She wanted to thank him for her gift but he did not come near her and she could not seek him.

When Heledd finished her turn at milking, she splashed the icy water standing in a jug by the door onto her face and rubbed the mud off with the corner of her scarf, before walking the distance to the house. Though the days were longer, the sun had not appeared at all that day and, now that the light was fading at the crest of the mountains to the west, the torches had already been lit in the yard. Though they gave off as much warmth as light, Heledd shivered as she stepped into the open expanse of the farm close.

"Are you cold, Heledd?" The northerner stepped forward to block her way. Heledd pressed her lips together, wrapping her arms more tightly around her waist to close the gap in her shawl. "I have a remedy." Heledd drew her head back as she raised her chin a fraction to meet his eyes, ready to offer a courteous reply. Before she could speak, he swept his arms around her waist and lifted her from the ground. Carrying her to the side of the *beudy* out of sight of the house and the barracks, he pressed her against the wall, staring into her eyes.

"What do you want?"

"I know your heart is not cold, Heledd. You are not indifferent."

Elis had seen them. She stared straight ahead, over the northerner's shoulder. The warrior's body exuded the scent with which she had become familiar. She felt his breath on her cheek and was mesmerized by his audacity. He lifted his head for a moment, gradually loosening his grip until her feet touched the ground. He gave her a long, soft kiss at the corner of her mouth.

"You have not missed my company, I see. Between myself and God, Heledd, I wish I could say the same." He caressed her chin with his thumb and slid his hand inside her shawl, to the small of her back, holding her against him. Every word Urien Macsen had said to him since her uncle had tricked him reverberated in his head. Every lie he knew about her now, now it was too late, damned him. Every word of honor and promise he had ever made was flung back at him from her green eyes, green as rich as the holly.

"Why have you come now? Why today?" The warmth of his hand radiated through her tired muscles.

"Why do you ask? Have you wanted me to come to you at any other time?" Holding her now, a thoughtless instrument of her humiliation, he wondered at his arrogance, his willful disregard for everything he believed of himself. Garmon blamed no one – he had chosen to be tricked, to believe the lies, to trust his course was honorable, to hope she would want the life he offered.

"No."

"I will look forward to the day you do. Until then, I will live in hope, *gwraig*."

"False hope," she said, pushing her blistered hands against his chest. She heard footsteps and bolted. Garmon locked his arm tighter around her. "Let me go." Out of the corner of her eye, she saw Elis closing in from the *beudy* with several women behind him. Her cousin sneered and nodded, folding his arms across his chest. The women gawked at her, the edges of their mouths forming grins.

"Hope all the same, Heledd Bannawg," the warrior whispered against her lips. "You would not deny a man that much, would you?" Even now, when he had lost, he could not give her up, although in doing so he failed her. He covered her mouth with his own, urging her to open to his kiss, but she clenched her jaw, raising her fist to strike.

"They're watching," Heledd said under her breath. "Don't do this, please. It means nothing to you and everything to me. They will laugh at me," she said.

"Do you think it is nothing to me to hold you?" Garmon glanced in the direction of the onlookers. When he looked at Heledd again, he shielded her from their spying, stroking her cheek with the backs of his long fingers. "Do you think it is nothing to have even the most meager hope you will smile for me when there is nothing else for which I can hope?" For a moment, he lifted his head but the clouds refused to reveal the sun and he closed his eyes. "You need not worry what they think of you, *gwraig*. It is what your friends think that matters. I still have not heard you laugh, Heledd. Will I?" She looked away, staring at the gray hills, always west, toward the Gurnos. "I don't believe you have no laughter in you. I have heard you sing." He caught a wisp of her hair and brushed it away from her face. "I know I have given you no reason to think well of me, but I have hope, slight as it is, that you will, one day. Lift your proud chin, *'ngwraig*, and let me kiss you."

When she refused, he laughed and held her hard, kissing her

again before he released her. Heledd slid along the wall away from him and ran past Elis and the women, toward the house, chased by her cousin's laughter. She looked back only once. Garmon Dolwyddlan leaned his shoulder against the wall and bowed his head. Elis's satisfied grin seared into her, driving surprise and wonder too deep for her to recall the tenderness of the kiss or the sorrow in Garmon's granite-hued eyes.

Her cousins fixed her with stares as she served them in Llew Talgarth's smaller, private dining hall that evening. She caught a glimpse of Alys with a mawkish smile on her pretty face but no one spoke to her. As she lay down beneath the black and red *carthen*, she wondered at their unending hatred. She had nothing that could hurt them. She had no weapon or power.

For weeks afterward, she could taste Garmon Dolwyddlan, feel him near her, his body shielding her from the cold. She woke at night with the taste of his lips on hers and the scent of his skin in every breath she took. No matter how often Heledd chided herself and warned against such foolishness, she could not deny she wished she had allowed him to kiss her as he asked – if there had been no witnesses. She wished she had given him the hope he wanted, as he had given her the hope he was not laughing at her.

Heledd waited longer outside the *beudy*, walked more slowly as she crossed the yard, went nearer to the barracks than she had ever dared before, on the chance she could thank him. She practiced her carefully fashioned words of gratitude, time after time, but no opportunity came. If he saw her or if he knew she waited for him, he never appeared. The taste of his kiss faded and her memory of the strength of his hand ceased to warm her or ease any ache.


The shortest month brought the coldest days with no promise of spring. Alys commanded her to join her in the small dining hall. Heledd could not refuse. After her work in the milking shed, she sat on the bench beside Alys, and took up the next skein in the basket. She wrapped it around her knees and wound the wool onto an empty shuttle. Her hands were not so chapped the winding made them bleed and she settled into a monotonous and soothing rhythm, the same monotony that made milking a comfort.

"I have news for you, Heledd."

Heledd pulled a burr from the wool and flicked it into the hearth.

"If you have no more interest than that, I will not tell you," Alys pouted.

Heledd glanced up, bringing interest into her weary eyes as if she had lit them with a spark from the fire. "What news do you have?"

"Very soon, I will have a *husband*." Alys straightened her shoulders. "I will not need to steal kisses behind the *beudy* as you do. We will be in our own house."

"When are you to wed?"

"In a few weeks. I know you will be happy for me."

Heledd laid the full shuttle on the bench beside her and picked up another.

"I will be Meilor Gwesyn's daughter-in-law." Alys said this with an iron glint in her eye. "My son will inherit part of all his grandfather owns. Dada tells me Meilor has been negotiating for this union for more than a year. Dada has driven a hard bargain and my bride-price was high, very high, but, of course, he was willing to pay that and more to have me for his son."

"Where will you live?" However much she longed for the freedom Alys enjoyed, Heledd could not afford to allow her cousin to know she did.

"Dada is building a house for us, just there." She pointed beyond the door to the courtyard where another house had once stood.

"Why will your husband be here?"

"He will train as a soldier, of course. Why do you ask that?"

"You were once interested in another soldier."

"What are you talking about? What soldier? I have never been interested in a soldier." Alys stared at Heledd for a moment and erupted into laughter. "Do you miss him?"

"Who?" Too late, Heledd regretted she had reminded her cousin of Garmon Dolwyddlan.

"You are hard. Well, I suppose if that northerner didn't bother to tell you he was leaving, he couldn't have cared much about you."

*Garmon does not want you.* She turned her head away from her cousin's close study, her proud chin shot upward so even the logs in the fire spit back at her – too proud, too hard.

"He left the day he took you behind the *beudy*, where everyone could watch you. How we laughed at you, begging him to stay."

"That is not true." Heledd turned her upper body to face her cousin, squaring her shoulders. "I did not beg him to stay."

"Of course, it is true. Elis does not lie to me. You do always whine so."

"I did not. He said nothing to me of leaving."

"No wonder that one refused to have you with him in the barracks."

"Who told you that?"

"Ach, everyone knows. My father told the northerner he had to take you to the barracks if he wanted to enjoy your company. He told Elis you were his to see where and as often as it pleased him. Apparently, it pleased him best not to see you at all," Alys laughed. "Still, I can hardly believe you have so little concern for the disappearance of a man for whom you may be carrying a child." Alys searched her older cousin's face. "Are you?"

"No," Heledd replied. "I am not."

"Oh, I had hoped we could help each other, since neither of us has a mother to advise us." Alys lowered her eyes for a moment. "I'm sorry you are alone now, Heledd. When you said so little and after what my brothers told me of your wicked—."

"is a lie. I have never been with him, or any man."

Alys shook her head, a smirk on her lips. She leaned toward Heledd and slapped her hand. "If he was so cruel to you, you have only yourself to blame. If you were sweeter, you might have been more fortunate. You will want to be kinder to the next soldier who buys you. By then, I think you will be used to the barracks and the ways of soldiers."

"What do you mean?" When Alys did not answer, Heledd flung the shuttle back into the basket and lurched toward the smaller girl. "I may be sold but I am not a whore and I do not see much difference between your high, very high bride-price and the selling of my bond. You are bought and your body is the chattel."

"To my husband, Heledd, traitor's daughter. My *husband*."


Betsan lurked at the doorway of Heledd's cell with a flat smile on her face and did not move when Heledd approached. "This is not your room now."

"Where am I to sleep?" She tilted her head to look beyond the maidservant.

"This is my room now," Betsan sang, whirling her shabby skirts, blocking Heledd's view. "You have no room in the house."

"What has happened to my belongings?"

"There is nothing here belonging to you. Goewin has cleaned the room for me. Anything that wasn't a rag has gone to others."

"My clothes... My purse!"

"Gone," Betsan giggled. "Go away. I am taking your place in the kitchen and *beudy*."

"What am I to do? Where?"

"How would I know the answer to that? Ask the steward. He was the one who told Goewin to take away your filth."

The kitchen was deserted. The fires had been banked for the night and the two boys were asleep on their straw heaps in the larder. Mice skittered between the legs of the boards and the tin wash basin, escaping from their hunter into the gaps in the stone wall. The cat stretched its front paws, raised its haunches and sprang. With one claw, it hooked its prey and dragged it from the gap, flexing the rest of its claws into the mouse's spine.

The northeast wind clattered against the slats covering the windows and thrust flecks of straw into her face. In the *beudy*,

Heledd gathered an armful of straw and pressed her back against the far wall, tugging the edge of her shawl up to her ear. She cringed when a rat lifted its nose at her and leapt away as though she were vermin.

Before any possibility of sleep came, the door crashed against the wall and Talgarth's sons stood in the opening, each with his sword drawn. Heledd pushed to her feet, hard against the wall. There were screams in her head and wails of horror. All around her, the walls were red, crushing down, roaring with flames, red beads flew in her face, hung from her lashes and she tasted her own blood in her throat. Her fingers dug into the mortar but Elis dragged her into the yard and Deion shoved her away from the house. They said nothing as they stalked her through the yard to the door of the barracks.

"Knock, Heledd, or they will not let you in."

"I will not," she whispered, staring at the door. Between the planks, she saw men in the light of the fire, in groups, sitting, talking. She heard the voices of women and recognized Heulwen's laughter. Elis twisted her wrist and forced her fist against the wood, driving splinters into her knuckles.

"This woman begs entrance," he shouted. Before the door was fully open, Deion propelled her through it and howled with laughter when she fell across the threshold at the feet of a warrior. "Another whore for you, from Llew Talgarth," her eldest cousin said. "This one is already paid for and broken."

The warrior grabbed her by the arms and stood her on her feet, turning her toward the back wall. With one hand, he pushed her into the crowd of men and turned back to the brothers. "Broken?" he growled.

"She'll be no trouble but if she is, you know what my father expects."

The wall of men had closed around her. She felt a hand on her arm and yanked away. No one spoke and the laughter of the women was silenced.

"I know what Llew expects," Urien Macsen replied. "He will have his due."

"When your men are finished—."

"You will be the first to know, Elis Llew. The first to reap the reward." The warrior slapped the door with such force it struck the jamb and shuddered through the low building so everyone felt the tremble in the floorboards. "Leave us to our work."

"Don't come near me. Never come near me." Heledd's plea was met with shrugs from those nearest her as Urien pulled men aside and caught her arms again. "You will have to beat me to death. You will have to kill me," she hissed in his face. He was laughing at her. She twisted her head – they were all laughing at her.

"I will need do neither, *merch*."

"I will not beg. Kill me. I will not beg for my life."

"Ach, no one has asked you." Urien beckoned one of the women toward him. While he still held Heledd, he bent his head to Elain and spoke under his breath. She nodded, disappearing to the far end of the long narrow room. "Have you eaten tonight, Heledd?"

She fought against the constraint of his grip and he let her go but there was no escape through the men and women who crowded around her. Heledd pulled into herself, willing her back to be as straight as the bolt that now barred her cousins' entry into the soldiers' quarters. Though the men spoke in loud voices, she could hear Deion's voice pestering his elder brother, even as they walked away. "I wanted her first. Why do you always give *him* the right?"

"Sit down, Heledd." A man dropped his arm over the speaker's shoulder, resting his hand on her swollen belly. Heulwen rested her chin for a moment on the brawny arm cradling her and smiled at Heledd. "Sit down."

Blackness crashed down on Heledd and she dropped to the floor. She awoke with the faces of Elain and Heulwen close to her. A damp cloth covered her forehead and her black and red *carthen* was spread over her.

"I have never known you to be so fearful, Heledd," Heulwen said, turning the cloth. "You are always the first to fight."

Her eyes shifted from their faces to the white-washed wall of the barracks and the thick, woven homespun separating her from the rest of the room. Heulwen leaned back and groaned, relieving the strain in her spine. Heledd extended her hand to the wall of muscle covering the unborn child and its mother straightened her back, pride filling her eyes. "How long?"

Heulwen shrugged but Elain said, "Hours. She is in labor now."

When they left her, Heledd turned onto her side to face the wall, clutching the black and red wool to her breast, shoving her fist half into her mouth to stifle the sobs racking her as the sounds of the men and the stench of their sweat swelled and receded through the last hours before dawn. When she next woke, the barracks was silent except for the soft voices of women and whispered gasps of breath, rhythmic as the loom clattering with each pass of the shuttle. Heledd held her breath, remembering where she was. She felt the *baban's* first cry reverberating through her body. Silence followed, a hush broken only by a woman's voice. "Let me see my son." A quiet cheer rumbled beneath the rafters and one man dropped to his knees at Heulwen's side.


Within a week, Elis's wife gave birth to a daughter. Alys was charged with the child's care but the work of washing the girl-child's soiled linen was given to Heledd. While his wife recovered, despite the resentment among the soldiers, Elis took comfort with Elain. Heulwen's boy flourished in the brawny arms of his father. When her child was two months old, Heulwen returned to her work in the *beudy* and slept in the barracks, with the father of her son.

One by one, Heledd's possessions were returned to her and she kept them hidden in the corner of the barracks that had become hers, into which no one ventured. Though no wall separated her from their drunken play or grim gambling, though she heard their grunts and prayers, no man followed her to her corner. Though she was always alone, she was always surrounded by soldiers – cursing, spitting, taking their pleasures, staring at her when no one else saw them.

In late spring, Heledd was a year older. She began another year on the same day Alys Llew was wed to Gwern Meilor. The priest joined the two on the same patch of ground upon which Ieuan Bannawg had met his death. Heledd kept her back straight and her eyes averted to the crest of the Gurnos. She had seen Meilor Gwesyn only once ten years before – on the day her uncle sealed their allegiance – but the butcher of her family ignored her as though he had never known she existed.

By summer, Alys was expecting her own child.

"You'll be glad now you helped with Elis's daughter," Alys commented. Heledd stood at her side, as they had nearly a year before, watching Gwern Meilor through another day of training outside the barracks.

"Yes," Heledd answered. The sun was high and the sky cloudless. Her body soaked in the warmth as though it was food for her soul while her skin browned like roasting lamb. "There are riders coming along the river. Many of them," Heledd told her companion, concealing any sign of hope the warrior leading the group was a tall man she knew. "It is not a war band," she said a moment later, "there are women with them." Her curiosity brought a wary frown to her face.

Alys laid her hand on her small, swollen belly and bent forward to get a better view. "They must be coming to see my father," was all she said.

Heledd watched them until they were allowed through the gate, counting two women, a warrior and twelve soldiers, but saw no more of them that day. Though there was music and feasting in Talgarth's hall that night, she was glad to stay in the kitchen when she saw the storyteller take up his stool in front of her uncle's guests. From her place in the pantry, she could see the two women and the warrior talking and laughing with Llew Talgarth, his sons and Urien Macsen. Alys and her husband were also in the hall and when the storyteller began his tale, the family watched their guests with eager expressions, just as they had watched Garmon Dolwyddlan.

"They've traveled far," Goewin said as she loaded another salver with mutton to be taken to the family's dining *neuadd*, "too far for it to be of value but they will hear the same tale. Llew Talgarth will ensure the whole of Hywel's kingdom hears how we are brought low. Our shame is no secret. Go, Heledd, lie at their feet to be kicked."

"From the north, do you think?" Heledd asked, ignoring the order. Though Garmon had abandoned her, her thoughts often turned to him unbidden. She no longer felt shame or guilt for the way she had been treated. Her life was better. Though the soldiers harried her, Urien Macsen was deaf to her cousins' demands for news she served as Llew Talgarth expected.

"Ach, who can tell? Unless over the Bannawg, there is only one way to enter this valley and that is along the river, upstream, from the south. They are from downstream as far as I can say." Goewin shoved the salver into the arms of the nearest serving boy and dusted flour from her hands, turning to start another task.

Heledd had forgiven Garmon for whatever had been his intention, bestowing on him an honorable character for his restraint, even if the cause of that restraint was drunkenness, or, as she had come to believe, had never wanted her in the first place. Her family had played some trick on him from which he escaped when he was sober at dawn. Heledd no longer held him accountable.

"What do you suppose is to the north?" Heledd asked, turning once again to her duties, plunging her hands into the tin basin to wash the wooden bowls retrieved from Talgarth's table. Since there was now no danger he would appear, she felt free to be honest, at least in the privacy of her heart. She was safe to think and dream about Garmon Dolwyddlan – he would always be kind to her, never disappoint her, mock or laugh at her. Though she had not understood at the time, she had come to believe he had cared enough to say good-bye. Although she still wished she had let him kiss her in the way he wanted, she was glad he had not forced her to do so.

"Murder and shame, nothing I ever want to see again,"

Goewin replied. "And neither should you, my girl. When you have finished there, you may go to your bed. They will retire soon, judging from the listless talk tonight."

Heledd did as she was bid, turning toward the barracks with Heulwen, Elain and all the others – women she had come to know by name. Closing her eyes on another day, she pressed her fingers to her lips and hunched her shoulder beneath the *carthen* the northerner had given her.

# FOUR

In the late afternoon of the following day, Talgarth joined his daughter and niece to watch his soldiers training. Heledd, standing at the edge of the wall, the sun in her eyes, was restless, watching another soldier train with Urien Macsen. The other soldiers in the guests' war band watched their fair-haired commander. Heledd had not seen the two women of the group since their arrival. Alys was intent on her husband and the child in her belly as she sat sheltered beneath the canopy.

"You are more like your mother every day," Talgarth told his daughter, patting her hand. Alys smiled up at him.

"Heledd." His tone was sharp, impatient. "I have accepted another offer for you." He waited a moment for the surprise to fade from his niece's eyes. "A reasonable offer," he assured her.

"No! You cannot do this, Dada. Who will be here when my child is born? Heledd is meant to help me, you told me yourself. You promised—."

"My purse does not stretch in all directions to meet your needs, Alys," Talgarth replied, turning his thin gaze on Heledd.

"Who has made this offer?" She was not fooled by his use of the words *offer* or *reasonable*.

"Huw Bro-Dawel," Talgarth told her. "I am glad you are determined to be sensible. The man has paid your bond. He drove a hard bargain, but I succeeded in getting a good portion of your worth from him. I also exacted a small settlement for you, so you need not feel slighted."

"You are satisfied with this offer, Uncle?"

"I know the man, Heledd. You cannot do better."

"Am I to meet him before I go?" Heledd glanced at the fair-haired warrior. He was near the same age as another soldier she knew and he was smiling. Urien never smiled – he bore the weight of his command in a scowl from dawn until darkness, even when he met Elain to walk away from the hill *caer*, he was a commander foremost. The fair-haired warrior grinned when she met his gaze and she thought she saw a twitch at the corner of Urien's hard mouth. Heledd dropped her eyes, but she couldn't hide the willful curve of her lips.

"He has sent his daughters and these warriors to escort you to him."

"His daughters are older than Heledd, Dada," Alys giggled, "and Heledd seems to prefer this golden creature, even to Urien. What is he like, Heledd?"

"What does that matter?" Talgarth demanded.

"Her new master must be very old. Does he know she is not a maiden?"

"He did not ask," her father replied. "He has had only one wife I know of," he told his niece. "He has been divorced for more than twenty years. A man needs companionship."

"He has been divorced longer than Heledd is old," Alys laughed. "You can teach him, Heledd. He will need encouragement. Will you tell him you prefer his emissary, Heledd?"

"When am I to leave?" Although the offer meant she would never be free, neither would she be waiting for a soldier from the north to return nor be at her uncle's mercy or his daughter's beck and call.

"Heledd, you cannot mean to accept. This is slavery ... of the worst kind."

Heledd did not respond but turned to Talgarth for his answer.

Talgarth smiled and said, "Your escort is leaving tomorrow. You will become acquainted with Bro-Dawel's daughters on the journey."

"Uncle," Heledd began, lifting her chin as she spoke. "What was the first offer you received for me?"

"What? What are you asking?"

Heledd's chin rose a fraction more. "You said you had now received another offer for me. There was one other before this. What was it?"

"Do not concern yourself with that. It was … withdrawn. You will leave tomorrow."

Heledd thought the sudden thud of her heart against the wall of her chest could be heard and her hands flew, clenched to her breast to silence it. *Withdrawn.*

As soon as her father had left, Alys turned on Heledd with a screech that attracted the attention of the soldiers in the field. "How could you do this to me? It is only because of me you weren't thrown out of my father's house years ago," Alys hissed. "Once that northerner was finished with you, Dada wanted to send you to the barracks – to get some worth from you – but I stopped him. I begged him for your sake. This is how you repay me? It was your own fault my father agreed to the soldiers' demands. Now you sell yourself to an old man you have never seen."

"I have not sold myself," Heledd answered. "I have been sold."

"More than once," Alys growled. "You with your wild ideas of who is sold and what is bought. I forgave you the first time—."

"You forgave *me?*"

"Yes, I did and this is my reward. Good riddance. Who knows what diseases you might bring into my house to infect my child? Who knows how long it would be before you seduced my husband? We'll see how long this old man keeps you before *he* abandons you like the northerner did. You couldn't keep him and he was as old as Urien Macsen. My father was forced to offer you to the soldiers without payment from their wages. And I have felt sorry for you. You *are* a whore," Alys screamed before she ran down the steps and across the yard.

Heledd felt the eyes of the soldiers turn on her and tilted her chin toward the rays of the hot sun crowning the Gurnos. *Withdrawn. Gone with no word in all these months. Such a fool, you are, Heledd Bannawg.*

Before dawn, Heledd was awakened by the sound of horses in the farm close. Her new master had bestowed gifts and, since it no longer mattered she now had finer garments than any Alys owned, she dressed in the fine, embroidered frock. She covered it with the mulberry-dyed tunic. Though the day promised to be hot, she also wore new woolen stockings and tied the black silk purse to her belt, wrapping all the rest of her few possessions in Garmon Dolwyddlan's thick, soft *carthen*. Goewin was waiting for her in the kitchen with a bowl of *cawl* and warmed ale. "You will have a long journey," she said when Heledd protested she did not have time to eat. "These people can wait for you to be fed, since they have not seen fit to speak to you in all the time they have been enjoying the hospitality of Bannawg."

"Thank you," Heledd murmured, sitting where the *beudy* mistress directed and surrendering to her fussing. Not a minute passed before a shadow filled the doorway.

"*Boneddiges*," the fair-headed commander said as he waited beside a gray-dappled mare. She held her breath at the formality, the graciousness of his greeting. She had never been offered the dignity of 'gentlewoman' before. "If we do not leave soon, we will not make our home by nightfall." She was on her feet, rushing toward the fair-haired warrior as though she had never had any fear of a man of his profession. He grasped her arm and led her toward the others in his company. The two women were already mounted, their horses stamping the ground.

"We have wasted enough time," said one of the sisters. "Throw her over that wretched animal's back if she will not mount. We have had enough of these false tears."

Heledd glanced back over her shoulder but Goewin was already herding the other women to the kitchen and their work. She clutched her few possessions close to her heart and lifted her eyes to the face of the warrior who held her arm.

"*Boneddiges*, if you will allow me," he said, standing by while she settled on the back of the docile animal. "Huw Bro-Dawel asks you to accept this mare as a token of his gratitude you have accepted his offer. If you have any need, you have only to ask me."

"What is your name?"

"I am Aled, a friend, Heledd *merch* Ieuan Bannawg," he replied.

Heledd searched his cheerful face, saddened he reminded her so soon of her father and her shame. When all of the soldiers had mounted, the travelers left the *gaer* and the gates were closed behind them. Heledd looked back but no one bid her farewell and she turned her face in the direction she was meant to go – not beyond the Gurnos as she had always hoped, but south, to follow the relentless Tywi.

Aled kept a silent vigil. Heledd grasped the opportunity to study her companions and surroundings on the journey. The soldiers were all dressed in linen shirts, dyed deep violet with gold sashes across their chests. They wore flannel leggings and short boots. Aled also wore a violet linen shirt, with a purple and gold-trimmed tunic, opened at the sides and fastened together by a leather belt holding his sword and hunting knife close to hand. His leggings were a fine, natural leather made to fit him like a glove. He was not as lean nor as tall as another man she knew but he smiled more often.

The sister who had spoken wore her brown hair in long, soft plaits, interwoven with the same violet and gold the men were wearing. Her frock was made from a delicate linen, with purple silk braid around her sleeve cuffs and the hem of the full skirt. Over the frock, she wore a long purple coat, fitted over her torso and flaring out over her hips with long, wide sleeves folded back to show the gold brocade lining. Her steady, blue eyes were inquisitive, judgmental and unforgiving.

The quieter sister was fair and dressed her golden brown hair with two plaits at the side drawn back to meet at the nape of her neck and fastened by a black ribbon. She had deep blue eyes that, to Heledd, seemed forlorn. Her garments were somber, from her brown frock to her black hooded cloak, even to her black woolen stockings and ankle boots.

At midmorning, they stopped at the place where the Tywi spread its surging, roaring power over the wide valley. Streams and rivulets flowed noisily from the hills and the Tywi swelled in violent eddies at every intermingling. Heledd had never seen the river turn back on itself, as swirls of water rushed upstream as forcefully as those coming down.

"If you have no objection, *boneddiges*," Aled said, "we will stop here for a while to rest the horses. We will eat and drink then press on to Bro-Dawel." While they rested, the elder sister called Aled to her. He excused himself from Heledd's company and stood before the two. "Where did you sleep last night?" Mared asked him.

"In the barracks with my command, *boneddiges*, where else?"

"Was *she* there?"

"I cannot say, Mared. Heledd *merch* Ieuan Bannawg is not my concern."

"Really? I was told Talgarth had sent her to Urien Macsen and he—."

"If you are so curious, you know whom to ask. Which of the Talgarth soldiers did you call to your bed?" While his soldiers laughed aloud, he avoided the hand Mared raised to strike him.

"You will regret that."

"When does a great pleasure not bring regret?" He gestured for his soldiers to mount. As Aled cupped his hands beneath Heledd's foot, he grinned and lifted her onto the mare's back. Whether Huw Bro-Dawel was tolerant of his soldiers' behavior or had no regard for his daughters, neither prospect relieved any of her misgivings about her new master. The sun remained high for the remainder of the journey but as dusk closed behind them, the horses sensed their stables, nourishment and rest. Her gray-dappled mare increased its pace as the smoke and flickering torch lights of a *caer* came into view when the company reached the brow of a hill. They rode into a valley laden with orchards, vineyards, woods between two rivers, fields stretching as far as she could see, grain in swathes of gold to the tops of the rolling hills in every direction.

As they approached, the gates opened and the sisters urged their mounts forward, entering ahead of the soldiers who kept pace with Heledd. When she pulled back on the reins, resisting the mare's desire to reach home, Aled waited beside her, laying his hands on the crown of his saddle, and gazed at her face.

"You have nothing to fear from our *pennaeth*," he said. "He is a good man. There is no reason for you to fear this place or any who live here."

Heledd glanced at him, swallowing hard. "Do you know of a place called Dolwyddlan?"

"Is it a place you know? Do you have reason to go there?"

Heledd saw his wide grin and her ignorance grated. "No. Never." Her chin was high and she raised the reins to signal the mare forward. Gritting her teeth, she said, "One final question." Aled nodded with another wide grin. "Is this place in the north?"

"No, *boneddiges*. We are to the south and far west of Bannawg."

"Good." *Bannawg*. Heledd turned her head toward the Gurnos, imagining she could see the rays of the setting sun on its face. *South and west. Beyond the Gurnos.*

As she directed the mare through the gates of the *gaer*, Heledd caught her breath at the hundreds of soldiers within the walls. Many wore their weapons openly. Others were off-duty and talked in groups everywhere she looked. They greeted Aled and stared at her. Some followed the returning group, murmuring amongst themselves, calling others to witness.

The sisters had already dismounted and rushed toward the large house surrounding a courtyard, at the center of the walled *caer*. One of her escorts helped her to dismount but left her alone by the mare, in doubt whether she should also go to the house. She heard her uncle's name often and those of her cousins. No one spoke to her. After a while, they began to walk away, leading their horses with them. Heledd feigned an interest in her purse. When Aled had given his orders and received others, he came toward her, a frown fading from his mouth.

"Huw Bro-Dawel cannot see you now, *boneddiges*, but has left instructions for your comfort. He welcomes you to your new home." Aled led her to the house and directed one of the women to take care of her.

Heledd's room, one of three along a corridor, had a window looking toward the hills and was many times larger than her cell. The floor was covered with oiled flagstones. There was a small grate in the wall with a fire already burning, filling the room with the scent of herbs. The solid door could be bolted and Heledd did not hesitate to slide the bolt into place, savoring the breath-taking sense of privacy.

Meat and drink were brought to her as well as a tub of warm water. The woman who helped her to undress handled her fine linen frock with a smile, folding it over a stool in the corner, gesturing for Heledd to sit down in the tub. The water was warmer than her skin and felt like silk. The fragrance of the soap was familiar and filled her with a sense of ease. While Heledd lathered the cloth and stroked it over her face and arms, she searched her head for questions that were not too ignorant to ask.

"What is this soap?"

"It is lavender, *boneddiges*. The *pennaeth's* daughter makes it."

"What is her name? What is your name?"

"Meini is the *pennaeth's* youngest daughter. I am Bethan. If you require anything, you can find me in the kitchen. Or ask any of the stewards," she added, laying a sleeveless nightdress on the bed. "Someone will always know where to find me."

"I have worked in the *beudy*," Heledd said, folding the cloth over the edge of the tub and shivering as she stood. Bethan draped the linen sheet around her and called two boys to take the tub away. The boys stared at Heledd but Bethan chased them from the room.

"Everyone is curious," she scolded at their backs. "Mind your eyes are not gouged out for your peeping."

"Who would do that to them?"

"The man who brought you here, of course."

"You mean Aled?"

"No, *merch*. But you have nothing to fear from boys. The

soldiers have talked of nothing else. And the women. Everyone wants to know something more about you."

"What do you know already?"

"Not much. You are from the East and your parents are dead," Bethan said, peeling the linen out of Heledd's hands and handing her the nightdress. The fabric was delicate and all of the edges were trimmed with narrow lace. It fell over her body like down, settling against her, clinging to her still damp skin. "Stand by the fire until you are warm and then go to bed. You have had a long journey."

"Where can I find Aled?"

"Ach, he will be with his wife by now, *merch*, having a meal with his children. But I can have him brought to you."

"No! I mean, I only wanted to ask a question."

"If I can answer," the woman said, "I will, *merch*."

"You have been very kind and it is late. I do not want to keep you."

"Have you eaten your fill?" When she nodded, Bethan said, "Then I will wish you a good night's rest. If you require anything, there will always be someone near."

The bed was high and so wide she could stretch her arms and not reach the edges. The webbing was covered with a thick, down-filled mattress, a linen canvas and a pile of soft, woolen *carthen*. Heledd sank into it but sleep did not come as easily as her surroundings soothed her. If Huw Bro-Dawel gouged out the eyes of boys, what would he do to her, she wondered, if she failed to meet his expectations? What had her uncle said of her to make a *pennaeth* want to pay her bond? What would be expected of her to earn all the gifts she had been given?

The glow of the fire cast shadows on the whitewashed wall opposite her but, stare as she would, she could find no answers. In the morning, she waited to be summoned but no word came from her new master. Closing the door on her room, she ventured into the corridor of the house to find the courtyard, careful to remember how she might return if she must. Retracing her steps from the night before, she took a deep breath of the late summer breeze. The aroma of baking bread filled her nostrils. She grew accustomed to people staring at her and returned their interest.

"What is your work?" she asked one man who was making a shoe. He stared back at her and said he was a cobbler. "Do you make only shoes or ... or do you also make saddles?" she asked, her chin rising a little higher with each faltering question. She could not blame her red cheeks on the heat of the sun.

"No, *boneddiges*," he replied. "I do not make saddles. I make shoes. When you want a pair to replace those," he said, gesturing with his awl at her clogs, "come to me."

Heledd gave him a weak smile and turned to walk away from her failure at idle conversation.

"If you wish to explore," Aled said to her as she approached the courtyard, "you should ask me."

"I did not know I needed permission."

"Not permission, Heledd. A guide. I am at your disposal, at whatever time or place you appoint."

"I would like to see Huw Bro-Dawel."

"Unfortunately, he is not available, but I will tell him you have requested a meeting."

"My uncle—. Talgarth has told me he knows Huw Bro-Dawel and you have told me he is a good man," Heledd ventured.

"That is true. He is a busy man, Heledd. Today, he hears complaints."

"What am I to do until he is ready to see me?"

"As you like," Aled said with a bow. "Bro-Dawel – the *gaer*, the village, the *ystad*, all await your pleasure. Would you like to ride? This *ystad* is pretty and the day is fine."

"No, thank you."

"Be at home, Heledd Bannawg," he said. "No harm will come to you while I live and all here wish you well."

"Save the *pennaeth's* daughters."

"Mared knows little of any matter of importance," Aled said. "She resents her ignorance where you are concerned and turns her resentment against the one she would do well to know. And Meini, ... Meini has other concerns."

"The result is the same," Heledd said.

"Aye," he said, "but don't be hasty to judge us. There is much to see and learn on both sides. Your arrival has been long awaited by many and a ride will help you become acquainted with your new home."

Five soldiers waited for them at the gates. All wore their hair cropped close to their heads, as though they had been shaved and a few weeks' growth of hair had returned. Their thickly padded jerkins were of the same purple as Aled's shirt. Each had a sword and hunting knife in their belts. They greeted her with smiles but their eyes betrayed a keener interest. Although they rode to the rear, she felt their scrutiny to the marrow of her spine. With effort, she fixed her attention on the fields of grain surrounded by hawthorn hedgerows woven to keep wandering animals, even to the smallest lamb, from escaping. The trees in the apple orchard were heavy with fruit. Vineyards sheltered on the west-facing slopes of the hills.

"All this belongs to Huw Bro-Dawel?"

"Aye," Aled replied, "and more. We do not have time to see the north and east today, but I will take you to the south before we return. You are to have your meal with the *pennaeth* and his daughters later."

"Then I should return to the house to make ready."

"That will not be necessary," Aled told her, continuing on the circuit of the boundary to the south. "This is the most beautiful part of all the *ystad*. It is wild and impossible to tame for farming. The *pennaeth* keeps it for hunting – his favorite pastime in recent years."

"Thank you, Aled," Heledd said, "but I cannot go to the *neuadd* of Huw Bro-Dawel as I am, straight from riding."

"*Boneddiges*, how you appear in Huw's *neuadd* will make no difference to him. Better that you know something of your home than waste fine weather where your effort will not be appreciated."

"Why? Why will he not appreciate such an effort?"

"He will not," Aled insisted. "He is not unkind, *boneddiges*, he is practical. He would prefer you to know your new home than

61

you waste time on frivolities." He urged her to take account of the beauty of the landscape into which their horses had plunged. As they trotted deeper into a green wood, all around them the air was cool and moist, fragrant with growth. Sunlight forced petals to flare open under its gaze, releasing perfume that attracted bees from the hives. The thud of the hooves of the seven horses was muffled by the thick layers of moss and leafy mold all along the well-trodden trail. Deer and other game shot across their path.

"Wait here, *boneddiges*," Aled commanded and gestured for the soldier nearest him to follow.

"What is it?" Heledd asked the soldier who had moved into Aled's place beside her.

"A warband," the young soldier said under his breath.

"I don't see anyone," Heledd whispered, her blood chilling so suddenly she shivered.

"The commander of a warband who would allow his troops to be seen by a woman is not a good soldier," he laughed quietly.

"I am not blind," Heledd said, raising her chin.

"You are not a soldier either," he said.

"Geraint," murmured another, "it's him."

"Who?" Heledd asked, straining to see, fear welling in her throat, cutting off her voice.

"There is nothing for you to fear, *boneddiges*," Geraint answered. "The warband is commanded by a friend." Though she stared hard into the wood, Heledd could see no one, not even Aled and the other soldier who had gone with him to investigate.

"How can you tell?"

"We know him," Geraint answered. "Sign of him is all around us."

"Where? I don't see anything." Heledd said, looking in every direction.

"You don't need to see him," said the second soldier. "With respect, *boneddiges*, if you could – if he was our enemy, he would be dead."

"Hisht, Nisien," Geraint ordered. "Aled returns."

"Where?" Heledd demanded.

"Here," Aled laughed, riding up from behind the group waiting for him. Aled smiled to reassure her then spoke to the others. "It is as planned. He won't come as yet, be wary. He expects visitors any day."

"Where is this warband? How did you know?" Heledd asked again. "What visitors?"

"The commander left a sign he wanted to talk. He is training new men."

"Where is this sign?"

"Back at the top of the trail into this *cwm*. Carwyn," Aled told her, nodding toward the boy-soldier who had accompanied him to meet the warband, "was the first to see it." Carwyn grinned at Heledd. "He has earned his mead today."

Heledd pressed her lips together and urged her horse forward a few paces, glancing through the trees in the direction Aled and Carwyn had gone but she could see nothing that was not bark and foliage. "Is that why we came this way?" she asked.

"Yes," Aled said. "The commander had reason to meet us."

"What reason?"

"His own," Aled answered, frowning. "He is not accountable to us, *boneddiges*. Only to the *pennaeth*."

"Are you also training?" she asked.

"We are always training, *boneddiges*. We are at war, not to train is to become complacent. Laziness means death," Aled said. "We have lost too many good men in recent months." Aled gazed into her dappled face for a moment. "You need not be frightened, *boneddiges*. No harm will come to you while we six are near. We are your protection – sworn to ensure your safety. Carwyn, Nisien, Geraint," he said, pointing to the soldiers in turn, "Rhodri, Daf and myself. We are the best warriors, save one, Bro-Dawel has to offer. At your command," he finished, bowing his head to her. "If you have any need, each one of us has been ordered to see it is done. At least one of us will be close at hand, with the others ready, at any time you require."

The work of the day was ending by the time the seven explorers reached the gates of the *gaer* and were granted entrance. Only a few soldiers remained in the yard and were turning their attention to their meat, mead and bed. Aled escorted his guest to the *pennaeth's* private hall and presented her to Huw Bro-Dawel. Two of her guards entered the room and took places behind the *pennaeth*, standing on either side of the doorway leading to another part of the house. Huw Bro-Dawel stared at the girl before him for several moments.

"Hmmm," he began, "you are not as pretty as I was told." His eldest daughter, seated to his left, giggled. Heledd studied him as closely as she was studied. He was near in age to her own father, had he lived, nearer sixty than forty. His gray hair was close-cropped, like his soldiers. The brown of his eyes was ringed with halos of luminous blue and his jaw was covered with a dark, day's growth of beard.

"I am as I am," Heledd replied, holding her chin high. "It is not for me to offer any comment on the opinions of others." Despite his age, he was still vigorous and strong, robust. His thick fingers grasped the bowl of the cup in his hand with a firm, steady tension.

"Neither are you as ugly as some have said," Huw remarked, his eyes smiled at her, though his voice was gruff.

"Her hair is the color of blood," Mared whispered to her sister. "That is ugly. And those blemishes." Though she hated the sight of her own hair, Heledd dropped her eyes for a moment. She had never been told she was blemished but she was not surprised to hear it.

"Sit by me, *merch*," Huw Bro-Dawel commanded, placing her on his right. "You will be safe enough here. Those two are not part of the bargain," he told her, holding out his hand to her. She accepted his hand, surprised when he clasped her fingers in a possessive grip. "You have met my daughters, I think."

"No, *pennaeth*, I have not." Huw gave her a sidelong look and shrugged.

"Widows, the two of them. And mostly childless," he said, his deep voice cutting across all conversation in the hall. "Both of their husbands preferred to die in war than live with them," he growled. "The older of the two is Mared. The second is Meini. They are much of a muchness and need not concern you." Heledd nodded her understanding, accepting the meat he put before her. "Meini will not remarry but Mared will soon be wed again and thankfully occupied by her husband's needs … as will you."

Heledd could not hide the blush that shot across her freckled cheeks. *Husband?* Her uncle had not mentioned anything about a husband. She pressed her lips tightly together as Huw laughed at her. He held up his cup to be filled and did the same with the cup at her fingertips. "You will like this mead. It is sweet enough for a maid and robust enough for even an old stallion." Heledd tasted the drink and agreed. Her cup was not empty for the rest of the evening but she drank little of the strong liquor, though Huw Bro-Dawel emptied his cup as many times as he lifted it to be refilled.

"What of Bro-Dawel have you seen? I gave orders, were they followed?"

"I do not know if your orders were followed, but I saw the western and southern boundaries. As well as a fine, green wood."

"Ah, my hunting grounds," the *pennaeth* said with obvious pride but taking no more interest in the matter. "What skills have you learned?"

"I have learned to make bread and milk cows," she said. Mared's laughter burst out of her mouth like sparks from pitch-wood. Her father turned a cold eye on her and she was silent.

"These are useful," he said. "Any others?"

"I have learned to sew but I am not skilled in fine work."

"Also good," Huw assured her, urging further disclosure with an open handed gesture. Heledd's cheeks burned. Behind him, Mared was mimicking her way of speaking, exaggerating the tilt of her chin, all watched by her guards, Rhodri and Daf.

"Spinning," Heledd answered Huw's encouragement in a

small voice.

"Excellent. Excellent," the *pennaeth* approved, patting her forearm. "You will be a great asset. Everyone works here," he said with a glance at his daughters. "Suitable employment is a boon, Heledd. We will find plenty for you to do."

Huw Bro-Dawel rose from the table, gesturing for her to leave ahead of him. She could feel the sisters' eyes stabbing into her back as she crossed the floor to the passageway. Before she laid her hand on the latch, Huw's fist came down on the table sending crockery crashing to the stone flags. Rhodri reached around her to open the door. Daf ushered her through to the safety of the corridor. Through the closed door, she heard the *pennaeth* rail at his offspring in vile language she had never heard spoken by a man of his rank before.

"Will he punish them?"

"Mared will wish he had," Rhodri replied and led her back to her room.

She did not question his orders, but wondered what Huw Bro-Dawel had in mind for her. That she would work was apparent and did not frighten her. Before she undressed, Heledd bolted the door.

# Five

"Where are you going?" Geraint caught up with Heledd in the *buarth* the following morning.

"To the *beudy*."

"Your horse is waiting." He blocked her path. "I have been ordered to bring you—."

"Tell Aled I have work today."

"*Boneddiges*, this is not how—. What am I to say?" he asked, tilting his blond head to peer into her eyes. "If the commander hears I let you work," he appealed, "I will have to explain."

"Tell him I refused to obey you."

"Obey? You do not—. You are not required to obey me." He stood for a moment then sighed. "I will go to the *beudy* with you."

"I'm sure I can be trusted to work without a guard," Heledd told him.

"I have my duty, *boneddiges*. I will be with you until my watch is finished."

"Who is on watch after you?"

"We were all to ride with you today, but if you stay in the *gaer*, Carwyn will follow me, then Aled."

"I hope you all enjoy the *beudy*."

"Aye, *boneddiges*," he replied, following at her heels.

After a moment she asked, "Do you think I will be allowed to work the cheese press?"

At the entrance to the *beudy*, Geraint stood with arms folded across his chest, observing her, as Heledd took her place by the side of the next cow to be milked, patted its belly and rubbed her hands together to warm them before grasping the animal's teats. The other women at the milking took little notice of her.

When she saw the red-haired girl quietly at her work in the stall opposite her, Mared leapt from her stool, unmindful of the amount of milk she spilled in the straw, darting across the *beudy* with her arm raised. Her scream terrified the animals and Heledd was knocked off her stool by the cow she milked, splashing some of the precious contents over her clothes. Scrambling to right the bucket before it fell into the hay, Heledd quickly soothed her animal and returned to her work.

"Serves you right," Mared screeched. "This is all your fault."

Heledd pressed her forehead against the cow's belly. The cow's muscles flexed and twitched, stamping its hind legs but Heledd was steadfast until the animal settled with the rhythmic motion of her hands and the returning quiet of the *beudy*.

"Put me down," Mared hissed. "You have no right to interfere with me, Geraint."

"I have my orders."

Heledd swallowed hard, closing her eyes. Her decision to face the wrath of the sisters had not had the result she hoped.

"Geraint," Heledd heard Aled's voice. "Go back to your post." The soldier set Mared's feet on the hay-strewn floor, released her and folded his arms across his chest as before. Aled crouched beside Heledd. "You are not required to work."

"I prefer work," Heledd said, lifting her head and continuing with her steady hands to fill the bucket. "I am not afraid of work."

"Neither should you fear anyone," he murmured. "When you have finished demonstrating your courage and willingness to labor, come to the *buarth*."

Heledd nodded and, having filled one bucket, moved on to fill another. When both were ready, she found the harness, hooked the buckets to the straps and lifted the wooden beam onto her shoulders to carry the milk to the vat. Geraint followed her at a short distance and sighed with relief when she hung up her milking apron and walked into the sunshine.

"There is a lot of work involved in getting cheese," he commented.

"Cheese is a wonderful thing and there is a lot of work involved," Heledd laughed. "I do not know enough but at least that much of my effort was not wasted."

"What do you mean, *boneddiges*?"

"You may now have some respect for the hard work women do to put food in your belly."

"I have not always been a soldier, *boneddiges*," Geraint replied, stiffening. "I am not ignorant of others' part in the life of the *gaer*."

"What has happened now?" Aled demanded, looking from Heledd's pout to Geraint's frown.

"Nothing," Heledd said. "Geraint has taught me a lesson, for which I was in need."

"What did you do?" Aled demanded of his soldier, stepping forward, his hand instinctively falling on the hilt of his knife.

Heledd stepped between them. "It is nothing. Nothing. I insulted him."

"*Boneddiges*." Geraint laid his hand on her arm.

"He is trained to accept insult without retaliation, especially from you," Aled told her, glaring at the soldier. "You are relieved of your duty."

"No," Heledd said. "I do not want that. Geraint and I are coming to understand one another. I want him to stay."

"Understand one another?" Aled questioned, narrowing one eye at the young man standing erect behind Heledd. "Are you mad? Do you have anything in your head but *uwd*?"

"Leave him alone. It is not his fault. It is mine and I am making it worse – I insulted him, his intelligence. He only told me what, if I was anything other than ignorant myself, I would have known. He did not breech any code, even yours. Now, let's go," she said, pushing Aled out of her way and demanding Geraint help her to mount the gray-dappled mare. "I am very sorry," she said under her breath, tears welling in her eyes.

"We will talk of this later," Aled told Geraint. "Return to your duties for now." Aled guided his auburn-maned warhorse through the open gates. Though she could hear whispering among the five, she could not catch any of their words and sighed, ashamed of her innate ability to anger everyone at Bro-Dawel. Her mood remained pensive throughout the journey upstream along the smaller of the two rivers. She took little account of her surroundings and failed to shake off her disappointment in herself until Aled halted and waited for her to catch up with him.

"If you are concerned an injustice will be done to Geraint on your account, you are mistaken. He will not be judged without evidence and since you have claimed the fault, there is no case against him." Heledd lifted her chin a little. "That does not mean he will not have to explain himself and the circumstances—."

"I can explain," Heledd said.

"You will not be called to explain. This is between Geraint and his commander."

"But—."

"*Boneddiges*, I have told you. He will be treated fairly and no harm will come to him unjustly. I give you my word."

"But, this is my fault. All of it."

"*Boneddiges*, trust me," Aled said, pressing her hand. "Geraint will put his trust in his commander, as he has always." Aled raised his head from his close scrutiny of her face and pointed ahead of them. "There is the northern boundary of Bro-Dawel's *ystad* – a natural boundary of the river beyond Tredeml. To the east is one of the cloister schools in this district. Huw Bro-Dawel is their patron here. Can you see the roof?" Heledd shook her head. "Just beyond that stand of trees below the hill? When the sun shines on it, it is like gold." Heledd could not see any sign of a building in the direction Aled pointed. He shrugged, glancing back at his soldiers. "The land for this school was given to the order by the *pennaeth*. For their service to his ... family."

"Does the family go there often?"

"Often?" Aled shrugged again. "When necessary. There is a chapel nearer the *gaer* for worship. Capel Non. You can go there as you wish. The priest is there on the Sabbath, but the chapel is open to all, every day."

"Thank you, Aled."

"You see that copse, between the rivers? Near the *gaer*?"

"Yes," she said, finding the copse easily.

"The chapel is there, in the center of that grove."

"I see it."

"It is a beautiful chapel – the walls are painted with saints, flowers, birds. Especially in the morning, when the sun shines through the window above the altar."

"I'm sure it is pretty."

Aled nodded his head and turned his attention once again to the view to the north. He told her the *ystad* included a village and the small market town. "Tredeml is only a small village. The people come to the *gaer* in winter, it is the same with the town. The *gaer* is sheltered, the village and town are not. Bro-Dawel is a noisy place in winter, and cheerful."

Heledd did not understand why Aled made the effort to give her the best impression of her new home. She was a bondservant and, although Huw Bro-Dawel had used the word 'husband', Heledd had no misunderstanding of its meaning where bondwomen were concerned. "I would like to return to the house," she said and pressed her knees to the mare's shoulders.

As if he read her thoughts, Aled said, "*Boneddiges*—, Heledd, there is not one man in this command who, for love of the man who brought you here, would not gladly give his own life to protect you."

"You flatter me," she said, "or you are courteous. Huw Bro-Dawel must be a good man to commit the lives of his finest to protect his chattel." She rode ahead and resisted Aled's attempts at further conversation. There was a trick in his flattery and she meant to know it. A sudden breeze shook the leaves high above her head and chilled her to the bone.


Despite the excursions to every corner of the Bro-Dawel *ystad* and the attention she received from her elite guard, Heledd puzzled over her position in the family and her relationship with the *pennaeth's* daughters. As the days wore on, Huw took even less notice of her than he had when she first arrived. Though she had her meals in the family's private hall, he spoke only in greeting but did not converse with her as he did with the stewards, soldiers and other officials of his household. Heledd resigned herself to being in the same category of importance as his daughters – beneath his notice.

There was always meat on the table. The wine and mead flowed. The bread was fresh and fragrant. The cheese was rich. As the time for harvest neared, the new apples began to replace the sauces made from the previous year's crop. Turnip and parsnip were prepared roasted with the meat or boiled and mashed with butter and herbs, sometimes with honey for breakfast. The cook made sweet oat cakes Huw Bro-Dawel pushed away but his daughters relished as much as Heledd.

She had discovered the small, iron-bound chest in her room contained more clothing. The *carthen* on her bed were as soft and as thick, but she kept the one from Garmon Dolwyddlan close to her skin.

At the end of another week on the *ystad*, she had become well acquainted with her surroundings beyond the *gaer* as well as most of the buildings within the settlement. When she also became familiar with the routine of the *gaer*, she took her breakfast with the other members of the household in the dining hall next to the family's private rooms.

On a fine morning at the beginning of the harvesting season, she walked beyond the paddock toward a longhouse standing apart from the other dwellings, behind a stone wall and slatted gate. Carwyn greeted her from the courtyard, running to catch up.

"Do I need a guard to stroll within the *gaer*?"

"I was told you are going to the chapel today," Carwyn replied.

"Am I?" Heledd shrugged. "Who lives in that house?"

"My commander," Carwyn answered and turned back the way he had come. "Our horses are ready, *boneddiges*."

"I would like it if you called me Heledd," she said,

Accustomed to long days of hard work, her inactivity vexed her. "I am not lazy, you know. I can be doing something useful. I could learn to make cheese."

"That is not required," Carwyn said. "There are plenty of people here to do work, especially now Mared has learned to milk." His grin did nothing to lift her foreboding.

"She does not thank me for that," Heledd said, pressing her lips together. Shielding her eyes against the sunlight, she glanced around the *buarth* but saw no one of whom she could ask for occupation. Although Aled had given her a glowing account, she had not thought to go to the chapel on her own and had not accompanied the family on the Sabbath. "We will walk?"

"If it is your wish, *boneddiges*."

"Heledd. Please? I think we can be friends, Carwyn, don't you?" Of the six soldiers who accompanied her, he was the youngest and seemed the most innocent. She did not see suspicion or cruelty in his eyes. He was younger than Heledd, tall and sure of himself.

"If you wish … Heledd."

"I do," she said, taking his arm with a skip in her step.

As the harvest drew near, the soldiers were honing scythes or repairing the carts, oiling the harnesses for the oxen, carving new handles for the short sickles. The air was filled with the blending scents of leather, oil and new wood shavings – more pleasant than the manure that made the *buarth* aromatic in the blaze of the sun.

Heledd and Carwyn passed through the gates and followed one of the roads toward the eastern part of the *ystad*, turning off onto a narrower path into the copse. From a distance, the chapel was pink in the sunlight, the lime rendering casting its hue through the whitewash. When they were closer, Heledd saw the door stood slightly ajar, as Aled had told her it would be, held open by a wedge at the base of the oak-plank door. She slid the wedge aside and entered the coolness.

Aled's description had not done justice to the wall paintings covering the narrow space leading to the altar. Where the wall sloped in toward the window ledges, there were motifs of birds and game, painted in a dark green and red, with black markings Heledd could not decipher. Some of the flowers were detailed in blue and the same yellow of the poppy growing in the hedgerows. The freshness of the paint and the breeze made the chapel a delightful respite from the odors of the *gaer*.

She sat for several minutes on one of the long benches at the front of the chapel, studying the murals and absorbing the tranquility. She did not worry her position was even less secure as bondwoman to Huw Bro-Dawel than it was as bondservant to Llew Talgarth. She understood Huw Bro-Dawel had paid her honor-price to her uncle as a prisoner of war. She was a servant, but without duties. Since she had no delusions about her position, until her bond master told her what he wanted from her, she was free to do as she pleased – with six guards. *I wonder what Alys would think of my band of soldiers?* The thought made her smile. She wondered, too, if report of her had reached her uncle. He would be outraged she was so free, so well-fed, so content. Her hands were not rough from work. She could keep her fingernails trimmed and smooth. Her face was not chapped from the wind or from the hides of cattle. She had no bruises or calluses from working the butter churns or carrying pails of milk. Her knees and the palms of her hands were not reddened. She was too soft, and that also made her smile.

For another few minutes, she let her sense of happiness wash over her. She could not remember another day when she had had time to listen to the breeze in the copse or be lulled into a sense of peace. She had not felt anything similar from her first memory – waking in the narrow cot of her cell in Bannawg on the day she was to begin her work in the house. Nothing remained of her family in her thoughts, only what had been put there by the storyteller. Her family did not exist for her except as the names Anwen and Ieuan, traitors and cowards. *I should not feel this. I should not be happy when they are dead and so many were killed because of them. I should not feel this when there is war and so many have been killed…* Her fingers pressed hard on her mouth to stifle her trembling breath. "Carwyn!" She ran from the place, throwing herself into the boy's arms.

"What?" he demanded, staring around him, trying to put her aside to reach his sword. "What?" He searched, staring into the copse but could see nothing that was not there when they arrived.

"Take me back," she cried. "Take me back." She pulled away and ran from the chapel, Carwyn at her heels, looking over his shoulder. He kept pace with her until she finally slowed, gasping for breath, and stumbled onto the main road.

"What has frightened you, *boneddiges*?" Carwyn asked, looking down at her as she crumpled onto the grass. Heledd took deep breaths for several moments before she met his gaze. "Heledd, what is wrong?"

"I should not be here," she said. "I should not have left Bannawg."

Carwyn glanced in the direction they had come. "Why do you say that?"

"I felt— I just know. I accepted this because I thought I could not bear to stay there."

"But why were you frightened?"

In her lungs, she could still feel the pressure of breathless sorrow. "I was frightened. I am a coward. I cannot believe … anyone."

"You are safe with me, *boneddiges*," Carwyn replied, a crease forming between his eyebrows. "If there was someone near, and I did not see him, I have failed. I must tell the commander what happened."

"There is no need to tell anyone, Carwyn. No one frightened me. There is no one here to frighten me. I have left them all in Bannawg." *Little girls, red beads soaking into the soil, bodies of small boys, a soldier raising his sword above his head, a white hand, so soft, lifting her chin so she saw beyond the Gurnos.*

Heledd lay back against the cushions lining the walls surrounding two sides of the bed, running her hand over the soft wool of the gold and purple *carthen*. Her eyes wandered around the room, taking note of the furnishings, the fine quality of the linens and woven fabrics, until her gaze fell on the black damask purse lying on top of the chest at the foot of her bed. Turning onto her belly, she took the purse into her hands, wondering how a soldier could afford such an elegant item. Stolen, she asked herself, from some woman he murdered? That was too evil to contemplate. Stolen, yes, she allowed, but not from the body of a dead woman. Such things are done, she reminded herself.

Thinking of the man who had given her so many gifts soothed her and Heledd allowed her thoughts of Garmon Dolwyddlan to wander. That she had fallen in love with him she denied, hoping denial would make it so. He was kind. It was natural she would feel gratitude – as she felt gratitude to Goewin, Heulwen and the other women who had been kind. She had hoped being away from Bannawg, so far south and west from any place he might ever be, would help her to forget him, but not his kindness. She wore the gifts he had given her but excused her weakness – it was sinful to waste such things in the effort to forget him. When she was honest with herself, she admitted loving a man she would never see again was childish, so much simpler than living with a man who disappointed and confused.

She had seen how quickly joy had turned to anger when Alys faced the reality of being wife to someone she did not know. Because he had taken nothing, expected nothing and gave without asking for anything in return, Heledd could love Garmon from a distance as someone who would never be in her life. Even as a bondservant, she could still love him, no matter what her master asked her to do. She could never know Garmon Dolwyddlan but he was the man against whom she measured all others.

As she stroked the silk purse against her cheek, she did not bother to caution her heart against bestowing on him magical qualities that made him some creature other than a man. *If he was, I would have had my child by him long before I left Bannawg. I would have dropped my wizard child as soon as my uncle laid a stick upon the ground to test me.* She blushed at the silly train of her thoughts and reminded herself she was a bondservant and a soldier would not be able to buy her freedom, even if he had wanted her. *Withdrawn.*

Still, kindness, if that was what the gifts had been, she thought as she gazed at the fine stitching and let the silken cord caress her fingers, was a gift in itself. The whisper of the silk on her fingertips reminded Heledd of Garmon's kiss and she blushed again, feeling the same weakness in her body she had felt when he pressed her fingers to his lips, the same warmth she had felt when he held her in his arms on that cold day outside the *beudy* while Elis watched. *If Elis had not been there ... yes, I would have kissed him.*

Whatever the intention of these precious gifts, they were the finest she had ever received and she refused to tarnish them with thoughts of any evil connected to them. However Garmon Dolwyddlan had come to possess them, he gave them to her as unfettered tokens of some care he had had for her then. She had been hard and unyielding, refusing him even the smallest show of appreciation – how could she be surprised he had abandoned and forgotten her? She could not blame him she was cold and hard, and gave him no foundation for his hope she was not as she was.

She was proud and disdainful. She was arrogant. She had escaped the barracks and Heulwen's life because none of the soldiers wanted her. *If no one wants me,* she thought, enjoying the pleasure of the black silk until her arm tired and her hand relaxed, dropping to her chest, *I will always be safe.* She held the purse against her heart and drifted to sleep – forgetting the sense of sorrow she had felt in the chapel.

In Heledd's dreams, the memories made her heart quicken and finally jump with the never-forgotten terror of war, brought a cold hand into her fingers, the white flesh hardening like a claw, red beads glistening, darkening. In the distance, horns broke the stillness of the dusk. The rhythmic beating of drums, steady as a heartbeat, stirred terror, little girls, boys, screaming. And silence.

Darkness had closed in on the *gaer.* Heledd woke with a

start, her heartbeat heavy, a thud. She turned onto her back, listening, holding her breath. Leaping to the door, she pressed her ear against the planks, stared over her shoulder at the black window. The thatch roofs on the houses were not burning. She heard people in the *buarth*, their loud voices in the courtyard of the *pennaeth's* house. She heard singing and laughter – the drunken soldiers, victorious? No woman's wailing. No screams. Her heart slowed. The horns were blown again and answered by drumming from within the walls. Heledd slid the bolt aside. When she reached the *buarth*, she saw all of the people of Bro-Dawel on either side of the road, waiting.

Heledd wrapped her shawl around her and moved through the crowd until she was able to see over the shoulders of the shoemaker and the wine steward. Across from her, she saw Carwyn, Daf and Nisien straining to see from among their fellow soldiers. Rhodri came up behind them, spoke and all four smiled at her. They acknowledged someone standing behind her with a nod. When Heledd turned her head, she found Aled near her, with a woman under his arm.

"There he is, Mared," she heard Meini call to her sister. "There is your husband." Heledd also strained to see which of the twenty men Meini singled out but saw only twenty similar men in helmets, carrying shields on one arm and their swords raised above their heads. Just soldiers, prepared to kill.

At the front of the column, without helmets or armor, she recognized two men who had been among those who came with Aled to Bannawg. Heledd pouted slightly, wondering why they had joined the warband after returning. Nowhere in the crowd did she see Huw Bro-Dawel. Thinking she should be with him, rather than standing among the revelers, eager to welcome their sons, husbands and brothers home from their weeks of training, she turned away to look for the *pennaeth*.

"Where are you going, Heledd?" Aled asked her, grasping her arm. "The feasting has just begun and Huw will be looking for you. He takes great pride in presenting his new soldiers to his people." He was already drunk and she attempted to pull her arm from his grasp without angering him. The woman he held whispered in his ear. "Are you?" he queried, searching her face. "Are you frightened of me?"

"No," Heledd said, startled, her eyes searching beyond him for escape. She pulled again and gently levered his fingers loose, keeping a smile on her lips, her eyes widening. "I was just going to find Huw Bro-Dawel. As you said, he will be looking for me."

"Ach, I will take you to him. Huw will want to present you to the commander of his army, where all can see how proud he is of—."

Heledd glanced in the direction of Mared who had been caught around the waist and was being carried toward the house. *They are all drunk. They have weapons and they are drunk.* "Let me go," she hissed at her captor, wrenching her arm so forcefully from his grasp Aled and the woman nearly fell as Heledd darted into the crowd and out of sight. There was no place she could hide that would not be discovered. She shot the bolt across the door of her room, gasping for breath. *Such a fool you are,* Heledd told herself, *to give any soldier the benefit of your regard.* The men whom she had begun to like and trust, the soldiers who claimed to protect her, were drunken soldiers like any others.

*How could I have been so stupid,* Heledd asked herself, *so foolish to think I might be safe here?* The laughter and carousing in the *buarth* went on, moving like the churning river into the rooms of the house, coming closer to her and receding, until she heard Huw Bro-Dawel's booming voice greeting his newly trained soldiers and inviting them to drink and eat in his *neuadd.* Rage began to push fear from her heart. *What can it mean?* she asked, pacing between the door and the opposite wall. *Why am I here if not—? A soldier dishonors me in my uncle's house, abandons me to whatever my uncle decides befits the whore he made me and ... and so I am easily traded to an old man, as a bondwoman for the rest of my life, to be a soldier's reward.* This was the only sense she could make of the weeks she had been given so much freedom.

If she was not to work in the *beudy,* she could not see how else she could be useful – presented to the commander of his army. She leaned her back against the rough beams of the wall and hung her head, all her thoughts of love and kindness draining away. *If Bro-Dawel can be so vile,* she thought, how can I allow him to succeed in what he has done? I will not let him think I am defeated, that I believed the lies, that I believed he meant me no harm.

"I hate them," she hissed at the door. "I hate them all." She stared at the fine bed linens and the silken cushions. "This is the only explanation. This is why I was paraded in front of all these people – the only reason I was taken to be seen by the warband – so Huw Bro-Dawel's commander could see ..." *me,* Heledd ended on a sob.

# six

"*Boneddiges*," Bethan called at the bolted door, "the *pennaeth* is waiting for you."

Heledd waited a moment before she could speak, lifting her chin, staring into the thatch above the pretty room. "Tell him— tell Bro-Dawel I will attend when I am ready."

"Do you need my help?"

"No, thank you. I am used to caring for myself."

"When you come, you can meet my son. He is very proud tonight, as are they all."

"I will not be long. Don't wait for me." When she heard Bethan's retreating steps, she flung herself at the door, slamming her fists on the planks. *Tell him he will have to beat me to death. I would rather die. I would rather ... be dead.* She scraped her fingers into her ugly hair, slumping onto the edge of the bed. *I will show them the mistake they have made to do this to me.*

She stripped out of her rumpled clothing, folding every item that did not belong to her into the chest. "I am not a whore," she told her blurred reflection in the silver-plate on the wall. "I am a milkmaid. I work in the *beudy*." She dressed again in her old frock and her brown everyday tunic – the only clothes she had earned by the work she had always done. "One day, I *will* learn to make cheese." After several deep breaths and a last glance at her reflection, Heledd opened the door of her room, her chin high. There was no sign of the terrified girl behind the haughty mask. *Even if he beats me, I will not let this happen to me.* She turned away from the corridor leading to the *neuadd*, in no doubt Aled and the five others were part of the conspiracy to humiliate her.

All of the foolish dreaming and happiness she had felt in the afternoon brought only hard rage. She repeated to herself all the reasons she hated soldiers, strengthening her armor with a catalogue of their treachery. How quickly they had turned against her father, their *pennaeth*, to serve another, wealthier master, she accused them. How easily they justified shaming a girl who had never harmed them. Some men had died with her father, she admitted, as she shoved through the door at the end of the corridor and strode through the torch lit *buarth* toward the *beudy*. "Only because they did not have opportunity to betray him," she sneered, slipping through the door. She pulled the apron over her head and took two buckets from the shelf, hooking a stool over her arm.

The milking was finished for the day. The cattle had been driven out and the parlor was silent except for the whisper of her skirt on the straw as she set her stool in the stall farthest from the door. Through the back door of the *beudy*, she led one of the newly-calved heifers into the stall and put the loop of restraining rope around its head. As she would have done had she been allowed to work, she set one bucket on the straw and hung the other over the rail of the stall. The legs of the stool sank into the muck as Heledd dropped onto it, exhaling a long, determined breath. She rubbed her hands together and laid her cheek on the animal's haunches.

"You will think I am strange," she said to her companion in the darkness, "and I know you have provided all that is required of you today but tonight, I hope you will forgive me." Heledd flexed her fingers, lamenting how soft she had let them become. When she gathered the teats into her palms, she winced at the loss of skill and strength. Over the many years of milking, calluses had made the work easier. Though they were not gone completely, she was soft and had no rhythm. The heifer kicked Heledd off the stool more than once and, by the time she was ready to abandon the work, her clothing was streaked with muck and her hair with straw. On her cheeks, she could feel the abraded skin begin to sting and her wooden clogs were wet with urine. Some of her manicured nails were broken and her palms ached from the hard work. "Now, I am ready," she told the heifer as she pushed it through the door into the pen with the other milk cows. "I will do a better job tomorrow."

Taking a deep breath, she pushed the doors to the *pennaeth's* grand *neuadd* open before her. The sea of bodies between her and Huw's table held no terrors for Heledd, bondservant and *merch* Ieuan Bannawg, coward and traitor. Without looking to left or right, she walked directly across the large room toward the place at the table the *pennaeth* expected her on the other nights she ate with him.

Mared sat in her usual place but Meini had been pushed aside one seat to make way for Mared's husband – every inch the soldier and all Heledd most hated about the breed: coarse, aggressive, cruel. Mared's adoration of him was evident. Heledd's place beside Huw Bro-Dawel was waiting for her with a cup standing ready to be filled. Huw ignored her, but her entrance had not gone unnoticed by his daughters who exchanged words around the drunken soldier who took the opportunity to kiss Meini as well as his wife. Heledd's chin rose higher.

Huw was nearly as drunk as his soldiers by the time the platters of meat, apples and other fruits were laid on the tables. He had not filled her cup nor cut her meat but his own cup was never empty. Heledd cut her own meat with the small knife at the side of her plate. She ate and observed the feasting host of bodies around her, holding her head high. The sisters' ridicule made no impression on her. She stank of muck and wet straw. Huw glanced at her once and stared, clenching his jaw. His fist crashed onto the table but he said nothing. Her hair was tied back in her usual fashion and covered with a scarf. Only her roughed cheeks cast any glow across her freckled face.

"Ah, there you are," Huw said. Heledd glanced at him but realized he was speaking to someone else. He gestured to the man to come forward. "As you see, the girl has arrived safely but I cannot say she is as pretty as you claimed."

Heledd stiffened, drawing her breath as she glared at her bondmaster.

"I can see that."

Heledd silenced her breath, stilled her body, gathering rage and dismay like a black cloak around her before she looked in the direction of the quiet voice. His hair was still damp and his face was newly shaved. He showed his respect by taking time to bathe before entering the *pennaeth's neuadd* to join in the celebrations. Heledd clutched the small knife in her fist, turning on the northerner eyes as sharp and as deadly as the blade trembling in her hand.

He faltered for a moment and his uneven gait became more pronounced. He greeted her with a bow. "*Boneddiges.*"

Heledd whirled her gaze away from him, shunning the offer of his outstretched hand.

"You see how rude she is," Mared hissed at her father. "Even Garmon cannot command her respect."

"The girl doesn't seem happy to see you," Huw said.

"I am not surprised," Garmon answered, taking the seat beside her. "We did not part on the best of terms." He laid his long fingers over the hand in which she clutched the knife.

Heledd dragged her hand from his grasp, gouging the blade into the table, as she would have liked to gouge his eyes. He turned his hand upwards, defenseless, displaying the scar she had left on the heel of his palm. Heledd clenched her jaw. After a moment, Garmon clasped one of the jugs, filling first her cup then his own.

"Your journey here was pleasant, I am told."

Heledd remained silent.

"Have you had opportunity to see much of the *ystad?*"

Convinced he had planned every moment of her days in her new home, she replied, "You know what I have been forced to endure." The northerner tilted his head to peer at her. "Aled has been thorough." She found Aled in the room and glowered at him. Garmon followed her gaze but his expression was impassive.

"Aled is a good soldier," Garmon said. "He follows orders."

Heledd felt her fury rise in hot waves over her cheeks. Seconds later, she said, "His orders must have been detailed."

The puzzled frown on Garmon's face encouraged her to believe she had found a weakness and she lifted her chin.

"To please you, *boneddiges*, they would have to be," Garmon replied.

"Nothing you have to say is of any interest or concern to me. I do not care what you or any of these think of me," she spat. "I am not so ignorant as you think. I am not stupid."

"Heledd, what has happened?" he whispered, laying his hand on her arm. "This is not— This is not Bannawg, *gwraig*. You have no reason to fear ... anyone."

She yanked her arm from his grasp. "I am not afraid of you or your kind. You cannot threaten me with anything worse than what I have already known."

"No one threatens you, Heledd," he said, glancing at the faces turned toward him – Aled, the elite guard, the two soldiers who had been at Bannawg, nearly all the soldiers in Huw's army.

Heledd closed her eyes for a moment. When she opened them, she stared into the cold, gray eyes of the man for whom, a few hours before, she had declared her love. Once, he had threatened her for her haughty behavior. Once, he had tarnished what little was left of her good name. From the moment he entered her room, Heledd *merch* Ieuan Bannawg was a whore as well as the daughter of a coward and a traitor, as well as a prisoner of war – disgraced and of less worth than a stock animal. And still, she had forgiven him – because he had not hurt her or sought revenge. Now, because of him, she was a bondwoman to strangers with no hope of freedom. *My father's crimes protected me in my uncle's house*, Heledd reasoned, *that is why Llew Talgarth chose a stranger to dishonor me.* "This is not Dolwyddlan," she accused the northerner.

"Had I known— I confess to stretching the truth," he said, "it was necessary under the circumstances."

"What was the purpose of your deceit?"

"Deceit is a strong word, Heledd."

She shrugged and picked up her cup, glad her hand did not betray her rage. *Here, no one knows who I am but they will and they will regret bringing the daughter of a wicked man among them.*

"A tale," Garmon continued, lowering his voice. She could feel his eyes on her face. "I have waited a long time for this moment," he murmured. "You are even more beautiful than I remembered."

"You must be mad to think my opinion of you has changed."

"I hoped—." He bowed his head for a moment. "For many things."

"Then you are much more of a fool than even I thought."

"Too much to hope we might be friends, Heledd, even now?"

"Never. We can never be that."

"Then allow me the courtesy of hearing my answer to your question, *gwraig*." He scanned the faces in the dining hall before he snatched a breath. "Deceit is too strong. I had a friend at Talgarth, who asked me to visit, to train with him. Urien Macsen," Garmon confirmed. "I had not seen him for many years and it was an opportunity to learn more of my profession. Since Huw Bro-Dawel was known to your uncle, Urien thought it best Talgarth did not know who I was." He drank from his cup. "I soon had other, stronger, reasons to keep my true identity a secret." He paused for a moment, but when she did not ask any question, he took a long breath. "It was not my intention to injure you, Heledd. That could not be avoided."

*How better to hurt me*, Heledd thought, *and escape any retribution, than to be someone who does not exist?*

"Why are you dressed like this?" he asked, seeming to awaken to her appearance as though from a trance. "What have you done?" He pressed her reddened hand palm upward on the table and spread her fingers open. "You were not expected—. Who told you to work in the *beudy*?"

His hand was as smooth and as gentle as she remembered. The scent of his clothing and his skin were the same. Her broken nails and the dirt ground into the crevices of her roughed palms were the same. She raised her chin and found the upper most corner of the *neuadd* upon which she could concentrate, to distract her from the distress of being near him.

His steady gaze burned into her. His arm rested on the table in front of her, a wall between her and the rest of the company. No one cared, least of all Huw Bro-Dawel, the warrior dominated her, spoke to her as though they were alone.

Huw had taken no more interest in her from the moment Garmon had seated himself beside her than he had when she first entered the *neuadd*. The threat of contact with him was like a living thing – a force between them that weakened her. *You fool*, she screamed inwardly, pulling rage around her like a wall. She shoved his arm away from in front of her, sitting as straight as an iron bolt, hatred for him and everyone else narrowing her eyes.

"I know I have not given you good reason to think well of me," Garmon began, once again placing his hand over hers.

"Think well of you? How could I ever have thought well of you?" Garmon released her hand the instant Heledd withdrew from him, turning his attention to the jug of mead.

"Now is not a good time to talk, *gwraig*," he said and filled their cups once more. He cut meat for her but Heledd refused to eat and did not take the cup into her hand again. While the two men on either side of her talked of war, training and hunting, Heledd blocked their words. Her thoughts settled on the happy moments of the afternoon and the curious comfort she had felt as she held the silk damask purse to her heart. As if to assure herself the giver of that gift could not be the man beside her, she glanced at Garmon and found her reflection in his gray eyes.

"Heledd," he murmured, leaning toward her.

Coming to her senses, she turned her face away from him. "You may think you are clever and you have won, hireling, but I will never be your whore."

"One day, *menyw*," Garmon told her, turning his gaze to study the people of Bro-Dawel, "you will know the truth."

"What do you think of all this?" Mared demanded in a loud whisper. Huw Bro-Dawel was leaning back comfortably in his large chair, amused by his people and proud of his soldiers, listening intently to the musicians and paying no heed to his daughter's conversation.

"Of what?" Garmon asked.

"Of that." Mared waved a dismissive hand in Heledd's direction. "No one knows what to do with her. She has changed the way things are done."

"What should I think?" Garmon asked, filling his cup again and spearing a large chunk of meat on his hunting knife.

"What is she doing here? What does my father want with her?" The warrior shrugged. "Garmon. How are we to manage with her here? She's a nuisance."

"There is nothing you need do," he commented, leaning back in his chair. "Nothing about Heledd is any of your concern."

"You approve this?"

"It is not my place to approve or comment."

"He will listen to you, he always does," Mared insisted. Garmon drank deeply from his cup. "I don't like her."

"I doubt your friendship is uppermost in Heledd's concerns," Garmon said.

"I am capable of answering for myself," Heledd snapped.

"No one was talking to you," Mared hissed.

"You are talking about me," Heledd observed, "I should therefore, at least, have the right to defend myself as you are so rude."

"I am rude? Are you going to allow her to speak to me like that?" Mared demanded of the northerner. "She is just a bondwoman after all."

"Heledd has a right to speak her mind. And you will find she is a *morwyn briod*, Mared."

"She is only a maiden of property by virtue of what my father has given her. And she is no maiden—."

"By her own virtue and more," Garmon said, turning his granite-hued eyes on Heledd for a moment. She met his glance with glaring eyes and a toss of her head.

"I know all about her and her family. I know what her father did to his own brother. Ach, I will not sit here to be insulted in this way." Mared leapt to her feet, knocking over her cup as she marched away. Her husband shrugged and turned his attention to Meini. The whole of the *neuadd* fell silent and Garmon signaled one of the boys to pick the pieces of the cup from the floor.

Goewin's few words and gestures of kindness came back to Heledd's thoughts and her eyes filled with tears for a moment before her anger at Garmon's deceit dried them as suddenly.

Garmon's attention had turned from her to Huw Bro-Dawel then to gaze at his soldiers in the *neuadd*. The celebrations resumed as he raised his cup in salute to his friends. Heledd turned her attention to scan the faces in the room, feeling sick to see all of her six guards were staring at her.

"Mared does not like me," Heledd said, though she had not meant to speak.

"I would have been surprised if she did," Garmon replied, giving her another of his sidelong glances before he refilled his cup.


For the remainder of the evening, Heledd was silent until Huw came to his senses enough to dismiss her. Though no one would have noticed in their drunken state, she bid him good night and retired to her room, all her dignity gathered around her in her haughty manner. *How am I to live in such a place?* she asked herself, nursing the ache in her heart. At dawn, the last of the revelers found their way to their beds and the *gaer* was quiet again.

Although her heart wished otherwise, Heledd could not justify hiding in her room. With reluctance, she had put all of the gifts she had received from Garmon Dolwyddlan, including the black purse, into the chest and dressed in her work clothes. She slipped her bare feet into the wooden clogs and took a deep breath before sliding the bolt free. No one awaited her outside her door. Though she was surprised, Heledd accepted she no longer had need of guards, their companionship was withdrawn.

She had slept many hours later than usual but entered the hall in time to eat in the company of the stewards and the womenfolk who had finished serving the *pennaeth*, his family and higher officials. Their courteous greetings surprised her. Heledd returned their pleasant words while she ate the *uwd* and drank the ale put before her, grateful no one seemed to recall the disagreement she had had with the *pennaeth's* daughter or her disrespect for his commander.

She helped to clear the tables and washed them down with hot water and soap, ready for the evening meal. No one commented on her willingness to work or prevented her from doing so. Their acceptance of her position among them encouraged Heledd to follow the women of the household to the *beudy* as she had on the first morning. Work kept her from dwelling on the events of the previous night and she was glad to be in familiar surroundings.

When the other women broke from their work to rest in the *buarth*, Heledd could not continue working without help. The sun was not as warm and the air had a tinge of autumn. In a few days, everyone on the *ystad*, from the smallest boys and youngest kitchen maids to the most brutal soldier, would be in the fields to help with the harvesting of the grain for the winter. As long as she worked and was useful, she could survive.

That the most vocal of the two sisters did not want her in Bro-Dawel was apparent. Meini's thoughts and feelings were still a mystery to Heledd. Although she did not want to think about him, she began to ask silent questions about Garmon. Even Mared seemed to respect him.

Some of the women had left the *buarth* while she thought about these matters. Heledd could see them gathering near the stables. Many of the soldiers were there, including her six guards who had now abandoned her. She knew who gave them their orders. She had seen their respect for Garmon in their behavior toward him the night before. *Who is he? If I knew the answer to this question, what difference could that make?*

More of the women went to join the others at the stables and Heledd resigned herself to being among them. One or two had spoken to her as they worked. If she could make friends of them, if she could be one of them … What difference could that make?

Heledd stood at the edge of the crowd watching a young colt in training. She couldn't see through the crowd or over their heads but she heard some of the soldiers urging their comrade on in his work. As she strained to see, the colt reared, slashing the air with its hooves. The crowd gasped then expressed their approval as the colt was brought down.

In a moment, Heledd found herself standing at the front of the onlookers, with Aled and Nisien on either side of her, though she had made no effort to push herself forward. Garmon held the colt, tethered only by a rope around his nose and ears, using only a light hand to encourage the animal to follow instruction. Heledd turned to the side to push her way clear of the crowd.

"Garmon has been hand training this one from birth, only days after his return from Bannawg," Aled murmured to Heledd. "Its sire is Garmon's warhorse. The dam," he said, smiling at her, "is the mare you were given. The colt will make as fine a warhorse as its sire, once he is trained."

Heledd lowered her gaze, feeling the quick blush spread over her cheeks. She had turned her back to the paddock but was prevented from moving through the crowd to return to the *beudy*. No one took notice of her effort to push past them.

"We thought you meant to sleep all the day," Garmon said. Her blush deepened. Everyone had now turned their eyes on her. She saw from the direction of Aled's gaze Garmon crossed the corral enclosure toward her, leading the colt beside him.

"I was only a little late," she said, without turning. "I have been in the *beudy*." She looked to the other women to support her and was surprised to see everyone in the crowd, including Aled and Nisien, had moved away, leaving her alone with him. She could feel the colt's excited breath on her shoulder.

"This little one likes you," Garmon said, his breath on her cheek.

"I have work," she said, taking a step toward the *beudy* as he swung over the fence rails and dropped beside her.

"At least show me the courtesy of looking at me," Garmon murmured, touching her arm. Heledd turned, raising her trembling hand to stroke the colt's nose. "If you had risen earlier, you could have taken your ride with me," Garmon said. Heledd stiffened and dropped her hands to her sides. "Do you approve of this one?"

"He is finely built," she agreed. "It's a pity he will be used for war."

"You prefer him to be gelded?"

Heledd lifted her eyes, knowing she would regret meeting his gaze. Garmon stood so near her she felt the heat of his exertion and, in the instant she looked at him, his beauty took her breath away. Spinning away on her heel, she headed for the *beudy*, shocked by her physical response and the image her response conjured in her mind, but she controlled her impulse to run. Garmon tossed the rope lead to Aled and strode after her, grasping her wrist.

"Are you always this rude when someone is speaking to you? Or just to me?"

"To you," she sneered, keeping her eyes on the ground. "Rude?" Heledd raised her head until she fixed her eyes on his. "Do you think I owe you courtesy? Do you think I owe you respect?" Out of the corner of her eye, she saw Aled and Nisien take a step forward and were halted by Garmon's calm gesture. "If I were a soldier—."

"I prefer you as you are, Heledd," he said, bowing his head to fill his lungs with the warm scent of her body. "Yet, if you were a soldier, I can imagine what you would want to do to me and even that is more pleasurable than these months without sight of you."

She leaned so close to him, her anger was so fierce she could have sunken her teeth into his throat. Her hands clenched and she pulled back her shoulder ready to strike. His friends moved to defend him. "I ... must return to my work."

"What work can you have more important than this ... discussion?" Garmon loosened his grip on her wrist. "Who told you to work?"

"I prefer to work," she said. "It is honest." He released her wrist with one hand and, with the other, raised her chin, but she kept her eyes averted, staring at the men who had tricked her into believing they were her friends.

Although he compelled her to meet his gaze, Heledd's own strength of will resisted the pressure of his thumb to turn her head and he relented, looking beyond her for a moment. "Why are you wearing that?" Garmon demanded, frowning at the frayed garments. "I know you have better."

"These are my clothes," she said, hardening her jaw as she glared back at him.

"You do not want those provided for you?"

"I do not need them." Heledd jerked her chin out of his grasp and turned on her heel. He caught her hand and pressed it against his heart. Heledd felt its warmth through her fingertips but she refused to turn to look at him.

"Will you share a meal with me tonight?"

"No." she gasped. "I will not."

"Your reason?" he asked, under his breath.

"I always have my meal with ... the *pennaeth*."

"The *pennaeth* is hunting. You cannot eat alone in your room, Heledd. I will send a woman to bring you to my house." He gave her no option and, because she was desperate to get away, Heledd nodded, grateful he released her as soon as she had agreed.

Heledd ran to the shelter of the *beudy* and her work there. For the remainder of the day, she was industrious, staying to clean the cheese vat long after most of the other women had gone. The solitude gave her time to ponder but she found no answers in the scrubbed surface of the tin vat, the lime-washed sink boards or the ruddy surface of her work-worn hands.

By the time she reached her room, she was light-headed with hunger and fatigue, sinking onto her bed to wonder what had come over her, how reckless she was to accept the invitation of a man who had paid for her. Only an idiot would consent to go near him. Heledd dragged her everyday tunic over her head, stripped out of her frock and shift to bathe away the grime of the day, shivering despite the warmth of the water in the tub Bethan ordered brought to her every evening. She stepped out onto the flagstones and wrapped the wide linen cloth around her weary body, aching where the impatient heifer had kicked her to the floor of the milking parlor. She had eaten little the previous night and had only *uwd* and ale for breakfast. The hour was already late and the cook would not welcome a beggar at the door. *I do not have to go. I am not his bondservant.*

She sat on the edge of the bed, staring at her hands. Her fingernails were clean again and trimmed, her hands were pink from the warm bath but still tender. Her belly was empty. Her best frock and the mulberry-colored tunic hung on the hook by the door, under her faded shawl. She could not wear either the brown tunic or the frock she had worn to work in the *beudy*. She had nothing else to wear. No matter what anyone thought of her, she had proved her point in Bro-Dawel's *neuadd*. She did not want to wear dirty clothes after she had bathed.

Hunger defeated her better judgment as she dressed in the simple shift and linen frock, reparation for Garmon's crime against her in her uncle's house. *This is who you are, Heledd merch Ieuan Bannawg. A bondservant who has accepted an invitation to share a meal with the commander of your bondmaster's army*, she scolded, *the man who is responsible for all that has happened to you in this year and you go because you are hungry.* She waited for the woman to come to the door. When the knock came, Heledd clenched her fists. *I have earned this meal by my toil today.*

# SEVEN

"If you are ready," the woman said, "I will take you to Garmon."

"I am ready," Heledd replied, recognizing the blonde woman as the one who had been in Aled's arms when the soldiers returned from their training. She was well-dressed in creamy linen and a silk tunic the color of the summer sky. Heledd could not remember seeing the woman anywhere in the *gaer* except with Aled. She called the commander by his first name, not by any title or other form of respectful address. These simple facts made Heledd think the woman was the soldier's equal or even his better, of a higher status than the women in the *beudy* or the kitchen. Heledd bit her lips as they crossed the *buarth* and hesitated when she saw they were headed toward the house set apart from the others.

The woman pushed the gate open and waited for Heledd to enter before she dropped a rope circle over one of the slats to keep it closed. The distance to the house was lit by two torches. The door, set in the middle of the front wall of the house, stood open, awaiting them. Heledd's heart pounded so hard against the wall of her chest she was certain it could be heard. Her impulse to run back to the safety of her room was so strong she stopped at the doorway as though there was a wall preventing her from stepping over the threshold.

To the left side of the door, there was a firelit room with a long table already laden with dishes, glazed jugs and a half-dozen or more cups. Heledd sighed with relief she was not the only guest but still could not move forward. To the right of the door, there was a wall, a passageway leading to the back of the house and another door into a second room. Behind her, she heard the wooden gate opened again and, despite her misgivings, she nearly cried out in gratitude to see Aled approaching. She turned to greet him. He nodded and turned his smile on the woman who had brought Heledd to the house. Aled was also dressed in fine garments with lavish embroidery, of a much higher quality than Heledd had seen him wear before. He bowed to her and gestured for her to enter the house ahead of him. Heledd braced herself, uncertainty weakening her. The flagstone floor was strewn with fresh rushes giving off an aroma of herbs and spices when they were crushed under foot.

"Garmon is late, as usual," Aled said.

"Am I?" Garmon rose from an armed chair before the hearth. "I think it is you who are late, Aled."

*He's in pain*, was Heledd's first thought when she saw the scowl he disguised with a broad smile for his friend. He too had taken care to dress in fine clothing. He had bathed and his sable-brown hair was loose, brushing his shoulders. He wore a finely woven linen shirt beneath an embroidered grey tunic. His black boots reflected the glow of the flames. The leggings he wore were flannel, dyed nearly as dark brown as his hair.

"Heledd," he greeted her with another smile. "You know Aled, but I do not think you have been introduced to his wife, Ceinwen." Heledd acknowledged the woman with a small curtsy and Ceinwen nodded her head once in greeting.

Heledd's eyes returned to her host, but she did not meet his gaze. After a few moments, she realized she was staring at his chest. Another blush flooded over her cheeks. She wished the thatches above her head would fall and bury her. Lifting her chin in her usual defiant manner, she fixed her eyes on the stone hearth.

"You have also yet to meet these guests," Garmon said, catching her hand and drawing her attention to the passageway. Heledd had to lower her gaze to meet the eyes of these guests – a trio of children: a girl of about six, a boy of five and another boy of about four years. "These are Aled and Ceinwen's children. The two youngest are, I have been told, already asleep."

Heledd greeted the three with a nod and a smile that pleased their parents. She hid her confusion and misgivings in her attention to the children. Garmon still held her hand and gave no sign of letting her go. After a moment, he raised her fingers to his lips as he had the first time he had invited her to share a meal with him. *Who are these people?* Heledd asked herself again, refusing to lift her eyes to his face though she was aware he gazed at her, willing her to look at him. Instead she watched as the children were seated by their age rank at the table. Ceinwen and Aled stood near the table, waiting for Garmon to invite them to sit by their children.

Though she struggled to draw her hand from his grasp, her effort was resisted and Garmon led her to the table to sit between himself and Aled. The passageway from which the children came into the room was filled with stewards who served the meal and disappeared. Half of the long table was empty except for the extra dishes and jugs. Heledd wondered at the intimacy of the gathering.

"I— I should not be here," she said suddenly, half-rising.

"Why do you say that?" Garmon asked, cutting meat to put on her plate.

"What will Huw Bro-Dawel think? And his daughters?"

"What they think is unimportant. Huw will expect me to do my duty to him."

"Should we not be in the *neuadd*?" Although she did not believe anything concerning her was of interest to Huw Bro-Dawel, she could not see how inviting her to his house could be a duty to his *pennaeth*.

"Only the *pennaeth* is host in the *neuadd*. This is my house ... and my *neuadd*. Do you dislike it?"

Heledd heard a note of uncertainty in his voice. She clasped her trembling hands together in her lap. "I do not want to be here."

"What do you dislike?"

"I cannot—." The group was too small and the children too young for a repeat of her outburst of the previous night. He did not care he endangered her and she did not want to give him the satisfaction of knowing she was frightened.

"Ceinwen, explain to her," Garmon said with a laugh.

"This was my suggestion, Heledd. I thought you would be more at ease here, in these rooms, away from the bickering while Huw Bro-Dawel is hunting. The *neuadd* is cold and uninviting when the *pennaeth* is away and his daughters prefer to take their meals in their private rooms. Aled and I would gladly invite you to our *hafod* but there is no room in a small house with five children sleeping along the walls. Garmon offered his house, so you would be among friends."

"Was I wrong? Do you object to my hospitality, as poor as it is?"

Heledd remained silent, staring at her hands, grateful she had no need to conceal frayed cuffs with her fingers. *Don't be foolish. Don't let him see how you feel, never let him see into your heart.* Any answer she gave could betray her somehow.

"Then sit and eat, Heledd," he whispered against her temple, "and enjoy the company of friends."

Again, she felt his breath on her cheek as she had the terrible night she had awakened and taken refuge in his arms. Shame washed through her like a river of ice. If she was not careful, she would be his victim again. Even though Huw had no interest in her, she could not afford to take the chance he would not send her back to Talgarth, demanding reparation. *What am I doing? This man knows I will be punished for refusing him, if not by Bro-Dawel, by my uncle.*

The conversation between the three friends was light and unguarded. There was no mention of killing or war. Garmon extolled the virtues of the wild colt. Aled extolled the virtues of the northerner's training.

"You are both forgetting," Ceinwen said, "the bloodlines of its dam are far better than those of the warhorse to which the mare was bred."

Heledd's attention was drawn to Ceinwen by Garmon's sharp glance at her and the sudden blush on Aled's wife's face when her husband squeezed her hand.

"Good bloodlines are not everything," Aled said. "Garmon's warhorse has always thrown true."

"Of course, there was that very fine filly in the last season *Diawl* was put to stud," Ceinwen murmured, "though the dam was not exceptional. And the season before …"

"That was good fortune," Garmon said, "more than good bloodstock. This mare will do for my purposes, for many seasons, if the owner is agreeable."

There was a long silence but Heledd found nothing to add to the discussion and was puzzled when Ceinwen and Aled averted their gaze when she glanced at them.

"Do you?"

Heledd swung her head and faced the commander's dark eyes, inches from her own. "Do I what?" Her voice was as weak as her spirit.

He leaned toward her and murmured, "Do you agree?"

"To what?"

He smiled and turned his attention to the meal, encouraging her to eat and drink as she pleased while he spoke with the children. After her experience as laundry maid to Elis's daughter, Heledd could raise no interest in the youngest two. She felt no maternal instincts and she could not force herself to pretend an interest the children themselves would know to be false. When the meal was finished, Aled's daughter was still talking to Garmon Dolwyddlan but Heledd left the table to sit with Ceinwen near the fire.

The woman was not talkative and Heledd could think of nothing to say or questions to ask. After a short while, the girl joined her mother and Heledd watched the girl make marks on the hearthstone, chatting the whole time as she had with the commander. As she expected, the girl was learning to sew and to weave, make stitches for embroidery, recognize herbs and plants, prepare medicines and remedies. To Heledd's surprise, the girl was also being taught to read and make letters. Neither of these wonders had been offered to Heledd as a child and she asked the girl to demonstrate.

"That is my name. Mairwen," she said, after she had made

the letters on the hearthstone.

"Can you make the letters of my name?" Heledd asked and watched while the girl scratched five marks on the stone with the charcoal: *H e l e th*. Though she could not recognize her own name, Heledd smiled and complimented Mairwen on her skill. In a few minutes, Ceinwen took all of the children away. Garmon joined Heledd at the hearth, gazing down at the names written there. With another piece of charcoal, he drew a line through her name and made five new marks: *H e l e dd*. "Why did you do that?" she asked.

"You were kind not to correct her, but she should learn what is right," Garmon replied, sitting in the smaller chair and resting his feet on the stool before him.

Heledd stared for a long time at the second spelling of her name, fixing it in her mind, trying to remember the movement of his hand as he had made the letters. She clasped her fingers together, surreptitiously making the strokes in her palm.

"Last night, did you mean to remind me of my bad behavior," he asked, breaking the silence that had lasted for several minutes. When she did not answer, he asked, "Did you decide to wear that for the same reason?" He gestured toward the mulberry tunic, fastened by small bone toggles from her breasts to her hips.

Heledd stared at him for a moment, a blush rose from her throat and spread beneath her jaw. Under her dappling, her skin was as pale as cream. The blush radiated like fire. "If you think I want to be reminded of that or anything else that concerns you, you are wrong."

Garmon stared into the fire for several moments, a trace of a smile at the corner of his mouth. "I," he said at last, "for my sins, can think of nothing else." He studied her profile, opening his scarred hand to her. "There are others for you. Have you looked in the chest?"

She hesitated before saying, "I only wore this because my clothes—. These are not mine."

"They are. If you want them."

Heledd turned her face away, keeping her eyes fixed on the

hearthstone. Neither spoke for a time. When the silence was more terrible than conversation, she said, "When I first saw Bro-Dawel, I thought I could be happy here."

"And now? You have changed your mind?" When she made no answer, he said, "I'm not surprised." After another few moments, he said, "Forgive me, Heledd. I am not good company for you this evening. I confess I am tired."

"It is time for me to go," she said, rising from the chair.

"Stay," he said, "where I fail, you succeed. You are good company for me."

"Where is Aled?" she asked, bolting away from the chair.

"He left with his family," Garmon told her. "You did not notice?"

"No. I must go."

"Of course," he agreed, pushing himself to his feet, a grimace flashing across his face.

"What's wrong?"

"Nothing. I will call someone to take you back."

"No. I can find my way."

"You cannot wander alone at this time of night," he said, straightening. He was in pain – a lot of pain. He wrapped a hooded jacket around her shoulders and opened the door, leading her through the gate and across the *buarth*. They met no one in the corridor to her room. Heledd was intent on every sound, movement and gesture Garmon made. At her door, he leaned his shoulder against the wall. "You will come tomorrow evening?" he asked, staring down at her from eyes dark with the effort of control.

"No," she answered.

"Will you come to the stables?"

"No."

"I understand, *menyw*," he murmured with a smile, gesturing for her to go into the room. "Bolt your door, Heledd."

"I always do."

"I will remember that."

With her heart pounding and a hot blush spreading through her, she darted into the dark room and shot the bolt in place, pressing her body against the door. She heard his laughter and then a sharp hiss. Heledd did not dare breathe or move from the door until she knew he had recovered. But he did not go and she could only listen hard, torn between rushing to his aid and leaving him his dignity.

"Go to bed," he urged her in a hoarse whisper. With a gasp, she leapt away from the door and sat on the bed, still listening. When he finally took steps away from her door, his gait faltered and she heard his curse as his shoulder slammed against the wall.

Heledd forced herself to remain silent until she was certain he had left the house. When all was quiet, she undressed and folded her clothes on the stool. She had seen men suffering in agony from wounds that would eventually kill them and she saw in Garmon's eyes the same torture, and the same proud denial. *Women are not so silly.* She crawled into the delicious bed. *If I were suffering such pain, the world would know it.* As she drifted to sleep, she recalled how Elis's daughter was born to the sound of his mother's howling and wondered how it would be to share a wonderful, wide bed with a man she loved.

She was awake at dawn and one of the first to be in the kitchen to help with the morning meal, waiting for Garmon's appearance as she ladled the *uwd* into wooden bowls. She served the soldiers and stewards, always with an eye on the door but Garmon did not come. No one close to him was present. Only after she had wasted the hour in the hall did it occur to her he would stay in his own house if he was unwell. By the time she realized her mistake, the women were going to the *beudy* and Heledd went with them.

"How dare you show your face?" Mared hissed at Heledd as she came out of the kitchen into the sunlight. "I thought you might have had the sense to keep yourself hidden after your shameful behavior in front of my father."

"What shameful behavior?" Heledd asked, turning to face her accuser.

"Don't think I did not see the way you flirted with Garmon, or the way you allowed him to caress you," Mared said, keeping her voice low. "Not everyone at my father's table was too drunk to see your attempt to entice him."

"He does not strike me as one who needs you to defend him," Heledd replied.

"Ach, you just show your ignorance, you little whore. If my father was here, I would drag you in front of him by your hideous mop," Mared hissed in her face, flicking her hand at Heledd's head. "I will not bother with you any longer. You will destroy yourself much quicker than any effort I or my sister can make to see you are put out of my father's house. Everyone knows you have lain with Carwyn, and Geraint. Do you take them together?"

"You lie," Heledd gasped.

"Ach, all I have to do is ask Garmon to repeat what he found at Talgarth. He will tell how you whored for him too. That will be a pretty story to keep us warm when the nights are long, how you threw your legs up for him—."

"Why are you doing this? What have I ever done to you?"

"You mean to set Garmon against my father and whore as you did in Talgarth," Mared said under her breath. "We know what Ieuan Bannawg was and you are the same. Your mother was a whore for Meilor Gwesyn."

"Who told you such a thing? My mother is dead."

"Your uncle told me about her," Mared gloated.

"That isn't true. He was lying."

"How dare you call your own uncle a liar, after all he has done for you? My father has paid your bond and this is how you repay him? Whoring just as you did in Talgarth – with how many of the soldiers?"

"Where did you hear these things?"

"Everyone at Talgarth knows. Elis told me how you seduced Garmon in the *buarth* with all the women of the household watching. Alys told me how you followed him around like a lovesick bitch. And how you went to the barracks. Traitor's daughter, you whore for hirelings. I know you have slept with Garmon," Mared whispered, close to Heledd's ear. "Your cousin told me, she described him perfectly but I did not tell her

I knew him. I could hardly believe it. Garmon. I cannot imagine why he allowed my father to bring you here, except for revenge." Mared leaned close to Heledd and smiled. "How funny you are. No doubt you think he might love you," she laughed. "Garmon wouldn't dirty his hands on you, not here where he has any woman he wants. You have no idea who he is, you ragged little slut. He's laughing at you. And when my father learns of your treachery, he will have you whipped like the lying strumpet you are."

Heledd cursed herself for her concern he suffered. She knew she would have to go about her work as before, as if nothing had happened, as if Mared had never spoken to her. Once she had recovered from the onslaught, she took a deep breath and strode into the *beudy* making herself blind to the stares of the women and took her place in one of the stalls to milk. Meini, in the stall next to her, glanced in Heledd's direction but did not make eye contact. Mared appeared at the door of the dairy where the milk was separated, her hands on her hips. Meini looked up for a moment and returned to her milking without greeting her sister.

"How can you work so close to that stinking whore?" Mared demanded. "That one is not content with our father, she must also have a soldier – or two. She does not even have the decency to leave Garmon alone," she whispered to one of the other women. A number of the women looked from Heledd to their *pennaeth's* daughter. Heledd bit her lips together, never doubting their allegiance. The day before, most had been at the stables to watch Garmon train the colt in the paddock. They admired him. She understood what it meant when several moved closer Mared. "She doesn't care he is ill." Heledd listened in silence, in spite of any better judgment, hoping to hear news of him.

"Is Garmon recovered?" one of the women asked.

"No, poor man," Mared said. "The surgeon has given him an infusion for the pain. Did that one care he was in agony? Not her, she enticed him to her room."

"That is not true," Heledd said, keeping her voice as calm as possible, standing to face her adversary. "Garmon would not let me go alone."

"Ach, you see. She does not even show him the respect of using a polite address. She thinks she can make him fall in love with her, just because she amused him when he was far from home."

"That is a wretched thing to say," Heledd said.

"But true. You— she thinks he can be tricked because he is crippled." Mared stopped speaking.

"And?" Garmon asked in a low voice.

"Garmon, are you well?" Mared asked, rushing toward him. Heledd studied him, crouching behind the cow. Garmon dismissed Mared with a flick of his hand and strode toward Heledd.

"Come out," he growled at her. "I have no patience for games." Heledd stood and stepped out to face him, holding the milking pail handle with both hands in front of her. "I am going to the paddock. Come with me." Heledd responded to the order, hanging the pail on the wall before following him into the *buarth*. Though his step was more uneven, she thought he had recovered from whatever ailed him the night before. At the fence around the paddock, he swung himself over and dropped to the other side, beckoning her forward. Heledd stood at the rails but he commanded her to climb, gesturing with impatience. She did as she was bid. He planted his hands on her waist and lifted her into the paddock, set her on her feet and released her as though she was covered in thorns. He walked a short distance away from her and turned. "You need not return to the *beudy* to work."

"But I must do something, some work ..."

"You are not here to work."

"If I don't work, I will starve."

"You will not starve, Heledd."

"I want to work. I have always worked."

"Then I will find work for you. Work more suited to your abilities."

"And what would that be? Why am I here?" she demanded.

"I do not want the kind of work you think is suitable for me."

"What do you think is?" he asked, lowering his head to hide a smile. When he raised his eyes, the smile was gone, replaced by a hard line. "There is no need for you to endure Mared's abuse."

"You heard what she said?"

"I may be crippled," he hissed, "but I am not deaf."

"I do not want to be chased from the *beudy*. I must show I can stand my ground."

Garmon gazed at her for a moment and smiled. "You can help Ceinwen."

"What work does she do?"

"She is with the small children, in the school."

"I would prefer to stay in the *beudy*," Heledd answered, lowering her eyes.

"That work is too hard, too—."

"I prefer it."

"I prefer—."

"It is not for you to decide or to tell me what to do. I am the *pennaeth's* servant."

"You are my—. That work is not worthy of you."

"I don't want to think what you may mean. I will stay where I am. The *beudy* is honest work, work I can do well. I am a farmer's daughter, no matter what others want to make of me. One day, I will make cheese and—."

"Why do you think you are here?"

"To work. Huw Bro-Dawel holds my bond and—."

"Is that what your uncle told you? Is that what he asked you to accept?"

"Yes."

"Nothing else?"

"Nothing else," she replied, pressing her lips together. Her uncle's mention of a child within a year and her suspicions of her true position remained unspoken. Garmon Dolwyddlan already knew her deepest fear.

Garmon gazed at her for a moment then said, "I am not surprised Talgarth asked you no other question." He raised his sword hand. As he laid it on her cheek, Heledd saw the scar she had left. "You are more than a servant, *gwraig*. I will send Ceinwen to bring you to my house tonight."

"You know I cannot," Heledd said, meeting his gaze.

"Neither she nor Aled will leave you alone with me."

"I will not." She drew away from his caress.

"I understand, *menyw*. I do not expect you to watch me at work," he said, bowing his head for a moment, "unless you are entertained."

"I am not," she replied.

"Is that the truth, Heledd?" He took a step closer, sliding his hand to the small of her back.

Heledd pushed his arm down and stepped back. "I am more useful in the *beudy*."

"As you wish," he replied. Though he offered, she refused his help to climb over the top rail. As she turned her eyes toward the *buarth*, he walked into the stables. When he was gone, she ambled back to the hot, stifling and noisy *beudy*, resuming her work, regretting her decision. No sooner had she pressed her head against the cow's haunches than Mared came to stand behind her. The moment Mared opened her mouth to speak, Heledd snapped at her. "You should not speak of a warrior like that. You show no respect."

"How dare you correct me? You are a fine one to talk of respect for warriors."

Heledd picked up the rhythm of her work once again, murmuring, "You bring shame on your family with your evil-tongue." Heledd heard several of the women laugh and, as suddenly, fall silent. She saw Meini's face blanch but Mared clenched her fists, fuming for a moment before she slapped the back of Heledd's head and burst from the *beudy*. The other women returned to their tasks without comment.

For the remainder of the day, Heledd had solitude enough to consider everything Mared had said to her, from accusing her of corrupting Carwyn to claiming Garmon had entertained the sisters with stories of his treatment of her. Heledd knew the first was untrue and was certain Carwyn had neither the guile

nor any reason to make an accusation against her. Regarding
Geraint, she was equally certain Mared lied. Though she had no
doubt Alys had taken pleasure in revealing her false knowledge
of Heledd's treatment at Garmon's hands, she doubted Garmon
allowed the whole of Bro-Dawel to know what he had done –
however arrogant he was, he was neither crude nor boastful.
Whatever he thought of her and whatever his intentions then or
now, Garmon would not reveal these to anyone, perhaps not
even his closest friends. Heledd pressed her forehead to the
cow's belly, overcome with sadness.

"Why are you crying?" Meini asked, in a whisper. "Don't let
Mared upset you. She is frightened."

Heledd turned her head to look at the younger sister, wiping
her cheeks with her apron. "Why is she frightened?"

"Ever since our mother—."

"What are you thinking?" Mared demanded of her sister,
slapping the side of Meini's head. "Don't you even think of
interfering," she warned as Heledd turned on her stool, "or I
will whip you."

"I am not afraid of you," Heledd said.

"You should be," Mared hissed, yanking Heledd's hair
before she dragged Meini from the *beudy*.

Heledd searched the faces of the other women for their
reaction but they had all gone back to their work in silence.
When they stopped to rest at midday, Heledd stayed apart,
sitting on the ground at the entrance to the *beudy*, with her back
against the door jamb and her knees drawn up to her chest.
Many of them had gone to the stables. The two or three who
stayed near the *beudy*, glanced at their friends and then back at
Heledd sitting alone. After a short while, they shrugged and
followed their friends. Heledd dropped her head onto her
knees, grateful for the peace allowing her to think without
interruption.

She had identified Garmon's closest friends and, although
his soldiers adored him and would die for him—. Heledd threw
her arms over her head. *How can I have been so stupid?* she asked
herself. On the second day after her arrival in Bro-Dawel, Aled

had told her everything she needed to know and she had been too stupid to understand. His words flew into her head at that moment, "There is not one man in this company who, for love of the man who brought you here …" That man, she knew, was not Huw Bro-Dawel. That man was Garmon, the commander of the warband who had left a sign to her guards to bring her close enough for him to see her. And, if it was true, she was—, Heledd could not bring herself to say, even in the silence of her thoughts, what she did not want to believe.

Locking her arms around her, Heledd buried her forehead against her knees, sitting in the dirt of the *beudy* doorway, her heart crashing against the wall of her chest as though it fought to break free, to desert her in despair. She was valuable only because he had been forced to pay twice to own her. Her uncle had not known – though it would not have mattered to him – he had profited from her sale to the same man and that man had never received his full measure. She understood hatred and revenge. That she was hated enough by her uncle and her cousins to be sold was a fact she had always known. That she was hated by a man who had been kind to her could be understood – she had repaid kindness with disdain and generosity with disrespect.

Despite her efforts to block her fears, her heart rebelled against her mind's tyranny. The bargain struck with her uncle was bondage. Though Garmon had told Mared she was a 'maiden of property', she understood she was his property. Heledd clenched her fists and gave her head a few knocks but it would not be silenced. To be his whore would not change that. Working her life away in the *beudy* would not change that.

# eight

*"Boneddiges?"*

Heledd raised her head and looked into Mairwen's face. "What are you doing here?"

"My mother sent me to find my father."

"Have you?"

"Yes. He was at the stables where she said he would be."

"Where are you going now?"

"Back to the school." Mairwen inquired, crouching beside Heledd and peering into her still reddened eyes. "Why are you sad?"

Heledd pushed herself to her feet and dusted the back of her brown tunic. "Your mother will be waiting for you. And I have work to do." She looked closely at the child. "Thank you for being so kind. As you can see, I am not sad now."

"You look sad."

"How do you know?"

"I have been sad."

"When are you sad, Mairwen?"

"When I have been punished for being naughty. Have you been naughty?"

"I must have been, or I would not be here," Heledd murmured. "Are you naughty often?"

"No, because I do not like to be punished," the six-year-old girl said, "but I can make myself happy again."

"And how do you do that?"

"I am most happy when I dance. Like this," and she demonstrated, taking Heledd's hands and skipping around her, flinging her arms wide and whirling in the doorway. Heledd copied her movements until both were dizzy and laughing as they leaned against the lime-washed wall of the *beudy* for support.

"Let's do it again," Mairwen giggled.

"No, we will be ill." Heledd said, placing her hands on the girl's shoulders. "I sing when I am happy."

"What do you sing, *boneddiges*?"

"I cannot remember."

"Do you know this song?" Mairwen sang a verse but Heledd shook her head, humming a tune in her head instead. "I do not know that one but I can teach you my song."

"Tomorrow. You can teach me tomorrow. Go back to your mother," she said and turned the child to go on her way.

"Everyone is happy here," Mairwen said over her shoulder.

"Everyone?"

"Yes, everyone, except Daci."

"Why is Daci sad?"

"I don't know. He has been sad a long, long time."

"Who is Daci?"

"The *pennaeth*," the little girl giggled. "When he comes to our house, we make Daci laugh. He is happy when he is laughing."

"Wait," Heledd called, catching up to Mairwen. "Will you show me how you write my name again?" The little girl drew Heledd's name with her finger on her palm. "And this is how to write Garmon. If you come to the school, I can show you all the names, of everyone in the *gaer* and all the names of all the villages."

"I will. When I can." Heledd watched the girl run the length of the *buarth* until she disappeared around the back of the *hafodydd* that stood near the wall surrounding Garmon's longhouse. Both the gate and the door were open. She looked at her palm but could not see the marks written there, she could only feel the movement of Mairwen's small finger to make the six letters 'G A R M O N'. *For what purpose will I ever have use of those?* She rubbed away the sensation of the marks on her worn tunic. When she looked up at the longhouse again, she saw Meini closing the gate before she went into the house.

Until dusk, Heledd carried buckets of milk to the dairy, separated cream for butter and drained the whey from the curds to be used for the morning meal. She wrapped curds in muslin, tied the necks of the bags together and set them ready at the cheese press for a woman skilled in the art. Between one life of slavery and threat and another life of slavery and threat, she could hope the second life was less worse than the first. She could choose to love the man who had, until then, never hurt her. She could choose never to surrender to his ownership. She loved him, like all of his many friends loved him and as many of the women.

Once she had stripped out of her filthy clothing and dropped them and her shift into the basket, to be washed, her day's work and the upheaval in her heart, exhausted her. The most she desired was to bathe and go to sleep. She poured some of the hot water from the jug into the tub, took one of the small cloths from beside the jug and let it fall into the clear water. As it sank, she wondered what made a man desire one girl over another – or desire any girl at all. The soldiers she had witnessed in the barracks at Talgarth-y-Bannawg had not seemed particular about the women they took to their beds.

Though Heledd knew what happened between a man and a woman as cows were mated to bulls and mares to stallions, she wondered what part love played in mating. *My mare to Garmon's warhorse.* A strange sensation swept upwards through her body and brought a tingle to her lips. *Stallions and bulls do not kiss the fingertips of their mates, or hold their hands to their hearts. Or give gifts.* She was already past the age to marry and had only ever been kissed by one man, only ever been held in the arms of one man, only ever been caressed by one man.

While she washed her body, she took stock of what she had to offer that was different to any other girl, assessing what made her desirable to Garmon ... enough to pay twice her value and give her gifts. From her cheeks to her toes, she was all *brith* – lightly dappled over her chest, abdomen and thighs. Wherever the sun had reached, she was brown-patched. She wondered if the dappled mare had belonged to him, scrubbing hard at her fingernails. The mare, she calculated, had been mated to Garmon's warhorse long before he reached Talgarth-y-Bannawg. He could not have known the mare would be given to her. She trembled again at the thought her mare had been mated to his warhorse and their colt was Garmon's to raise. *Ach, Heledd, you are dreaming yourself into danger. Think, do not swoon so.*

She noted her calves were strong, solid and straight and her thighs were plump. Her belly was round and her hips as well. She thought her waist was thick. Though her breasts were not as full as Alys or many other women she had seen, she believed she would be able to nurse whatever children she bore. If a man, such as Garmon – if a man had an opportunity to sleep with her, what reason would he have not to take from her what he had bought? Heledd chewed on her lower lip for a long time, pondering this experience.

She placed her hand on her hip where Garmon's hand had rested through the night, a full year ago. The feel of her own skin was pleasant. Her hand, like his, was cold and her hip was hot by contrast. She wondered if he would have noticed the difference and felt the same wonder. Heledd flung her arms wide and began to dance according to Mairwen's instructions.

At the sound of a knock on her door, her eyes flashed to the bolt and she sighed in relief she had secured it.

"Heledd, open the door," Ceinwen called. Heledd swept a *carthen* from the bed and wrapped herself from her breasts to her ankles before sliding the bolt open. "You are not dressed," Ceinwen commented with a frown.

"I am going to bed," Heledd replied, stepping back to allow Ceinwen to enter.

"Without a meal?"

"I am too tired to eat," Heledd told her, shutting and bolting the door again. "Tomorrow, I have asked to make cheese."

"Tomorrow," Ceinwen said, "you and all the rest of Bro-Dawel will be in the fields. The farmers have chosen tomorrow for the harvest. Tonight, you will need to eat."

"But," Heledd began, staring at the basket of her dirty work clothes.

"Get dressed and come with me."

Heledd dropped the *carthen* onto the bed and pulled her only shift from the basket. Ceinwen took it away from her and threw it back. Lifting the lid of the chest, she pulled out a clean linen shift and handed it to her.

"You have not bothered to look at anything in this room," she scolded.

"They are not mine," Heledd replied, tightening her lips.

"There is no time this evening but I suggest you look at what is here. Put that on and this frock, they will have to do for now. Nothing can be done about this tunic," Ceinwen said, tossing a blue garment into her hands, "until after the harvest. Put it on and follow me."

"Where are we going?"

"To Garmon, of course."

"I told him I could not," Heledd began. "I will not."

"He told me and your reasons. Since you refuse to go to his house, he, at great trouble to himself and Huw Bro-Dawel's household, has come to you," Ceinwen snapped. "Now, get ready. I will see to your hair." While Heledd tied the ribbon at the neckline of the frock over the new shift, Ceinwen braided her hair. The linen was nearly white, soft on her skin and, although it did not fit her perfectly, it was close enough. The blue tunic fell heavily to the middle of her calves and was belted at the hips with a wide embroidered band. Ceinwen finished the braid and secured it with a silk cord from the chest. Heledd twisted her head to look into the chest but Ceinwen pushed her through the door.


Garmon had opened the *pennaeth's neuadd* and many of the inhabitants of Bro-Dawel were already there. The stewards were scowling and the kitchen was buzzing with shouts and curses. Aled, Rhodri and Daf stood by the hearth at the other end of the room, near Garmon. When she entered, he nodded in the direction of the table. Ceinwen had left her and gone to Aled.

Heledd watched as Ceinwen greeted her husband with a slight nod of her head and allowed him to touch her cheek. From the direction of Aled's gaze, Heledd surmised there would be another mouth to feed at Bro-Dawel by the spring. She suddenly wondered if Alys was well, calculating her child was due in late winter – the child who was destined to bind Bannawg to Gwesyn. None of that matters to me, nor has it since my father sought to murder his brother. I should be glad to be away from that place.

Garmon's attention had returned to his friends. Heledd was deep in thought as she walked to the end of the table. When she lifted her head, she was in the kitchen. Though the workers in the kitchen gave her sidelong looks when she put on an apron, her place among them was not questioned and her help was accepted. She had worked often in the kitchen at Bro-Dawel and knew enough to be of use as she tore the round loaves of bread into quarters and tossed the quarters onto the flat baskets to be taken into the *neuadd*. She had filled four baskets when one of the stewards said, "Your place is ready at the *pennaeth's* table, *boneddiges*."

"I will go when I finish this," she replied, filling her arms with bread to be quartered.

"They cannot start their meal without you," the steward told her, creasing his brow.

Heledd smiled at him. "I understand," she said, taking up one of the filled baskets and asked one of the boys to take another.

"*Boneddiges*," the steward began, raising his hands to take the basket from her. Heledd avoided him and led the boy from the kitchen, still wearing the apron over the blue tunic. She directed the boy to the *pennaeth's* table while she served the soldiers and the clerks at their table on the opposite side of the wide room. Daf, Carwyn, Nisien and Geraint stared up at her as she handed them bread from her basket and they peered around her to see what their commander thought. The clerks held up their platters and she smiled as she gave them bread for their meat stew. When they had all been served, she turned on her heel to go back to the kitchen with the boy and met Garmon's eyes. He was still standing at the table though Ceinwen, Aled and Rhodri were seated. To her surprise, Heledd saw Meini was also at the *pennaeth's* table, seated between Garmon and Rhodri. The *pennaeth's* chair was empty and pushed back, as was the chair in which she normally sat. Aled and Ceinwen were watching her with the same intensity as Garmon.

Heledd gave her empty basket to the boy, removed her apron and sat on the bench, between Garmon and Aled. Once she was seated, Garmon sat down by Meini and poured himself a cupful of ale. Aled filled Heledd's cup, tore her bread and invited her to take the bowl of stew waiting for her. With the exception of the clerks and stewards, Heledd did not believe there was anyone in the room who believed she was the *pennaeth's* bondservant.

She pondered the elaborate fiction Garmon had prepared to keep all but his closest friends from discovering Heledd *merch* Ieuan the Traitor, was *his* bondwoman. That his friends were prepared to die to keep her for him was less surprising now she knew how proud he was and how much they loved him. Though she might have welcomed some conversation from Garmon, his attention was given solely to Meini, whose anxious glances toward the doorway convinced Heledd Mared did not know her sister had accepted the warrior's invitation. *Invitation? Meini visits him in his house.* Heledd almost laughed aloud. *No patience for games*, she recalled Garmon's own words earlier. Heledd turned her shoulder away from him and leaned forward to speak to Ceinwen.

"At Talgarth-y-Bannawg, we begin the harvest before dawn," Heledd began. "The cleric blesses the crops and everyone is fed as the sun rises."

"Our way is similar," Ceinwen replied. "Tonight, there will be a service of supplication in the chapel. At dawn, the field workers will be fed and they will work every day to bring down the grain until the last stalk is cut."

"At Talgarth-y-Bannawg, only the women thresh."

"Most of us will be threshing, and the young boys. That

begins in a few days, when all of the grain is down."

"There is so much to bring down?"

"If the crops are good, the cutting can take a week or more," Ceinwen replied with pride.

"Will you be threshing?" Heledd asked.

"Not this year," Ceinwen answered, glancing at her husband.

"That is what I thought," Heledd replied with a smile. Both Aled and Ceinwen stared at her. Heledd returned her attention to her meal without responding to their astonishment. Their quick exchange of glances with Garmon did not escape her notice but she ignored them, draining her cup and inviting Aled to refill it. She ate until she was satisfied and then rested her elbows on the table, feeling at ease in her new home. She knew what and who she was – at least she believed she knew. The shift was pleasant against her skin and she looked forward to exploring the contents of the chest later that night.

"What makes you smile?" Garmon asked, leaning toward her and searching her face.

"Was I?" Heledd asked in return.

"Something has pleased you?"

Heledd had looked into his eyes for only a moment when she realized it was a very dangerous thing and immediately turned her head away, cursing her wayward blushes in silence. With a heavy sigh, she shook her head and stared into the cup she held in front of her on the table.

"Mairwen told her mother some tale of dancing at the *beudy*," Garmon persisted. "What do you know if it?" Heledd could not restrain her laughter and nearly spilled the contents of her cup over her tunic as she did. "So, you were happy today," he murmured.

"Mairwen was happy," she said, still refusing to look at him. Did she love him? Did he place a value on her? What did either mean? The only people from whom Heledd could have learned the answers were dead. Had Anwen *gwraig* Ieuan Bannawg loved her husband? She chose to die at the same time rather than live in slavery but that was no measure of her affection for her husband. Heledd could find no memory in her thoughts of them together. Anwen and Ieuan Bannawg had seven children. Only one child had lived to remember them and she now failed.

"You laugh," Garmon said, calling her back from her reverie. "I had begun to think I would never hear it. Will you tell me what caused your happiness?"

When Heledd raised her eyes to look at him, they were filling with tears. For a moment, he watched them spill onto her cheeks then lowered his own gaze. Without looking at her again, he returned to his conversation with Rhodri and Meini. Heledd stared at his back for several moments. He had turned away from her. The first tears she had ever shed for her parents and family dried as suddenly as they had come.


When the inhabitants of Bro-Dawel walked along the road leading to the chapel in the copse, they were accompanied by torches and small bells, ringing in the darkness, their cheerful sound carrying for miles in every direction. Heledd walked with Rhodri and Daf, keeping her eyes on the ground. Garmon walked at the front of the procession with Meini on his arm. Mared and her husband walked behind them. The older sister pestered the younger with a pretense of straightening her scarf and clothing. Garmon's step was uneven but Heledd did not think he was in pain as she had seen him before.

Garmon spoke the responses on behalf of the gathering in the language of the Church. The cleric was a benign, thin little man with large white teeth who smiled readily when he met the gazes of his flock. Mared played with a strand of her brown hair and Meini craned her neck to see beyond Garmon's shoulder. The heavy fragrance of the incense made Heledd sleepy. She breathed deeply to keep herself awake and fought the fatigue in her limbs. People murmured their responses to the prayers and supplications. Garmon's rich, meditative voice expressed their wish for a good harvest to sustain them during the winter to follow.

The cleric made his entreaty in a lyrical prayer that nearly undid all of Heledd's efforts to stand upright. Rhodri swiftly took her arm when she swayed and Daf stepped forward to lend support. Heledd shook the drowsiness away with impatience but was grateful for their strong arms. With a blush that could not be seen in the candlelight, she smiled at each of them in turn.

"Disgraceful," Mared whispered to Meini, as they walked out of the chapel, "coming to this holy place in such a state. She must have swallowed as much mead as any common soldier. Any excuse to throw herself in a soldier's arms."

"Heledd drank no more than I and she has worked hard today, like the rest of us," Meini told her sister. "I nearly fell asleep myself. If not for your husband's support, I also would have fallen."

The sharp intake of Mared's breath nearly made Heledd laugh aloud but she knew that was as dangerous as meeting Garmon's deep, gray eyes. Both Rhodri and Daf had offered their arms for the long walk back to the *gaer* and Heledd had slipped her hands in the crooks of their elbows. She thought Garmon would have preferred to offer his arm but, when the long procession reached the gates, he held Meini's hand where it was and they walked together toward his house.

Horns blared for what seemed like hours just before dawn. Heledd held as many cushions as she could reach over her head but she could not block out the incessant demand to rise. With a growl, she threw off the cushions and *carthen*, rubbing her face as she sat up in the too comfortable bed. Only then did she remember all of her work clothes were in the basket to be washed. Her new shift was too fine to wear in the fields. She growled again at her own laziness. In the dim light of the dawn, she flung open the chest and searched its contents for anything as serviceable as her dirty clothes. Everything she examined was finer than the garment before it and she realized her mulberry-hued tunic was more suitable for laboring in the fields than any garment in the chest. Even the very fine shift she had worn for the first time the night before was less fine than the three others she found in the chest.

"I have no choice," she sighed to herself as she folded all of the frocks, shifts and tunics back into the chest and put on her a garment that only a few days before she had sworn never to wear again until she had paid for it, somehow, honestly.

By the time she reached the dining hall, the room was full to the corners with farm hands, many she recognized from her explorations of the *gaer* and its outlying lands. She slid onto one of the benches with some of the other women, the shoemaker, the chief steward, four of the serving boys as well as two soldiers and helped herself to the bread and cheese being passed among them. The atmosphere in the hall was joyful and the chatter filled the hall as though she was beneath a waterfall. She saw Meini at another long table with Geraint and Carwyn. The younger of the *pennaeth's* daughters met her glance with a smile and then her gaze shot across the room toward her elder sister. Mared had not seen her sister's friendly exchange. Her glum features were intent on the crust of bread and ale Ceinwen set in front of her. All of Heledd's band of warriors were there and she was surprised to see Garmon, dressed in a plain shirt and leggings, seated at a table in the far corner of the room, talking with Aled and a number of other men she did not recognize.

Garmon and his companions were the first to leave the hall and were followed by everyone else, as they stuffed the last crumbs of bread into their mouths and took their last swigs of ale before running into the *buarth* to be given their assignments. Mared was one of the last to appear, clinging to her husband's arm. For her trouble, the two of them were assigned to one of the fields furthest from the house. Despite her grumbling, her husband seemed cheerful as he planted her in the cart and swung up beside her, happily resting his dark, curly head in her lap for the journey to the far field.

Heledd was not surprised her assignment was in the same field as Garmon, Aled and the rest of her guards but she was surprised Meini would be among the women to work with them. Each crew of field hands was overseen by a team of farmers and no one was in doubt of the hierarchy of command.

Garmon, the warrior, listened to his instructions and went to one edge of the field with the scythe over his shoulder. Aled, Rhodri, Daf and Nisien took their positions at the same edge. Each warrior had a team of gatherers assigned to their wide ribbon of grain down the field to the opposite end.

The contest began as soon as the warriors were in position. Heledd was in Rhodri's team, Meini in Garmon's. All of the teams had women and boys to help them.

"We will win," Heledd assured Rhodri. "I have done this since I was this high," she said, marking a place on her thigh. Rhodri grinned back at her and waited for the shout that would begin the race. When it came, he swung his scythe in an easy arc cutting the wheat stalks as close to the ground as he could. To help them, women sang verses loud enough for the reapers to pick up the rhythm and swing their scythes with it. At the same time, the women swept up the fallen grain stalks and when their bundles were large enough, passed them to the boys who set them in crossed stacks.

Before long, Rhodri's team was pulling ahead of the others. Sweat ran from every pore in his body. Heledd gave him ale to drink and wiped his brow as often as he asked. At the end of the row, Rhodri's team gave a cheer and ran along to the end of the field to cut in the opposite direction on the next row the farmers assigned to them. Rhodri was a full quarter length ahead of the next fastest. Although Garmon was taller, stronger and more experienced than Rhodri, his team was slower to support him.

As Rhodri came to the end of the third row, he flung himself on the ground and threw his arms over his head. "What are you doing?" Heledd demanded, standing over him. She dropped to her knees and, leaning close to his ear, she said, "If you think I'm going to let you lose this, you are mistaken. On your feet, soldier, and get back to work."

Rhodri opened his eyes and stared at her. "But, Garmon always wins ."

"I always win," Heledd grinned, grabbing his shoulders and tugging at him. Rhodri leapt to his feet with a curse. He had lost half of his lead and his team had lost their momentum.

"At your command, *boneddiges*," Rhodri said, fitting the strap of the scythe around his shoulder. Heledd pushed him forward and clapped her hands to the rhythm of the verses until the rest of the team had regained their pace. When Garmon's team finished their third row and were starting the fourth only a few cuts behind Rhodri, Heledd increased the rhythm just enough to quicken their progress.

Rhodri made up the time he had given away to his rival and led his team to victory with one final mighty sweep of the scythe before he collapsed with a cheer at the bottom of the field. The women finished their gathering and turned everything over to the boys, cheering them on as the last baton of the race passed into their small hands. When the boys fell on the ground beside Rhodri, the women gave a great cheer and Rhodri's team collapsed together in laughter. Heledd threw her arms around Rhodri and kissed his forehead.

"*This* is the happiest day of my life," she told him, and fell on her back to watch the rest of the race.

Moments later, Garmon planted the blade of his scythe on the ground and folded his arms on the top of the handle, waiting for his team to finish. Although they were happy at coming in before the other teams, they were not cheering as loudly or laughing as happily as Rhodri's team. Garmon thanked them for their hard work and received their praise with grace. Heledd watched the dignified behavior of the commander's team and thought their behavior would have been the same if they had won.

"I'm sorry, Garmon," Heledd overheard Meini say. "I have never done this before."

"Then why did you come?" he asked, peering at her. Meini glanced in Heledd's direction and looked away again. "You do not belong here, Meini," he murmured, stroking her cheek. "This work is for farmers," he said, "and their offspring."

Heledd tossed her head and turned her attention to the farmers – men who did not kill or plunder for their livelihoods.

Excitement returned to the field when Daf and Nisien were

fighting each other to avoid the last position. Heledd cheered for both in turn and thought the race between them was a draw. As soon as the boys finished stacking on both teams, the farmers surveyed the results of all five teams. To Heledd's dismay, they declared Garmon's team the winners on the grounds the cuts were clean and low, and the stacks were tidy.

"What do you mean?" Heledd demanded. "I see no difference between them." The judges were taken aback and looked to Garmon for explanation. "Oh, I see," she said, "he always wins, so he wins." She turned on her heel and returned to her team. "We won, but we are not the winners," she commented. "Now I know what the game is, we will win tomorrow."

"*Boneddiges,*" Rhodri murmured, "we will die of this." His half smile relieved her of a moment of guilt and she laughed. "We will do better tomorrow," Rhodri offered to appease her disappointment.

"The field is yours, soldier." Heledd curtsied to Garmon, slipped her arm through Rhodri's and, to the sound of the commander's laughter, walked with her team toward the *gaer*. As the circling birds descended to peck at the fallen seeds littering the ground, the farmers threw sacking cloth over the stacks to keep the grain dry and ready for the carts. The other teams picked up their tools and followed.

At the end of the day, all of the teams returned from every corner of the *ystad*, and gathered in the hall as they had at dawn to be fed before going to their beds. Mead and ale flowed freely into the workers' cups. Bread, cheese and apples were stacked in baskets on the tables for them to take what they wanted and find a place to sit or lie while they told stories of their day's work to their friends.

Heledd sat beside Daf, sympathizing with him at the unfairness of his loss. Nisien sat across from her, monumentally unsympathetic, but encouraging Daf to drink himself into a happier mood. The shoemaker, sitting on her other side, rose from his seat and Garmon took his place, wrapping his sun-browned fingers around the nearest empty cup and holding it up for a girl to fill it. He drank the mead in one swallow and held his cup up again.

"Well done, Gar," Daf conceded, saluting him with his own cup. Nisien did the same. Heledd's cup was empty but she graciously tilted it toward the warrior, acknowledging his victory.

"This is no longer the happiest day of your life, I see," he said, turning his head to look at her.

"Tomorrow, perhaps," Heledd said, a smile forcing itself to the corner of her mouth. "If not, the next day."

"Hope is a good thing," he said. "Have you eaten your fill, *gwraig?*" She nodded, setting her cup on the table and folding her arms, resting on her elbows to resume her conversation with Daf. Garmon swung his right leg to the outside of the bench, behind her, so his body was facing her as he held her cup for the girl to fill it with mead. One by one of her band of six joined the group at the long table, including several of the women as well as Meini. Heledd returned her shy smile and wrapped her fingers around the cup Garmon had set in front of her. He had turned his body so he could talk to Aled, sitting on his left, and his thigh pressed against Heledd's back. Though she arched her lower back to pull away, his thigh moved with her. Except for jumping up or sliding under the table, she could not escape the contact and resigned herself to it.

The numbers in the hall dwindled gradually as the exhausted farm workers found better reasons to go to their beds than to drink their *pennaeth's* free-flowing ale and mead. No one at the commander's table seemed inclined to leave and their jovial conversations continued with the sound of their laughter filling the long room to the thatch.

"Look," Geraint said to Meini and Carwyn, "Rheinallt's choosing his prize." All heads at the table turned to watch Mared's husband drag himself to his feet and onto the bench where his wife was sitting beside him. "She'll kill him with her bare hands if he makes a mistake," Geraint laughed.

"What's he doing?" Heledd asked Geraint, leaning forward.

Geraint looked to Garmon before he answered. "Rheinallt

won in the north field today. He's choosing which woman he'll sleep with tonight."

"But he's Mared's husband," Heledd said.

Geraint smiled at her, glanced at Meini, saying, "And Mared will never let him forget that. He wouldn't dare choose anyone else, but he's entitled to any willing companion tonight and he'll enjoy making Mared jealous, but not too jealous," he finished with a laugh. Meini and Carwyn shared his amusement but Garmon was silent as he laid his hand on his knee, still resting against Heledd's back. After a pause, he placed his hand on her shoulder and let it slide over her back to rest on her waist.

"The winning reaper has his pick of the willing girls," Rhodri muttered. "It doesn't mean anything," he added quickly. "It's an old custom, no one takes any notice these days."

"You didn't say that when you chose Meleri," Meini said in her soft voice.

"Who is Meleri?" Heledd asked him, pretending she felt nothing when Garmon leaned against her to fill her cup once more.

"My wife," Rhodri answered, "now."

"Oh, I— I didn't know," Heledd said, biting her lip.

Rheinallt continued to look around the hall for several more moments before he jumped down from the bench and took a long stride away, swung around and scooped Mared into his arms. He threw her over his shoulder to thunderous cheering from the remaining revelers and ignored the pummeling his wife was inflicting on him.

Several other soldiers and farmers made their choices as the fires at both ends of the hall began to burn to embers. The conversation among Garmon's friends had turned to other matters while the serving girls brought the last jugs of ale and put them on the table so they could also go to their beds, ready for the early call in the morning.

"I saw fresh signs of wanderers when I rode through Tredeml yesterday," Aled replied to Nisien's similar comment. "What have you heard?" he asked Garmon.

"The usual. Huw's gone so we can expect our guests in the

next few days. If the hunting is as good as it promised to be when we were training, he won't be back for at least two weeks."

"I'd rather be hunting than this," Geraint admitted.

"Me too," Carwyn agreed, grasping the handle of the jug.

"You've had your fill," Garmon told the boy-soldier, "and you're on duty."

"No, I'm not," Carwyn protested.

"Yes, you are. Take Heledd to her room and then go to your bed, Carwyn."

"Yes, Commander," the boy groaned, getting to his feet to obey the order.

"If," Garmon whispered in Heledd's ear, "you leave your door unbolted tonight, you will have only yourself to blame."

Heledd slid along the bench away from him. As she pushed herself to her feet and dusted off her skirt, she replied, "I will never be so careless." As she followed Carwyn from the hall, Garmon threw his head back with laughter and turned back to the conversation with his friends.

# NINE

When the horns sounded the following dawn, Heledd stretched her body under the linen bedclothes and winced. Every muscle in her back, arms and legs ached. She glanced at the bolted door. If I leave it bolted, she mused, they might let me sleep. Along the passageway, she could hear some of the workers dragging themselves toward the hall, regretting their thumping heads and stiff knees.

Her mulberry tunic hung on the hook near the door and her frock lay folded on top of the chest. Neither Mared nor any of the other women chosen by champions would have been so tidy.

Throwing off the *carthen*, Heledd took a deep breath and inspected the state of her shift. She pouted for a moment, then shrugged. Before she washed or dressed, she made certain of the bolted door, then hastily prepared for another day's labor in the grain fields. By the time she arrived in the hall, most of her fellow field hands had finished eating. Garmon was not at any of the tables but Aled and the others were scattered among the stewards, farmers and women. The men who directed the work were leaving the hall and Heledd finished the flagon of ale before filling the skirt of her tunic with bread and cheese.

She looked for Garmon in the *buarth* but could not see him in all the confusion. She was sent to one of the fields beyond the rise, again with Aled, Rhodri and the others. She hadn't heard Garmon's name called and he didn't walk along the road with them. When they reached the field, she expected to see him waiting, but no one from his team of the day before was there.

"Garmon won't come today," Aled told her as he joined his team.

"Why not?"

"He has business elsewhere," he said.

"Nothing that one does surprises me," she said partly to herself, hitching up the skirt of her tunic and relaxing her aching shoulders. She greeted her fellow reapers with a smile, noticing they were already smiling at her. To Rhodri, she said, "Our victory will be less sweet but I'm sure we will be able to swallow it."

"*Boneddiges*," he replied, "any victory we have today will be meaningless. Garmon has already claimed the prize."

"Does that mean we need not make any effort? You said he always wins," Heledd reminded him, "does that mean no work is done the next day?" She cocked her head at him. "What prize was that?"

"He's never claimed his prize before," he admitted. "He has always before granted the honor to the next best." When she asked him why, he stiffened slightly and replied, "Garmon takes his pleasures in private."

The deep frown on his face warned Heledd he did not want to discuss his commander with her. Rhodri's answers only raised more questions for Heledd, all questions she could not ask aloud. Both she and Rhodri were relieved when the other teams were in position to begin.

As hard as she tried and no matter how grueling the work throughout the day and the eventual victory Rhodri earned, Heledd could not drive from her thoughts the images the soldier's comment had placed there. How many of the women with whom she worked in the *beudy* were among Garmon's 'pleasures', Heledd wondered. How many of those she had grown to like were more knowledgeable of him than she was? Which woman working in her team that day was to his liking. *Ach*, she scolded, *you should not care. But why didn't he claim me as his prize? Nothing he does should surprise you, Heledd, and you are better off he did not. What could you have done but refuse?*

At the end of the day, when the teams were walking along

the roads, their numbers swelling at each crossroads, Heledd was tempted to ask Rhodri if he meant to claim his prize that night. Before she opened her mouth to be so foolish, she took a place in the hall where she could see everyone who came in from the *buarth* or the kitchen. The meal was quieter than the night before. There were still another two days' work of reaping and she could not guess how long the threshing would take. While she and the others reaped, the older women and men had been loading the carts and taking the grain to the mill. Heledd realized the threshing floor would be her next task and turned to the woman sitting next to her.

"Will you be threshing?"

"Yes, *boneddiges*. Will you?"

"It is hard work," Heledd said, "but I enjoy it."

"I cannot say I enjoy it but it is not as rough as reaping."

"What will the men be doing after this and we are threshing?" Heledd asked.

"The boys and younger men will be at the mill, handling the stalks for us. All the others will be in the fields."

"Why?"

"With the oxen, to turn the grass into the soil, ready for grazing in the spring."

"I have never heard of that," Heledd admitted. "At Bannawg, the fields are left over winter and turned in spring for another crop."

"Perhaps you do not have as many to feed," the woman suggested.

Heledd furrowed her brow in thought. "I did not pay much attention," she laughed. "I know we were not cutting the grain for as many days as this."

"Are you weary, *boneddiges*?" the woman asked, taking more of the bread and soaking it in the stew in her wooden bowl.

Heledd shrugged. "What is your name?"

"I am called Rhian."

"Do you have a husband?"

"My husband is Nisien *mab* Iori," Rhian replied, "so I am Rhian *merch* Hywel *gwraig* Nisien."

"I am Heledd *merch* Ieuan Bannawg."

"You have been kept busy since you came here, Heledd, so we have not had opportunity to meet. You know my husband."

"Yes. Nisien has been very kind," she said and to ensure Rhian did not misconstrue her meaning, Heledd added, "as have all of the soldier's in Aled's command."

"Nisien is very proud he was chosen for that duty."

"I was told they are the best, most valuable soldiers of all here," Heledd said, cocking her head a little.

"They have all been hand-picked to serve with Aled. Even the youngest, Carwyn, had to meet Garmon's strictest measure to be selected."

"Why is that?" Heledd queried. "I mean, what does Garmon have to do with Aled's command?"

"Garmon is the commander of all the soldiers. Aled is his foster brother," Rhian said. "He commands the five best, chosen to serve close to Garmon. None of the others have earned that privilege."

"Garmon is highly regarded by all the soldiers," Heledd commented.

"I think Nisien loves Garmon more than he loves me," Rhian confided. "There is no man he loves more, certainly."

"And there is no man Garmon loves more than Huw Bro-Dawel."

"There is no doubt of that," Rhian told her, taking her bowl in her hand and standing to go. "Garmon is like a son to him."

"I have not seen either of the *pennaeth's* daughters today."

"I do not know about Mared, but Meini has been with Garmon most of the night, and all of today."

Though her heart missed a beat, Heledd gave no outward sign of her flash of jealousy. Rhian leaned closer to Heledd and said, "Meini's husband was one of the five best until he was killed while Garmon was at Talgarth-y-Bannawg. Mared has always been jealous Meini's husband was chosen and neither of her husbands have been."

"How was Meini's husband killed?" Heledd asked, rising to walk with Rhian from the hall. "I thought Huw said he … well, he wasn't very kind."

"The *pennaeth* is not kind to his daughters. Meini's husband was killed by marauders from another *ystad*. Garmon returned as soon as he was told, for Meini's sake. Gwyn was another of his foster brothers – all but one of them was raised here."

"Who is the other?"

"I don't know. He left many years before I came here to wed Nisien."

"So there were four foster brothers," Heledd said. Rhian shrugged.

"What is your work here?"

"I am in the school, with Ceinwen."

"That is why we have not met," Heledd said, understanding the 'five best' also had the best, most educated wives. "Does Meini also work in the school?"

"No, Meini is a *meddyg*, she knows everything about medicines and remedies." After a moment, Rhian confided, "Nisien has only ever had one ambition – to be one of the five. He would gladly die for any one of them, but especially Garmon."

"I have heard they all feel the same. I wonder why."

"Because they know he would die for them."

"How do they know that?"

"Garmon has proved that to them many times. He would have taken the blow that killed Gwyn if he had been here. Meini knows that and he returned to make sure she did not bear the grief alone. Aled was the only one who knew how to reach him and Garmon returned the day after. He has always loved Meini," she concluded. "I must go, Heledd. Nisien will be wondering what has happened to me."

Heledd watched the young woman, a full year younger than herself, run off in the direction of her *hafod*, eager and blissful to be returning to her husband's bed. Heledd sighed in dismay. Apart from asking blatantly, she could not think of any way to be sure of her position. Barely able to lift her feet from the ground, she went to her room to bathe and sleep.

As she lay alone in the dark, she could not help but wonder

how long Meini would stay with Garmon. Heledd remembered then she was the reason Meini gave for joining the field hands on the first day of the harvest. She wondered if Meini was Garmon's 'business elsewhere' that had kept him from defending his title of champion reaper? She wondered if Meini had been his 'prize'. She wondered if Meini thrilled to the touch of his hand on her body. She wondered how Meini could bear he was not hers alone—or was he? *Is it Meini who keeps him from me?* she asked herself. Meini, so quiet, so subdued, so easily silenced. *Is that what he prefers?*

*I am haughty. Meini is not haughty. I am stubborn and talkative, difficult. I'm sure he thinks I work in the beudy to annoy the others because I am too sure of myself. I'm domineering too, happier to take over and push even the soldiers around. Look how I behaved on the first day of harvest. I wonder Rhodri didn't complain. Perhaps he did,* Heledd considered. *Ach, and my hair is so ugly and look at my skin, I am like a farmer's boy. My hands are rough. And,* she said finally to herself before sleep released her from her complaints, *my father turned on his own brother and sacrificed all his family, but one, to his treachery.*

When the horns were blown the following morning, Heledd was already in the hall, rushing between the kitchen and the tables, to put large bowls of *uwd* and flagons of ale ready for the workers as they entered and took seats with friends and their teams.

"Do you never stop?" Rhodri asked as he accepted the wooden bowl from her.

"I am as I am," Heledd replied, and moved on to the next man. She was among the first to go to the *buarth* to be assigned a field. Garmon and Meini were still nowhere to be seen. Heledd was again in the same field as the elite and began her walk along the road with people she recognized, including Mared and her husband, taking her sister and Garmon's place in the team. Though she regretted not being with the man she had come to love, she felt ready to face this new challenge of working alongside a woman who despised her. As she walked among her fellow workers, she lifted her chin – just another of her qualities men did not like.

Heledd was relieved when she was not put in a team with Mared. During the course of the day, she learned Mared's husband was called Rheinallt *mab* Rheinallt. Even to Heledd, who had judged him coarse, aggressive and cruel, Rheinallt proved to be a cheerful laborer and worshipped the ground Mared tread. More surprising was the discovery Mared was fond of her husband. *Whatever his abilities as a soldier, he has found a way into that woman's heart*, Heledd thought to herself, as she gathered one of the final cuts of wheat for the day. And for all Mared's faults as a sister and a daughter, Rheinallt *mab* Rheinallt loved her as a wife.

Heledd was still pondering these mysteries as she collapsed on one of the benches along the wall of the *pennaeth's* house to catch her breath and relax her muscles in the last rays of sun of the long day.

"Look at the state on you, Heledd *merch* Ieuan Traitor," Heledd heard Mared's voice in a whisper. "You may as well be one of the barracks whores."

Heledd opened her eyes, shielding them from the sun with her hand so that she could see Mared's face.

"I could say the same of you, Mared *gwraig* Rheinallt." Mared stiffened but stood her ground.

"My father will return soon. I wonder what he will think of you."

"Probably no more than he did when I came here, have no fear," Heledd replied, pushing to her feet. "I do not know why you dislike me, but you have no cause. I was not brought here to take anything away from you or to be anything over you. If I have a place, it is of no consequence to your life or the life of your husband. I only want to be useful," she finished, "and to be left alone, in peace."

She straightened her tunic and had started to walk toward the hall when Mared said, "You really don't know, do you?"

But when Heledd turned to ask what Mared meant, the woman had turned on her heel and was running toward the house. *What weapon have I given her?* Heledd wondered as she sat beside the shoemaker to eat.

"You have worn those shoes every day," the shoemaker said after a while. "Do you want another pair?"

"I can't pay you," Heledd admitted.

"I will be paid. Come to my workshop after the harvest is done and I will judge your size. You will have a new pair before the end of next month. I have some good leather that will suit you."

"How can I pay you?" The shoemaker touched the side of his nose and winked at her. Heledd decided not to pursue whatever the gesture meant but thanked him and ate her meal in silence. Too tired to worry over Mared or to think about Meini anymore that day, Heledd went to her room and bolted the door. The work clothes were still in the basket but she had no energy to wash them or the clothes she was wearing. She washed her face, soaked a cloth to bathe the rest of her body and slid into the bed.

Self-pity did not encroach often on Heledd's heart and when it did, it passed quickly, but when she awoke the following morning, many hours beyond the time the day's work had begun, the former inhabitant of Talgarth-y-Bannawg rebelled. God had not intended her to slave her life away in a foreign place, she decided, or He would have ensured she awoke on time. Turning comfortably onto her side with her back to the door, she looked up through the narrow window to see the cloudless sky and marvel at how soon the fortunes of girls are changed by the decisions of men. Only two, or was it three, days previous she had claimed to be the happiest child of her wretched father. Her mood had swung so far from that joy she felt she could not sustain the misery any longer. Foolishly, she had given her heart, and yet even more foolishly, she had thought a heart might be given in return.

There were women at Bro-Dawel younger than she who had infants and husbands who loved them. There were women at Bro-Dawel, selfish and cruel, who had husbands who adored them. There were women at Bro-Dawel who had already had one husband and would have another. Even such a haughty, stubborn girl as she was could have had a husband if not for her uncle's malice toward her.

Not being wanted was one thing when she did not like the people who did not want her. Not being wanted by the one on whose love she had set her heart was another. Heledd was so heart-sore she could not cry, only stare out at the sky and wonder when the sorrow would end.

She was deaf to the sounds in the *gaer* outside her window and in the passageway outside her door. She did not hear Ceinwen's call or the knocking at her door until it was accompanied by a heavy thud on the latch.

"Go away," she said, burying her head in the pillows.

"Heledd, it's Ceinwen. Are you ill?"

"No, go away," she said again.

"The day is nearly finished. What have you been doing?"

*All day, I have lain here alone and now they come.* She didn't answer Ceinwen's question.

"Open the door." For answer, Heledd threw the nearest object she could reach toward the door. The silk purse fell soundlessly on the floor and Heledd heaved a sigh. "Open the door, or we will have to break it down," Ceinwen warned her. She knocked quickly several times. "What is wrong with you?" she asked in a whisper. "Is it your time?"

"No. Go away," Heledd replied. "I want to sleep."

"You have slept all day."

"And I want to sleep the rest of it." Ceinwen was silent for several minutes and Heledd hoped she had gone but before long she heard her whispering to someone. "Leave me alone," Heledd said, making an attempt to sound as though she were giving a command, not begging.

"I would," Ceinwen assured her, "but I cannot. I have been asked to see you are well. I won't go until you open the door."

With a snort, Heledd whipped the *carthen* off and leapt to the door. She shot the bolt back, dragged the door open and said, "There. Are you satisfied? I am well." She slammed the door shut again but before she could secure the bolt, the door was pushed open. Although she put all her weight into keeping it shut, she was forced back and finally let the door fly open so

Garmon nearly fell on top of her. "What do *you* want?" Heledd demanded, her fists clenched on her hips. He stared at her for a moment, then made an angry gesture for Ceinwen to enter. He was controlling his rage, taking deep breaths, gritting his teeth. "Ach, get out. Both of you," she hissed and flung herself back into the bed and pulled the *carthen* over her head.

When she finally heard them leave and the door was closed behind them, Heledd released the breath she had been holding and stared at the wall.

"Heledd," Garmon murmured, laying his hand on her shoulder. "What has made you so angry?"

Knowing she would weep if she spoke, Heledd remained silent, focusing on the tiny cracks in the whitewashed mud as if she could read them, just another quality she did not have. Forcing herself to hold back her tears, her throat ached and her breathing was erratic.

"Heledd, tell me what has happened."

"Go away," she whispered, not trusting her voice.

"Is that what you want?"

"Yes."

His hand fell away from her shoulder. When he turned toward the door, she almost sobbed aloud but held her breath until he opened the latch.

"Huw Bro-Dawel's sister and her sons have come to meet you. The meal will be in the *neuadd*. Ceinwen will help you to dress," he told her and walked out, tossing the black purse onto the top of the chest. Heledd was still holding her breath when she heard Ceinwen close the door on the sound of his uneven step away from her room.

"So you have changed your mind," Ceinwen said, pulling the *carthen* away from Heledd's head. "I knew he could talk sense into you. We don't have much time and you will need a bath."

Heledd stared at Ceinwen for a moment. "Why do I need to meet them?"

"You cannot be rude to Huw's family, *merch*, no matter how any of us feel about them. Huw is not here to greet them, so the task falls to you."

"Why not Mared, or Meini?"

"They will be there, of course. But it is your place to be their host."

Heledd's heart sank lower. "I don't understand. How is it my place to be host?"

"You look as though you have already met them," Ceinwen laughed. "Come, Heledd, it will not be as bad as that. It would be better if Huw was here but you will soon know what to do, what is expected."

Dressed in all of the best clothes Ceinwen selected from the chest, Heledd took a deep breath, closed her eyes and prayed she could endure another hour. Despite the disadvantage of her education and the restrictions of her upbringing, graciousness and hospitality had been bred into her. As Rhodri and Nisien waited for her command, she lifted her chin just a fraction more and gestured with her right hand for the doors to be pulled wide.

Ceinwen had done as best she could with Heledd's hideous mop – at least she could not see any strand of it to remind her of its color. Beneath the ochre-dyed frock, she wore the finest of the shifts which fit her better than the one she had been wearing to work in the fields. Over the ochre frock, she wore a sable-brown coat, laced at the front and back to pull in at the waist. The sleeves of the coat were fitted at her shoulders and widened at her wrists. Ceinwen had folded them back to reveal the deep gold silk lining and the tapered, heavily embroidered sleeve of the frock. At the bottom of the chest, Ceinwen had found a pair of black silk slippers and Heledd had agreed to wear the silk damask purse on the gold cord around her hips. On her face, she hoped she wore a pleasant expression. In her green eyes, she prayed she revealed nothing of her terror.

Garmon's was the first face she found in the room, though she had not intended to seek him. He wore his fine gray tunic and tall black leather boots, polished to a soft sheen – as the first time she had seen him. *At least, I am better dressed than I was then.* He, too, wore an expression of hospitality. Heledd's eyes narrowed only slightly when she saw Meini standing beside him.

Meini wore a simple linen frock and gray tunic, her golden brown hair pulled back at her temples with plaits braided into black ribbons. Mared, as finely attired as Heledd, stood on the other side of Garmon, an expression of dismay on her face.

Heledd nodded once in the direction of the group of three and turned her attention to the strangers in the room: a tall woman dressed in a heavy, red brocade coat and two young men – two handsome young men, Heledd noted with a slight lift in her spirits – each dressed in dark green tunics with brown leggings. For a moment, she almost pitied their attempt to impress her and crossed the *neuadd* toward the strangers with her hands extended toward the woman to welcome her to her *pennaeth's* home.

"Forgive me for being so late," she said to the woman, "the harvest has taken its toll on all of us, though I have been truant today, I confess." Heledd took the woman's hands and gave her a kiss on each cheek, before standing back to smile at the two men.

"You're a child," the woman said. "Huw will eat you alive. Ach, my brother is a fool. What's your name, girl?"

"Heledd," she answered, still locked in the woman's grip.

"Heledd what? Are you an orphan? No father's name to protect you from old goats?"

"I am the daughter of Ieuan Bannawg and his wife, Anwen. My parents are dead."

"Ach, that explains everything. You'll never survive it. I'm not surprised you agreed, of course, but you will be dead within the year, I'm sorry to say." Heledd's eyes widened momentarily. "Of course," the woman continued, "Huw did not see fit to tell me what he plans for you. Mared is convinced you will be her stepmother and has made her objections known, but I think Huw has something else in mind for you. Ach," she laughed, "you do not need to look so frightened. I'm sure he does not mean for you to be Garmon's consort."

Though she was certain she had expressed no fear that could have given the woman reason to say such a thing, Heledd withdrew her hands from the woman's dry grasp. Both Mared and Meini had glanced at Garmon, moving closer to him.

"Please excuse me for a moment, *boneddiges*. There are a number of matters which require my attention." Heledd turned on her heel and strode to the doors, flung them open and met with Rhodri and Nisien. After a few moments of discussion, both warriors nodded and went in different directions, for once without glancing into the *neuadd* to confirm their orders with their commander. Heledd turned once again to face Huw's sister and his nephews. "For guests of such importance to Huw Bro-Dawel, I must ensure all is as he would wish. Forgive me if I have been in anyway discourteous to you or your sons."

The two handsome young men beamed at her and stepped forward from behind their mother to take her right hand in turn and bow over it. Neither brought her hand to his lips nor held it against his heart.

"May I present my eldest son, Aeron *mab* Cenfyn. And my youngest, Wyn *mab* Cenfyn," Huw's sister said.

"And this, *boneddiges*, is our mother, Llinos *gwraig* Cenfyn," Aeron said with a bow to the imperious woman who stood behind them. The woman's name was not one Heledd would have chosen for one with an eye like a hawk.

At that moment, the doors swung open again and Heledd turned with a smile as she said, "And may I present the rest of our guests for the evening." One by one, Heledd's band of soldiers, with Aled and Ceinwen at the fore, entered the room, Rhodri came to stand by Heledd and she smiled at him. The chief steward also entered and gave orders to his juniors to arrange the tables as Heledd had requested. Before Huw Bro-Dawel's deputy was satisfied, the last of her guests entered. Mared's tiny sigh as Rheinallt *mab* Rheinallt joined the group of three, was all the expression of gratitude Heledd expected to receive before she invited the *pennaeth's* sister and her sons to take their places at the table.

Satisfied the changes to the company were in place, Heledd gave the honor of saying the Grace to Aeron – to appease his sense of offense. While he was eloquent, Heledd's first impression of him did not change. Heledd made no attempt to engage Garmon in conversation, allowing him the freedom to converse with Meini, Rheinallt and Mared without interference. Though Rhodri was nervous and uncertain, Heledd was pleased to have him as a buffer between her and the visitors. She squeezed his hand as he placed meat before her, a gesture that did not go unnoticed by anyone at either table. Rhodri returned a small smile, glancing beyond her at his commander.

"I hope you have had a pleasant journey," she said to the *pennaeth's* sister. "Have you traveled far?"

"Our home is further north, child. My husband's *ystad* is better for cattle and grazing than this. The work of the herdsmen is more skilled, of course." Llinos studied Heledd for a moment and smiled. "I see you are familiar with the work of the field. I wonder my brother would have thought to combine youth and beauty with practical skills."

For once, Heledd's readiness to blush did not betray her. "Everyone works at Bro-Dawel," Heledd replied.

"Not everyone," Llinos replied. "There are some who play on my brother's kindness and betray his trust."

"I have only been here a short time, but I have seen no evidence of betrayal. We have all worked to bring this harvest – as poor as it has been – into the grain stores."

"My brother has never had a poor harvest, not unless someone has stolen from him." Llinos stared at Garmon's back with narrowed eyes and a pinched face, as though she could force him to admit guilt by her hatred. "I have neglected to ask after the health of your uncle, Heledd *merch* Ieuan Bannawg," Llinos Cenfyn said when the meal was finished and the mead began to flow more freely amongst the men.

"I have not heard any news other than what I knew when I left his house," Heledd said. "He was well then."

"So much sadness in such a small country," Llinos commented. "And what joy your cousin has wed Meilor Gwesyn's son. I hope her happiness is not a bitter drink for you, Heledd," she continued, "to know her joy comes at the hands of your father's executioner."

Heledd stared at her hand, clasping the cup of mead, and

was surprised she summoned the control to keep the cup on the table and not to throw it in Llinos Cenfyn's face.

"Heledd Ieuan's father died in battle," Garmon said, "not as Llew Talgarth claims."

"And who are you to change the story we have all come to know and use to teach our children the consequences of betrayal? You of all men should know and appreciate the worth of cautionary tales."

"There are more truthful witnesses to what was done at Bannawg," Garmon replied, though he had not turned to face Llinos Cenfyn. He spoke to the room and the company, his quiet voice filling Heledd's heart with the hope he told the truth and was not merely offering her false protection from the ill-mannered monster sitting at the *pennaeth's* table.

# ten

*What does he know?* No one had ever disputed her uncle's story of her family's slaughter and the reason for it. She had always understood her father, the traitor, had been hung and his body left to rot on the gallows. Heledd stared at Garmon but when he glanced over his shoulder to look at her, his expression had not changed from when she first walked into the *neuadd*. Hospitable and dignified. She could not tell if he meant to give another 'more truthful' account or was merely pulling the claws from the cat.

"I'm certain Heledd would not want to call her own uncle a liar," Llinos declared, "just to raise herself. After all, what does it matter to a woman what men do? She will soon have enough trouble of her own, if my brother has anything to say about it, and a good name for her bastard children will not matter, in any case."

Heledd knew she should say something in her own defense but her mind had locked on to Garmon's words and she could not think beyond 'more truthful witnesses'. The cup in her hand shook and she watched the contents spill across the planks of the table. Rhodri was quick to throw a linen cloth over the rivulet threatening to run into her lap.

"Have I upset you, child?" Llinos asked sweetly. "I'm sure I did not mean to cause offense but if Garmon is so ill-mannered to contest what we all know to be true, the blame is surely with him."

"You mistake my reaction, Llinos *gwraig* Cenfyn," Heledd said. "You are here as guests. May I respectfully suggest you refrain from insulting me and your brother's friends? I am under no obligation to show you any hospitality, Llinos *gwraig* Cenfyn, as Huw Bro-Dawel did not see fit to inform me of your intention to visit here. How am I to know whether you are welcome, without his word, unless," she paused a moment, "unless you show yourselves to be guests worthy of my esteem?" Heledd had only to glance in Ceinwen's direction to know her words had received their approval, including Garmon. She did not have to look at Llinos Cenfyn to know she had hit her mark there: Llinos had taken in such a sharp breath she nearly choked.

"You are a haughty child," Llinos said with sickening charm.

"So I have been told, by more than one, I can assure you," Heledd replied, gesturing to Rhodri to fill her cup again. She noted he glanced over her head at Garmon for his approval. Heledd turned her head slightly toward the commander and lifted her chin. Out of the corner of her eye, she saw her defiant chin had made him smile.

Though Llinos Cenfyn made an effort to engage Heledd in conversation with her eldest son, Aeron Cenfyn seemed more interested in filling his cup with mead and his eyes with Nisien's delicately pretty young wife. His attention to Rhian enraged Nisien who looked often to Garmon for direction. Heledd noticed Rhian was also wary, keeping her eyes down to avoid Aeron's lustful stare.

"You both have work at dawn," Heledd declared to Ceinwen, after a few moments. "Your husbands need not return." Heledd was annoyed Aled sought his foster brother's approval before he instructed Nisien to follow her orders. With a smile, Heledd acknowledged she could become accustomed to giving orders. Daf and Carwyn glanced at one another and exchanged a silent communication with Garmon. Curiosity forced Heledd to look at him and she was surprised to see he was studying her, with a deep frown on his brow.

"There is no reason to stare, Garmon," Llinos chided him. "The poor child cannot be expected to know how to behave. This is obviously beyond her education in the field and stockyard."

Heledd turned in her chair to face Llinos Cenfyn, giving her one of her sweetest smiles, though she was conscious of Rhodri's growing anger.

"I am glad you are not offended by Garmon's harsh nature," Llinos confided. "He has always been thus, ever since he was a young boy, but especially after his terrible deed. He is crippled and embittered," Llinos continued in a tone low enough to be construed as an attempt at private conversation.

"Ach, I have heard all that more often than I can count. And to be truthful, I have found there to be no foundation in it. Garmon has always been the kindest, most generous and patient man, honest and forthright," she added for good measure.

"You are fortunate, child," Llinos Cenfyn told her, "My nephew—."

"Aunt," Meini interrupted as she rose to her feet. "Allow me to walk you to your rooms. They are the prettiest, of course, the rooms you always prefer."

Heledd stared at Meini for a moment, saying, "Yes, *boneddiges*, forgive me for keeping you so long after your journey. You, *and* your sons, must be eager for your beds."

"I am eager for one bed," Aeron said to his brother.

Heledd also rose to her feet to encourage them to leave the *neuadd*. "We are all required to work tomorrow as you realize. I'm sure you will understand this is a difficult time to offer the hospitality Huw's guests might otherwise expect."

Llinos Cenfyn pushed her stout body up from the bench. Her sons made way for her but when they turned to accept Meini's offer, both Garmon and Geraint blocked their exit from the *neuadd*. Garmon made a sharp gesture and four of the stewards directed the brothers through the other door of the *neuadd*. They left but not before they mimicked the commander's uneven step. With no further reason for pretense, Heledd sat down and asked Rhodri to fill her cup once more. Again, he sought Garmon's approval but Heledd had ceased to care. For several minutes, when everyone else had left, Heledd sat in silence with Garmon, drinking from the cup of mead and searching its contents for something to say.

"You did well," Garmon said, "though you had no knowledge of these people." Heledd inclined her head to accept the praise without comment. "There will be a price to pay for your keen observations. They are not ones to forget an injury."

"What injury did I cause them?" she asked, turning her head to look at him. Once again, he was studying her, resting his head on his hand as he relaxed in the large chair.

"You recognized them for what they are. They will not thank you for it, *gwraig*."

"What will they do?"

"You need not concern yourself, Heledd," he told her, filling his own cup. Heledd drained hers and reached for the jug but he laid his hand over her cup. "You have had enough."

"I do not think so."

"I think so."

"You think too much," she said, pushing his hand away.

"And you are too drunk."

"That is my own business," she said, "and it is always you who are too drunk."

"I have not had reason to regret that on any occasion. I do not want you to have reason to regret tonight."

"What do you regret, Garmon?" Heledd asked, leaning toward him, lifting her chin so her lips were just below his jaw. If he chose to kiss her, he need only to bow his head. Instead, he drew slowly, deliberately away. Heledd sank back in her chair with a scowl. She was not too drunk to understand her offer was rejected. "You are right," she said, "I *am* too drunk." Heledd saw, when she met his gaze, her sarcasm had cut him and she was satisfied. She realized too late hurting him gave her no pleasure. Mustering a semblance of sobriety, Heledd pushed herself to her feet, resting her hands on the table until the dizziness passed.

"I will walk you to your room," Garmon said, gesturing for the chief steward to clear the tables. Heledd was grateful he did not make her ask for his help and held onto his arm with both hands, leaning heavily against his shoulder. Her head was swimming and she could not focus her eyes on any object without feeling ill. By the time they reached the corridor to her room, all of the mead had found its way to her head and her legs refused to carry her further.

"Between myself and God, Heledd *merch* Ieuan Bannawg, *gwraig*—," Garmon murmured as he caught her and lifted her into his arms, "you will be my death." Heledd was not too drunk to hear this declaration. Neither was she too drunk to hear him whisper her name again. She was not too drunk to feel his lips brush her temple or his cheek pressed against her brow. Nor was she too drunk to feel his arms tighten around her or to sense he was reluctant to let her go as he laid her on the bed.

Armed with the proof of these few signs, Heledd turned toward him as though in sleep, letting her arm fall across his shoulders. She felt his heart stop as though it was her own. She felt his breathing falter as though her own lungs refused to take air. "Garmon," she murmured, her lips brushing his neck. He made no movement for several moments, and then lifted his head to stare down at her in the darkness. Heledd opened her eyes and saw his expression in the moonlight. Her arm slid listlessly from around him and she turned her face away. Whatever his feelings for her might be, her invitation had not made him happy.

"Bolt the door when I'm gone," he said, rising from the bed and crossing the room. "Do you hear me?"

"Yes."

"You will feel better in the morning," he assured her as he left the room. "Bolt the door, Heledd," he reminded her. When she made no move to do as he ordered, he growled, "Bolt the damn door, *menyw*."

"Yes, sir," she hissed as she obeyed.

Contrary to Garmon's assurances, Heledd felt worse in the morning. Not only did she have a terrible head and a queasy feeling in her stomach, but she remembered everything she had said and done before Garmon left her. She was ill. She had an excuse to stay locked in her room. She had slept in her clothes and the beautiful garments were not fit to wear again without attention. Careful of her head and her stomach, she undressed to her shift and crawled back under the *carthen*, hiding from even the tiniest shaft of light coming through the window. To her shame, she could not forget how she had felt in his arms and she had to press her fingers to her lips to keep them from trembling.

She also could not forget the anger in Garmon's eyes and she could not understand how he could kiss her so tenderly, hold her so lovingly and be so angry with her for wanting him. Every muscle in her body had ached for him, her blood had been like fire and she felt she would be burned alive if he did nothing. His response was like ice, a cold blade in her heart.

From the *buarth*, she heard the shouts and laughter of Bro-Dawel. *Threshing*, she remembered with a groan. Rhian would be waiting for her, expecting her. With a heavy sigh, Heledd rolled onto her side and sat on the edge of the bed. The room had stopped spinning and her head was no longer throbbing. The cool autumn breeze through the window refreshed her and her stomach was less troublesome. *I am also untidy, just another fault to add to my growing list.* Looking at her rumbled clothing on the chest and her old work clothes still in the basket, Heledd straightened her mulberry tunic and frock so they did not look so much like she had used them to clean under the bed and stripped off the shift she had worn the night before, replacing it with the other. She closed the neck of her frock, slipped the ruddy tunic over her head and cinched the cloth belt around her hips. She wondered if Garmon had noticed she wore his gift on her belt. Wearing it gave her pleasure, even empty, and she fastened it to hang down her left side, over her thigh, as she had the previous night.

The sun was already climbing above the hills when she commanded her legs to stride into the *buarth* on her way to the mill. She kept her eyes slightly closed to block out as much of the light as she could. The pain was like a needle through her forehead. She had not walked far when, out of the corner of her eye, she saw a soldier's boots keeping pace with her a few feet away. Her head hurt too much for her to lift her eyes.

"What are you doing here?" she asked.

"I am going with you to the mill," Carwyn answered. Heledd nodded and brought her hand to her brow to smooth away some of the pain.

"Where is your commander this morning?"

"Aled is in the fields with the oxen. Garmon," he said, "is there as well."

"Nisien?"

"He is already at the mill with his wife. You are so pale, *boneddiges*. Are you ill?"

"I'm— I feel like I have been kicked by a horse. No. Worse than that."

"Meini told me you may want to drink some of this," Carwyn said, holding out a small clay pot. "This will help, I think."

"Why would she want me to drink that?"

"Garmon told her you would need one of her remedies."

"Good of him," Heledd said, taking the pot to smell the contents. "What is it?" Shading her eyes with one hand, Heledd put the clay pot to her lips and drank the liquid, gasping and nearly spitting it out. "That's poison."

"I don't think so, *boneddiges*," Carwyn said, his brow furrowing. "Meini knows how to make remedies." Heledd gave him the pot and he slipped it inside his shirt again.

"Where are Huw Bro-Dawel's guests?"

"They have had their breakfast and are still in the dining hall."

"I have heard the *pennaeth* say everyone works here, Carwyn."

"Yes, *boneddiges*."

"Tell the chief steward—."

"*Boneddiges*, I am not to leave your side until Geraint comes on duty to take my place."

"Who gave that order? Ach, never mind, I can guess." She glanced around the *buarth*. "They will make trouble."

"Aye."

"What should I do, Carwyn? If they refuse and even

Garmon cannot persuade them, what could I do that would make any difference?"

"You are the *pennaeth's* deputy. I know what Huw would expect, I know what he would do."

"Then we will do that."

Although he was less than half the age of some of the soldiers in Huw Bro-Dawel's army, Carwyn commanded with authority when he called three of the soldiers from their work in the stables to follow Heledd into the dining hall. When she saw them, she stepped behind Carwyn.

"Are you sure this is wise, *boneddiges*?" one of the soldiers asked.

She looked into his scarred face and pressed her lips together. "No, but I believe it is right under the circumstances." The needle in her forehead twisted and her right eye felt the point. "Will you do it?"

The man lifted his heavy hands in a shrug, nodding to his comrades to follow her and the boy-soldier. The mother and her sons had commandeered a long table laden with baskets of bread and jugs of ale. One of the girls from the kitchen set a jug near Wyn Cenfyn's hand and he thanked her but when she curtsied and turned away, he caught her wrist. "Is that all I get?"

"I think," Heledd said, "that is more than enough. Rahel, take that jug away and ask the steward to send boys to clear this table, as all the others." The girl yanked her hand away and grabbed two jugs before she darted into the kitchen.

"We have not had our breakfast, Heledd, come join us. You are so pale," Llinos Cenfyn said. "Did you not sleep well?"

"I slept well enough. The time for breakfast is long past, *boneddiges*."

"When you did not join us earlier, we felt it was not polite for us to eat before you."

Heledd peered at the corner of the mother's mouth. "You should have eaten when you had opportunity. At Bro-Dawel, we use our time suitable to the opportunity. Now it is time to work. Here are two strong men," she told the three soldiers behind her. "They will do for the work you have to complete today. *Boneddiges*, you may come with me to the mill or attend the needs of the sewing room. I give you the choice. The *pennaeth* has left instructions."

"My brother has never 'left instructions' in all the years we have visited him, child. I can guess who has influenced this odd behavior. Was Garmon very unkind to you last night? Is that why you are doing his bidding today? Where did he strike you, child?" Llinos Cenfyn stretched her hand toward Heledd. "You can trust I will not take offense on this occasion, nor will I complain to my brother. It is all the work of that whore's bastard."

"On the contrary," Heledd felt the outrage of the soldiers at the insults to their commander, "Huw Bro-Dawel does not tolerate indolence of any kind. I repeat your choice, *boneddiges*, the sewing room or the threshing floor."

"You poor child. You have no idea of the wrath my brother will bring down on your head when he hears of this insult to his family."

"Moc, see these two work as they are required." The two other soldiers pulled the brothers from their seats on the benches and propelled them through the doors. "Unless you want this soldier to treat you like a sack of grain, I suggest you follow him to the sewing room. Ceinwen Aled will set work for you." Heledd spoke briefly to the scarred man. When the dining hall was cleared and the boys emerged from the kitchen, she sank onto the bench for a moment, looking up at Carwyn through half-closed eyes. "That felt right."

She rubbed her temples with both hands before taking his arm to walk to the mill. The wooden ladder beside the wall leading to the threshing floor was covered in chaff and stalk dust. Carwyn laid his hand on Heledd's shoulder and went up the ladder before her, searching the threshing floor. He nodded for her to follow him then took his place by the shaft from which the other boys and young men were dragging the wheat stalks to hand to the women and girls. She took a deep breath to clear her head then joined Rhian in the far corner of the floor. The wheat heads split away as the six women flailed the stalks on the threshing floor, with movements that were a kind of rhythmic dance. The wheat berries fell through the square opening in the center of the floor into the baskets on the level below, ready for chaffing. Little girls scooped the heads that hadn't reached the baskets into their small hands from the stone floor or picked them up with their fingers so no grain was wasted.

The threshing continued for another hour before they were all given an opportunity to rest. Mairwen emerged from the mill house, her small body covered in dust, even her eyelashes were white. When she saw Heledd lying with Rhian on the grass by the millstream, she trotted over, scattering mill dust like snow behind her.

"What are you doing here, Mairwen. Why aren't you in the school?"

"I am in the mill," Mairwen declared. "I am old enough now."

"I see," Heledd replied with a smile, wondering when her head had stopped aching. A few yards away, Nisien and Carwyn rested on their sides, their elbows planted on the grass so they could watch their charges. Heledd welcomed Mairwen to sit beside her and turned her face toward Rhian. "Do others of Aled's command have wives?"

"All but Geraint and Carwyn, yes."

"I haven't met them," Heledd said.

"Meleri *gwraig* Rhodri and Camwy *gwraig* Daf are close to their time. They stay near to their *hafodydd* and the midwife."

"Who is midwife?"

"Meleri's mother, Tegwen Talog. Her *hafod* is near the *beudy*."

Heledd nodded and brushed some dust from the tip of her nose. "When is your child to be born?"

"Ach, I told Nisien not to tell anyone yet."

"He didn't," Heledd smiled, "you just did." Rhian blushed and gazed at her husband. "Where— does Garmon also have a wife?" she asked, turning her head to watch the clouds. When Rhian did not answer, Heledd glanced at her. "Does he?"

"In name," Rhian answered after a moment.

"What does that mean?" Heledd inquired with a laugh she hoped sounded indifferent.

"Ceinwen says he has chosen his wife, *boneddiges*, but that has not been announced."

"I see … I didn't know. This is such dry work," she complained, turning onto her belly and drinking from the stream with her cupped hands. She laid her head on her folded arms.

"Everyone believes he has chosen Meini. I hope that is true," Rhian said in a low voice, glancing at Mairwen. The little girl had also turned onto her belly and laid her head on her arms.

"Why?" Heledd asked, swirling her hand in the stream.

"She has been so unhappy for such a long time, since Gwyn was killed. She has always been close to Garmon. She's been so much happier since he came home."

Heledd turned onto her back, staring up at the bright sky, wondering how much more pain she could endure before her heart broke. And yet, she asked, "Why does everyone think he has chosen Meini?"

"He has spent almost every spare moment with her. He asks her opinion about everything – especially the house he has built. Meini chose nearly all the furnishings. And," Rhian leaned closer to Heledd, whispering, "he chose her to be with him after he was declared champion reaper. That is always a sure sign."

"Did he? It was a sure sign for Rhodri," she rushed to add.

"Was it?" Rhian asked.

"Apparently. At least, that's what Meini said." Heledd turned onto her belly again and dipped her hands in the stream, letting the cool water run through her fingers. She smiled at Mairwen who was doing the same.

"That's something *I* didn't know. I wonder if Camwy knows. Anyway, everyone is happy Garmon is finally wed – except all the women who were in love with him."

"Truly?"

"He may be old, but he is still handsome, and kind. When he came back from university—."

"Where did he go to university?" Heledd interrupted. She had never known anyone who had been so educated.

"In Paris," Rhian said, as though that city was the only possibility. "When he came back, he had property as well as knowing everything about law. You know," Rhian said, lowering her voice, "I think he wanted to marry Meini years ago but the *pennaeth* wouldn't allow it. I think that's why he has been unwed for so long. When Gwyn was killed this year, Garmon was here in less than two days – he rode all night to be with her. Nothing could keep him away."

"You must be right then," Heledd said.

"Of course, he had to make sure you got here safely for the *pennaeth* but Aled went in his place, with Meini and Mared ..." Rhian said, pursing her lips for a moment. "Camwy says Meini is the only woman Garmon has ever loved, and he's loved her since he was a boy."

"Why didn't he marry her before this?" Heledd asked.

"That's obvious. He has no family. His mother was a whore," Rhian whispered. Heledd glanced at her. "Everyone knows and he doesn't hide it. Once the *pennaeth* returns, there will be a wedding and everyone will be so happy for them."

"Yes, I'm sure. How old is Garmon?" She had had enough of wives.

"No one knows. But he must be at least twenty-five because he's older than Aled and *he* celebrated his twenty-fourth birthday in early summer."

"When does Garmon celebrate his birthday?"

"He doesn't."

"Should you be threshing?" Heledd asked suddenly, lifting her head to peer at Rhian. "Ceinwen is not. You should not. Nisien," she called across the mill yard. When he came to her, she said, "Take your wife to the school where she belongs. She should not be here." Though he frowned, he extended his hands toward Rhian and pulled her to her feet. "And see she goes to Tegwen Talog as well."

"Yes, *boneddiges*," he said, turning a questioning glance on Rhian.

Gazing over her shoulder, Heledd watched them go. Her questions, she knew, would reach Garmon and she wondered if he would regret how he treated her from the beginning. A man with a wife had no right to kiss a maiden or hold her in his arms or give her cause to love him. Heledd dropped her head to her arms again and tried to rest until the millers called them back to work.

When dusk made the work too difficult, Heledd rolled her shoulders as she waited for Geraint, who had relieved Carwyn in mid-afternoon, to descend the ladder ahead of her. All the other women and girls were gone on their way to the hall to eat. Geraint stood near the door, wary and on guard.

"I do not want to go back to the *gaer* as yet," she told him. "Walk with me."

"*Boneddiges*," he began, looking at the people making their way toward rest.

"I will not keep you from your food too long."

"That is not the reason," he replied, offended.

"What is the reason? Am I a prisoner? Am I never to have any fun?"

"*Boneddiges*," he said. "I am at your command." When she turned toward the copse between the two rivers, he gave one last look toward the *gaer* and followed her, staying close and watchful. Heledd crossed the clearing near the chapel and went to the shore of the second, wider river. She sat down and removed her shoes. "What is your intention, *boneddiges*?"

"I want to swim. Turn your back until I tell you."

"I cannot, *boneddiges*," Geraint said, a worried frown in his blue eyes.

"Orders?"

"Yes, *boneddiges*."

"Well then, forget what you see." She undressed in front of him and dove into the gentle current. He had lowered his gaze and crouched by the edge, watching her and every movement around them. Heledd swam upstream for a short distance then turned onto her back to float down. When she drew close to the spot from which Geraint watched every move she made, she dove under the water and changed direction, surfacing out of sight but, seeing the panic gripping him as he jumped to his feet, she was sorry and swam into view. "Geraint," she began, swimming closer.

"Yes, *boneddiges*?"

"How long have you been here, in Aled's command?"

"Five years, come winter."

"You must have been very young."

"Nearly fourteen, a little younger than Carwyn is now."

"Why did you choose to be a soldier, a warrior?"

"I do not know, *boneddiges*, I have never asked myself that question. My father was a warrior. I only ever wanted to become a warrior."

"Where is your home?"

"Here, *boneddiges*, but I come from a district in the east, like you, much further east and to the north. I came here to train with Garmon Dolwyddlan."

"Is it a good life, being a warrior?"

"I have work that suits me, I eat," he answered. "I have friends."

"That sounds like a good life. But what happens when there is war and one of your friends is killed, or your life is threatened?"

"That is not so good," he admitted, "but it is part of the work." He peered into the woods in the copse to locate a bird and made its sound in answer.

"Were you with Meini's husband when he was killed?"

"Yes."

"Where does this *pennaeth* who attacked your warband live?"

"You need not concern yourself with him, *boneddiges*," Geraint answered, rising from his crouched position. Geraint shrugged, turning his head at the sound of another bird and mimicked its song. "There is a treaty between Bro-Dawel and Tŷ Gwyn now." Heledd opened her mouth to ask another question just as a ruddy-hued warhorse crashed through the undergrowth and reared at the edge of the water. Heledd dove and swam upstream to a place where she could watch, concealed by low hanging branches.

"Go back," Garmon told his young warrior. "I will deal with her."

"The *boneddiges*—."

"There is no reason to explain, you have done your duty," Garmon assured him. "I do not need to hear details to know what happened." Geraint turned on his heel and disappeared into the copse. Heledd could hear him running toward the chapel. "Come out, *menyw*," Garmon growled, crouching by the riverbank, looking straight at her.

"How did you know where to find us?"

"I taught Geraint everything he knows," he replied. "Do you think he would not leave signs? Come here," he ordered, pointing to a spot in front of him. Heledd swam to face him but remained in the deep water. "Come out. Have you forgotten you have guests?"

"No, but—," she bit her lips together, using her arms to keep her footing in the eddies.

"The meal will not be served without you. Where are your clothes?" Heledd nodded at the pile and Garmon scooped them in his hand. He pointed again to the place he wanted her to emerge from the river.

"I can't," she protested. "You have my clothes."

"How did you get in?" he asked. Heledd answered with a blush. "You undress in front of a man in my command, why should it bother you to dress before me?"

Heledd glared at him. "You do not frighten *me*," she said, swimming toward the bank.

"Why is that?" he asked, stepping closer to the edge of the river. "I have always frightened you before."

"You have always given me good reason."

"You are not frightened of Geraint or Rhodri, the others."

"They have proved I can trust them."

"So now, you are not frightened of me? Why is that?"

"I know you would not treat your wife with such disrespect," she said, straightening her legs to stand out of the water. Before she had fully emerged, he fixed his gaze on her face. She walked steadily toward him. He did not avert his gaze from her face. He simply looked into her eyes, as though he had seen her standing naked before him every day of his life, as though he did not see her.

# eLeven

Heledd selected the shift from among the clothes gathered in his hand and let it drift down her body, smoothing it carefully wherever it caught on her damp skin. She wrung the water from her long plait and tossed it back over her shoulder. She walked away to find her shoes and hosan, taking her time to ensure the stockings were pulled well over her knees.

When she returned, she drew the frock from his grasp, dropping it over her head, sliding her arms into the long sleeves before wriggling into the skirt. Standing squarely in front of him as he had ordered, she fastened each cord, from below her hips to her breasts. Not one muscle in his face gave her any sign he saw her. *I may as well be made of stone.*

He had confirmed he had a wife whom he respected enough not to look on another woman. Although her heart ached, she was glad he was not a man who did. When she took the mulberry tunic from his hand, there was no resistance in his release of it. *Perhaps he is the one who is made of stone.* Heledd fastened the silk purse to her belt, turning to begin the walk back to the *gaer. Foolish girl, a man who loves his wife cannot be tempted by a farmer's daughter. If he had ever wanted you …*

"You cannot return that way," he said in his quiet, steady voice.

"Why not?"

"Because that is the way you came and the way Geraint has returned."

"What does that matter?"

"It matters," he said, mounting the warhorse and riding toward her. "I will take you back." He pulled her up to sit behind him, instructing her to hold on to the horse's belly with her knees. Heledd sighed and dropped her hands behind her onto the animal's long back.

*You are such a fool.* She dropped her chin to her chest and letting the swaying movement of the horse's slow walk soothe her agitation. "Why does it matter?" she asked as they followed the path into the green wood.

"It matters because they believe you will be the *pennaeth's* wife."

"But I'm not, am I? And no one who has met me believes that."

"The *pennaeth's* wife does not go to the river with one of his soldiers, however high that soldier's rank."

"But the *pennaeth's* wife would go to the green woods with the commander of the *pennaeth's* army?"

"The *pennaeth* is hunting, *menyw*, in the green woods. No one will question your return from a meeting with him there."

"Of course," Heledd said.

"Do not be despondent. They will not think you have been with me."

He urged the warhorse to a quicker pace and Heledd threw her arms around his chest to keep from falling to the ground. She stared at the back of his head, shocked by what he had said and certain he knew she *did* want to be with him. *He has a wife. Why doesn't he take his wife to him and leave me alone to be with my old goat of a 'husband'?*

"Why do you care what people think of me? Huw Bro-Dawel does not care. I do not care. Let them think as they please. The *pennaeth's* sister is not going to believe this fiction. She's cruel but she is not stupid. She'll wonder why her brother has left me alone and eventually, she'll know what I am. What they don't know, they will invent, in any case."

"I have always found that to be true myself, *gwraig*, and it is always useful. And you are wrong about Huw Bro-Dawel. He cares much more than you think."

"He doesn't show it. Ach, I'm tired of this," Heledd snapped, jumping to the ground. The warhorse to screamed and reared, tearing at the air.

"*Uffern*." Garmon hissed, fighting to bring the terrified animal under his control. The warhorse bucked and screamed, thrashing with his huge hooves. Heledd ran to the safety of the trees and hid, watching as the warrior calmed his skittish mount with the force of his will and a steady hand. When the danger was over, Heledd sank to the ground, sobbing. Garmon dropped to the ground and tied the reins to a branch. "Heledd, get up," he said, standing over her. "I am to blame … I did not foresee …" He crouched beside her and laid his hand on her shoulder. She shrugged him away, covering her ears.

"Leave me alone," she cried, wiping away the tears with the palms of her hands. "It is all lies and treachery. Leave me alone."

Garmon stood and walked away to his horse, wiping the blood from his forehead on his shirt sleeve. He mounted again and directed the horse back to her. "You're right, it is. If there was another way, I would consider it. Get up, *gwraig*, your guests are waiting."

"You're bleeding," she said when she lifted her eyes to meet his gaze.

"This scratch will not be my death," Garmon said, offering his hand. When Heledd mounted, she sat with both of her legs drawn up, wrapping her arms around Garmon's body and laying her head on the back of his shoulder.

"Another way for what?" she asked.

"What do you mean?"

"You said if there was another way, you would consider it."

"The *pennaeth's* sister and her sons descend on Bro-Dawel like vultures, when they smell opportunity. Huw is not here to contain them and you are the only one, because they believe you are his wife – or soon will be, who can prevent them from causing great harm."

"Why me? You command an army of warriors, surely …"

"These vultures do not respect my authority."

"I noticed," Heledd said with a faint smile, as she rubbed her cheek against the soft flannel of his tunic.

"Everyone notices," Garmon said with a laugh, straightening his back. "Since they believe you have Huw's authority, they will respect you until … until they discover your weakness."

"That will not take long."

"It will take longer provided you play your part and do not allow yourself to be distracted."

"Why can't Mared … or Meini do this?"

"Mared makes herself blind to their faults. Meini … is not strong enough. I would have told you all this, to prepare you, yesterday, but you were not in a mood to listen."

"They will not believe a great *pennaeth* has chosen a farmer's daughter, a bondservant, as his wife."

"These people will believe anything," he said, "if the actress gives a good performance. The stage is prepared, Heledd, resume your place on it."

Heledd was silent for a long time. "I'm sorry about your head," she sighed, wiping away a final tear with her fingertips.

"It is nothing. I have endured much worse."

"Forgive me."

"You have done nothing requiring forgiveness," he replied, arching his back as he urged the warhorse to continue the journey through the hunting grounds, back to the *gaer*.

"What happened?" Aled demanded as soon as Garmon rode into the *gaer*. "Geraint told me she went to the river. What happened to you?"

"The *boneddiges* went to the *pennaeth's* hunting camp," Garmon told his friend and foster brother. "It's a scratch. The horse was frightened by a rabbit."

"A rabbit?"

"Yes," Garmon declared, dropped Heledd to the ground and dismounted. "Change your clothes, *gwraig*. Your guests are already in the *neuadd*."

"Will you be there?"

"If you require."

Heledd nodded and walked away to her room, asking a girl

to find Bethan.

"Do you know what you're doing, Gar?" she heard Aled ask.

"Yes," was Garmon's answer. "No," was the final word he said before both men walked away toward his house.

Heledd's hair, dressed with a twisted cord of purple and gold with purple beads at the ends, was still damp when she entered the *neuadd* with Rhodri. Garmon, Meini, Aled and Ceinwen were already there. The scratch on Garmon's forehead had been bathed, half hidden by his dark wave of hair, and he wore a clean shirt and tunic. Both Meini and Ceinwen stared at Heledd when she crossed the threshold of the long room. Her chin rose and Garmon bowed his head, she saw, to conceal a smile. On Bethan's advice, Heledd had chosen to wear a second frock from the chest – a simpler, less elegant design than the ochre one she had worn the night before. The next time she went to the river, she had reminded herself, she would have to take all her frocks and tunics to be washed. The gold damask tunic she wore fell to just above her ankles and she had wrapped a purple silk scarf around her waist, tying it and leaving the ends to trail over her hip. She had left the damask purse in the chest. Garmon had not seemed to recognize it and she had begun to think Goewin told her the story only to make her feel better about his behavior. *Another lie.*

Though the *pennaeth's* sister and her sons were also in the *neuadd*, Heledd chose only to acknowledge them before she walked directly toward Meini. Seeing she was the destination, Meini took a few steps away from Garmon. From the corner of her eye, Heledd saw Garmon hesitate to take a step toward Meini and she warned him off with a narrowed gaze. Surprised he obeyed her and puzzled he did not prevent her, Heledd backed Meini further from the others in the room, confronting her with a searching stare.

"What," she began in a normal voice then continued under her breath, "was in that clay pot you gave to Carwyn for me?"

"You drank it?"

"Was I not supposed to drink it?"

"Yes, but, I thought— Did he tell you it was from me?"

Heledd nodded. "I thought, once you knew it was from me, you would pour it on the ground."

"Why would I do that? Do you have something against me? Did you intend harm?"

"No."

"Then why do you think I believe you do?" Meini lowered her eyes and Heledd gritted her teeth. "Ach, just more lies. Will you, at least, tell me what was in that pot?"

"Peppermint, chamomile and lavender."

"Thank you. It was vile but I felt better." Meini bowed her head to accept Heledd's thanks. "I doubt I will need it again," she admitted with a smile.

"It is usually effective when someone is—," Meini began.

"Too drunk? Very drunk?" Heledd asked, "or not drunk enough?"

"In pain," Meini answered, looking beyond Heledd to exchange a glance with Garmon.

"What is his part in our conversation?" Heledd demanded, glancing over her shoulder at the commander who kept his head bowed as though listening to Llinos Cenfyn standing next to him. "Meini," Heledd gasped, "forgive me. I have only recently heard you lost your husband. I am sorry." Meini's eyes had begun to fill with tears and Heledd grasped her hand. "I'm sorry. I didn't mean to upset you." Meini shook her head and turned slightly away, wiping her tears away with her fingers and again peering at Garmon as if for aid.

"Why do you look to Garmon?"

Meini pulled her hand from Heledd's grasp. "Do you think a few kind words will win my friendship, Heledd, after all you have done?" Heledd was surprised by the anger in Meini's tone and stiffened. "My relationship with Garmon is of no concern to you, or anyone else," she hissed and pushed past Heledd to rejoin her friends.

*All I have done?* Heledd pouted momentarily before she turned to face the rest of the company, meeting Aeron's gaze with a cool smile. She crossed the room toward him and extended her hand to him. Aeron clasped her hand in both of his and raised it to his lips but Heledd restrained him with her other hand on his wrist. "Tell me what you accomplished today, *bonheddig*," she said, taking his arm and allowing him to escort her to the table.

"I will tell, if you promise you will tell me all you did," Aeron Cenfyn answered, leaning his head so close to hers she felt his lips brush against her ear. "I have learned a skill I believe will please you."

*Ach, you do not play these games well, Heledd.* Outwardly, she smiled. Aeron Cenfyn assumed the place beside her to her right. Garmon ordered Rhodri to take his place, while he and the others of his friends took places at the lesser table opposite. Heledd had no doubt his purpose was to watch her performance. Rhodri was in the *pennaeth's* position and his discomfort was evident. "Please attend to your mother, *bonheddig*," Heledd told Aeron. "Rhodri is accustomed to my preferences and I can be difficult."

"I would be honored to learn how to please you," Aeron said, again brushing her ear.

"Then you will not take offense when I say I detest having my ear bitten." Smiling sweetly into his frowning eyes, she turned to Rhodri with relief. "Tell me something about your wife," she said, gesturing for him to cut her a portion of the mutton joint set before them.

"What would you like to know, *boneddiges*?" He found a tender piece and cut it with his hunting knife.

"Since I have not met her, tell me what you would like me to know."

"Meleri is the daughter of Talog Bardd, the *pennaeth's* storyteller."

"Her mother is Tegwen Talog."

"Yes, *boneddiges*."

"And the wife of Rhodri."

"Yes."

"And soon the mother of Rhodri's child?"

"Yes," he said with a proud smile.

"But who is Meleri? You have only told me what is known

by anyone. What do you know of her?" Rhodri frowned slightly, glanced at Garmon and was surprised when Heledd laughed. "Don't tell me you must ask for permission to speak of your own wife."

"No, *boneddiges*," he replied. "I have never been asked about her."

"And Garmon can answer for you?"

"No, *boneddiges*. I can answer for myself." Heledd encouraged him with a nod and he said, "Meleri is very pretty, to me anyway. She is dark, tall for a woman and strong. She is clever as well."

"What does she like to do, what skills does she have?"

"She does not like the work her mother does, although she has been taught. She prefers to be a scribe for her father. She is also skilled in needlework."

"Did she make this?" Heledd asked, fingering the cuff of his embroidered shirt. Rhodri nodded. "She is talented," Heledd commented. "And your tunic?" Again, Rhodri nodded. "Does she make clothes for all of your friends? For Garmon?"

"No, *boneddiges*, not now." Rhodri said. "Only for me and the *baban*."

"Do you think she would consider making something for me? When she has time?" Heledd was so surprised by her question she blushed from the top of her collarbone to her forehead and dropped her chin. "I'm sorry. I don't know why I asked that."

"I'm sure Meleri would be delighted to make more garments for you, when she has time," Rhodri whispered, peering up into her face. Heledd pressed her forehead to his shoulder. When she had recovered from her embarrassment, she sat up, exhaled a deep breath and turned back to her meal.

"You have certainly taught him how to please you," Aeron Cenfyn commented aloud.

"I cannot take credit for that," Heledd replied. "To some men, these things come naturally." Her glance fell momentarily on Garmon whose bowed head could not hide another smile. *Why does he smile when I am at my worst? Why do I care?* Though she knew he did not care about her, Garmon's lack of jealousy, though she had not intended to use Rhodri in that way, was still hurtful. She was jealous of every look and gesture between him and Meini, or any other woman with whom he had occasion to converse. *If he does not care, why should I not find pleasure in the conversation of someone who likes me?* She glanced speculatively at Aeron Cenfyn and decided against entering into any discussion with him.

"I understand you visited with my uncle today," Aeron said, changing tack.

"Do you?" she said, not wishing to confirm the lie.

"Was the visit to your liking?"

"The *pennaeth* is hunting," she said. "Do you think any discussion with a man intent on hunting is agreeable?"

"Not for a woman like you," Aeron Cenfyn said, under his breath.

"And just what sort of woman do you think I am?" Heledd asked in a normal tone. Aeron's eyes widened and as suddenly narrowed. "If you do not want all of my friends to know what you say, then you should not say it."

"I will remember that," he replied, pouring mead into her cup to the brim. Heledd looked at the cup for a moment and then at him. "I have noticed you like the taste of my uncle's mead," he said.

"The *pennaeth's* mead is good, but I have lost my taste for it tonight."

"Is there nothing I can do to please you?"

Heledd bit the side of her lower lip for a moment but decided against asking him to leave the *neuadd*. "I beg your pardon, *bonheddig*, I have had an eventful day. There is little anyone here can do to please me when I am in this state."

"What state is that, *boneddiges*?" Aeron laid his hand on her arm. "Are you ill?"

"Not at all," Heledd replied, turning toward her attendant. "If you would be kind enough, Rhodri, I would like to return to my room." Heledd rose to her feet and made her apologies to Huw Bro-Dawel's sister before taking Rhodri's arm and walking from the room.

"No doubt you had something to do with this," Llinos Cenfyn said to Garmon before Heledd had reached the door. The farmer's daughter slowed her pace slightly to hear more. Though Garmon made no reply, Llinos continued, "You cannot even allow the child a peaceful meal with friends without your spying."

When Rhodri turned into the corridor to her room, Heledd stopped and looked into his eyes. "Why does Llinos *gwraig* Cenfyn hate Garmon so much?"

"She blames him for the death of her nephew," Rhodri replied, meeting her gaze.

"Is that true? Was that his 'terrible deed'?"

"Huw Bro-Dawel is the one to ask on that matter, *boneddiges*. He was the only one who was there when Rhydderch, his son, was killed."

"The only one besides Garmon, you mean."

"Yes, *boneddiges*."

"Garmon blames himself as well," she guessed. Heledd continued to look into Rhodri's clear, brown eyes. "Rhydderch *mab* Huw took the blow meant for Garmon?"

"Perhaps, *boneddiges*."

"And Huw witnessed his son's death."

"That is what I understand," Rhodri nodded.

"And Garmon was injured?" Again, Rhodri nodded. "Rhydderch was another of Garmon's foster brothers. There is another, a fifth?"

"Yes. But only Garmon and Aled know him. And the *pennaeth*, of course."

Heledd stood quietly for a long moment, working through the complications of so many brothers. "Huw does not blame Garmon."

"No, he never has. Garmon is like a son to him."

"Thank you, Rhodri. I hope you do not mind these questions."

"No, *boneddiges*. Garmon told us you are inquisitive," he answered with a broad smile.

"What else did he tell you?" Heledd asked, laying her hand on his arm and searching his guileless face.

"That we should not let your arrogance keep us from our duty."

"Anything else," she asked, unconsciously lifting her chin.

"He did say, once, when he was very drunk, you were … beautiful, *boneddiges*."

"He would have to be very, *very* drunk to say that," she commented, her wayward chin rising to the level of her dismay.

"If you do not mind, *boneddiges*, if you have no further need of me this evening, I would like to go to Meleri. She was not well when I left her."

*Beautiful.* Heledd scoffed, as she paced from one side of her room to the other, staring at either the door or the slatted window. *Very drunk. Not just too drunk.* She wondered if he recalled saying such a stupid thing in front of his soldiers. *Who else heard him say it? How they must have laughed when they saw me.* With effort, she put the matter out of her mind to concentrate on her performance. She could not prevent 'great harm' unless she had all the pieces of the complicated puzzle of Bro-Dawel.

There were now two things she must know: who killed Rhydderch *mab* Huw and who was the fifth foster brother. If they were one and the same person, her task would be simpler but she could not imagine a foster brother killing another – such a crime was more often committed by brothers in blood. As she paced her room, she realized Garmon would know of all the questions she had asked that day and before. Aled's command would keep Garmon informed of everything that concerned him. He would know she was close to solving the mystery of his relationship with Huw Bro-Dawel. He would know she knew he had a wife. He had heard Llinos Cenfyn tell her he had been crippled when he committed a 'terrible deed'.

One question she could not answer was why he had allowed her to discover so much, knowing she was so inquisitive. And that question led her to wonder why he wanted her to know anything about him. The only person who had refused to answer her questions was Meini. Heledd wondered why it mattered so much to Meini she remained ignorant of Garmon's relationship to her. Perhaps she had asked Meini the wrong question.

Heledd already knew the foster brothers were sanctioned to kill their *pennaeth's* enemies, so she was certain the fifth brother was not Rhydderch's murderer or they would have hunted him to his death. Boys were sent to foster fathers between the ages of seven and fourteen. Though two of her brothers might have been old enough, before they were murdered, to have left Bannawg, Heledd could not remember them well enough to know if they were involved. If they had been, that would answer her question about why she had been brought to Bro-Dawel. *But, if that was the reason, I would be dead by now.*

Any other boy at Bannawg at that time would have been killed as well. The only survivors had been a few women and girls, most of whom had been taken away to live as the bondservants of Meilor Gwesyn. These were all facts the storyteller included in his tale. But there were 'more truthful witnesses', Garmon had said. If some of them were still alive … Heledd shook her head. There was no point thinking about Bannawg. Nothing that happened there could help her understand Bro-Dawel. *Unless, unless the friend … Garmon's friend at Bannawg … was someone who might have been known at Bro-Dawel. The fifth foster-brother, Huw Bro-Dawel's foster-son, the one who was unknown to the five elite.*

Aled had known where to find Garmon, to bring him home to Meini. Heledd reasoned the foster-brother had to be at Talgarth-y-Bannawg, perhaps a man who was a 'more truthful witness', more likely, as Alys had told her, was the son of a man who had been betrayed by her father, a man who hunted and executed Ieuan Bannawg. *Possible.* The only man at Talgarth-y-Bannawg with whom she had seen Garmon Dolwyddlan was her cousin, Elis. They were close in age. *Possible.* But not a truthful witness, nor his father. Her mind ceased to work. There were no other men in her uncle's army who had any sympathy or care for her. She was despised. None of the soldiers had ever shown her kindness or respect. *Ach, it is too hard. I am too dull and too tired.*

For once, Heledd undressed and folded her garments with care. She extinguished the oil pot by the door. As she moved toward the bed, she heard footsteps in the passageway and someone tried the latch. Her eyes shot to the bolt, her heart wild. She held her breath as the bolt held against the attempt to enter her room. The footsteps, the uneven step, retreated and Heledd breathed again, realizing she had heard the same sound on previous nights. Although she had not realized it at the time, she had heard the sound outside her cell in Talgarth-y-Bannawg.

She had heard the same sound, the same step, outside the chapel in the copse and had not recognized it. Now, the sound had become so engrained in her sleep she would have awakened in alarm if it did not come at some point in the darkness of night. *But why does he come?*


The leaden sound of rain on the thatched roof of the house and the *hafodydd* woke Heledd early the following morning. The rain would not keep the women from their work in the mill but it would keep Aeron and Wyn from the work she had arranged for them in the high fields. All of the farmers and warriors would be idle. Heledd did not think Aeron Cenfyn had any real interest in her except that which his mother demanded of her son to annoy Garmon. Her next thought was for Rhian. His interest in Rhian had been intense. Nisien, she knew, would be close at hand but she did not put any store in Aeron Cenfyn's decency to keep away from another man's wife, if the opportunity presented itself.

Heledd dressed quickly in her work clothes and ran to Garmon's house at the far end of the *buarth*. When she entered through the gate, she had decided what she would say and knocked on the door, expecting it to be answered by one of the stewards. Instead, she found herself staring into Meini's pretty face. Recovering from her surprise, she said, "Is Garmon here?"

"Yes."

"May I speak to him?"

"I will ask but I doubt he will want to speak to you." Meini half closed the door as she went back into the house, toward the closed door of the second room. When she returned, she said, "As I suspected, he regrets he cannot see you now." Behind Meini, Heledd saw the door open and Garmon stood in the passageway, looking over Meini's head at Heledd as he pulled his shirt over his head.

"I think he will," Heledd said, putting her foot over the threshold though Meini barred her entry.

"Meini, will you bring us some ale?" Garmon asked, closing the door to his bedchamber and gesturing for Heledd to go to the hearth. Meini turned on her heel and Heledd watched their silent exchange. The tenderness of their communication shocked her and she turned her gaze to the hearthstone. Her name, as Garmon had written it, was still there though the letters Mairwen had written had been scrubbed away. "You are awake earlier this morning," Garmon said, taking a seat in the smaller of the two chairs facing the fire. "Did you not sleep well?"

"The rain woke me."

"Why? What concerns you?"

Suddenly her worry and her plan seemed idiotic and she remained silent. Garmon put another log on the fire, grimacing as he sat back in the chair. "Forgive me, I should not have disturbed you."

"You might have thought of that sooner," Meini said, handing Heledd a flagon of ale. "The damage is done now."

"Meini," Garmon said, "Heledd would not be here if she did not have good reason. What is it, *menyw*?"

Meini huffed at him and set his flagon on the stool by his chair.

"I— it's raining—."

"Ach, a brilliant observation."

"Go about your business, Meini or be silent," he commanded. "And?"

171

"And, all of the men will be idle."

"That worries you?"

"In the case of two, yes." Garmon nodded and drank from his flagon. "I think— I worry these two will cause trouble. Soon. Today."

"You have a suggestion, *gwraig?*"

"It is—. I'm sorry, it is asking too much. I should have thought about it longer before I came to you." She stood to go.

"Ask," Garmon said.

Heledd turned to Meini as if for support. The *pennaeth's* daughter shook her head, her eyes fixed on Garmon, with an expression of frustration on her pressed lips. Heledd walked around the chair, putting it between her and the commander. "I think they will cause trouble with Nisien, just for sport. And, for Rhian's sake, I thought, if they could be distracted, somehow, taken away from the temptation for mischief," Heledd faltered, and sank into the chair.

"Men will fight, Heledd," Garmon said, "for what they value or for what they want."

Heledd looked at him for a long time. "Is there nothing to be done to prevent it?"

"You can delay it, divert it, displace it, but you cannot prevent it."

"But you said—." She exhaled heavily. "I disagree with you," she said. "There is no logical reason for this fight."

"Aeron wants Rhian. Nisien is in his way," he shrugged. "Nisien values his wife. Aeron is a threat."

"So you will do nothing?"

"I did not say that," Garmon assured her. "Just so you understand the wanting and the having will not be resolved by keeping these two apart. They will find a way to settle their rivalry."

"Did you know Rhian is pregnant?"

"No," he said with a frown. "How do you know?"

"I asked her."

"You are always inquisitive," he laughed. "That will change the balance for Nisien."

"What if he is killed?"

"That is unlikely, Heledd."

"Others have been killed," she said, forgetting Meini was still in the room. "Who will take the blow meant for Nisien, if it comes?"

"I will."

"Garmon," Meini cried, kneeling beside him and throwing her arms around his neck. Heledd turned her eyes to stare into the flames, stunned by Meini's distress.

"I am not going to allow this," Heledd said, springing to her feet. "You can be a soldier, as you please, and get yourself killed, if you want, but it won't be because some bastard son of an ugly cow wants to take another man's wife." She slammed the flagon down on the table and ran from the house.

# twelve

"Heledd," Garmon shouted, putting Meini aside and leaping to the door. Though she heard him and heard the stream of curses he shouted in her wake, she ran all the way to the barracks, threw open the door and flung herself inside. She stopped long enough to catch her breath, blind to the several women who ducked under the covers of the beds from one corner of the room to the other.

"Blessed God," she said under her breath. *I am about to ask two men to put themselves in danger to prevent injury to another. How can I do this? What else can I do?*

"*Boneddiges*," Carwyn said, covering the head of the girl in his bed. "What is it?"

"Is Geraint here?"

"I am, *boneddiges*," the blue-eyed warrior replied, as he planted his feet on the ground, dragging a corner of the *carthen* across his thighs.

"I can't," she cried. "I can't do it." She fled from the barracks and stood alone in the *buarth*, not knowing which way to turn. Carwyn and Geraint, in their short *trwsus*, ran after her, stopped in their tracks by a silent order from their commander as he walked to meet them.

"Heledd," Garmon said, extending his hand. "I won't let you put these men in danger. You know that, not for this."

"If not for this, what?" Heledd turned away from him.

"You know the answer," he said, standing at her side, sliding his arm around her and pulling her to him. His shirt was already soaked through to the skin, outlining the curvature of his shoulder muscles. Heledd stood in silence for a moment, allowing her shoulder to rest against his chest and laying her hands on his arm, calming herself with slow breaths. Drops of rain clung to her hair like beads around her face.

"Are you," she asked after a long moment, "drunk?"

"Not drunk enough, *gwraig*," Garmon replied, gesturing for his soldiers to return to the barracks. "Not drunk enough," he murmured against her temple, "not yet."

Reluctantly, she pushed his arm away from her and turned to face him. "This is not finished," she said and, under her breath, "Garmon *llysfab* Huw." She turned on her heel and walked back to the house.

She believed she had guessed correctly, or near enough, to his relationship to Huw Bro-Dawel. That Huw would have made him his stepson after Rhydderch's death made sense to her. Shaking some of the rain from her hair, she twisted the braid over her shoulder and went into the hall to have her breakfast. Because driving the oxen through the mud would be impossible, the rain signaled a much needed day of rest for the field workers and only a few of the men had troubled to rise.

Unbidden and only for a moment, Heledd wondered if the feel of Garmon's skin would thrill her as much as being held in his arms. She took the empty place by the shoemaker and opposite the wine steward. Before she had a chance to enter into their conversation, Llinos Cenfyn swept into the hall with her sons in her wake. Huw's sister gestured for Heledd to join them at a table in the far corner. Excusing herself from her preferred company, she took a seat beside Llinos. At first, Aeron paid no attention to her as his eyes scanned the hall for another woman.

"I cannot understand my brother's thinking," Llinos complained, "leaving you here alone and at the mercy of that brute." Heledd glanced at her. "I saw the assault he made on you in the *buarth*, child. You did well to get away when you did. Imagine," Llinos sighed, "calling soldiers to trap you for him."

Aeron turned his languid eyes on Heledd's face, letting them slither over her as though he could see through her shawl and frock, as though she was undressing before him, his smile was as slow as though he licked his lips. He was not looking at her as if he had seen her naked every day and did not see her.

"What did you say to him to force him to let you go," Llinos coaxed.

"That was nothing," Heledd said. "A trivial remark from our first encounter."

"Oh? What was it?"

"I merely asked the commander if he was drunk," Heledd replied, after considering her answer.

"Was he?" Aeron asked, leaning across the table.

"He claimed he was not," Heledd said, rolling her shoulder and laying her hand on her throat. *I can play this game of sacrifice.* Heledd watched Aeron's eyes darken. His fair hair hung over his brow like a blanket, partially obscuring his pale, red-rimmed eyes. Though he was handsome, he had the face of a boy, an indolent, sulking boy. She left her hand resting at the opening of her frock, her fingers playing with the top fastened cord while she bit into one of the newly harvested apples.

"When did you first meet Garmon?" Llinos asked.

"I have known Garmon Dolwyddlan since he trained at Talgarth-y-Bannawg, a year ago. We met again when I came here at Huw Bro-Dawel's behest."

Carwyn and Geraint entered the hall, taking places at one of the empty tables, within striking distance. *He will sacrifice his soldiers to protect me, but not for the wife of one of their own. How can I understand this?* Her confusion showed in her face as she stared at the planks of the table.

"Don't worry, child," Llinos Cenfyn whispered, "My sons will keep them away from you. I'm surprised that whore's bastard has the nerve to assault you like that. Huw is a matter of a few minutes' ride away and yet that one thinks he can attack you with impunity."

Heledd watched Aeron shift on the bench and realized he was not made of stone.

"Which whore is this?" Heledd asked. "Which bastard?"

"Ach, there are so many of her kind here. Garmon's mother is long dead, from all her whoring and the brats she bore. Why my brother allowed her to stay, I cannot understand. Pity, I suppose, though she never showed him the slightest gratitude, constantly throwing her legs in the air for any man who had a coin or a crust of bread."

"Did she have a name?" Heledd asked, dropping her hands to her lap.

"Child, why would I know the name of a barracks whore?" Llinos laughed. "Although I did, at first, feel sorry for the boy – before he showed his true nature. The whore used to take him with her to the barracks while she sold herself. He held the coins she was paid."

"Barracks whores are not paid in coins," Heledd said.

"How do you know this?"

"Everyone knows this, *boneddiges*. Some work in the kitchen as well, and take turns at night, or whenever they are wanted, in the barracks."

"You are knowledgeable for one so young," Llinos said, smiling at her eldest son.

Rhian, Rhodri, Geraint had all told her the same story. Garmon's restraint, his use of drunkenness as an excuse – he had wanted her. She knew that. His body was her evidence. He had chosen not to make a whore of her as her uncle intended. He protected her while he could but she could not understand why he troubled to bring her to a place where she was safe from that life for as long as she chose. Aside from the fiction of being the *pennaeth's* wife, it seemed possible that, as Rhian had told her, he was kind ... and the *pennaeth* was kind to him, loved him enough to indulge such an act of generosity – to offer her a home where she was free to make her own life.

Heledd glanced at Geraint and Carwyn, neither of whom had taken their eyes off her without knowing the other kept guard. Aeron, she knew, waited for her to give him the slightest encouragement and would not care what became of her. Even distracting him for a day, she began to comprehend, would not be enough of a sacrifice for Rhian's sake. She was not what Aeron Cenfyn wanted; she was a temporary diversion. As Garmon had told her, she could not prevent the fight in his eyes, only divert his lust to herself, and delay the inevitable. Garmon, for whatever reason, would protect her with his own life and the lives of his friends. Carwyn and Geraint would be in harm's way as well as herself. *Ach, I am such a stupid girl.*

"Please excuse me, *boneddiges. Boneddigion.* I am needed in the mill," Heledd said. If she had aroused Aeron's interest, someone – either Rhian or some other unfortunate woman – would pay for her stupidity. *I have only caused more trouble for everyone.* Her responsibility was to prevent 'great harm' and she could not do that by being even more stupid. Looking straight into Aeron's eyes, she said, "Moc expects you and your brother."

"I have been released, *boneddiges,*" Aeron replied, standing when she rose from the table, "into your custody." Llinos Cenfyn smiled at Heledd and urged her elder son to follow her when she left the hall. At the door of the house, Aeron caught her wrist. "Where are you leading?"

"If you are in my custody, you will work as I work." Though he nodded, he glanced over his shoulder at the door leading back to the hall. "What about them?"

"Why do you ask?" Heledd questioned, drawing her shawl over her head and walking in the direction of the mill. Aeron walked beside her though he glanced over his shoulder often until they reached the low door of the mill house. Carwyn and Geraint had not left the hall. The women, girls and little boys were already at work. Heledd ducked her head to enter but Aeron caught her wrist again, turning her to face him.

"What is your game, *boneddiges?*" he asked, glancing at the waterwheel and the men carrying bundles of wheat into the mill.

"This is the work I do," she said, pulling her hand free. "As all the men and women here who work for what they have."

"This is not what I had in mind," Aeron said, stepping closer to her, sliding his arm around her waist. "It is not what you have led me to expect from you."

"*Boneddiges.*" Geraint and Carwyn shouted as they came around the corner of the building. They had not yet drawn their swords but their hands were ready.

"They will kill you if you persist," Heledd said, turning her face away from his attempt to kiss her. He released her and turned to glare at the two youngest of Aled's command.

"You tricked me, wanton," Aeron said under his breath. "I do not dirty my hands with toil. I allowed you to amuse yourself at my expense yesterday, but not again."

Carwyn waited at the corner of the mill as Geraint came forward to stand beside Heledd.

"Forgive us, *boneddiges*. We had to deal with another matter in the hall," Geraint said. "We will report to the commander but you have a right to complain about our performance. Are you hurt?"

"No," she said, meeting Aeron's angry glare. "But I have learned what I needed to know."

"My uncle will hear about this," Aeron said to her, backing off when Geraint threatened him with the back of his fist. "And that," Aeron scoffed, walking away. As he passed Carwyn, he spat in the boy-soldier's face.

"Between myself and God," Heledd moaned, crouching at Geraint's feet. "I have made such a mess of this."

"They always cause trouble when they come here, *boneddiges*. It is not you, or any of us," Geraint told her, crouching beside her. "Carwyn, tell Aled what has happened. I will stay with Heledd Ieuan. Put a guard on the two of them, and their mother."

She peered at Geraint through her tears. "I am sorry for the trouble I caused you yesterday too."

"That was no trouble."

"Was Garmon angry?"

"No, *boneddiges*. He laughed," Geraint said with a smile, but his cheeks were pink.

"He is always amused when I am at my worst."

"Aye, *boneddiges*," Geraint replied. "He said I needed better training than he could provide."

"Geraint," she began, drying her cheeks with her shawl, "do you know what Garmon's mother was called?"

"Yes, *boneddiges*, her name was Creiddwen Owein. She was a whore, as you have heard."

"I do not believe that," Heledd said.

"That much is true, *boneddiges*. Garmon *llysfab* Huw has no father he can name, but I believe there are a few who, if they met him, would be proud to claim him as their son."

"Is Huw?" she asked, a slight smile at the corner of her mouth.

"Aye, *boneddiges*," Geraint replied. "What will you do now? I am at your command, as ever." Heledd wrapped her arms around her legs and let her breath out. "The river? The green wood? The chapel?"

"Ach," Heledd laughed, "you're making fun of me." She threw her shawl back from her head. "I do not get into so much trouble when I work. I will go back to the mill." Geraint nodded and helped her to her feet. "Will Rhian be safe?"

"She has never been in danger."

"I should have trusted she would not be," Heledd admitted. "I should have trusted Garmon would do what needed to be done."

"Aye, *boneddiges*," Geraint agreed, ducking as he entered the mill behind her.

"How many children did Creiddwen Owein have?"

"I do not know the answer to that question, *boneddiges*."

"Does Garmon know?"

"You may ask."


When the day came to an end, Heledd did not want to go back to the house to face her guests or their complaints. Her hair was covered with dust and she longed for the river. The evening meal would not be ready for an hour or more.

"Geraint," she began in a supplicating tone he recognized and groaned in response. "Would it be too much to ask …?"

"*Boneddiges*, I have no authority to deny you any request," he said, looking down at her, his hand resting on the hilt of his sword. He too was covered in dust. "But I do not think the river is the best place for you this evening. There is a better, safer place though it may not suit you to go there."

"What place is that?"

"I will show you," he said and led her back toward the *gaer* for a short distance then onto a wooded path leading down the hill. Heledd could hear water rushing and crashing over rocks. She heard voices and laughter. Geraint pushed aside the heavy foliage and motioned Heledd to go before him. At the foot of a fall of the millstream, the women, girls and little boys were swimming in the pool. Heledd removed her tunic, shoes and frock, sliding into the pool in her shift as the other women had done.

Geraint washed the dust from his head and neck under the waterfall, stretching out on top of a boulder to keep an eye on Heledd. She played no tricks on him, happy to be welcomed among her fellow threshers and befriended by Mairwen. All the talk was about Meleri *gwraig* Rhodri's newborn son. The little girl climbed out of the pool and stood, shivering, on the bank, her small body turning blue. "When I am a wife, I will manage a big house and have lots of people to h-help m-me."

"Wrap yourself in my shawl," Heledd told her. "Your mother will not be pleased if I allow you to catch a chill."

"That will not surprise her," Mairwen said, pulling the woolen shawl tight around her shoulders. "She says she doesn't believe you can do anything right."

Heledd dropped her chin for a moment but when she saw everyone else nearby had heard, she lifted it again. "We cannot all be as clever as you and your mother," Heledd said with a laugh. Soon after, the women began to come out of the water, wringing the water from their shifts and hair. They wrapped their shawls around their shoulders and started their walk back to the *gaer*. Heledd followed their example, walking a little ahead of Geraint. When they reached the top of the hill, she turned and said, "Please do not tell Garmon what Mairwen said about me."

"*Boneddiges*, I am not a spy. None of us have been asked to report any word you say or any question you ask. We report only what threatens you or our own failures. If you choose to complain about the child or her mother, that is for you to decide," Geraint said.

"I would not do that," Heledd declared. "Ceinwen has a right to her opinion." She thought a moment then turned toward the road again. "You told Garmon about the river," she reminded him.

"He was there, *boneddiges*," Geraint reminded her in turn. "And I had failed to bring you back when he expected."

"I know that," Heledd said, pulling her shawl tighter. She did not know whether to feel relief or disappointment. "What I do not know," she said, "is what Huw Bro-Dawel intends for me. He is so much more interested in his hunting than in anything I do."

"I cannot enlighten you," Geraint replied.

"I didn't think you could, Geraint," she said with a grin, slipping her hand through his arm, "but it is good to be able to say these things aloud. I think too much because there's no one I can—." She dropped her hand to her side. "Have you seen Rhodri's son?"

"Not yet. Meleri will not allow Rhodri to take the baby out of her sight."

When they reached the *buarth*, Heledd asked, "Which is Rhodri's *hafod*?" Geraint led her to a small house near the far end of the *buarth*, not far from Garmon's longhouse and she knocked on the door. A woman, whom Heledd guessed was Tegwen Talog, opened and stepped back.

"Please come in, Heledd," she said, "my daughter and her son will be happy you have come to visit them." In the corner of the one room, in the wide bed, Meleri *gwraig* Rhodri rested against a mountain of pillows, nursing her baby. Her long, black hair was braided at the sides and the braids were held back by a ribbon at the nape of her neck. Tegwen Talog closed the door, leaving Geraint outside.

"I'm sorry to intrude like this, I'm not even dressed properly."

"No matter, *merch*. You are welcome in this house in any guise. Meleri, look who is here," Tegwen Talog said as she brushed a curl from her daughter's forehead and bent to kiss her grandson's head. Meleri smiled briefly at Heledd but all her attention was on the wonder of her baby.

"He is very beautiful, Meleri," Heledd commented, noting the black crop of hair shooting from the tiny head like needles.

"Thank you," Meleri said, slipping her finger into the boy's fist. "I think he looks like Rhodri, but Mam says he looks like me."

"Come, Heledd, you will be ill if you stay in those wet clothes," Tegwen said. "My life would not be worth living if I allowed anything to happen to you when I could prevent it." She handed Heledd a linen sheet and waited for her to remove the clammy shift. "This is as good a time as any to have a look at how you are made. I have been too busy with these two and Camwy to see to you as yet, but judging from what I can see now, you will not be troublesome." Heledd gratefully wrapped herself in the dry linen and submitted to the midwife's scrutiny. "You have a good back," Tegwen told her, and your hips are flexible. They are also straight. You are wide here, yes, that's good," she continued placing her strong hands on Heledd's belly and the small of her back, pressing firmly into the young woman's abdomen. "You'll have an easy time, but don't tell your husband that," the midwife laughed. "How old are you?"

"I will be twenty in the spring."

"That's a good age, eh, Meleri. There's no good in having a baby too soon, before your body is ready." Her daughter smiled and went back to gazing at her baby. "How old were you when..." Tegwen began, studying Heledd's body. "When did you first lie with a man?" she asked softly, though Meleri heard nothing but her baby's cooing.

Heledd shook her head. "I have not."

"That will not be the case for much longer, I'll be bound."

"I see no reason for you to believe that," Heledd said, lifting her chin.

"No man is made of stone, *merch*. Even the strongest are weak where a girl as pretty as you is concerned."

Heledd stated at Tegwen Talog for a moment. "Am I?"

"Are you what, Heledd?"

"Pretty?"

"Pretty enough for most, I suspect."

"But I am all *brith* and my hair is so ugly."

"In whose opinion," Tegwen asked, "your own?"

"And others," Heledd said.

"Ask one who loves you," Tegwen replied.

"I would, if such a one lived," Heledd answered as she dressed in the frock and mulberry tunic. "I thank you, Tegwen Talog, for your assessment. If I ever have occasion to require your skills, I will be at ease."

"I will see you long before summer, Heledd Ieuan."

"Please tell Meleri she has a beautiful baby," Heledd said, storing the midwife's comment in her wishful heart, "and I look forward to seeing them again."

As she closed the door to the *hafod*, Heledd heard the midwife say, "She is as haughty as we were told—."

"Thank you, Geraint."

He bowed his head with a smile. "Is Rhodri correct in his judgment – 'the best boy ever born'?"

"He is very beautiful, of what I saw, like his mother," Heledd replied. "Rhodri can be proud, in truth."

"Don't let him hear you praise the boy," Geraint laughed. "He is already insufferable. Garmon has threatened to drown him."

"Rhodri or his son?" Heledd asked as she opened the door to her room.

"*Boneddiges*," Geraint said as he bent his head to whisper in her ear, "do not believe all you hear about Garmon. He is hard but he is not unkind, or unjust."

"Thank you, Geraint," Heledd said, laying her hand on his arm and kissing his cheek. She stood, looking into his eyes for a long time, wondering what he saw when he looked at her. Geraint blushed after a while, but endured her study. Heledd touched his cheek with her fingertips, realizing that she embarrassed him. "I hope you are right," she said, closing and bolting the door of her room.

Though she was no longer surprised by their loyalty, Heledd

was surprised by the strength of their love for a man others despised. The 'whore's bastard' inspired ridicule and adoration in equal measure. On her account, there was confusion and apprehension. She did not want him to be kind. She did not want him to be generous. Most of all, she did not want him to love Meini, to only ever have loved Meini.

While she listlessly dressed for the evening meal, she studied her body according to Tegwen Talog's scrutiny. Heledd did not know how she was 'pretty' compared to any other girl. The girl she had seen with Carwyn that morning was pretty. Ceinwen was pretty. Alys was pretty. Was a 'good back' pretty? Were 'straight hips' pretty? How would she not be 'troublesome'? She was strong, could work as hard as a man, could fight like a man, was as tall – hideous, no one could tell what she was. She was not pretty – *beautiful?* He, when he was very, *very* drunk, told his friends she was beautiful.

Heledd bathed in the tub and washed her face in the cold water from the jug. When she ran her hands over her nose and cheeks, she felt no blemishes or scars. Her nose was straight and her lips were below her nose as other girls. Her eyes were on either side of her nose, like everyone else. Her forehead was higher than some and lower than others. Apart from her freckles and her ugly mop of hair, she was the same as Meleri, though not as skilled. She was the same as Ceinwen, but not as fair. She was the same as Meini, but not as quiet. She was the same as Mared, but not as mean.

All these women had husbands or had had husbands or would soon have husbands who loved them and called them beautiful.

By the time Bethan came and she had dressed in the simple frock with the blue tunic that fell below her knees and was too big for her, Heledd was convinced she was unlike any other woman in the *gaer*, in addition to being *brith* and having ugly hair. She did not look at herself in the silver-plate while Bethan plaited her hair and tied the end with a gold cord. Her eyes were lowered when she opened her door.

"*Boneddiges.*"

"How long have you been standing there, Carwyn?"

"Since I was told to come for you," he answered. "Since Geraint went off duty."

"Why didn't you let me know you were waiting? I would have hurried if I had known you were here."

"There was no reason for you to hurry and Garmon told me you were not to be disturbed," the young soldier said.

"Why not?" The boy soldier shrugged but she guessed the commander had no great longing to see her. "Where are we going tonight?"

"To the *neuadd*," he said, offering his arm as he turned in the corridor. Heledd pressed her lips together, closed the door of her room and followed. The gathering in the *neuadd* turned as if they were one person when Carwyn opened the doors and Heledd walked past him. She had not expected Rhodri or Daf to be waiting for her. The only one of Aled's command who was not in the room was Geraint. Meini stood near her sister, in a group that included Aeron, Wyn and their mother. Garmon stood alone by the hearth and, although she sensed from his brief smile she amused him, when Heledd started to walk toward him, he turned away to look into the flames. Carwyn took his post on guard at the door. Llinos Cenfyn was smiling at her. Mared was jubilant. Meini hung her head and glanced occasionally at Garmon, only to be pinched by her sister.

Though she wondered what trap had been set for her, she continued across the room toward Garmon, acknowledging the *pennaeth's* family as she walked past them. By the time she had reached the commander, Mared was whispering to her aunt and cousins. Heledd stood in front of the hearth, facing Garmon, her hands clasped behind her back. "Why did you tell Carwyn not to disturb me? It is obvious I am late and everyone has been waiting for me. I would not have chosen to be so rude, if I had known."

Garmon raised his eyes from inspecting the flames to gaze at her. "These can wait for you, *gwraig*," he said quietly, turning to face her, surveying Bethan's efforts to present her in clothing that did not emphasize her manliness. "Did you enjoy your swim this afternoon?" He smiled when she blushed. Whether he had heard what everyone in the *gaer* thought of her lack of ability or whether he was referring to the humiliation of her escapade in the river, Heledd could not guess. "I know of a prettier, more private place. You need only tell me when you wish to go there."

His tone was hard. His words fell in the space between them like stones and she drew back to avoid them. "Garmon?" Heledd bit her lower lip, once more swaying toward him.

"You are not as late as Geraint."

"Why? Where is he?"

"Mared has a theory."

"Garmon," Mared said, "I warned you. We agreed."

He inclined his head to acknowledge her and returned his gaze to the fire. Heledd turned to look at the others in the room. Ceinwen glared at her with the same ill-feeling as Mared had always shown her. Rhodri glanced at her, a sad smile and a question in his eyes. Rhian didn't raise her eyes at all. Heledd was so relieved when Geraint came through the door, she almost ran to him. When she greeted him with a warm smile and bowed her head, she saw from the corner of her eye Llinos Cenfyn was exultant. Heledd stared at the floor for a fraction of a second, turned to Garmon and said, "This is your doing."

She strode across the *neuadd* toward Geraint, ignoring the young soldier's attempts to warn her away. Instead she took his arm, kissed his cheek and walked with him toward the table. The chief steward scowled at the long delay but was gracious when Heledd finally called her guests to their meal.

"*Boneddiges,*" Geraint began in a low voice, "this is not good."

"Sit with me, Geraint," she said quietly.

"Do you think this is wise?" he asked under his breath.

"We have no choice." She spoke briefly to the chief steward and watched with satisfaction as the *pennaeth's* family were all seated at the table opposite her. "Have you done anything of which you need be ashamed, Geraint?"

"No, *boneddiges*."

"Neither have I." In a normal voice, she said, "I hope you enjoy your meal, Geraint. Rhodri and Garmon can both attest I am a demanding partner." She leaned forward and said to Rhodri, "You have a beautiful son." She sipped the mead Garmon had poured into her cup, thanking him with a nod. "Did Meleri tell you I went to see him today?"

"Yes, *boneddiges*," he answered, after he had looked over her head for Garmon's clearance to answer.

"I couldn't tell if he was like you or his mother."

"He is like Meleri," Rhodri said.

Heledd pointed to the portion of the joint she preferred and smiled at Geraint before continuing her conversation with Rhodri. "You will soon have a rival for the handsomest *baban* when Daf's little one is born."

"Do you think his offspring could possibly be prettier than mine," Rhodri asked with a laugh. "Look at his face."

"At least mine will be intelligent," Daf said.

Heledd's instinct had placed Meini at the end of the family table, far from her Cenfyn cousins but she witnessed the quick exchange between Garmon and Huw's youngest daughter. It was akin to terror and its relief on Meini's part and reassurance on his. Neither he nor Meini seemed perturbed Heledd had separated them – they maintained a level of private communication that was still expressive. If there was any intimate relationship between the *pennaeth's* youngest child and the son of Creiddwen Owein, both were skilled at concealment. Heledd laid her hand on Geraint's arm before she turned to speak to him, leaving it there though she noticed Huw's family – all except Meini – held their breaths with unaccountable glee in their eyes.

"What is it we are supposed to have done?" Her voice was less than a whisper and, when Geraint spoke, he turned his face away as though his words could be read from his speech.

"We have spent the whole of the day together, *boneddiges*, and parted with a kiss."

"Are we accused?"

"Not yet. There is only one in the room whose accusation will mean anything to either of us. If Garmon believes we are innocent, we have nothing to fear from those."

"Are we," she asked, searching his earnest face, "innocent?"

"Why do you ask, *boneddiges*?" He lifted his cup from the table and drank, peering over the edge at her for a moment before looking beyond her to his commander.

*How could it be other than innocent, Heledd, traitor's daughter?* She bowed her head for a long moment. When she turned in her chair to face her accusers, there was no sign in her hardened, fine-boned chin she had asked any question to which she had received an unsatisfactory answer.

# ᚳhiᚱᚴeen

Heledd was surprised to see Meini bowing her head to conceal a smile she had shared with Garmon. *What have I done now to make them laugh at me?*

"If his nephews are worked like common soldiers to please a whoremonger's chattel, this *ystad* has truly sunk to the depths I have always expected under the guidance of that murderer," Llinos Cenfyn murmured to her niece.

Heledd resisted the impulse to search Garmon's expression but noted the knuckles grasping his cup were white, hard as stone, though his manner was relaxed in his conversation with Ceinwen and Aled, as though he was deaf to everyone but his closest friends.

Heledd was certain Tegwen Talog was wrong about the strongest of men. *This one is granite.* A thought came so unexpectedly to Heledd's mind she stared at Garmon. He met her shocked gaze without response. *Struck with the right tool in the right place at the right time, granite can be cut like butter.*

"Where is this place?" she asked him, in a low voice.

"What place?" Garmon asked, pouring mead into his cup.

"The prettier, more private place you mentioned," she murmured.

"Not far," he replied, smiling. He studied her for a moment, taking stock of every detail, from her severely restrained waves of dark red hair to the tilt of her chin, as though he counted each freckle across her nose and the lashes framing her eyes.

"What's wrong?" she asked, touching her cheek, blushing furiously. "Is my face dirty?"

"Look at the way he stares at her," Llinos scoffed. "What

can you expect from him – raised in barracks in every *ystad* from the north to Tŷ Gwyn?" she asked those at her table. "Take no notice of the whore's bastard, Heledd. He knows nothing better."

Heledd's eyes met the flash of cold hatred in Garmon's granite-hued eyes. She felt the hot outrage of all those sitting near her. She saw Meini's ineffectual compassion as she clenched her hands together in front of her on the table.

For good or ill, she had given Garmon *llysfab* Huw her heart. With a trembling hand, she touched his wrist as it rested on the arm of her chair, as lightly as leaves falling, clinging to the branch of the tree. Garmon gave her only a brief glance before he drew his hand away to the table, leaving her fingers empty on the arm of the chair. He turned his shoulder to her to involve himself more keenly with his friends. Heledd gazed at her hand for a moment then brought it to the table to clasp the cup of mead. Geraint leaned nearer and she turned her ear to him.

"Hard but not unkind," he reminded her.

Heledd smiled and said softly, "I know." She had forced Garmon to look at her and she had not been mistaken about the intensity of his study. When their eyes met, she felt as though he reached into her soul, somehow he knew what she felt and spoke to her in a way that did not need words.

Garmon did not refill her cup but his own was never empty. She smiled to herself, wondering if he would choose to be too drunk, not drunk enough or very drunk that night. Either way, Heledd was certain he would not sleep easily. She would hear his footstep outside her door and, that night, she was determined to be fearless. That night, she was determined to know the truth he had promised her. He did not want a whore. If Meini was the wife he had chosen, theirs was a partnership of easy familiarity – of friendship. Garmon was not Meini's lover. She rested her head on her hand for a moment, smiling at Geraint. "Is there a girl here you like?"

Geraint grinned back at her. "Yes, *boneddiges*."

"Will you wed her?"

"If she will have me." He had not looked beyond her for his

commander's approval to answer and their conversation was not overheard, though they were studied by the *pennaeth's* family.

"I'm sure she will. If not, she is a fool."

"She is not a fool, *boneddiges*, but that is no guarantee she will have me. She may prefer another man."

"Is that likely, when you are so handsome and thoughtful?"

"*Boneddiges*, I am certain of only one thing. She is the woman upon whom I have determined my future. If she does not feel the same, that is my misfortune but will not lessen her in my esteem."

Heledd leaned nearer to him and whispered, "If she does not see your worth, Geraint, there will be others who will."

"No other will do as well as this one."

Heledd pouted for a moment and murmured, "I'm glad we understand one another, Geraint."

"Do we, *boneddiges*?"

Heledd laughed and kissed his cheek again, saying aloud, "Yes, you know we do. Very well. If only these others were as understanding." She waved her hand in a sweeping arc and grasped his arm. Before Heledd had an opportunity to say any more, the meal was interrupted by a young woman in a cloak. The rain had returned and she pushed the wet hood away from her round, rosy face. Her bright eyes matched her smile as she crossed the room toward Heledd. "*Boneddiges*, I have come to ask Dafydd return with me."

The warrior was already on his feet and halfway around the table. "Now we will see," he said to his fellow warriors and went to his wife. Heledd glanced at Garmon. He had already given the expectant father leave to go. One after another of them asked to be excused until only Heledd, Geraint, Garmon and Carwyn remained with the *pennaeth's* family. Finally, Meini, stood and left without a word.

Heledd also stood, pushing her chair out of the way.

"Where are you going?" Garmon inquired.

"To be useful," she said and, to Llinos Cenfyn, "Pardon me for leaving you but I have missed the birth of one new Bro-Dawel resident and do not want to miss another."

"Surely you are not going to assist in this ... this—." Llinos puckered her face and stared at Heledd before turning her scorn on Garmon. "Another mouth for my brother to feed from one of your rutting brutes."

"Huw Bro-Dawel has always welcomed the children of this *ystad, boneddiges*," he replied.

"How dare you? I can assure you he does not welcome the mewling, puking—."

"Aunt," Mared interrupted, "if you will also excuse me." She stood and darted past Heledd at the door of the *neuadd.*

"*Boneddiges*," Heledd said, "This is a happy night in Bro-Dawel. Stay and feast as you please. We have work."

"With your permission," Garmon said to Heledd. She nodded and strode ahead of him. When they reached the *buarth*, both Geraint and Carwyn ran toward the *hafodydd* but Garmon held her back. She looked down at his hand gripping her elbow, but when she raised her eyes to look into his face, she was surprised to meet black fury. "You have given that woman more weapons than she will ever need," he growled. "Never do that again."

"What? What did I do wrong?"

"Do not touch me. I am dead. Do you understand? I do not exist."

"I never believed otherwise," she spat back at him, turned on her heel and ran with the others to Dafydd's *hafod.*

In the middle of the yard at the center of all the small houses belonging to the married warriors, men had begun to build one of the first of the *Calan Gaeaf* bonfires that would also welcome the birth of Daf's *baban*. Soldiers from the barracks were gathering with the married warriors, bringing with them their jugs of ale and mead as well as their women. Celebrating the end of the harvest and the beginning of winter meant drunkenness and happy revelry in every *gaer* and village throughout the land. Heledd thought it was a good night to be born.

The air was fresh and silvery in the yard. Heledd rapped lightly on the door of the *hafod* and entered. At the foot of

Camwy's bed, the low birthing chair waited. Camwy was lying on her side, facing the door, her dark-rimmed eyes fixed on a spot somewhere to the side of Heledd's knees. Her face contorted as she groaned from the depths of her being – a sound so full of wonder and distress Heledd felt it in her own belly as she unlaced her tunic and replaced it with a linen *ffedog* she wrapped around her from breast to knee.

"Open your legs, Camwy," Tegwen told the young woman. "Let your body go with these waves. Don't fight so hard against them."

Camwy's whole body glistened and her blonde hair was dark with sweat. Her lips were bloody. Tegwen knelt by the bed and held Camwy's legs apart.

"You are almost ready," the midwife said. "A few more like that and the *baban* will come."

Camwy howled from somewhere deep in her soul and her legs trembled in convulsion. Her hands clutched the bedding, tearing at it and her own flesh. Ceinwen clasped the woman's hands in her own until the convulsions came to an end. Heledd helped Mared to make the chair ready and comfortable, covering the slanted, narrow back with a layer of sheepskins. On the curved seat, they draped linen and spread the midwife's kneeling pad within the half-circle of the chair. Tegwen, Meini and two other women helped Camwy from the bed and brought her to the chair.

Mared and Heledd made her comfortable before the next wave of convulsions swept over her. As the muscles in her abdomen contracted, the *baban's* passageway from her body was forced open. Tegwen sat on her heels between the woman's wide spread knees, directing all of the women to support Camwy as the *baban* began to push out of her.

"Get this out of me," Camwy sobbed. "Take this out of me." Two women held her knees apart as Tegwen worked to free the *baban's* head.

"When you are ready, Camwy *gwraig* Dafydd, bear down to help your child into the world."

With a great moan, Camwy gave birth to her daughter. The

*baban* slipped from her mother's womb into Tegwen Talog's strong hands to the exclamations and sobs of the women in the room. Heledd released Camwy's hand and wiped the blinding tears from her eyes.

"One more push, Camwy, *mam merch* Dafydd, and you will be done," Tegwen murmured as the afterbirth slid onto the linen cloth she held out. A rush of tears followed from the new mother as her *baban* was laid to her breast and began to suckle. "Heledd," Tegwen said, "you may tell Camwy's husband Medi *merch* Dafydd is born."

Heledd exchanged glances with the other women who, she believed, were better placed to bestow such information but none of them questioned Tegwen's choice. She took a deep breath before she opened the door to face the mob of drunken, joyous soldiers.

"Are you mad?" Mared exclaimed, catching Heledd by her braid, pulling her back before she opened the door. "Don't you know anything about men? If you go out like that, half of them will faint and the other half will be sick. If Daf sees the blood on your *ffedog*, he will think Camwy is dead."

"But they are soldiers."

"Their own blood is one thing. The blood of their enemies is another. This," Mared said, gesturing toward the stains on Heledd's *ffedog*, "is something else."

As she closed the door behind her, she scanned the crowd for Dafydd but the first face she found was Garmon's. He stood at the side of the bonfire, facing her, in his right hand, he held a flagon. His left was draped around the shoulders of a small, fair woman. As he tilted the flagon to his mouth and drained it, he kept his eyes on Heledd. He held it out to be filled again and Heledd noticed the small, fair woman clung to him, her arm wrapped around his waist.

The woman adored him, as she laid her hand on his forearm and poured ale from her jug for him. She was so much shorter than Garmon she had to tilt her head nearly horizontal to look up at him and the top of her head did not reach his shoulder. Garmon had continued to stare at Heledd, his usual stony gaze enflamed with drink. *He's drunk enough, but not for me.* He lowered his gaze slowly from her face, so slowly over her body she felt as though he used the tips of his fingers. He fixed his gaze on her belly as he took another long drink. When he smiled, her legs weakened beneath her. *It just the drink, he does not want me.*

Daf threw his arms around Heledd's thighs and lifted her into the air, twirling with her into the mass of bodies. She grinned down at him, holding onto his broad shoulders, and said quietly, "You have a beautiful, intelligent daughter, Dafydd." He shouted for joy and set her feet on the ground. He kissed her mouth and danced with her on the spot. He was swept away by his friends and she retreated to the steps of the *hafod*. When Heledd found Garmon again in the crowd, he was in deep conversation with his ale woman and another full flagon. *He will be too drunk.* Heledd sighed to herself and shut the door of the house.

Camwy had already been bathed and was lying quietly in her bed with her daughter at her breast, a tiny red hand patting her mother's flesh in rhythm with her suckling. By the time the *hafod* was clean and cleared of all the utensils Tegwen Talog used to help women to give birth, the sky had turned from gray to deep blue as night descended from the east.

"You did well," Ceinwen said, as the women prepared to leave Camwy in the care of her husband.

"Thank you," Heledd replied, tempted to say she could do some things right. "I have not helped in many births. In fact, none," she confessed. "It is a wonderful thing," Heledd murmured.

"It is unusual for a woman who has never had a child to attend," Meini said, "unless she has a particular skill." When Heledd glanced at Mared, Meini whispered, "Can you imagine anyone keeping my sister out?"

"As you all know, I have no particular skills," Heledd replied aloud, shivering.

"Except for making trouble," Mared joined in, "between men."

"That is not Heledd's fault," Ceinwen said. "Your cousins

make their own trouble every time they come here, or have you forgotten what they did to you?"

"You have no right to talk about them," Mared complained. "This one causes trouble for your precious Garmon, remember."

"Garmon can take care of himself," Ceinwen replied, glancing at Heledd.

"Can he? It seems to me he needs Meini much more often now *she's* here. Is he whoring more often or—." Mared was silenced when Tegwen yanked her hair.

"You forget Camwy has had a hard time, my girl. Leave your bickering in the gutter where it belongs," the midwife cautioned, shoving Mared out of her way so Camwy could get some sleep. "Tell Dafydd he can see his daughter but he must not disturb Camwy."

Mared did as she was told. Ceinwen wrapped herself in a shawl and left the house with the two other women. When Meini sat with Tegwen near the fire, Heledd realized she was no longer needed or wanted. Daf, much too drunk to be useful or cautious, stumbled over the threshold and shushed himself several times before he crept forward to look at his daughter and his wife. Heledd looked on in wonder as he knelt by the bed and buried his face in the folds of the *carthen* to weep.

"Why do you stare?" Meini whispered, beckoning Heledd to come away from the sleeping area. "Have you never seen a man shed tears?"

"No, never," Heledd murmured. "Have you?"

"Yes, many times." Meini brushed her skirt and gazed into the small stone hearth. "You had better go to bed, Heledd. There is no reason for you to stay now."

"Don't let Camwy's difficulty turn you against having a child, my girl. You will not have such a hard time," Tegwen told her. "You are well-built for breeding."

Being 'well-built' for breeding did not mean she ever would, Heledd reminded herself as she opened the door of the *hafod* and stepped out into the cool breeze. The bonfire was blazing, a plume of pale smoke streaked into the sky as far as she could see, trailing after the breeze to the west. A faint glow of pink crowned a gap between the hills. A flock of birds rose into the air like a cloud of dust. The fragrant wood smoke filled her senses and she would have taken a long walk into the copse near the chapel but some of the clerks and stewards were still at work. The cooks were banking the fires in the kitchen and Heledd could smell bread as she strolled toward the house.

The expression on Camwy's face when her daughter took her first breath came back to her and filled her with amazement. Heledd laughed out loud, wondering how she might feel to carry a child for a man she loved. *Be honest, the child you want to carry is the child of Garmon llysfab Huw. Ach, you are foolish, Heledd merch Ieuan Bannawg, he only looks at you when he is drunk enough and he only comes near you when he is too drunk.* Though it crossed her mind to look for him, Heledd did not want to find him with another woman.

A sudden gust of wind reminded her she had no shawl and she hastened to her room, bolted the door and lay down with a laugh. Bolting the door had become a habit. *Garmon is too drunk, in any case.* She lifted her chin in the darkness. *I don't want a man who has to be drunk to want me.* Heledd pressed her hands on her belly and gazed through the narrow, slatted window. Long hours of toil and tension overtook her and she slept deeply a moment after her head dropped on the cushions.

*The child took her mother's hand as soldiers broke through the gates of their village. She felt her mother crumple to the ground at the door of the beudy and saw her father fall in the buarth. She stood by her mother's body, still holding her cold hand, staring into her mother's green eyes but there was no light or laughter in them. A red necklace stained her throat, spreading over the bodice of her frock and the muddy ground. Llew Talgarth grinned down at the child and held out his hand. She heard the familiar sound of footsteps outside her door and a hand on the latch as soldiers set fires in the thatches. In the flames, her blue tunic caught alight and floated with the smoke into the sky.*

"My tunic," she gasped, sitting up. Half asleep, she tumbled from the bed and unbolted the door. Heledd felt another kind of unrest in her body. She had unbolted the door. Terror flooded through her. She had opened the door. She fought to clear her head, to explain what she had done but she could not speak and a hand groped in the darkness, grabbing her hair. She heard the bolt slammed back into the metal hasp. She gasped for breath but a hand covered her mouth. Her eyes were open but she couldn't see. *Something is wrong. This is wrong. He would not do this to me.* Her hands were heavy, pinned to her sides. She struggled to drag them free, to push the hand away from her. He laughed under his breath and tightened his grip.

"Do you want the whole of Bro-Dawel to know I am here? Do you want so many witnesses?" he whispered against her throat, tearing her frock from her shoulder, scratching her as the fabric ripped open. Heledd fought to hurt him in some way but he would not let her go. "You need not make a show of resistance," he murmured, forcing her down onto the bed and holding her hands against the wall above her head. "Keep guard," he hissed at someone behind him. "You can have her when I'm finished."

Heledd screamed. She could feel the screams tearing at her throat but no sound came even when his hand released her mouth and he tore the frock from her body. She heard the wood crack and the other man cried out, screamed in pain. Suddenly her hands were free and her attacker was gone. She heard a thud and a moan. Bolting upright, gasping for breath, she saw Aeron in a heap against the far wall. His brother lay on his back at the foot of the bed, half of the door lying across him. Heledd crawled into a tight ball at the head of the bed, holding the *carthen* against her like a shield, staring at Wyn on the floor, afraid to lift her eyes to the man who stood over her, dragging air into her lungs as though he breathed fire. She had no voice and she couldn't breathe, she heard only screaming in her head.

"You opened your door to them," Garmon hissed at her.

"Shall I leave them here for you to nurse?" Heledd curled up against the wall, turning her face away. She heard another moan from Aeron and cried out in terror. "A moment later," Garmon growled at her, "and your lovers would have found me in their place. Whether I was first at you or last, they would be there." Her eyes fell on the broken hasp, hanging from the door frame. "If I ever wanted to enter, do you think a bolted door is any more of barrier to me than a ragged curtain?"

Heledd neither wept nor protested. In her mind, she could see only soldiers, killing her family, ransacking her home, dragging the girls from the *beudy* – the smell of burning and Heledd *merch* Ieuan Bannawg staring into her mother's eyes … her own eyes.

"Llew," she whispered, her throat felt as though it was ripping apart, drowning in blood.

"What?" Garmon demanded, bending over her.

"Llew Talgarth," she whispered again. "Llew killed my mother." For a moment, Garmon was silent.

"Did you invite these dogs to your room?"

"No."

"Why did you open your door to them?"

"I didn't," she murmured, turning her face to the wall again. "The door was bolted. It is always bolted."

"I know, Carwyn assured me you had bolted it tonight. How did they get in?" Heledd shook her head. "You opened the bolt." She nodded. "But not for them?" he demanded. "For someone else? For Geraint?" Again, she denied the accusation. He pulled her off the bed and set her on the floor in front of him. "Who?" he asked, sliding his hand into her hair, holding her chin up so she had to meet his eyes. "Who did you want, Heledd?"

"Leave me alone," she whimpered. "No one."

"You refuse to give his name?"

"No one. There is no one."

"Tell me, *gwraig*, and I will bring him to you."

"One who loves me," Heledd replied, lifting her chin away from his grasp.

"Who would that be, Heledd?" She swallowed hard and closed her eyes. "Find yourself a bed, *gwraig*," he told her, "this is not your room."

"What have I done wrong?" Heledd cried, staring at him. "This is not my fault. I thought ... I didn't know ... I thought I heard ... someone. I was dreaming and ..."

"Go," he ordered. "Go to my house, Heledd. You will be safe there. I will take care of this vermin." He nodded toward the brothers' unconscious bodies. "Be gone when I return," he said and disappeared into the dark passageway. Heledd wrapped herself in her *carthen*, gathered all her possessions into the basket still holding her soiled work clothes and went in the opposite direction into the *buarth*. She hesitated a moment before running toward the only place she knew she would be safe.

She opened the door of the longhouse, stepped across the threshold and took a deep breath of the scent of herbs and applewood embers before closing the door. The shouts of the stewards and bailiffs drowned the baying of the three staghounds bounding from their beds in the corner of Garmon's bedroom. The shouts of the soldiers merged with Heledd's scream. Within moments, Bro-Dawel was silent again.


The three gray-brown dogs, their hackles on end, stood in a half circle, snarling, creeping forward, lowering their heads. Heledd's basket lay on the stones, its contents spilling at the hounds' feet. The largest of the dogs sniffed the sable-brown coat, growling at its owner. Heledd pressed her back against the door of the house, keeping her eyes fixed on the hunters whose heads were as high as her waist. Their fur stood out from their bodies in rough curls and their black eyes were as hard as their master's heart. The biggest of them sank its teeth into the edge of the basket and tossed it around its head, emptying all of the contents onto the flags. The other dogs skulked closer, sniffing her clothes. When the youngest sank its teeth into the black damask purse, Heledd cried, "No."

The three staghounds pricked their ears and stared at the

intruder, lowered their heads and hunched their shoulders. The youngest shook the silk purse.

"Put that down. Down." Heledd commanded. All three dogs growled, shaking whatever they held in their jaws. Heledd took a slow step forward. Again they were alert, stretching their necks to sniff at her. "Ach, I am not going to cower here all night, hoping to be rescued," she growled back at them. "I'm too tired and I've suffered at the hands of bullies long enough. Tear me to pieces if you're going to, but I'm going to bed." She strode forward, leaving everything on the floor until she reached the youngest hound. "That's mine," she said, holding out her hand. The dog sniffed her hand and let the black purse drop into it. Heledd walked past them, closing the door to the bedroom behind her.

The dogs darted to the door and began to dig at the bottom. "Down," she commanded. Though they stopped digging, she could hear them sniffing under the door, pacing to the front door and loping back again. Heledd hung her shawl by the door, ripped off her frock and shift, throwing both into the corner near the small hearth. She scrubbed her face and body hard to get rid of Aeron's stench and filled her lungs with the scent of soap and herbs. Even her hair carried the stale smell of his sweat. She unbraided it, washed it in the basin on the table, wrung it dry and combed it through with her fingers.

Wrapped in her *carthen*, she sat close to the fire, drying her hair. Heledd turned over in her mind all of the memories her dream had brought back to her, images that, as an three-year-old child, she had buried to survive without her family. All her brothers and sisters had been murdered by soldiers, slaughtered. So many years after their deaths, their youngest sister watched in her mind's eye, as she had watched at dawn on the day, her sisters' tiny bodies savaged and tossed like offal into the river. Heledd saw her brothers huddled together, holding each other as, one by one, the soldiers butchered them. She looked on while their corpses were nailed, by their ankles, on the wall of the house to rot, as a reminder to Bannawg her father had not protected his own sons. She held out her hand to see her mother's white hand clasped there, lifeless. Staring into the flames, she could see her father holding his sword above his head, staying his blow, as his younger brother slashed his body, the last to die.

In the safety of Garmon's bedroom, she saw the women who had survived the battle and its aftermath, who were not taken to Gwesyn, enslaved by Llew Talgarth, as whores for his warriors and as bondservants in the household. Everything that had once been Bannawg was stolen. She remembered Goewin on her knees, her face bruised and bloody from the beatings she had endured, begging Llew Talgarth to let her keep Ieuan's youngest child who was too young to survive on her own.

"Since I have more use for her alive than dead, I give you leave. You know the conditions," her uncle had said, laying his hand on Heledd's small head. Heledd remembered crying aloud, great sobs. "Shut her up or she'll be killed like the other bitches in her family."

She remembered she had lived with Goewin in a hut built against the side of the *beudy*. She slept shielded from the wind and rain by Goewin's thin body and shared Goewin's meager rations. Soldiers came at night. As soon as she could fend for herself, she was put in the cell near the kitchen and taken to be with Alys whenever the younger girl wanted companionship. She was encouraged to be as haughty and arrogant as her cousin toward the Bannawg people, schooled from that early age to believe Llew Talgarth had been wronged by his brother, taught to believe she was spared out of his kindness and true, unselfish love for his elder brother.

That night, in her dream, all the lies had fallen away. She was one of the 'more truthful witnesses' Garmon had mentioned. She had remembered only the brutality of Gwesyn's soldiers – the murderous, hate-filled violence that had left her an orphan. She had always known she was a prisoner of war and held in bond as reparation for her father's treachery. She had not known she was a hostage to ensure Bannawg kept her uncle's stolen *ystad* profitable for his own family's benefit. *How much did Bannawg suffer for my sake?* How badly had she, in her ignorance, treated them? How many were her father's warriors who had sacrificed their families and their own lives for her family and her life?

That morning, the weight of responsibility was too heavy for her and she wept with grief for her brothers, sisters and parents, for all the women, men and children who had suffered so long under Llew Talgarth's tyranny, for the arrogance and indifference with which she had repaid her debt to them. She heard the hounds whimpering at the door, scratching at the panels. "Down," she called to them, wiping her eyes on her *carthen*.

She was such a selfish, thoughtless girl that, even in guilt and misery, she dared to think if Garmon knew the whole truth about her father and mother, perhaps he would like her more. "Heledd," she chastised herself aloud, "nothing changes the fact you are the cold creature he has always known you to be." *You are probably all the things he most despises in a woman: too haughty, too arrogant, too selfish, too tall, too willful, too thoughtless …*

# Fourteen

All three of the dogs jumped from their watching positions and run snarling to the door of the house. Heledd steeled herself to face the scorn and disdain she had earned and heaped on herself. She dropped her chin to her knees and did not turn her head when the bedroom door opened and was closed again.

"I could not come sooner," Meini said, crossing the room, "Camwy has had a bad time since you left."

"Will she be all right?" Heledd asked in a small voice.

"Tegwen will have to be with her for some time."

"And her daughter?"

"Medi is a good, strong girl. Garmon sent me as soon as I had finished there. He told me what happened and you have been injured." Heledd glanced at Meini and turned her face away. "I see he did not exaggerate. I have brought some ointments that will help." Meini emptied the contents of a small basket on the table and busied herself with their arrangement. "You are not the first to have found out the truth about my cousins," she said, "but I am surprised you allowed him, both of them, to enter your room."

"I did not," Heledd declared, glaring at Huw Bro-Dawel's daughter.

"Then why did you unbolt you door?" Meini demanded. Heledd turned her face back to stare into the fire. "Did they rape you? Hurt you? If so, I will have to bring Tegwen as she is the only one who can treat you."

"No."

"If you refuse help, you will suffer more, Heledd. Aeron is a violent man, there could be damage—."

"I have seen what happens to women who have been raped," Heledd said, struggling to hold back a sob, "I have not suffered that."

"You are certain he did not hurt you?"

"Yes, I am certain," Heledd said.

"That is a mercy," Meini answered, bringing several small pots and a cloth with her when she knelt beside Heledd. "I know you dislike me, but I am good at healing. If you will allow me, I will do my best for you."

Before Heledd allowed Meini to touch her, she looked into her eyes and asked, "What is in your ointments?"

"This is an infusion of comfrey to treat your bruises," Meini replied, holding up a round pot, "and this is a salve of aloe for the scratch on your neck and shoulder."

Heledd placed her fingers where Meini had indicated and felt the inflamed skin from her jaw down to her left shoulder. "Is it bad?" Heledd whispered. "Will it show?"

"It will heal," Meini assured her. "For now, you can wear a shawl or leave your hair loose."

"I would not do that," Heledd said. "My hair is uglier than any scar."

"I don't think many would agree with you." Heledd turned her face away. "Ach, I told Garmon this would happen," Meini said, shaking her head. "You are not in danger, Heledd, except for the danger you cause for yourself. Even so, no harm will come to you. Garmon has sworn to protect you. Look around you, Heledd. You know there are men here who are sworn to give their lives to protect you. Trust Garmon. He will do nothing to cause harm to you." Heledd studied her for a long moment. "Let me treat your bruises first," Meini said, reaching out her hand but Heledd caught her wrist.

"Why should I trust you?"

"Because I would not be here if Garmon had not sent me. From now on, no one will be allowed near you without his permission."

"Why? Am I a prisoner?"

"Think as you choose. Garmon trusts me with his own life.

He also trusts me with yours."

"He trusts your sister as well?" Heledd asked.

"Mared blames him for our brother's death, as does Llinos and my cousins."

"And you love him?"

"Yes. He has protected me all my life, even when I have been unkind to him. I would do nothing now to hurt him. My husband loved him. And I have loved him since I was a child."

Heledd closed her eyes but the tears still came. Her mother, her father, everyone she had ever loved and who could have ever loved her, even as ignorant and willful as she was, were gone.

"I don't blame you for weeping," Meini said. "I told Garmon he risked too much using you to stand up to them. They were bound to retaliate, especially when you humiliated Aeron in front of Geraint and Carwyn. He is not the kind of man to forget such a thing. You are very lucky Garmon could not sleep, otherwise no one could have helped you."

"How do you know he could not sleep?"

"He is often restless, more so in the past few weeks, but ever since I have known him, he has wandered at night, keeping watch. I think he became used to that when he was a small boy, when he and his mother wandered. It is habit and, of course, occasionally, the pain."

"I know about his mother," Heledd said when Meini closed her mouth suddenly. "I know about your brother too."

"There are only three people in the world who know the truth about Rhydderch and you are not one of them."

"How do you know?"

"I know. Are you going to let me treat you or are you going to be a martyr to your own stupidity?"

"I am not stupid."

"Ach, so I have been told, but I can see no evidence you are intelligent."

To disprove Meini's assessment of her, Heledd said, "Your husband was Garmon's foster brother."

"Yes. When he asked my father for me, it was Garmon who

argued on Gwyn's behalf."

"Why was that necessary?"

"Because my father did not, does not believe I am worthy of a good husband. God must also agree," Meini replied, her expression hardening.

"I'm sorry," Heledd said, releasing Meini's wrist. "How long were you married?"

"Not long. A Year. Now, I have only his child."

"I have never seen you with a child."

"My father has taken my child from me. She is nearly a year old now but I do not see her often."

"That is cruel," Heledd said. "Why did he do that? Why hasn't Garmon—."

"It is not for Garmon to question my father. He spoke for Gwyn, not for me. My father has reasons for his actions. Will you let me treat you or do you prefer to be scarred – to carry Aeron's brand on your flesh for all to see?"

"I do not care," Heledd sighed.

"Garmon will care. He is already blaming himself. Do you want to punish him?"

"Ach, we would not want to cause him any displeasure, would we?"

"No, we would not," Meini scowled. "You would do better, Heledd, if you were less haughty toward those who wish you well." Though she raised her chin, Heledd submitted to Meini's care, allowing her to treat her several injuries and to examine her for the others she received in the struggle, soothing her hands with oil infused with lavender. "Aeron is both stupid and arrogant, a dangerous combination for any woman. He does not learn from mistakes. One day, he will be killed for assaulting another man's wife. Still, I cannot understand why he chose to attack you so openly. He is a coward, he waits until there can be no witnesses."

"Perhaps he thought, since everyone was so drunk …Why does Huw Bro-Dawel allow him to come? Who else has he assaulted here?" Meini met Heledd's questioning gaze in silence, but Heledd could see the answer in her eyes.

"They come like locusts when my father is grieving."

"Why does he grieve? When is that?"

"At harvest, at the time of the year he lost his wife."

"Your mother," Heledd said.

Meini bowed her head over her ointments. "He cannot bear to be here and so his sister takes advantage and torments Garmon in my father's absence. I was only seven the first year they came. I have been in debt to Garmon ever since. I have been his *meddyg* since I was eleven. By then, I had learned enough to help him."

"What happened to him?"

"He was wounded at the time my brother was killed."

"Your brother took the blow meant for Garmon?" Heledd asked, remembering the tale she had heard from Rhodri.

"No. Rhydderch struck the blow that crippled Garmon."

"Oh. But—."

"There are too many things you do not know, Heledd, and Garmon has been playing a dangerous game." Meini folded her cloth several times before she said, "My brother murdered Garmon's mother."

"Garmon killed your brother for that?"

"Garmon never lifted a finger against Rhydderch, he loved my brother. Garmon defended his mother and her other son."

Heledd stared at Meini then dropped her eyes to consider what she had been told. Finally, she asked, "How was your brother killed?"

"My father struck him down. My mother went mad after that."

"I am sorry, Meini."

"There is no need for your concern, Heledd. Rhydderch deserved to die, Garmon did not deserve to be crippled. My mother was fortunate she went mad, else my father would have killed her too."

"But you said your mother died— your father grieved for her."

"My father grieves for Creiddwen Owein. *You* said my mother, I did not correct you. My father had divorced my mother, when I was very young. He took Creiddwen Owein to him as his consort. Rhydderch murdered her to avenge our mother. I only know my father had left my mother long before Creiddwen Owein came here. When she did, my father fell in love with her and raised Garmon as his stepson. Creiddwen was kind and loving to me, to Mared as well. At first, Rhydderch was glad to have a younger brother, until my mother filled him with hate and jealousy." Meini pressed her lips together for a moment. "Creiddwen was already dying when my father reached them. He killed Rhydderch with a blow to the heart and held Creiddwen in his arms through the whole of the night until Talog Bardd persuaded him to let her go. Tegwen Talog and the physician from the cloister school saved Garmon's life but he could not stand or walk for a long time."

"You said Creiddwen Owein had another son," Heledd commented.

"Yes. Garmon's brother. My brother. And Mared's brother."

Heledd thought for a long time, staring into the flames. "He was killed?"

"No. He lives."

"Why are you telling me these things?"

"The more you know, the less troublesome you will be. Your ignorance and curiosity will get Garmon killed. I love him as my own brother. Creiddwen was the only mother I knew or ever want to know. One day, my father will forgive I am not Creiddwen's child. When he does, I will have my child again. My daughter is as precious to me as Mairwen is to Ceinwen – she is all I have of my husband. If Garmon dies, I will have no hope of holding my daughter in my arms ever again."

"Who raises her?"

"She is in the care of another woman here. I am allowed to see her once a month, but not without someone close at hand."

"Why?"

"My father believes I will kill her or poison her mind, as my mother poisoned Rhydderch against Creiddwen. If not for Garmon, my younger brother would also be dead. Rhydderch believed he was to be disowned and Creiddwen's second son, my half-brother, my father's only living son, would be *pennaeth.* Rhydderch fulfilled his own and my mother's fears."

Heledd was silent for a long time. After a while, she asked, "You saw all this?"

"Yes. It was my screaming that brought my father in time to save Garmon and my half-brother."

"Where is he? Your younger brother."

"It is better you do not know. Llinos has, until now, believed Huw will make Garmon his heir, so she has done all she can to discredit and destroy him. Now, she believes you will be my father's wife to give him another son. She will always delight in tormenting Garmon, for a crime he did not commit."

"And Garmon suffers this for his younger brother's sake," Heledd said.

"Yes and you have given Llinos and her sons many additional opportunities. It was my father's idea to bring you here under the pretense of marriage. Garmon agreed."

"How could I have known?"

"I told Garmon this would be the result. He— he believed he could protect you from them. He has taken their abuse for a long time and has become—."

"Like stone," Heledd finished for her.

Meini nodded, helping Heledd into a clean shift. Heledd raised her hands to tie the bodice and paused to finger the softness of the fabric, surprised such a simple, functional piece of clothing was so fine.

"A gift from ... a friend," Meini smiled.

"Meleri made this?"

"Ceinwen, I think," Meini replied. "It is hard to say."

"Please tell all of them their gifts are appreciated," Heledd said while she secured the silk ribbon above her breasts. Seeing her fingers were scratched and reddened from her fight with Aeron, she dropped her hands to her sides, out of sight.

"You will be all right here. The dogs will keep everyone but Garmon out of the house until he returns tonight."

"When?"

"When he has done what needs to be done," Meini replied.

Heledd did not ask what that could be. She clasped Meini's hand. "Thank you."

"Take this pot," Meini instructed, handing Heledd the pot of oil she had used on Heledd's hands, "he is likely to be in pain tonight."

"What should I do?"

"He will not want your pity, Heledd, but he may not be able to do this for himself. This oil relieves the ache in the scars on his thigh. Pour a small amount into your palm and rub it into his skin. Don't let him suffer for his pride's sake."

"I understand," Heledd said as she took the pot into her hands, remembering the first time she had witnessed Garmon's stone-like endurance of pain.

"Try to sleep. The next few days will be hard for you. Remember what I said. Trust Garmon – he will protect you at all costs."

When Meini had gone, she stared into the dying embers until she struggled to keep her eyes open and her head from falling forward. Fearfully, she pulled back the *carthen* on Garmon's bed, slid beneath it and prayed he would not be angry with her, prayed no one else would find her there. Before she fell asleep for a second time that night, Heledd committed to memory every object in the room – from the oak table and the high, wide bed to the simple, armed chair and iron-bound chest, the white washed walls and the black and red *carthen* – in case she never saw them again.

When she next woke, the wooden shutter over the small window high above the side of the bed was fastened so she could no longer see the sky. Although the fire had been built up while she slept, she had no idea how long she had been asleep. She knew she was not alone in the house. The dogs made no sound in the room beyond. She turned her head on the pillow, her cheek brushing against something cool and fragrant. She lifted her head and found a sprig of lavender on the white linen. Picking it up between her fingers, she wondered at the tenderness of the gesture.

She threw off the *carthen*, ready to express her gratitude to him, when she heard one of the dogs whine, followed by a soft gasp. From beneath the door, she saw the shadow of a dog's legs moving silently across the flags and then a larger shadow blocked the hearth light that had shone through the narrow cracks between the planks of the door. The latch on the door lifted soundlessly and Heledd pretended to sleep as Garmon entered the room. Through half-closed eyes, she watched him put another log on the small fire, another soft hiss escaping him as he stood erect again.

Heledd watched as he slowly removed his shirt and doeskin leggings in the warmth of the fire. He stood in his short linen *trwsus* and braced his hands on the wall above the fire, stretching and straightening his back, relieving the pain in his body. He lifted his head to look at her and Heledd held her breathing steady while he studied her. She wondered how bruised she was, whether the scratches on her neck and hands were visible – she wanted to be beautiful and knew she wasn't, would never be. She held the lavender in her fingers. *Why am I here?* Nothing Meini had told her could answer that question but there was an answer, somewhere in all that had happened since the night she had cried herself to sleep and been awakened by a soldier's soft breath on her cheek. *He is kind, just kind. I don't want him to be kind. I don't want him to be generous. He loves Meini. He has always loved Meini.*

Granite crossed her mind. He had had years of practice hiding what he thought and felt. With a deep sigh, she let her arm fall back over her head, her fingers still curled around the sprig, letting it slip into her hair. Garmon remained motionless, she could feel his gray eyes fixed on her face. Knowing if she opened her eyes, he would leave her, Heledd turned away from the center of the bed to face the wall, praying he would accept her invitation.

She heard his slow, controlled breathing. After several minutes, she heard a soft moan and, finally, a curse. Knowing something was wrong, Heledd turned onto her back as quietly as she could to see he held the small pot Meini had left and rested his shoulder against the wall above the hearth for support while he tried to open the stopper. Heledd sat up and threw off the *carthen*.

"Go back to sleep," he ordered, closing his fist around the pot.

"Are you in pain?"

"No. Go to sleep, *gwraig*."

"Don't be a fool," she snapped, sliding out of the bed and hissing as she dropped her feet onto the cold floor.

"What are you doing?"

"Don't worry," Heledd assured him, taking the pot of ointment out of his hand, "Meini told me what to do."

"*Uffern*," he hissed, "that meddling girl." When Heledd knelt beside him, he glared down at her. "I don't need you to nurse me. Go back to sleep."

"I have discovered many things about you, Garmon *llysfab* Huw, but this is the first indication I have seen of such a strong tendency toward stupidity." He glared at her for a moment as his expression began to soften. "Garmon, let me do this. I am not as incompetent as everyone thinks."

He studied her for a long time before saying, "You will not like what you see."

"I don't expect to," she replied waiting for him to be ready. "I am very dull," she said, "and, as you know, there is very little I can do right, but I am not wholly useless, even to you."

"Heledd," he murmured, his eyes reflecting the glow of the firelight. "You don't know."

"I do. I do know," she whispered, laying her hand on his wrist. "Do you want to lie down?" Garmon let a slow breath escape his lungs before he limped to the bed and eased his long body onto the mattress. Sitting on the edge of the bed, she pulled the stopper from the small pot and poured a small amount into her palm. As she did, Garmon rolled onto his side away from her, clenching his fist. Heledd carefully pushed the leg of his *trwsus* out of her way. With her finger, Heledd touched the longest scar on the back of his thigh. "Tell me if I hurt you." Smoothing the fragrant oil into the proud flesh, she blocked all of the images Meini's tale had created in her mind, suppressing any show of compassion. "You haven't given your colt much attention in the last few days. Will it forget its training?"

"No," he said, turning his head to watch her.

"When it is grown, who will ride it?"

"I will ride it," he breathed and after a pause, added, "or one of the others."

"I haven't ridden my horse for days and days, not since the first weeks I came here. The mare has probably forgotten me." Heledd worked the oil into the muscles of his thigh for several moments then poured more into her hand to apply to the other scars. Even with no medical knowledge, she could see how badly he had been hurt as a boy. She shook the images away angrily, not allowing herself to show any of the sorrow she felt. "Does the mare have a name?"

"The horse is yours."

"Do you think I should give it a name?"

"If you choose," Garmon answered, closing his eyes.

"What is your horse called?"

"*Diawl.*"

"Is that its name or are you cursing me?" Heledd laughed, rubbing her hands together to warm them before she worked them into the muscles of his thigh.

"Its name," Garmon answered.

"Good, because it would be a bad thing if you cursed me every time I touched you."

"You will not be asked to do this again," he said through clenched teeth.

"Shall I name my horse 'Angel'?" Heledd asked, leaning over his back to whisper in his ear. "Or perhaps—."

"Will you finish so I can sleep, *gwraig*?" he growled. "I have not slept for—."

"I'm sorry," Heledd snapped, sitting erect once more to concentrate on her task, reminding herself he was made of a type of granite that was harder than his heart, "you do not need to remind me of all the trouble I have caused. Meini has done that for you." When she had used all the contents of the small pot, she asked, "Is there anything else I need to do?"

"Yes," Garmon replied, turning onto his back and sitting on the edge of the bed. "Go to sleep. Here," he commanded, throwing back the *carthen* as he rose to his feet. Heledd put the pot on the table and walked around the bed, watching him as she laid down where he commanded. Garmon tossed the *carthen* over her, plucking the sprig of lavender that had fallen from her hair and flicking it into the flames.

"Why did you do that?"

"Sleep," he growled again, taking a long quilted robe from the cupboard and gathering a pile of *carthen* under his arm.

"Where are you going?" she asked, sitting up again.

"To find a bed," he said and shut the door. Heledd held her breath for a few moments, listening to every movement and sound in the other room. He allowed himself one sharp intake of breath before he relaxed his body into the large chair in front of the hearth. He called the staghounds away from the door. "She wants to be left alone," he murmured to them.

*No, I don't. I don't.* Heledd lowered her body into the thick mattress and pulled the *carthen* tight around her head, stifling the sound of her weeping with her fist. One of the hounds whined at the door and its master gave a sharp snap of his fingers. The hound sank to its haunches burying its nose under the door.


When Heledd awoke at dawn, her eyes were stinging and her throat raw. She set her feet on the cold flagstones. Her clean clothes from the basket were folded on the edge of the oak table. More logs had been added to the fire and breakfast was waiting for her on a tray on the stool brought close to the bed. She filled her lungs with the fragrance of the medicinal oil from Garmon's body. As soon as she started to dress, the dogs were alert, trotting like small horses back and forth in front of the door, sniffing and yelping. Just as soon, they were silenced and motionless.

She ignored the bread and cheese. She had no appetite and prepared to face Bro-Dawel, thinking through what had happened in the last few days, certain they knew everything she had done to deserve their scorn. As she tied her precious silk purse onto her belt, she stared at it as though seeing it for the first time. The sudden recognition caused her to cry out and she fell to her knees by the table, mourning her mother's terrible death.

Heledd did not hear the door open or see the hounds peering at her from behind a pair of black boots. Her blood red hair fell like a curtain on either side of her face as she bowed over her mother's black damask purse. It had hung at her hip when her brother-in-law cut her throat. "Forgive me. Forgive me," Heledd sobbed as she rocked in long buried grief.

The youngest of the hounds forced its head between the open door and its master's leg but was warned back with a gesture. When Garmon knelt on one knee beside her, Heledd sobbed, burying her face in his shirt, closing her fists in the cloth. For a moment, he remained frozen, staring down at the black purse she still held in her hand.

"What have you done that requires forgiveness?" he asked, finally laying his hand on the back of her head.

"I— I had forgotten. I had forgotten them all."

"Who? Who have you forgotten?"

"My mother. My family. I am the only living child and I forgot them," she sobbed, burying her face in her hands. "I forgot what happened to them."

Garmon lifted her chin and pulled her hands away, cupping her face. "You had no part in their deaths," he told her, caressing her cheek with the back of his fingers. "You were a child. Why should you remember their deaths?"

"I am their only witness. I am the only one who knows their story. If I cannot tell it, if I forget, they will not exist except as my uncle wants them to be remembered and hated."

"You are not the only witness, Heledd."

"But I am the only one who knew them. I am the only one who saw how my mother loved my father. I am the only one who watched my father teach my brothers how to be men – good men. No one knows that. No one knows how we were as a family, together, in our own house when the wind screamed at us and my mother sang so we were not afraid."

"You have not forgotten now, *gwraig*."

Heledd smoothed the silk damask over her thigh. "My mother always wore this. She wore it on the day she died. She was so proud when my father gave it to her – I don't remember why or when. I never saw her without it, except when she went to bed. Then it was folded on a shelf above her head. I didn't recognize it, not until this morning."

"I didn't know." He straightened his legs and pulled her to her feet. "Goewin said you would like it."

"She must have found it ... when my mother was put in her grave. If she had a grave. They hung my brothers on the wall of the house and threw my sisters' bodies into the river."

"Heledd."

"I do not want to forget that – or any of it, Garmon." She stared into his eyes. "There was no other witness to what my uncle did and ordered his soldiers to do. Goewin remembers what happened to her. I remember this. I am the last witness. My father howled in torment when Llew Talgarth slit my mother's throat but he could not strike his brother. Llew asked my mother if she wanted to live or die – he gave her the choice. She answered him and smiled at my father. The soldiers who forced my father to watch while his family was slaughtered gave him his sword and told him to fight. He believed we were all dead. He raised his sword above his head, like this, and never moved while his brother gutted him like a pig."

Heledd bowed her head for a moment, pressing her brow in the hollow of his shoulder, accepting Garmon's arms around her, the pressure of his cheek at the side of her head.

"His own brother did that, his brother whom he had always loved and protected since they were children, his brother who was always in our house, taking his meals at my father's table – he killed my mother because she said she would rather die than be his whore. He wanted her and when she would not have him, he slit her throat. What kind of man does that? Kills what he loves?"

"I have known only a few," Garmon answered. "What we most want is not always what we most love."

Heledd lifted her head from his shoulder. "No, but sometimes, perhaps, rarely …. No, not often."

# FiFteen

Strengthened by her memories of her family, Heledd folded the damask purse and laid it on top of the pile of her clothing. She was not the daughter of a coward or a traitor. She was his niece. She pressed her hands on the pile of beautiful clothing and tilted her head to look at the northerner. "Thank you for helping me. I can never repay your kindness and generosity."

"Heledd. *Boneddiges.*"

"Did you know?" She heard his formality, noted the change in his voice, saw the way he stood away from her.

"I learned part of the truth at Bannawg."

"From Goewin?"

"And others."

"Not my uncle," she said with a laugh. "Or his children."

"No. I doubt your cousins know or will ever accept the truth."

"Is that why you left?" she asked, turning her back to him to go to the small hearth. She extended her bruised and bloodied fingers to the warmth. She was conscious she had no reason to lift her chin. She had no reason to assume arrogance or to defend her sense of dignity. Except for the trouble she had caused and her unaccountable ability to make people hate her, she had no reason to feel the shame and loss that had been her companions from her earliest thoughts. But she did. They lived and breathed in her heart. *He loves Meini. He has always loved Meini.*

"No, *boneddiges.* It is the reason you are here."

"Why did you leave?" *Fool. You know the answer.*

"Because I knew I could not stay without committing a

220

crime – more than one."

There was no solace for her in his answer but she did not see scorn or pity in his eyes when she looked at him over her shoulder. "I must go back," she said.

"To Bannawg? You are safe here. I know I have … failed you, but—." He cradled her face in his large hands. "I will not fail you again."

"I have a duty, to my family," she said, raising her hands to his wrists to free herself. "And to my friends."

"Your life is here."

Heledd clenched the fabric of his linen shirt as he lowered his head and pressed a kiss to her lips. She tilted her chin to accept, holding her breath. Heledd felt the sudden, rigid tension spread through his body as his hands slid from her face, her shoulders and around her waist, pulling her into his arms, until nothing separated her from him. More than all she had ever wanted to be with him, she was pulling away from him, whimpering like a child, her eyes wide. His kiss was more insistent, fierce, merciless the further she withdrew. *Not like this, not like this.*

"No," was the only word Heledd said aloud. She felt the battle he waged between lust and reason. His hands trembled and he cursed her under his breath.

When he lifted his head, she dropped her forehead to his chest, gasping for air. After what seemed only the blink of an eye, Garmon released her but Heledd clung to him until, with a broken sob, she came to her senses and let him go. He stood away, turning her to face the hearth. "Your breakfast will be cold," he said, once more like stone, and left the room. In a few moments, she heard the door of the house slam behind him and she sank to the hearthstone, resting her head against the warm, smoke-stained granite.

The youngest of the staghounds crawled closer to her on its belly.

"You love him too, I suppose," Heledd sighed, dropping her hand onto the dog's shoulder when the hound laid its head on her thigh. "If he loved us even one hundredth as much, we would be happy, yes?" The hound lifted its head to stare at her then lay down again. The only sound in the longhouse was the crackle of the fires in both rooms. "Did you want to go with him?" she asked after a while. The dog turned its head more comfortably in her lap and closed its eyes. "What do you think he meant? Why did he kiss me like that?" She pressed her fingers to her lips, still feeling the pressure of his mouth. "He has never done that before, not even in Bannawg, when there was nothing to stop him." Heledd stroked the dog's shoulder. "Did I fail some other test I knew nothing about? What do you think will happen to me now, Dog?"

The staghound jerked its head, ears alert and leapt to its feet, bounding from the room, baying for blood. Heledd pushed herself to her feet, looking for a way to escape when she heard a sharp command and a sword drawn.

"Call off the dog, *boneddiges*, or I will have to kill it."

Recognizing Geraint's voice, Heledd flew to the door of Garmon's bedroom. "Down," she commanded. The hound dropped to its belly, still watching the soldier as he crossed the room toward Heledd, sheathing his sword in his belt again.

"Garmon told me you had frightened his dogs," he said, grinning at her. "That must have been a shock to him. He didn't tell me they take their orders from you as well. I'd be dead if this one didn't."

"I didn't mean to frighten them," Heledd said. "Is he angry?"

"With you, *boneddiges*? I doubt it."

"Where has he gone?"

"To join Huw in the hunting."

Heledd stared at the floor. "Oh," she murmured, "I thought … I mean …." she ended on a sigh, wondering how she had ever believed she might have understood Garmon *llysfab* Huw. "If these dogs are trained to kill," she asked suddenly, "why did they not kill me when I came here to the house last night?"

Geraint shrugged, "Garmon must have trained them to recognize you."

"Why would he do that?"

"You are not his enemy, *boneddiges*."

"But you thought this one would kill you," she said, looking at him askance.

"It protects you," Geraint replied. "If Garmon was here, it would have been the same. No one enters this house unless he has granted permission."

"Meini entered."

"Meini is always here," Geraint said, "when she is not in her father's house or the apothecary. The dogs know her as well as their master."

"Are you hungry?" she asked, covering her distress with a flurry of hospitality.

"I can eat," Geraint chuckled, "I can always eat."

Geraint's unquestioning acceptance of her presence in Garmon's house confused her. His lack of surprise when she came from the bedroom confused her. Meini's residence in Garmon's house filled her with hot jealousy and she wondered where the *pennaeth's* daughter had slept the night before, since Heledd had taken her place in Garmon's bed. Why hadn't he gone to Meini to find a bed? Heledd went into the bedroom and brought back the breakfast she had not touched.

"There is ale here," she said, pouring a full flagon for him. "Should I put another log on the fire?"

"Sit down, *boneddiges*," Geraint said, as he took a seat at the table. "There is no need for you to be anxious. Garmon has put me on duty in the house. Rhodri is close at hand. Nisien and Carwyn are just outside. Llinos Cenfyn is in the *pennaeth's* house, with Mared."

"That is a dangerous combination," Heledd commented, sitting across from him.

"It is worse than that, *boneddiges*," Geraint said. "You should also know the brothers were attacked last night. Just a few hours after Daf's daughter was born. Stewards found them both senseless on the floor of the dining hall."

Heledd did not know how to answer. She stared at the grain of the oak table, tracing her fingers over the patterns. Geraint had to know something more than he was saying. He must have been told they had been in her room, everyone would see the door was battered down and she had fled. Garmon had had Carwyn's assurance he had checked she bolted the door before he went off duty. Geraint must have also known she opened the door. For once, she was glad of the mop of red hair behind which she could hide from his gaze.

Though he did not seem to scorn her, Heledd's sense of her own stupidity grew. She had refused to allow Tegwen Talog to examine her to prove she had not been raped. If Aeron and Wyn claimed they had been with her, Heledd had no evidence to refute them or to prove her innocence. Garmon could not be certain he arrived in time to prevent them from causing harm to her. Her word would never be good enough. Heledd dropped her head onto her folded arms.

"Are you ill, *boneddiges*?" Geraint queried, leaning to touch her shoulder.

*This is how women die. This is how women are forced to become whores.* Heledd covered her head with her arms. *Is that what I am meant to be?* She groaned in misery and rage. *Is that what Garmon believes I am? Is that why he kissed me?*

"*Boneddiges*, are you ill?"

"No." Heledd lifted her head and stared into Geraint's eyes. After a moment, she stood and walked toward the door.

"Where are you going?" he demanded, following on her heels. He reached the door ahead of her and blocked her escape. "You cannot leave the house, *boneddiges*. My orders are clear. You do not leave and no one else enters."

"No one?"

"No one," he replied.

"I am a prisoner?" she asked. "I can see no one? Even if I must?"

"Those are my orders. Until Garmon returns, you are confined to his house."

Heledd turned away, staring at the floor. "Blessed God," she sighed. "It is worse than I could imagine."

"Why do you say that?" Geraint barked at her. "Do you think this was intended? Do you think Garmon wanted this? It is not bad enough that—," he broke off, cursing.

"What? What is not bad enough?" she shouted.

"That you have given Llinos Cenfyn all she needs to destroy him," he shouted in return.

"How? How have I done that?"

"Between myself and God, Heledd, I thought you loved him as we do."

The violence of his response silenced her. She lifted her chin high and walked back into the bedroom, allowing the staghound to follow her, slammed the door shut, throwing the empty oil pot at it for good measure. She heard Geraint curse again, stride across the room and bang on the door.

"Garmon told me you wanted to see me," he growled. "Why?"

"Go away," she murmured. After a few moments, he flung himself into a chair, scraping his boots on the hearthstone. Not long after his outburst, someone knocked on the outside door and Geraint yanked it open. Heledd heard their voices but could not distinguish them one from the other. The door was closed once more and Geraint returned to the chair by the hearth. Even if he fell asleep, she knew she would not be able to get past him or the two who were on guard outside.

If she could, she would be caught by someone in the *gaer*, or worse, caught alone by Llinos Cenfyn, her sons or Mared Rheinallt. She crossed the room to the shuttered window but, even with all her anger-fuelled strength, she could not unfasten the latch that locked it shut. In frustration, she growled and slammed the side of her fist against it. Her reward was a splinter in the soft flesh of her palm. Though she cried out, only the dog lifted his head to peer at her. Heledd threw herself on the bed, buried her head beneath the cushions and wept.


The embers in the bedroom hearth were cold and black when Heledd opened her eyes at the end of the day. The hound lay at the side of the bed, beneath her feet. When she lifted her head, the dog jumped up, wagging his tail. Heledd turned onto her back and stared around the darkened room, beginning to feel the chill in the air. She pushed herself to a sitting position and felt the stab of pain from the splinter in her hand.

"Ach, Dog, this place will get the better of me," she complained in a whisper, pulling at the splinter with her teeth. The splinter was large enough for her to feel and remove, large enough to bleed when it was gone. She moved as quietly as she could to the table and found the cloth Meini had brought with her. The dog followed her every move around the room, sitting when she stood still and shadowing her wherever she walked. "I cannot say I am any happier here than I was at Bannawg, you know. I suppose that is my punishment for forgetting my family and friends. But I wonder if it also means I must die of starvation and cold?" She wrapped her hand in the cloth and found the door. With a heavy sigh to prepare herself to face Geraint, she drew the door open and peered from behind it into the larger room. The fire in the hearth was blazing and a meal had been set out on the table. When she stepped into the room, Carwyn leapt from the chair facing the flames.

"Good evening, *boneddiges*," he said, bowing at the waist. His face was glowing from the heat and his hair was damp around his forehead. "Are you well?"

"I am well enough," Heledd replied, experimenting with a slight smile.

"I thought you would sleep through the night."

"Is it late?" She crossed the floor and looked down at the food on the table. "Where is Geraint?"

"He is not on duty. Do you want him to come back? Rhodri can bring him for you, if you want to see him."

"No," she replied. "No, thank you." She glanced at the door for a moment, a thought crossing her mind, before it had fully formed, she asked, "When did he go?"

"Only a few minutes ago."

"Why was he here so long?"

"Garmon told him you wanted to see him. He waited through his watch and Nisien's, *boneddiges*, but he will come back if you want."

"When will he be on duty again?" Heledd's partially completed thought had become clear. When Carwyn told her Geraint was scheduled to return that night, she said, "Tell Aled I do not need to speak with Geraint again today. Someone else can take his watch. This dog has been well trained by his master," Heledd said, patting the hound's head. "I think I will be safe."

Although Carwyn frowned slightly, he nodded, and asked, "Will you eat now?"

"I'm not— yes, I might as well," she said, sitting on the bench and taking one of the platters to fill with meat and bread.

"May I join you, *boneddiges*?" Carwyn asked, staring at the tray and all the meat, bread and cheese piled on it.

"Haven't you eaten?"

"I was waiting for you, *boneddiges*. I can wait until you have finished, if you prefer." Carwyn continued to gaze at the tray of food and the jug of ale.

"Sit down, Carwyn. I'm not going to eat while you starve."

Carwyn grinned as he jumped to the table, sat down on the bench opposite Heledd and took a platter. She gestured for him to help himself to whatever he wanted and then began to eat herself. After a short while, bewilderment returned and she dropped her hands into her lap. The hound cocked its head at her and Heledd gave him the slice of meat on her plate.

"Garmon won't like that you've given your meal to the dog," Carwyn said, with a laugh. "These dogs eat well enough without your help."

"He has so many reasons to be angry with me," she sighed, "I do not think one more will make much difference."

"Yes, *boneddiges*." Carwyn dropped his eyes and concentrated on his own meal, devouring everything, throwing the bone to the hound, and cleaning the platter with a hunk of bread. "Should I go now, *boneddiges*?" he asked suddenly. "I'm sorry, I didn't think ... except about the meal. I will tell Aled your wishes now," he exclaimed, jumping to his feet.

"Rhodri can pass my request to Aled. I am glad you are all here to help me," she said. A catch in her voice made her look away from him.

"Of course, *boneddiges*, I understand. Garmon told us what happened, so it's understandable you would be concerned when Garmon is not here – he is the best warrior of any of us, even Aled admits that."

"What did Garmon tell you, Carwyn?" she asked, peering into the young man's face.

"No one else in the *gaer* knows, *boneddiges*," he assured her.

"What do you know?"

"Aeron and Wyn broke into your room, in the *pennaeth's* own house. Garmon dealt with them and they were found in the dining hall. You will be safe here, in Garmon's house," he said, "until the *pennaeth* returns."

"Where are they now, the brothers?"

"No one has seen them since the stewards found them at dawn."

"Do they know where I am? Does Llinos Cenfyn know I am here?"

"No, *boneddiges*. Only Garmon's friends know you are here. If anyone asks, we have been told to say he has taken you to the *pennaeth*, to see the hunting and, if they ask when you left, you have been gone since Camwy's baby was born."

"He's very clever, your friend," Heledd mused aloud.

"Aye, *boneddiges*. He is that."

"How long will … the *pennaeth* be gone?"

"He will return tomorrow or the next day. If the hunting has been good, and it always is," he said with pride, "there will be a feast."

"Huw Bro-Dawel enjoys feasting," Heledd said with another experimental smile. She stood up from the table and called the dog to follow her into the bedroom with a gesture of her hand. She turned at the door and said, "The fire in my room has died."

"I will set it for you now, *boneddiges*," Carwyn said, collecting hot coals from the hearth in a bucket and filling his arms with logs. "It is likely to be cold tonight," he commented, kneeling by the small hearth. "The hunters won't be pleased, especially if it rains. I'm glad Garmon didn't want any of us to join him."

"Why not? I thought you all enjoyed killing," she said, sitting on the edge of the bed, watching as he blew on the coals to kindle the dry bark of the logs.

"I don't enjoy killing, *boneddiges*. Some take pleasure in war, but that is not why we are soldiers."

"Why are you soldiers then?"

"I know why I am a soldier, *boneddiges*, but I cannot answer for others. I want to protect my family from those who would steal from them, kill them for what little they have. If I can do that without killing, I will. But there are many, some in the *pennaeth's* own family, who would murder my mother and father for the clothes on their backs. While I am able, I will safeguard their lives and those of my sisters."

"How many sisters do you have, Carwyn?"

"Six. Seven. They are all younger than I am. That is a lot of protection for one soldier."

"Why aren't you protecting them now instead of keeping me a prisoner?"

"My sisters are not in danger from anyone while my comrades are alert and at the gates, as they are every night, every day. Why do you believe you are a prisoner?"

"If I am not a prisoner, why am I not as safe as your sisters? Why am I not allowed the freedom to leave this house?"

"No one in Bro-Dawel has any interest in hurting my sisters. They are unimportant in that way. You are threatened by Llinos Cenfyn and her sons. I have been ordered to keep you safe from them. That is what I will do until one of the others takes my place through the night. Nisien, probably."

"Nisien has a wife. He should be keeping watch over her. She has been threatened by Aeron Cenfyn, too."

"Rhian Nisien is not important to Aeron. Llinos Cenfyn gave him warning to fix his mind on you."

"How do you know that?" Heledd asked.

"I am a good listener," he laughed, sitting back on his heels as the bark flared, outlining his profile. Heledd stared at him for a moment and lowered her eyes immediately when he turned to meet her gaze. "I do what is necessary," Carwyn said in response to her astonishment.

"I understand," she said, gazing at his features. "What will you do when you are off duty tonight?"

"I will go to the barracks and get some sleep." He leapt to his feet and dusted his knees. "Garmon will be back tomorrow or the next day," he said with a smile.

"Should that matter to me?" Heledd watched his expression change from a confident, cheerful young man to a frowning boy.

"I didn't mean … to …"

"Will you have company tonight? Do you have a favorite among the girls?"

"I … " he faltered. "I don't know. I've never thought about it."

"Who is your favorite?" she asked.

"I like one or two better than the others."

"Why?"

"They are nicer, prettier. They make me feel good."

"When you feel good, what do you do?"

"I laugh. Some of the women make fun of me but one or two like to laugh with me, or make me laugh. And then we make love."

She could see, even in the dim light of the fire, she had embarrassed him. "Forgive me, Carwyn. I should not be asking such questions of you." He kept his head down and his eyes averted. "Don't worry, I wasn't making fun of you. I'm very sorry. Please forgive me."

"Of course," he said, glancing at the door.

"You can go. I will be all right now." Before he had closed the door, she had covered her face with her hands in shame. The hound sat on its haunches in front of her and she smiled at his quizzical expression. "How can I know anything without asking stupid questions?" she whispered to him. "If I knew how to make Garmon feel good, if I could make him laugh, would that be a good thing, do you think? Or would it make no difference?" She stroked the dog's ears for a few moments.

"You're probably right, Dog. It would make no difference to him. He only smiles when I am at my worst. Dog," she exclaimed under her breath, dropping to her knees and holding his head in her hands to stare into his black eyes, "does he think I love Geraint? Is that why he kissed me like that?" She pressed her forehead against the hound's brow. "Does he think I'm a whore for others, but not for him?"

She began to undress, studying her body in the firelight. "What sort of women do you think he likes? Who comes here to give him pleasure, to laugh and make love with him?" She measured her height against the wall and judged herself too tall in comparison to the small ale woman. "Did the ale woman sleep here the night Camwy's daughter was born? Do you know? Have you seen her or another?" She removed her shift and the rest of her undergarments.

"Would you tell me, if you could? Ach, I don't know why I am making myself so unhappy. One minute I am certain and the very next I am in despair. I believe one thing and he proves the other is true. Well, there is only one thing to be done and I will do it tomorrow," Heledd declared, crawling into the bed and settling the *carthen* over her body. "Would you like to have a name, Dog? A name I can call you so we are not strangers? I will think of a name for you tonight and we can be better friends in the morning. As long as you do not mind having me as a friend, that is," she finished with a small laugh.

In the other room, Carwyn settled into the chair by the hearth. Heledd stared at the blackness of the thatch above her, recalling everything Meini had told her about Garmon's mother and younger brother. She had seen the likeness for the first time in the sudden flare of the fire. Carwyn was fair and slight in comparison to his elder half-brother, but the similarity was there if one saw them both in the glow of a warm, agreeable light as she had done.

The knowledge gave her a terrible sense of responsibility – a responsibility she could not carry lightly. After all, she had neglected every other person who depended upon her. She made so many mistakes, she did not want to make one that would cost Carwyn his life. She listed the names of those who were privileged to know Carwyn was the son of Huw Bro-Dawel and Creiddwen Owein. Heledd believed she was one of only four – Huw, Garmon, Meini and herself. Carwyn's life was as much in her hands as theirs and she vowed she would not endanger him.

Heledd's first task in the morning was to train Bleddyn, the young staghound, new commands she would need. The dog was not as stupid as its mistress and by the time breakfast was brought to Garmon's house, Bleddyn knew what she meant when she pointed her finger and what to do when she dropped her hand to her side. She opened the door to the outer room just as Nisien was putting on his cloak to return to his wife and his hafod.

"Did you sleep well?" she asked, taking a seat at the table, gazing at his short, light brown hair, wondering why all of Aled's command had the same short hair, when Garmon and Aled wore their hair to their shoulders, even Huw wore his hair closely cropped.

"I was on duty, *boneddiges*. I did not sleep. Did you sleep well?"

"Very well, thank you. Will you have breakfast with me or are you anxious to return to Rhian?"

"As you prefer, *boneddiges*. Geraint is just coming."

"But I asked… Geraint will breakfast with me then. Thank you, Nisien. I know it is an onerous task to stay awake all night when your prisoner sleeps so comfortably." His puzzled look made her smile. "Don't concern yourself with my bad mood, Nisien. I am often haughty and arrogant, as you have seen. Good day to you and I hope Rhian is well."

"She is fatigued and changeable. I am told that is normal for a woman at her stage."

"I wouldn't know," Heledd replied, biting into one of the apples she picked up from the tray. "Would you ask if Meini could visit with me?"

"Are you ill?"

"I would like to see her, although I am not ill. And, while I think of it, I would also like to see Tegwen Talog." Nisien smiled slightly. "Not for the reason you think," she said, with a thin smile. Geraint entered the house and the two soldiers exchanged only a brief word before Nisien shut the door behind him. "Have you eaten?"

Geraint narrowed his eyes. "As you know, I can always eat," he said, taking the seat she offered on the other side of the table.

"Carwyn told me the hunters will be returning soon."

Geraint nodded, drinking from the flagon of ale.

"What sort of feasting will there be?"

"If the *pennaeth* and his huntsmen have been as successful as in past years, they will eat and drink for days. To make up for all the time they have lost while in the woods."

"Do you wish you had been able to go with them?"

"Yes and no." Heledd encouraged him to tell her more. "Yes, because it is good fellowship to hunt together. No, because sleeping in the trees is not comfortable."

"It doesn't sound very comfortable, especially for some."

"Huw keeps a lodge there. The *crac* sleep in comfort. And," he said, looking into her eyes, "Garmon can endure as much discomfort as any other man, more than most."

"Not always," she said.

"Not always, that's true," he admitted.

"What causes him to feel pain?"

"If he wants you to know, he will tell you," Geraint told her, draining his flagon and putting it firmly down on the table. Heledd doubted Garmon wanted her to know that and she shrugged in response.

"Then it will be a good thing when he marries Meini."

"Garmon will not marry Meini," Geraint said.

"That's what Rhian believes. And Camwy." Heledd said, refilling both their flagons and choosing another apple to go with her cheese.

"I do not mean any disrespect to Nisien's wife, but she has not been here long. And Camwy has a good imagination," Geraint answered. "When Garmon chooses a wife, they will be the last to know."

"Rhian is certain he chose Meini on the night of the harvest, when he was declared champion reaper."

"They are like brother and sister – she was with him, but not to be in his bed," he laughed. "He wanted you that night, everyone saw that, including Meini. Ach, don't look at me like that," he said, grinning. "You knew it yourself or you wouldn't have made sure he knew you were bolting your door, when he invited you to leave it open for him."

"He was drunk," she answered.

"Aye, he was very drunk," Geraint chuckled. "So drunk, he didn't feel any pain until dawn – when Meini was called to him."

# sixteen

Meini was the first of Heledd's invited visitors to enter the house and Geraint glanced from one woman to the other. "Who told you to come?" he asked the *pennaeth's* daughter.

"Nisien said Heledd wanted to see me."

"What reason do you have to see the *meddyg*?" he demanded of Heledd.

"I hurt my hand yesterday. It needs attention," Heledd said, showing him her roughly bandaged hand.

"When did you do that?" he inquired with a frown. "I heard nothing."

"You were angry," Heledd reminded him.

"So were you," he retorted.

"Let me see that, Heledd," Meini intervened, holding out her hand. "It is nasty. Why didn't you ask for it to be treated? Didn't you have any ointment left?"

"She threw it against the door," Geraint said.

"The pot was empty," Heledd said in her own defense. "And I fell asleep."

Geraint whirled toward the door when Tegwen Talog entered. "What is this?" he demanded of Heledd. "You know my orders. Are you determined to cause trouble?"

"Carwyn said I am not a prisoner. So, I believe I can speak to whomever I please. If you want, you can ask Garmon's permission but I have need of both these women and unless you insist on watching, I will see them alone."

"Garmon told me you frightened *him*," he said. "Now, I know why."

When Geraint finally allowed Heledd to go to the bedroom

alone with Tegwen Talog, she closed the door and turned to face the older woman. "Is your daughter well? And your grandson?"

"Both are very well."

"And Camwy? Is she better? I'm sorry if I have taken you away from her care," Heledd said, biting her lips together.

"Camwy is better," Tegwen replied, studying Heledd with interest.

"Do you remember telling me I had a good back?"

"Yes, you are well-built."

"What else can you tell by looking at me?"

"You have good hips, as I told you – you are well-built for breeding." Tegwen turned to take a seat on the stool by the bed.

"Can you tell other things?" Tegwen shrugged in answer. "Can you tell if I have been hurt, injured by someone?"

"In what way?"

"If I have been forced … against my will …to lie with a man?"

"Have you? By whom?" Tegwen asked, frowning.

"Can you say for certain if a man had done this?"

"There are some signs, if the act is recent, or if the man was violent. Why do you ask such a question, child? Do you fear Garmon would do such a thing? He is not a violent man, Heledd. He would not hurt you, and he would not touch you ever against your will."

"I know that. It is not Garmon," Heledd said, surprised Tegwen had heard nothing of the brothers' assault on her. "A man, another man."

"When did this happen? Does Garmon know?"

"Yes, he knows," Heledd admitted, sinking onto the bed and covering her face. "I have no witness to my innocence except the evidence of my own body. If you cannot confirm he has not touched me, I fear he will accuse me of a crime. I should have come to you when it happened," Heledd cried. "I was too proud …"

"Did you cry out?"

"I was prevented … I couldn't, I had no voice."

"What has Garmon done about this?"

"I do not know."

"Has Garmon slept with you since?" Tegwen inquired. "If so, there is nothing I can do for you, child."

"He has not," Heledd said. "He was in the house, in the outer room, nothing more."

"I will accept your word on that," Tegwen said with a gentle smile, glancing at the bed. "And Garmon's word, of course."

"Garmon *llysfab* Huw has no interest in me."

"It is more than interest, child," Tegwen replied. "He has invested—." When Heledd turned away, the midwife said, "I see your chin is bruised – the other man did this?" Heledd nodded and pulled the neck of her frock open to show the red scratch on her neck. "I am surprised this man has not been flogged for what he has done. Take off your clothes, child. I will do my best to determine all that has happened to you. If there is doubt, I will tell you, but no one else."

"You are very kind," Heledd said, removing her clothes and standing near the hearth while Tegwen washed her hands before beginning the examination with experienced eyes.

"You will need to lie down now, Heledd, so I can see if there is any other sign."

"I should tell you," Heledd said before she complied with Tegwen's request, "when I was younger, before I came to Bro-Dawel, my uncle gave me to one of his soldiers as payment for his service."

"Then there is no point to this examination, child, you must realize that," the midwife replied angrily. "If you think I will give a false report, you are mistaken. Did you cry out then? If not, you have no case in law."

"I fought him," Heledd said after a long pause. "I injured him and he was very drunk. I thought I had been spared but my cousin found evidence. She said it proved he had prevailed. Can you know if this is true?"

"Don't you know the answer from your knowledge of your own body?"

"I felt nothing different, *boneddiges*. Should I have?"

"Many women feel discomfort the first time they are mated. The degree depends on many things. The man… her own body."

"How? How does that depend on him?"

"If he is careless, if he is violent. If he is a very big man."

"He was none of those," Heledd answered. "He was drunk."

"Drink sometimes fuels a man's passion. Too much drink and he sleeps," Tegwen laughed.

"Very drunk or too drunk," Heledd murmured pressing her lips hard together.

"Some men think drink gives them license to commit any crime – they are dangerous and liquor is their courage. Other men drink to curb their passion. Most men drink for the pleasure of drinking – sometimes too much pleasure means a full night's sleep and a bad head."

"I have had a bad head," Heledd admitted with a blush.

"Then you know even more. We are what we are, drunk or sober."

"Granite is always granite," Heledd said.

"Just so. Lie down across the bed, my girl and bring your hips to the edge. This will not be pleasant," Tegwen warned as she washed her hands again. She lifted Heledd's knees and positioned her feet wide apart on the edge of the bedframe. Heledd threw her arms across her eyes as if she could block out what was happening to her by not seeing it done. She bit her lips and cried out in dismay when the midwife penetrated her with her strong fingers. Tegwen patted her patient's knee when she had finished her examination. "As near as I can say, you are as you were born, child. There is no evidence any man has used you. Do you wish me to testify to this to Garmon?"

Heledd shook her head. "I do not think that will be necessary." She drew her legs together and turned onto her side.

"You are probably right about that, child." Tegwen gave Heledd her shift and soaped her hands. "You will be a little uncomfortable but I have caused no damage. You are still a maiden. I'm surprised your mother did not tell you more about your body."

"My mother was killed when I was a small child." Heledd took a deep breath, pulled her shift over her and pushed it down her body. "Thank you, *boneddiges*, for being so kind to me. I hope there will never be need for you to be asked to give evidence on my behalf but I am grateful to you for your help."

"The more *I* know about your body, child, the more I can help you when you give birth to your first child." Heledd returned the midwife's smile with a quiet, uncertain glance. "You will need my services long before summer, Heledd, as I told you when I first examined you," Tegwen insisted. "When you first suspect your husband's seed has taken and your *baban* grows, come to me. There is more to birthing a strong, healthy baby than what you have seen in Camwy's house." Heledd nodded, though she doubted she would ever need such help, and held her frock against her breasts. When Tegwen left the room, she sank back onto the bed and hid her face in the frock, stifling the noise of her weeping.

The staghound sat by her, laying its head on her knee. "I have been so foolish, Bleddyn," she said, sitting up again and patting him, "but I intend to improve."

When Meini returned with her replenished basket, Heledd was sitting on the edge of the bed, listening to the midwife's happy conversation with Geraint, describing her grandson's intelligence and Medi's beauty. Heledd wondered at the capacity of some women for love. Tegwen's generosity reminded her of the women of Bannawg, especially Goewin, to love even those who injured them. It was a wonder to her they had found room in their hearts to care for anyone, after what they had suffered – especially for someone who was so careless of them.

"Did you truly use all of the oil I gave you for Garmon?" Meini interrupted her thoughts. Heledd lifted her head and nodded, pointing to the fragments of the clay pot half hidden by the bedroom door. "He must have been in agony," Meini commented.

"Why do you say that?"

"I gave you enough for a week," she replied.

"I used too much." The color beneath her freckles was as

dark as her hair.

"I'm sure Garmon had no complaints," Meini laughed. "That oil is potent. No doubt he slept very well after your treatment. I think he will prefer you to be his *meddyg* from now on."

"He said my help would never be required again."

"Ach, that is just his pride. He has said the same to me. No doubt, he will say it to you more than once."

"I doubt it," Heledd replied, holding out her hand for Meini's treatment, keeping her eyes averted. When her hand was bandaged and Meini was packing her basket, Heledd asked, "Do you think—? I mean, if—. You told me Garmon spoke for your husband when your father refused his permission for you to wed."

"Yes, that's true."

"Would Garmon do the same for me?"

"What do you mean, Heledd. Speak for you how?"

"What will happen if I ask to return to Bannawg?"

"Why? Why would you want to do that?"

"Bannawg is where I belong. I came here prepared to work, to be a good servant as I should, but now—. I never meant for this to happen, Meini."

"What?" Meini exclaimed. "What are you saying?" Meini stared hard at Heledd, her blue eyes flashing with rage. She took a threatening step forward. The staghound lifted its head, rising slowly, its whole body like a coil, and its teeth glistening.

"Bleddyn," Heledd said, laying her hand on the dog's head, "down."

"I will not be your messenger, Heledd, not for this. If you have reasons to break your contract with my father, I do not want to know them. I will not do your dirty work with Garmon. Whatever you have to say to either of them, you must say for yourself."

"The man you loved, loved you in return," Heledd said. "Can you blame me for wanting that?"

"I don't want to hear this." Meini hissed and stormed from the room.

"Then who am I to tell?" Heledd asked Bleddyn. The hound cocked his head from side to side and laid his paw on her lap. "I know," she sighed, "but I am a coward as well as all my other faults." She heard a sharp exchange between Meini and Geraint, but couldn't hear what they said to one another. "I do not know very much but I am not afraid to test my knowledge. Are you ready for some exercise, Bleddyn? We have been in this house too long."

Geraint lifted his eyes from his contemplation of the fire and, when she walked toward the door, he leapt to his feet.

"Unless you are prepared to knock me down," Heledd warned him, "I am going out."

"You know I cannot allow you to leave."

"Then you have a problem, Geraint, because I have been idle too long."

"Can you not find occupation here where you are out of harm's way?"

"Ach, harm will find me wherever I am," Heledd laughed.

"Not in this house."

"Here as well. Come with me, Geraint. You are a good guide."

"You will lead us both into trouble, *boneddiges*, but I have no authority to refuse you. I will have to account to Garmon for this. And if anything happens to you—."

"If anything happens to me, I can account for myself. And I have always felt it is better to face what you know will come. I am ready to face whatever waits."

Geraint frowned but picked up and sheathed his sword. Heledd raised the hood of Garmon's long black cloak and patted Bleddyn's head. The afternoon sun was dazzling to her eyes after being shut in the house. Heledd pulled the hood further down onto her brow and turned in the direction of Camwy's house to recover her tunic. Geraint followed her lead, watchful and unhappy. The staghound trotted, keeping close at her side, his shoulder at her left hand. At the door of Daf's *hafod*, Heledd went up the step but did not have to knock. Daf's voice was hardly audible when he invited her to enter.

"I saw you from the window, *boneddiges*," he said, opening the door. Heledd commanded Bleddyn to sit by the door and Geraint followed her into the room. "Camwy is sleeping. Have you come to see her?"

"Don't disturb her, Dafydd," Heledd replied. "May I see your daughter again?"

Daf led his guests to the wooden cradle by the bed and bent over it to lift Medi *merch* Dafydd to greet her visitors.

"She is just as beautiful as I remember, Dafydd."

"No thanks to me, I'm sure," he said with pride.

"May I hold her?" Heledd asked, surprised at herself. When the baby was handed into her arms, she held her as though Medi was made of the most fragile glass. Daf brought a chair and Heledd lowered herself into it. When she felt more confident, she stroked the baby's brow and bent her head over her to fill her lungs with the fragrance of Medi's skin. "She is perfect," Heledd murmured. "So perfect." She kissed the top of the baby's head. "My mother bore seven children, I can hardly believe such a marvelous thing to have even one," she said, smiling up at Daf.

"Nor I," he answered and took his daughter into his arms when Heledd offered her back to him.

"Thank you, Dafydd, for allowing me to hold her." Heledd found her blue tunic, folded on the stool by the door where she had left it, and called Bleddyn to her side. She turned to catch Daf and Geraint in quiet conversation and smiled down at the staghound. He pricked his ears and raised his paw, scowling. "Yes," she whispered, "I would like to know what they say about me too." Both men were quick to fall silent but revealed nothing. "If you're ready, Geraint, we have one other infant to see."

The walk between the warriors' *hafodydd* was short and Heledd was glad to see Meleri was already out of bed, sitting by the hearth with her baby in her lap.

"What have you decided to call your baby?"

"We have chosen to call him Tegwyn Talog *mab* Rhodri."

"That is a splendid name," Heledd said, touching the boy's

black spiky hair. "He's very strong now and you look well."

"My mother is good at her work."

"Yes, I know," Heledd replied, unthinkingly, but when she saw the knowing expression on Meleri's face, she resigned herself to being misunderstood whenever her relationship with Garmon was in the question. "There is a very good midwife at Bannawg as well. She cared for me when I was small and is caring for my ... my friends." Heledd could see from Meleri's distant look Goewin could not compare with Tegwen.

"My mother told me she has seen you and you are in excellent health."

"That is good to hear," Heledd said. "I think it would be a good thing to have two such skilled women in Bro-Dawel," Heledd commented. "Once my cousin has given birth safely to her child, I will ask the *pennaeth* to invite Goewin here." She was surprised at how simple it was to assume a rôle so false.

"Do you not have faith in the women of Bro-Dawel to bring your child safely into this world?" Meleri asked. Heledd detected resentment.

"If I ever have a child, I will trust Tegwen Talog with both our lives," Heledd assured her, "but Goewin is the only mother I have ever known. I would like her to be with me."

"I can understand that," Meleri said, taking her son's fingers into her hand. "I'm certain Garmon will not refuse you."

Heledd dropped her eyes to gaze at the baby to conceal the pleasure surging through her blood to have even this imperfect evidence Garmon, not the *pennaeth*, determined matters concerning her. Meleri was unaware of the effect of her words on her visitor and Geraint made no comment. Until Garmon himself confirmed it by some deed she could not mistake, Heledd reminded herself she had been certain before and he had proved her wrong each time.

Meini had urged her to trust him and insisted he would not cause her harm. If Garmon was a man she could trust, then he would not take her to his bed, or break into her room, or force her against her will. He had done none of these though he had opportunity. She had interpreted his distance for a cold, hard heart. Now, she believed he ruled himself with iron discipline, only occasionally wavering when he was a little drunk.

He called her *'gwraig'* more often than he called her by name, though he was, no doubt, the only man at Bro-Dawel who could testify she was still a maiden, and no one's wife. Though he did not call her *his* wife, he addressed her as such and Heledd thought, by doing so, he was providing her with a clue. Finally, she believed he was allowing her to make a choice – to accept him as her husband in her own time or to return to Bannawg. His preference seemed clear on the morning he found her weeping. *"Your life is here,"* he had said. Though his control had faltered when he kissed her and he had not said *"with me"*, Heledd wanted to believe that was what he might have said had he not been able to exert his self-control.

*"Boneddiges,"* Geraint said, taking her elbow. "We should go," he nodded in the direction of Meleri who had turned her attention to her suckling baby.

"And now we can begin our adventure," Heledd said turning to leave with Bleddyn close at her heels.

*"Boneddiges,"* he warned, "you make light of a situation—."

"I assure you, I do not," she said, studying his face, "I want to ride the mare given to me. I have neglected her."

"The hunters will return soon, *boneddiges*," Geraint said, joining her on the step of the *hafod*. "Can you not wait for Garmon to take you for this ride?"

Though she could discern no new information from his response, she answered, "I know I ask too much, Geraint, but I must do this."

"Must? Is there something wrong, *boneddiges*?"

"Will you come with me, or must I go on my own?" she pushed. Geraint bowed his head in acquiescence, but not without a sigh of protest. Heledd clapped her hands with glee. "I will take full responsibility, Geraint. I know Garmon will understand."

"I hope you are right," he laughed. "If not, he will take off my head and put it on a pike at the gate."

The mare, Angel, stood in her stall, opposite that of the colt, covered in a light blanket. Neither the colt nor its sire, *Diawl*, were in the stables. Heledd petted the mare's forelocks while Geraint prepared her for the ride. Angel tossed her head and snorted. While Geraint readied his own horse, Heledd led Angel out of the stall along the open area of the stables toward the stalls where the warhorses were kept, apart from the mares and geldings. *Diawl's* empty stall was the furthest from all. "They must all think I am very stupid, or they are very clever, since it has taken me so long to understand." She pressed her head against its shoulder.

"What did you say, *boneddiges*?"

"I have apologized for neglecting my horse," she replied, using the rails of the warhorse's stall to mount Angel. "Are you ready, Geraint?"

"Yes, I'm ready," he answered with no enthusiasm. "To meet my death, I have no doubt."

"Do not be so hard on Garmon," Heledd laughed. "I'm sure I can convince him to punish me in your place."

"Never, *boneddiges*, in all God's creation, would he consider that."

"I'm glad to hear you say that," Heledd smiled as they rode out of the paddock, Bleddyn trotting ahead of Angel. "I wish I was as sure."

"Where have *you* been?" Mared demanded as Heledd and Geraint rode past the house. The *pennaeth's* eldest daughter strode toward the riders, her fists clenched on her hips and her brown hair flying behind her. She was soon joined by Llinos Cenfyn and Meini.

"I have been where I should be," Heledd replied. "And now I am going for a ride," Heledd said, glancing at Meini. "Would you like to come with us?"

"The hunters will be back in a few hours," Meini said. "Why don't you join us in the *neuadd* to await the feast?"

"Thank you for the offer, Meini, but I would rather ride while the afternoon is bright and the breeze so fresh."

"You slut," Mared gasped.

"Let her go," Llinos Cenfyn sneered. "If she is in such a hurry to bring your father's wrath on her head, especially after the attack on my sons, let the whore go. I wonder she has waited this long before throwing herself at these men, as well as that whore's bastard."

"I warned you," Geraint said under his breath.

"I cannot think what you mean, *boneddiges*," Heledd said. "I have been busy with the two *baban* born this week. Of what attack on your sons do you speak?"

"You do not fool me, Heledd *merch* Traitor, and you will not fool my brother. Your father's crimes are in your blood. You are born of a traitor and are one yourself. I know your game. You play men for fools, but it is you who will be brought to justice this time, as your father was and the rest of his bloodline."

Heledd listened to the woman's tirade and then urged Angel forward so she could speak to her, commanding Bleddyn to sit beside the horse. "You know nothing of me or my family but the lies you choose to believe. Carry on in this vein and I assure you, Llinos Cenfyn, you will never enter this place again. I will ensure you and your vermin sons are turned away like the criminals you are," she said, "to starve to death as you deserve."

"You dare now, but you will sing differently when Huw Bro-Dawel has you flogged for your whoring. My sons will make their case against you and their attacker. Garmon will finally receive the justice long overdue for the murder of my nephew."

"No good will come of blaming a boy for the deeds of a man."

"You know nothing of what happened to my brother," Mared hissed.

"I have been given a full account."

"By the murderer himself no doubt," Llinos said.

"By another, truthful witness," Heledd replied, pressing her knees into the mare's sides and urging the animal to turn back toward the road.

"You have not heard all the witnesses against that whore's bastard. Ach, you deserve each other," Llinos spat.

"I have heard enough," Heledd said, "and I know what I must do."

"Nothing you have to say will make any difference to my brother," Llinos snarled. "And I will ensure you regret *forever* the moment you agreed to come to my brother's household, you haughty, whoring slut."

"Call me whatever you choose, Llinos Cenfyn, there are many more truthful voices in Bro-Dawel who will speak for me." As they passed through the gate, she asked Geraint, "Which pike, do you think, will bear *my* head?"

"If it comes to that, Heledd Bannawg, you will have plenty of company."

Heledd was not surprised to see Carwyn, Nisien, and Rhodri were waiting for them at the top of the road when they reached the bridge crossing the mill brook surrounding the eastern border of the *gaer*. The five of them trotted along the road until they had reached the ford across the smaller of the two rivers, then turned to the east to climb the road leading away from Bro-Dawel toward the River Tywi. They rode along the edges of the harvested fields at a gallop, free now to exercise their horses where they had toiled to bring in the coming year's supply of grain. Beyond the fields, they rode through the scores of beehives at the edge of the grazing meadows. The head beekeeper raised his fist, threatening them with violence. The warriors laughed and shouted their apologies as they raced past.

Geraint turned his horse toward the road to Tredeml and Heledd threw her hood back from her head to see the beauty of the river valley she could now call home. She heard the distant howls of staghounds and the crash of horses' hooves on the forest floor.

"Bleddyn," she said softly to the excited hound trotting beside Angel. "Down." The hound glanced up at her, his ears pricked and twisted toward the sound of the hunting dogs. "Not today," she said, "this is not a good time for either of us to be near your master." When Geraint frowned at her, Heledd smiled and said, "Even I know when I'm not wanted."

# seventeen

All along the valley of the Taf, the fields were golden, cropped and a haven for feasting birds and field mice, feeding on the grain berries the reapers of the *ystad* had lost on the way to the mill. As the five riders galloped past, flocks of birds rose into the air, black swirling clouds across the face of the sun. Behind the riders' backs, the flocks dove and rose again until assured they would be left in peace. Heledd laughed aloud to feel the cool breeze on her face, lifting her red hair behind her, like a banner. On such a day, even that could not bring her spirits down. Knowing how her parents, sisters and brothers had died had lifted a bloody shadow from her heart.

Although she grieved for their loss, their deaths were no longer a shame she had to bear. Her hideously colored hair was no longer a terrible reminder of a day she had forgotten. Wearing it loose no longer filled her with dread she might catch a glimpse of their bodies strewn across the *buarth* of her father's home farm. She could see them in her mind's eye and feel their loss, but she was no longer guilty of forgetting they had lived. She could see the face of each member of her family in happier times – the girls pretending to be their mother, the boys playing at being farmers and warriors, their proud father gathering them all in his arms when he came into the house at the end of the day, their patient mother scolding him for making them too excited to sleep. She could see her mother lying in Ieuan Bannawg's arms in their bed in the corner furthest from the hearth, turning to him when he wanted her, their bodies glistening in the firelight. Heledd could even see, without loathing, the sword he kept close at hand, ready to protect them.

Until the day of their deaths, none of them felt fear or dread or hunger in their father's house. Their happier times were too precious to lose and Heledd clung to them with all her heart. They would fuel her love for Garmon *llysfab* Huw and make her strong enough to be patient, to have hope.

Once they had reached the crest of the hills beyond Tredeml, Heledd could see the valley of the Tywi stretching far into the east, deep, green and wide. All along the river, villages burst their boundaries with fertility and growth. Smoke from chimneys plumed into the air, tempting her with visions of the happy residents celebrating the bounty of their harvests and their good hunting. And her impressions were all so different from her fearful arrival a few months before.

"*Boneddiges*," Rhodri said under his breath, touching her arm as he brought Angel to rest. "There is danger ahead."

"No, don't tell me that," she pleaded in a whisper, gesturing for Bleddyn to come back to her. "The day is too perfect and I am so happy."

"Geraint and Nisien have gone to investigate. Wait here with Carwyn."

She turned to look at the boy-soldier, leaving him to keep watch over them both, while she examined his face for likeness to Garmon and his father. She wondered how, once she saw the likeness, anyone could miss he had Huw's nose and eyes and his older brother's mouth. His hair was the color of oak, not yellow, but a softer, richer fairness – his mother's hair? Garmon, Heledd thought, had his mother's eyes – as gray as granite. Creiddwen Owein's eyes would not have been as hard, Heledd thought, more like the smoky-hued warmth of the hearthstone. She could imagine Huw Bro-Dawel falling in love with her from the first moment she arrived in his *ystad*. She could imagine him holding her in the safety of their bed and making love to her, creating the life of their beautiful son. Heledd could imagine Huw's grief and his desperation to keep their son safe. She could also imagine his love for Garmon – Creiddwen Owein's natural son. The Huw Bro-Dawel Heledd saw in the sons of his beloved wife was not the cruel, embittered tyrant he was to his daughters.

"Why are you staring at me?" Carwyn complained.

"I'm sorry," she gasped. "I was thinking about— about Garmon," she said honestly. The boy-soldier blushed. "You just happen to be there," she laughed. "It's a good thing he is hunting."

"Why is that?" Carwyn asked, bringing his horse to stand by Angel.

"Because he makes me laugh." Heledd replied, blushing in her turn.

"Laughing is not a bad thing. So why are you glad he is not here?"

"Now, it is your turn to embarrass me."

"I didn't mean to do that," Carwyn replied. "It's just Garmon is – aside from my own parents— important. He's— he's my friend. And my foster father."

"I know that, Carwyn," Heledd replied, touching his arm.

"They've found someone," Carwyn exclaimed, urging his horse toward the three others returning. Heledd turned to see her companions riding toward another warrior – a man alone, with no visible weapon. She nudged Angel to trot forward. When she was close enough to recognize the man, she backed away.

"I know him," she cried, "he is from Talgarth. He is my uncle's commander. Why has he come here?" Heledd urged Angel to stagger backward, to the safety of the woodland undergrowth. Urien Macsen stared in her direction but, after he had spoken to the three Bro-Dawel warriors, he turned his horse and rode alone toward the *gaer*.

"Do you know the warrior?" Rhodri asked, watching her face.

"He is from Talgarth," Heledd replied. "I have known him all my life."

"A friend?" Carwyn queried.

"He was Garmon's commander. They were friends. Geraint," she commanded, "tell Garmon Urien Macsen has come. Take Bleddyn with you." As soon as Geraint did as she ordered, she turned the mare away from Bro-Dawel, urging Angel deeper into the wood. Carwyn and Nisien followed but Rhodri followed the Talgarth warrior. "Where can I go?"

"Why are you frightened of this man?" Nisien asked, studying her face and glancing over his shoulder as Rhodri caught up with the stranger.

"He's here to take me back," she murmured. "He's my uncle's man."

"He said he had come to see the *pennaeth*. He carries no weapon."

Heledd shook her head, a cold shiver running through her body. "He is smart. He's killed before. Take me to the chapel. When Garmon comes tell him—. No, don't tell him. Urien will find me if Garmon knows. They were friends."

Nisien and Carwyn exchanged a frown but followed Heledd toward Capel Non. Once there, she slid from Angel's back and into the quiet sanctuary. Although the day was ending and the place was darkening, the sun shone through the window above the painted ledge, directing her eye toward the image of the saint and her young son, born at the edge of a cliff in shame and terror.

"Heledd," Carwyn murmured in the cool, solitude, "Garmon will not let anyone harm you. If this warrior is Garmon's friend, he is not here to harm you."

"Garmon is not here. This man is." She heard Carwyn's murmur and the hoof beats as Nisien rode away. She sighed without relief or solace when Carwyn entered the chapel to sit beside her. "Where has Nisien gone?"

"To bring Garmon here, to you."

Heledd bowed her head into her upturned hands but Carwyn's kindness could not dispel the fear Garmon had sent a message to Urien Macsen to take her away – as she herself had told him she wanted. As the long wait stretched into the darkness, she struggled to be awake when Garmon came and put no shawl around her shoulders so the chill in the air might keep her alert. When that tactic did not work, she began to talk aloud about Bannawg.

"I remember a winter when Alys fell from her horse and came into the house, covered in snow. We could only see her eyes. I have never seen a girl so angry." Carwyn nodded, his eyes focused on her face but his attention was keen on sounds of the night. "There was another year. Deion was learning to handle a spear and nearly killed the shoemaker. My uncle laughed when the man complained. That reminds me, I have promised to be measured for a new pair of shoes." She glanced at Carwyn as his body shifted, alert, his hearing intent on a silence she could not fathom. "Llew Talgarth didn't laugh for long when the shoemaker left, taking all his leathers with him and my cousins had no new shoes for winter."

"Where did the shoemaker go?" Garmon asked, standing at the door. Heledd jumped at the sound of his tired voice but he dismissed her with a sharp gesture. "I've only come to see Urien. Nisien insisted I come here first."

Heledd recognized the hard line of his jaw and did not wonder what she had done to make him turn to stone. "I thought you would want to know, since you knew him at Talgarth." She dropped her hand to her side and Bleddyn trotted away from his master to sit by her.

"Yes." Garmon peeled his gloves from his hands and slapped them on his palm. "Thank you." He loosened the neck of his shirt and opened the front of his hunting jerkin. "Did he say what he wanted? Why he has come here?"

"I didn't speak to him. He came to see the *pennaeth*," Heledd told him, glancing at Carwyn's face after each comment. "After all that has happened, I didn't want—." She swung away, biting her lip. "I've caused too much trouble," she murmured.

Garmon had walked the length of the chapel to stand by the window but when Heledd looked up, she saw his eyes were on her. Defiant in the face of his anger with her, she raised her chin and turned her eyes on Carwyn's gentle smile, asking herself why Garmon *llysfab* Huw could not be more like his younger brother.

"Come with me, Heledd," Garmon said, "we will only know

what he wants when he tells us."

"You didn't send for him?"

"No. Did you?"

The relief she felt danced through her heart and gurgled like a brook but his face did not change from stone to that of a man by the time they reached his house. Heledd was reluctant to enter but Garmon propelled her through the door, spoke under his breath to Carwyn before he stood for a moment alert, holding up his hand to signal her silence. She heard nothing other than the rustle of the staghounds' tails as they held, waiting for their master's command, their heads lowering, their forelegs bent to spring. Heledd caught her breath and received a sharp gesture in response.

At the door of his bedroom, he took a long breath, lifting his hand to remove the belt around his waist. A sweeping glance and brief sniff told him all he had to know. No one had slept in his room, in his bed, other than Heledd. For a moment, he stared at the disorder, the rumpled bedding, her clothes lying wherever she had removed them. He had not slept or eaten, thinking of her in his house, his bed and the memory of her lying near him, in his arms, snared him – only once had he held her like that. Every night since, he had dreamed of it. Garmon swallowed hard and motioned her into the room. "Go to bed."

"Where? Where am I to sleep?"

He dragged his hand over his face, closing it into a fist. "Where have you slept? Where did you sleep last night?"

"Here," Heledd answered, thrusting her hand in the direction of his bed. "This has been my bed," she said, following him into the empty room. Garmon stared at her. "It is also your bed, of course." He did not see the humor in her statement and she shrugged.

"There are *carthen* in the chest," he said. "I will take them."

"Take them where?" Granite is always granite, not like other men.

"To the other room, *menyw*."

"But there are insects and ... and ... I would rather sleep—"

"Heledd, do as I say, this once, please."

"Yes, Garmon. Forgive me."

"You have no reason to beg forgiveness," Garmon sighed.

"I must have done something," she snapped, taking an extra few *carthen* and flinging them into his chest, pushing him back, holding her breath when his rigid body expanded. Her fingers locked on the woolen blankets, refusing to allow her to release them. She stared into the fire of his rage. He released his grip and she stumbled, catching the *carthen* before they fell on the floor between them.

Garmon lurched forward, yanking her against him, dragging long breaths into his lungs. "Between myself and Satan, Heledd, if you were not already taken, nothing could stop me." He thrust her away. "Go to bed."

"Where are you going?" She watched in dismay as he threw the *carthen* against the wall and left her alone in the house. "You are always going," she sighed. As she laid down in the bed, Bleddyn crept toward her and dropped his head on her knees. *Taken? Does he believe Aeron's lies?* Heledd laid her hand on the staghound's head. "Can I do anything more wrong? He will be glad to be rid of me and I only have myself to blame for that."

The instant Geraint Padarn entered the house, Heledd jolted from the bed and whipped her shawl around her. When Bleddyn began to growl, she held up her hand. "You know me better. I am not this timid child who cowers in her bed when there is trouble to face."

"*Boneddiges.* Heledd," her guard huffed, "Garmon told me you were asleep."

"I know you will object so I command you to walk with me to the *pennaeth's* house. I will see that warrior now."

"Oh, you will?" Geraint chuckled, dragging his sword belt from around his waist. "And if I prefer to stay here in comfort?"

"You may do so, but I will go. Bleddyn is as good protection as ever you are."

"There is no reason to insult me," Geraint said. "Between you and Garmon, a man could begin to doubt his worth."

"Why? What did Garmon say to you?"

"No word, his frown is enough. He thinks I'm only good for taking headstrong girls for walks on a whim."

"That isn't what he thinks," Heledd said with a sigh. "Walk with me to the house, Geraint. I have to face this trouble now before anything worse happens."

As Heledd and Geraint reached the courtyard, a long band of boys and drummers came to the bend in the road from the hunting grounds. For a moment, Heledd strained her eyes to find Garmon among the hunters following the drummers before she remembered he would not be returning from hunting. Behind the hunters, Heledd saw the carts bearing the carcasses of game they had killed to feed the people of Bro-Dawel through the long winter months. The carts also carried the women who had been in the hunting camp with the men, and among them, Heledd saw the small, fair ale woman. Heledd felt a weight drop in her stomach, like a stone, making her dizzy. *Of course, he would have taken a woman with him.*

"There will be a great feast tonight," one of the wives told her. "None of the men will be sober and whomever they catch will be carrying a *baban* by morning. Bolt your door for certain tonight, Heledd."

"What are you doing there?" Llinos Cenfyn growled at her. "You're not satisfied with seducing Aeron, you want a hunter also?"

Geraint shrugged his shoulder at the insult, lifting his hand to ward off the woman's venom but Heledd searched the faces of the other women around her. None of them reacted to the slur. As the band of men rode through the gate, she kept her chin high, watching the extinguishing of the thin line of the sun behind the Penfro hills.

Aled found Ceinwen as soon as his horse touched the hard-packed soil of the *buarth*. After a tender greeting, and gathering his children near him, he turned to Heledd. "Urien? I would have come with Garmon," he said, "but he wanted to come alone. He was … worried."

"Why?"

"He thought Urien had come to take you back to Bannawg."

"It doesn't matter," Heledd assured them both. "I don't know why Urien is here but Garmon is gone."

"He's never where you expect him," Aled laughed.

As soon as all the carts were within the gates, all of the warriors' wives followed the hunters to the hall. Aled ushered Heledd and his family after them and urged her to stay among them. Aled spoke briefly to his *pennaeth* and Heledd saw Huw Bro-Dawel was in a better mood to celebrate after their conversation, inviting everyone in the *gaer* to eat and drink in his house. He called one of the women from the hunting band to follow him to his room on the other side of the house.

Llinos Cenfyn stalked Heledd in the hall and cornered her. "I see my brother has rejected you for another. At least that one is content with one man. I wonder you can be so free with your whoring while Huw is away. Even Garmon has bedded you. Your uncle has sent his commander to give evidence. My sons have been injured and I have no doubt their injuries are your doing," Llinos said, raising her hand to strike.

"Whether that is true," Garmon warned, "it is not for you to judge nor avenge."

"Let me go, Garmon," Llinos sneered, tugging her wrist free. "My brother will hear of this – all of this." She clasped Mared's arm and pulled the *pennaeth's* daughter away with her.

"Are you all right?" Heledd asked, rushing forward. "Where did you go? I was so worried when you left without—." She pressed her lips together when she saw the line of his jaw. "What is wrong now? What have I done now?"

"Why aren't you in the house?"

"I'm not a prisoner," Heledd replied, lifting her chin. "Why?" For a moment, she dropped her gaze to the stone flags, letting a slow frown take over her expression. She could still feel his arms encircling her on the morning after Medi was born. She could still feel the exquisite excitement that was almost terror as he lowered his head to kiss her, his gray eyes studying her so intently. Heledd wondered what he had expected from her, what he had wanted her to do she failed to understand. She recognized the dark rage still in his eyes.

"Heledd?" She lifted her eyes, surprised he had moved so close to her. He stroked her cheek with the back of his finger. "What is wrong?" She shook her head. A wall of people had closed around them, shielding them in the crowded room. The women and their warrior-hunter-farmer husbands had created a wall of their bodies and a barrier with their voices so Garmon spoke to her without being overheard. He let his hand fall away from her slowly. "What troubles you?"

"I'm frightened."

"Of?" he asked, his body stiffening.

"I have been so foolish," she answered, fighting back tears.

"In what way?"

His tone was gruff and she felt she could not answer truthfully. She shook her head, lifting her chin slightly.

"Garmon." Huw Bro-Dawel bellowed. "Where are you, *diawl*?" The wall of bodies parted. "Come here. Bring that girl with you."

Garmon took her hand and led her toward the *pennaeth's* table. All eyes in the room turned to watch the pair approach Huw. Llinos Cenfyn had already taken a place beside her brother at the table. Next to her, Aeron and Wyn stood ready to take their seats near their uncle. Heledd, despite her proud bearing, held back and she felt the persistent draw of Garmon's hand as he moved through the crowd. Although she prayed the weight of bodies would break his grip and she could escape, she knew he would not let her get away from him. Whatever was to come, she had no choice but to face her accusers but that gave her no comfort. She raised her chin further and straightened her back, searching beyond them for Urien Macsen but couldn't see him in the crowd.

Heledd gripped Garmon's hand like a vice and he turned his head once to look at her. His expression had returned to the stony glare she had seen earlier. The concern he had shown was buried once again. Once they had broken through the mob,

Heledd could see that, behind Huw Bro-Dawel's back, his nephews were mocking his stepson. Such ignorance drove Garmon *llysfab* Huw to bury concern and banish compassion from his outward appearance. She was not as sure of the effect of *her* behavior on him. She wondered if it was jealousy or anger that made him so difficult to understand. If he was angry with her, he only had himself to blame. *If he had been honest with me from the beginning...*

"Sit down, *merch*," Huw told her. He leaned close to her and whispered, "You are still a maiden, I presume." Heledd met his brown eyes with a gasp. "I thought as much. I don't know which one of you is the most stubborn."

"You are not without blame," she replied, grasping the cup before her and thrusting it out to be filled by the steward.

"Ah, at last, some spirit," Huw laughed. "I will enjoy this after all. I had feared Garmon had found a chick where a hawk is needed."

"I cannot imagine he wouldn't have brought you a full account of the worst aspects of my character," Heledd answered, throwing the heavy shawl off her shoulders and shaking her mane of dark auburn hair.

"How did you get that?" Huw asked, lifting her hair off her neck.

"I'm sure you will hear the story, soon enough."

"I know one man who could not have done this," Huw said, looking at Garmon. "I know another who would take pleasure in it."

"Then you know and we do not need to discuss it further." Huw nodded and clasped her hand.

"I think we will understand one another well enough, Heledd Bannawg."

"It is a pity you did not give me an opportunity to understand you earlier."

"You are not so much a hawk as an owl," Huw laughed. "I will watch my step with you from this moment. Now, what have you decided, *merch*?"

"Regarding?"

"Regarding this man," he queried, nodding his head toward Garmon.

"That is between Garmon and me," Heledd replied, draining the cup of mead and holding it up to the steward again.

"Just so," Huw said. "Put him out of his misery soon, Heledd, or he'll have to be put down." He patted her hand and turned away when his sister demanded his attention.

"Good health, Heledd," Garmon said, touching the lip of his flagon to her cup.

"Good health to you, Garmon."

"If you decide to drink your fill tonight, I will have to do the same," he told her with a slight smile. *A crack in the granite.* Heledd smiled to herself.

"Too drunk, very drunk or drunk enough, Garmon *llysfab* Huw *mab annwyl* Creiddwen Owein?"

"You have been studying," he commented, setting his flagon on the table.

"I may lack useful skills, as Ceinwen has rightly said, but I am not without some native intelligence. I learn what is necessary."

"Have you learned enough?"

"I have," she replied, pushing her plate toward him and pointing the cut of meat she wanted to begin her meal.

"And?" he asked, cutting into the joint where she directed. Heledd raised her finger to her lips, turning her attention to the meat on her plate. "You won't tell me?" Garmon persisted.

Before she answered, Huw snarled at his sister, "These events are best discussed in private. I will hear all you have to say tomorrow. Tonight, we can feast in celebration of a good harvest and excellent hunting. And," he finished, clasping Heledd's hand and holding it up for the crowd to witness, "the joining of two great houses."

# eighteen

The *neuadd* filled with gasps of dismay from some and exclamations of joy from others. She also saw puzzlement in the eyes of many. When she looked at Garmon from the corner of her eye, she read in his face what she had come to expect – silence. Huw released her hand and called the stewards to fill all the flagons and cups of his family and guests.

"To the memory of the woman who bore my only son," he said and drank from his own flagon until it was drained. Heledd lowered her eyes for a moment, feeling the enormity of his grief. She also felt the enormity of the privilege entrusted to her of knowing the truth. She did not dare lift her eyes to look at Garmon, whom she knew would also feel grief for the loss of the same woman. Their shared loss was only part of the strength of the bond between them; their determination to protect Creiddwen Owein's second son was another. But, Heledd believed there was a stronger bond than either of these – their love and respect for one another.

Llinos Cenfyn pursed her lips with satisfaction, assuming her brother spoke of Mared and Meini's mother, Rhydderch's mother. Heledd glanced at her, narrowing her eyes at the woman's assumption her brother meant to injure Garmon with this tribute. Heledd glared at her, then turned toward Garmon and slid her hand into his. Although he did not welcome the gesture, he did not withdraw from the contact as before.

"Blessed God," Heledd exclaimed under her breath, leaping to her feet.

"Where are you going?" Garmon asked, standing with her.

She did not need to see Urien Macsen to know he was

present, coming toward her. Meini saw him, lifted her eyes to welcome him and as quickly looked away when her father studied her.

"Come with me," Heledd murmured. Garmon stared after her fleeing figure for a moment then turned a puzzled frown on Huw Bro-Dawel. He met the stare of his elder foster brother and the *pennaeth* made a single, abrupt gesture.

Garmon followed Heledd from the dining hall. By the time he reached the *buarth*, he could see Heledd running toward his house, her hair streaming behind her, shining like red gold in the moonlight.

Heledd slipped through the door, pressing against the wall. Three pairs of black eyes followed her through the dim room, their owners stretched to their haunches and were alert as soon as their master burst through the door in her wake.

Heledd heard his distinctive footstep outside the bedroom. Bleddyn trotted into the room but his master and the two other staghounds stayed at the doorway.

"Why have you left the *neuadd*?"

"I didn't want to be there," Heledd answered, staring around her at the chaos she had made of his room and his life. "You need sleep," Heledd said. "If you need anything, I will be in the next room." Garmon glanced at her, an uncertain frown in his eyes. "I am used to this," she said. "You are not."

"Used to what?"

"I will sleep by the hearth." She collected the *carthen* from the floor but he followed her from the room. She spread several *carthen* on top of each other on the floor in front of the hearthstone. From the pile of logs, she chose two and laid them on the embers. "I hope that's enough."

"Enough for what? What are you doing?" Garmon asked, his voice low.

"Going to bed," Heledd answered, unlacing her long tunic and unfastening the toggles of her frock. She folded the garments on the table and bathed her face and arms, keeping her back to him. When she crossed the floor to stand beside him, Garmon turned his head slowly away from studying the fire, raising his eyes to look into her face. Heledd lifted her hand to touch his cheek but he clasped her wrist. "I have been studying, as you observed," she said, letting her arm relax so he released her. Heledd turned away and sat on the *carthen*, wrapping one around her shoulders. "I still have questions. Will you answer them?"

"If I can," Garmon replied, so visibly relieved Heledd almost laughed. *I do frighten him.* Heledd turned her face to the warmth of the fire and thought for a moment, sighing heavily to relax her body, deciding where to begin.

"Tell me about your mother."

"What do you want to know? What do you know already?"

"I know she came here when you were a boy, Huw fell in love with her and made her his wife. I have heard she was a whore."

"She was," he said, leaning back in the armed chair and stretching his legs out on the hearthstone. "I do not know who my father was, is, of among men she could name and others she could not."

"Where did she live before coming here?"

"In the north," he answered. "Dolwyddlan."

"So you did not lie to me," Heledd said, dropping her chin to her knees.

"No." Garmon glanced at her for a moment then returned his gaze to the safety of the flames. "My mother was the daughter of a good man. My grandfather might have raised me if she had stayed there."

"Why did she leave her father?"

"The man who was her first lover forced her to go rather than accept his responsibility to her. He paid my grandfather compensation."

"Why did he do that?"

"He didn't want to marry her, she was only the daughter of a cleric in a religious house. My grandmother was dead and my grandfather was old. They had nothing of value and had no claim on this man – my mother chose not to accuse him. To live, she sold herself to other men. One of them was my father."

"How did she come to Bro-Dawel?"

"We had traveled from the north for a long time. She was tired and the *pennaeth* here had a good name. She offered herself to him."

"And he knew how she had been living?"

"He knew. Huw had divorced his wife only a few months after Meini was born. He applied for my mother's pardon. She was absolved of guilt so he could take her as his lawful wife. My grandfather was already dead so Huw paid her bride-price to me."

"Was she very beautiful?" Heledd asked, patting Bleddyn's head when he came to sit with her. The other dogs remained in their corner, keeping their ears pricked.

"Huw thought so," he said with a smile.

"He loved her very much," Heledd said, looking up at Garmon. "She must have been beautiful."

"He loved her honesty." Garmon set another log on the fire and poured ale into a flagon. "And he knew she loved him."

Heledd smiled to herself. "That is always very important." Garmon glanced at her for a moment then took a long drink from the flagon. "She had another son." He nodded, keeping his eyes fixed on the fire. "Carwyn." Garmon turned his eyes on her, searching her face. "He looks like you. And his father. I saw the likeness only a few nights ago, when he was here. I embarrassed him and he reminded me of you. From then on, I saw how much he resembled you, and Huw, in everything he said and did. I was surprised so few others have seen."

"They don't know to look," he replied, taking a deep breath, holding the flagon in both hands against his chest. "Carwyn doesn't know either."

"I thought as much. He's very happy as he is."

"Huw will tell him when the time comes."

"When will Huw stop punishing Meini?"

"Is there anything you don't know?" Garmon laughed.

"Very little." Heledd stifled a yawn. She closed her eyes for a moment then gave in to the fatigue of sleepless nights, laying her head on her arms and stretching out beneath the *carthen*. "I would like to have eight children."

"Why eight?" he asked.

"One for each of my brothers and sisters. One for me. And one for my husband. That's five boys and three girls," she yawned. "One for Gerwyn to be the first, then Arianwedd, Ieuan, Tomas, Meddwen and Marlais. After that, another boy. And then a girl."

"Will your husband want so many children?" he asked.

"If he wants me, those are my terms, among others."

"What others?"

"Bleddyn?" Heledd called softly, patting the *carthen* beside her. The staghound trotted around her, wagging its tail. Heledd wrapped her arm around the dog before she took a slow, deep breath and closed her eyes, smiling to herself before she fell asleep when Bleddyn growled as Garmon moved toward her.


The *buarth* was bright with laughter and, although the day was well advanced, the men who had been hunting were still groggy from their triumphant return. Bleddyn shot across the open space between the stables and Huw's house, his tufted tail straight out from his back like a spear. When he returned to Heledd's side, he sat for a moment then thrust his head under her hand and lifted it. "I know you're there," she whispered, "and I'm glad of it. You may be my only friend." Although Meini was overjoyed Urien had come, Heledd regretted. "If I had insisted he be chased away," she told the staghound, "this would not have happened. I can understand why Garmon is angry with me for being so foolish about Urien, but why did Urien threaten to kill him?"

Once Garmon had left his house, Heledd had tried to follow but he had ridden away before she got to the stables. Putting the bridle onto Angel had proved to be a skill she could not learn quick enough to ride after him. She had stood helplessly at the stable door as Garmon urged *Diawl* to a gallop at the gates and watched him disappear over the crest of the hill toward

Tredeml. "He isn't even wearing a coat," she lamented to Bleddyn. "Ach, I am so stupid. I should have cracked that granite wall of his last night, when I had the chance." She took a step into the sunlight of the paddock. "I'm no good at this terrible game. I don't understand love at all. How did my mother manage it?" Heledd glanced down at the young hound's black eyes. "I would have, you know, if he hadn't held me away from him. All I wanted to do was touch him, to let him know I loved him. He wouldn't let me do even that. Just to touch his cheek. How could that hurt him?"

Heledd looked over her shoulder at the colt in its stall. When she turned her eyes again toward the hills, there was no sign of Garmon and her heart gave a thud in the cavity of her chest with such force she cried out in pain. The staghound barked and nudged her hand with its head. "How shall we keep ourselves out of trouble today, Bleddyn?" she asked, turning her eyes in the direction of the barracks. As she drew nearer, Geraint met her, on his way to the longhouse.

"What are you doing here, Heledd Bannawg? Shouldn't you be in Garmon's house or with Meini and your friend from Bannawg?" he asked, a puzzled frown on his face.

"Meini doesn't need my help."

"She might," he said, opening the door of the barracks and announcing her presence before he entered. "Your friend is strong, willful. Meini is neither."

"Meini knows what she is doing."

"Why have you come here?" he murmured as Heledd stepped into the long, wide room. "This is not the best place for a girl, even at this time of day. Garmon will not be happy."

"When is he ever? I intend to keep out of trouble."

"How? I do not think that is the wisest idea you have had today." When she did not answer, Geraint said, "What was your purpose, Heledd? Garmon does not visit any of these women. You have no reason to be jealous."

"I am not jealous or even curious, Geraint. It is courtesy. These women, no less than I, depend on one another and Garmon's mother was one of them. How can I not show them the same respect I would show her, if she was alive?"


Garmon rode into the *caer* hours after darkness had fallen, riding at a pace reflecting his weariness. Heledd watched him from the door of the longhouse, warned of his arrival when the staghounds leapt to their feet and pranced to the door. Bleddyn stayed behind with her while the others met their master in the paddock. When Garmon crossed the length of the *buarth* toward his house, Heledd left the door open but took her seat at the table to wait for him. She heard his voice when he was not far from the gate but did not hear the voice of the person to whom he spoke. She had ceased to wonder who was on duty to confine her. When he closed the door, she was pouring a flagon of ale for him.

"You need not wait for me," he said, accepting the flagon. He drank half of the contents before he turned away to wash his hands and face in the basin by the passageway. "Have you eaten?"

"Only a little."

"Is Meini here?"

"No, she is in the house, with Urien Macsen."

Garmon glanced in the direction of the door and, when he returned his gaze to her, he slumped into the armed chair and stretched his legs toward the hearth.

"Where did you go?" Heledd asked, picking at the crumbling edge of the cheese.

"To the town," he replied and drained the flagon. "Eat," he commanded. "I will have a meal later."

"Huw's principal clerk was here earlier this evening." When Garmon turned his head toward her, she said, "Llinos Cenfyn has made a complaint against me. Tomorrow, I will have an opportunity to hear the accusations and to present my defense."

"What are her complaints? Of what are you accused?"

Heledd was surprised by his tone. She had thought he would be angry. "I don't know."

"How are we to prepare a defense if we don't know the

charges?" he asked. "I know how her mind works. There will be no surprises, Heledd."

She was surprised he seemed unconcerned. *He doesn't care. He can be rid of me after this.* "I'm glad you're confident."

"You do not believe Huw will find you guilty, do you?" he asked, a slight smile turning the corner of his mouth.

"I don't know what to expect. He has no reason to believe me more than his own flesh and blood."

"He has reason enough," Garmon assured her. "And I will be there."

"I don't want that. I don't want you to hear what they say."

"I know what they will say," he answered. "She will say you seduced her sons. Her sons will claim they were victims of your sorcery. All of them will claim Aeron and Wyn were attacked in the *pennaeth's* house – by me – and will demand you are flogged and I am jailed."

"Flogged! I have seen a woman flogged," she cried, covering her head with her arms.

"Jail is no pleasant thing, either," he laughed, moving to sit opposite her at the table. "Huw will never allow you to be hurt, I swear to you, Heledd."

"How can you be sure? You don't know what they will say, who they will call as witnesses."

"You have witnesses."

"Who? Who will speak for me against the *pennaeth's* sister?"

"More voices than you know. I will, I was there, remember?"

"Excellent. My co-accused is my only witness."

As soon as breakfast had been served in the longhouse, Meini helped Heledd to dress in her ochre linen frock, sable-brown coat and dressed her hair so the scratch on her neck was not visible but could be shown if the *pennaeth* asked. Garmon had gone to tell his foster brother the news Heledd was required to defend herself against the accusations of the *pennaeth's* sister.

"Garmon will not let you down, Heledd. He will act as your

attorney and you must trust him," Meini told her, as she tied the lacings of the brown coat.

"I do. I will," Heledd said. "I feel sick."

"It will be worse before it gets better," Meini said. "Urien is here as well. He will be a witness for you, against the lies Llinos has told about you."

Garmon returned to the house, dressed in his finest, most somber gray woolen tunic and leggings. His hair was tied back with a black strip and his boots were polished. "You'll do," he said to her, with only a slight flexing of the straight line of his mouth.

"Whatever you do," Meini said, "don't let them make you say anything foolish. My father is a tyrant in the *llys*, as judge and jury most often. Keep your head."

Heledd nodded as she followed Garmon toward the *llys*. Bleddyn trotted beside her. For several hours the previous night, Garmon had explained all the procedures likely in the *pennaeth's llys*. Heledd was only a little more confident his knowledge of the law could never be exceeded by his aunt's cunning. Garmon waited at the gate and they walked together through the *buarth*, acknowledging greetings from soldiers and tradesmen as they went. In the courtyard, they were met by the principal clerk.

"The plaintiffs are already here, Garmon, if you want to wait in the dining hall. Otherwise, you can wait in the anteroom with them."

Though the courtyard was sheltered, an east wind whipped down on them from the thatch and they walked together into the dining hall, sitting for a short time, in silence, on a bench along the north wall. Heledd longed for activity to occupy her trembling hands and had to restrain her impulse to run to the kitchen. When they were called to the *llys*, the plaintiffs were already standing before Huw Bro-Dawel. Garmon waited for Heledd to bow her head in greeting to the *pennaeth* before he took his place beside her, nearest the Cenfyn trio.

"Your attorney has explained to you the way this will be done, I presume."

"Yes, *pennaeth*," she murmured.

"Just as well she is contrite now," Llinos whispered to her sons.

"You will be silent in my *llys*, sister, until I give you permission to speak," Huw growled at Llinos. "Heledd Bannawg, you have the right to hear the charges brought against you. These will be read before all present," he said, indicating the clerks, stewards, tradesmen and soldiers who stood around the walls. "Is there anyone present you may wish to call as witness in your defense?"

Heledd looked at the faces of the men who would hear the case against her and whispered to Garmon.

"If it please you, *pennaeth*, the defendant wishes to exclude the following men as witnesses for the defense. Elwyn Chief Steward, Carwyn, Geraint, Rhodri, Nisien, Dafydd and Aled. Also, Silien the Miller and Martyn the Shoemaker."

"I object, *pennaeth*, there will be few to hear the case for the plaintiffs or the charges against this wanton," Llinos complained.

"I will hear and you will refrain from prejudicial statements or I will throw you and your accusations out of my *llys*. The witnesses so named are excused to be called at an appropriate time."

"I reserve the right to call these witnesses for the plaintiffs," Llinos Cenfyn said and her brother assented to her request. Aled's command all looked at Garmon before leaving the room.

"The defendant will hear the charges," the principal clerk announced. Garmon placed his hand under Heledd's elbow and assisted her to step forward with him to face the *pennaeth*.

"Heledd *merch* Ieuan Bannawg, you are charged with two counts of entrapment, two counts of wanton solicitation, two counts of false imprisonment, as well as two counts of assault. How do you plead?"

"The defendant, while not wishing to give credence to any of these accusations, respects the authority of this *llys* and enters a plea of not guilty on all of these fallacious charges," Garmon replied on her behalf.

"Let the record show the defendant has entered a plea of not guilty on all charges. And," Huw continued, "a little less of the legal finery would be appreciated by all present, Garmon."

Llinos smiled broadly at her brother's snipe at his stepson but Heledd's attorney was not perturbed.

"If it please the *llys*, I, on behalf of the defendant's husband, also enter a counter charge of assault with intent to commit rape against Aeron Cenfyn and Wyn Cenfyn."

"I object." Llinos exclaimed, stepping forward.

"I can well understand your objection, *boneddiges*. I regret, Garmon, that will not be allowed at this time, as the husband in question may be seen to be biased with regard to the charge brought by his wife."

"I do not see the case for bias, *pennaeth*."

"I do. That charge will be heard in a separate *llys* under another adjudicator. *Boneddiges* Llinos, call your first witness."

"You didn't tell me you were going to do that," Heledd whispered.

"It was necessary," Garmon murmured without taking his eyes from his stepfather's face.

"Why?"

"Now they know the *pennaeth* cannot be seen to be prejudiced against their case. It is also established your husband is in the *llys*, therefore, they will do their best to present a compelling case but without excess – they do not want to offend him unduly."

"How can the *pennaeth* judge fairly?"

"He is *pennaeth*. Except in cases of murder or offenses against the king, no one else has a right to judge in matters concerning his family."

Wyn *mab* Cenfyn had stepped forward and Heledd steeled herself to hear his lies, spoken before the people of Bro-Dawel. Though only in extraordinary circumstances would a woman's testimony be heard, the *beudy* girls, seamstresses, mill girls and barracks women were present. Wyn told a story Heledd only partially recognized. How they gained access to her room and everything he told the court were fabrications of their wicked imaginations. When the opportunity came, Garmon declined to ask the witness any questions.

Huw shrugged and Aeron *mab* Cenfyn stepped before the *pennaeth*. Heledd held her hands steady at her sides as Aeron described his version of the events, beginning with her words to him on the second evening of their stay in Bro-Dawel. "I was invited by the defendant to discover ways in which I could best please her," he said. Heledd pressed her lips together but Garmon expressed nothing. "On the following morning, she invited me to do so."

"To do what?" Huw asked.

"To please her." After writing something on the parchment by his hand, Huw nodded and Aeron continued. "However, when two of the soldiers set to watch her appeared, she, the defendant, changed her mind. One of the soldiers threatened me with violence."

"What is your understanding of 'the soldiers set to watch' the defendant?"

"I was given to understand the defendant's husband had selected a number of his soldiers to guard her."

"By 'guard', what do you believe is meant?"

"Objection," Garmon said. "The interpretation of the meaning of a word is irrelevant to this case. The husband's intention with regard to his wife is not on trial here."

"I believe there is cause to examine the plaintiff's interpretation of the word, Garmon. You may answer," Huw told Aeron.

"As the defendant could not possibly be in danger within the stronghold of such a renowned warrior, he may have intended to protect his property from poachers."

"In other words, you believe they were set to ensure her status was not compromised by interference from another man?"

"Yes."

Huw motioned for Aeron to continue his statement, while he wrote.

"On the night Dafydd Llanarth's daughter was born, my

brother and I were celebrating the birth with members of the *pennaeth's* household. As we passed the defendant's room on the way to our own, we were talking quietly so as not to disturb anyone in that part of the house. When we were near the door of Heledd *merch*—."

"The defendant," Huw reminded him.

"When we were near the defendant's room, the door opened and the defendant invited me and my brother to enter."

Huw made a note and motioned Aeron to continue.

"We were about to decline the invitation, when Hel—, the defendant, made a provocative gesture."

"What gesture?" Huw asked, looking directly into his nephew's eyes.

"I would rather not say, *pennaeth*, as I do not want to offend her husband."

"You accuse this girl of serious offences but you decline to offend her husband in your cause against her?" Huw demanded. "What do you claim the defendant *did* to provoke you?"

"She toyed with the fastening of her gown and let her hand rest on her throat, and her breast."

"I—," Heledd gasped and Garmon cautioned her not to react.

"You will have your opportunity to speak, *merch*," Huw said. "And then?"

"And then she caught my wrist and pulled me through the door."

"You could not resist?"

"I was provoked, *pennaeth*," he said, turning a brief smile on the men in the *llys*.

"*Pennaeth*," Garmon said, "I request the record show the plaintiff, Aeron *mab* Cenfyn, has shown disrespect to this *llys*, and to my client, by his expression."

"Let the record show this witness sought to influence the *llys* by exhibiting a prejudicial expression during testimony. These are serious allegations, Aeron Cenfyn, and may have dire consequences for this girl. You will desist from this behavior or I will have your testimony declared unsafe."

"Yes, *pennaeth*. The defendant encouraged me and my brother to enter her room by an unmistakable physical action."

"Were you aware at the time the defendant was – is – the wife of another man?"

"So, apparently, my mother had been informed, but I was provoked by this incident. And, I had been told by a member of the husband's household the defendant was only a bondservant."

"And you still entered her room, though you were aware – as far as you knew at the time – she was the property of this man, who has since been shown to be her husband?"

"Uncle—." Huw turned a cold stare on his nephew. "I entered only because I did not wish to offend the defendant or leave her in that state to be molested by another, less sympathetic person. She appeared to be in an agitated condition."

"What was your intention?"

"Only to ensure she was not harmed."

"What happened after you and Wyn Cenfyn entered the room?"

"She – the defendant – bolted the door and demanded we – my brother and I – have intercourse with her."

"Did you?"

"Yes."

"What happened after that?"

"While we were sleeping with her, someone broke into the room and assaulted us."

"You were asleep, both of you, in the defendant's bed?"

"Yes. The attack was ferocious, *pennaeth*. We only recovered our senses hours later."

"Is it your contention the defendant attacked you?"

"I believe she was assisted by another, but, yes, I believe the defendant struck us."

"Do you have anything else to say in this matter?" When Aeron shook his head, Huw dismissed him and gazed at his sister. "Do you have any other witnesses?"

"Yes, *pennaeth*, the plaintiffs call Mared *gwraig* Rheinallt *merch*

Huw to give testimony."

"That does not surprise me," he replied, gesturing for one of the clerks to bring his daughter to the *llys*. When Mared stood before him, he inquired, "You know your testimony in this case is heard in sufferance."

"Yes, *pennaeth*."

"And you know every word you say will be subject to scrutiny?"

"Yes, *pennaeth*."

"What do you have to say in this matter?"

"If it please you, *pennaeth*, I have asked this witness to testify as to the character of the defendant. I have detailed the questions to be asked," Llinos said.

"That is not usual, however, I will allow it in the case of this witness. What have you to say, Mared *gwraig* Rheinallt?"

"I will answer truthfully, according to my knowledge, *pennaeth*."

Reading from the scrolled document, Huw asked, "When did you first become acquainted with the defendant and under what circumstances?"

"At the end of summer, before the harvest," Mared said, glancing at her husband who stood among the soldiers. "My sister, Meini, and I went to Talgarth-y-Bannawg to escort the defendant to Bro-Dawel. We were not introduced to the defendant at Talgarth, nor did we make her acquaintance on the journey home. I had made enquiries about her while at Talgarth and was told a number of details."

"Can you give eyewitness to any of these details?"

"No."

"Then, they are inadmissible, as you know."

"You refuse to hear what this witness knows about the defendant?" Llinos exclaimed.

"This witness 'knows' only what she has heard. Hearsay is not admissible."

"I request you ask her the next question, *pennaeth*."

"I will, but if her answer is more hearsay, her testimony will not be allowed. Since the defendant's arrival at Bro-Dawel, have you witnessed any behavior that is inappropriate for a woman of the defendant's position?"

"In my opinion, yes. But since I was never privileged to know her position, I cannot judge whether what I witnessed was inappropriate."

"Your opinion is irrelevant to this case, Mared." Huw read through the questions on the small document in silence, giving no indication of his reaction to them. "There is nothing here that will add to the knowledge of this *llys* which is of relevance to the case at hand. However, I will allow you to make any statement you think will do so."

"Objection," Garmon said, stepping forward. "This witness should not be allowed free reign to prejudice this *llys* with her opinions."

"You will confine your remarks to knowledge, not opinion, is that clear?"

"Since I was given many details of the defendant's behavior from members of her own family, I have conducted my own investigations into her character," Mared said, facing her father with a proud bearing. "On numerous occasions, I have tested the intentions and caliber of the defendant by accusation, implication, threats and actual violence. I have taunted and insulted her, shamed her publicly, thrown aspersions on her status and character. I have accused her of behavior fit only for outlaws of society."

"Why?"

"I believed that, if she was destined to be a member of my father's household, I had a duty to ensure the defendant was fit for any rôle she might play here."

"You did not think others may have already assessed the defendant's character and judged based on their knowledge?"

"I have never been privileged to know the intentions of my family."

"To what conclusion did your investigations lead you?" Huw asked, studying his daughter with care. Heledd glanced at Rheinallt and realized he was proud of his wife. When she again looked at Mared, Heledd pressed her lips together, holding her breath.

"The defendant, Heledd *merch* Ieuan Bannawg, is no better," Mared declared, "than any of the rest of us, and no worse."

"I object," Llinos screeched.

"You cannot object to the testimony of your own witness whom you have specifically called to attest to the character of the defendant, *boneddiges*. Do you have another witness?" Huw dismissed his daughter. Mared swept past Garmon and Heledd with her head held high, received a kiss from her doting husband and left the *llys*.

"I will testify myself," Llinos declared, stepping forward.

"Did you witness the actions of the defendant on the night in question? Were you there in the room with your sons and this girl?"

"No, of course, I was not, but I did witness her shameful attempt to—."

"Come forward, *boneddiges*," Huw growled. He leaned forward over the high table and spoke only to her. When she stepped back, he said, "What is your testimony?"

"On numerous occasions, I witnessed the defendant attempting to attract the attention of my son, Aeron *mab* Cenfyn. The first was the evening which he has already described. I heard her taunt him to find ways to please her. On another occasion, she drew attention to her body while my son was discussing matters of the ordinary business of the harvest and the running of the *ystad*. Also, I saw her running from the house on the night my sons say she seduced them, half-naked, to the house of her attorney. On that same night, I witnessed Garmon *mab* Creiddwen Owein and two others whom I could not identify, carrying the bodies of my sons from the defendant's room to the dining hall."

"Come forward," Huw commanded his stepson. In a few moments, he motioned Garmon back to stand by Heledd. "This is a different matter and will be heard at a later time."

"But—."

"You did not name Garmon *llysfab* Huw in your complaint, *boneddiges*. Had you done so, he would not have been allowed to act as attorney for the defendant. I should throw the complaint against Heledd Bannawg out of my *llys*. However, that will serve only to prolong the unpleasantness for all concerned. Does the defendant have witnesses she wishes to call?" he asked Garmon.

"The list of witnesses is here, *pennaeth*," Garmon said, handing the document to the principal clerk. Huw read the list and handed it back to the clerk with instructions.

"While we wait for the defendant's first witness, I suggest the plaintiffs wait in the anteroom and the defendant and her attorney may wait in my office. The clerk will call you when we are ready to proceed."

Before Heledd said a word when the door of the *pennaeth's* office closed behind them, Garmon sank into one of the chairs in front of the desk.

"Are you in pain?" she asked, kneeling beside him and laying her hand on his arm.

Garmon closed his eyes for a moment. When they opened, he turned his gaze on her face, raising his hand and letting it drop. "Did you do that?"

"What? Did I do what?" Heledd demanded, understanding the note of dismay and accusation in his voice. *He is more than jealous. He is hurt.* Heledd sat back on her heels, bit her lower lip and dropped her chin to her chest. "I thought I could protect Rhian," she said. "And then, when I saw I couldn't, I knew I had made a terrible mistake only I could rectify." When he did not respond, she said, "Geraint understood—." She did not see what he threw across the room, but the crash against the wall behind his stepfather's desk made her reel backward, throwing her arm over her face to ward off a blow. When no blow came, she lowered her arm and looked from beneath her brow at her attorney. She opened her mouth to speak.

"You do not need to explain," he said. Heledd leaned forward, reaching out her hand but he rose from the chair and stood at the window with his back to her. "Huw will not make too much of that, but you may be asked to explain your thinking where Rhian is concerned."

"I understand," Heledd said. The clerk's interruption

brought both of them back into the *llys*. Meini entered to stand before her father. Unlike her older sister, Meini's countenance was subdued and timid.

"There are only a few questions for this witness," Huw told the *llys*. "When, after the birth of Dafydd Llanarth's daughter, you were called to attend the defendant in her attorney's house, what did you observe of her state?"

"The defendant was still weeping when I entered the house. I was delayed for several hours and she had already bathed."

"Destroyed the evidence," Llinos commented.

Her brother gestured for one of the officers of the *llys* to stand beside his sister. "Another word and you will regret speaking without permission. Go on with your testimony, Meini Gwyn."

"The defendant was frightened and anxious."

"I object," Llinos said. "The witness cannot know the state of mind of the defendant."

"Did she tell you she was frightened or anxious?"

"No, *pennaeth*. I presumed based on the account I had received from my stepbrother and of my own experience."

"Confine your testimony to your observations of her physical state, please."

"Yes, *pennaeth*," Meini murmured. "I saw her hands were bloodied and scratched. She had another scratch the length of her neck to her breast, here," Meini demonstrated, "and a bruise on her chin. I also found bruises on her arms, back, and legs."

"Could these injuries have been caused by a struggle?"

"Yes."

"Could they have been caused by the defendant making an attack on an individual?"

"Some of them, yes."

"How can you tell?" Huw asked, peering into her downcast face.

"The scratch on the defendant's neck is the same as the tear in the frock she was wearing at the time."

"You have this item to show the *llys*?"

"The frock is here," Meini said, placing the garment, folded into a parcel, on the table in front of her father.

"I will examine this later. Did the defendant tell you what happened?"

Meini lowered her eyes, biting her lips. "She said she had not 'allowed' my cousins, Aeron and Wyn, into her room. I suggested Tegwen Talog be called but the defendant told me she had not been raped."

"Anything else?"

"Nothing that is relevant, *pennaeth*."

"When she told you," Llinos asked, when her brother gave her permission to question the witness, "she had not been 'raped', did you not think, based on your knowledge of the defendant, perhaps, she meant she had sought intercourse with the plaintiffs."

"No, I did not," Meini declared. She turned on her heel and left the *llys* the moment her father granted.

"As the next witness will give testimony of concern only to me as adjudicator, I will hear this in my office. The *llys* will remain here." Huw retired to his office and the witness was taken there from another part of the house. Only Garmon, Heledd and the principal clerk knew Huw would hear the account of Tegwen Talog. Only Heledd knew what the midwife was likely to say and she waited for the *pennaeth's* return with much less anxiety than her adversaries. Garmon had not asked to know, even as her attorney.

Heledd understood where Garmon had learned to conceal his emotions when Huw Bro-Dawel opened the door of his office and took his chair once more. "I see no further need for witnesses in this case. Both parties have presented their cause in accordance with the requirements of the law. I will now consider each side and give my decision tomorrow, at this time." He called the principal clerk to him and the officer dismissed the *llys*.

Heledd turned to Garmon to ask what Huw meant but her attorney was already walking out of the *llys*. The Cenfyn family stared at her, standing alone, and their collective smirk drove the shard of abandonment deeper.

"I'll walk with you back to Garmon's house," Rheinallt said, offering his arm.

"Will you thank Mared for me," Heledd said.

"She did not do it for you, *boneddiges*," the soldier told her, "but that does not mean she is not glad she was able to help you as a member of her family. Mared knows what her father expects in his *llys*. She would have told the truth regardless of its consequences to you or anyone else."

# ΠΙΝΕΤΕΕΝ

"That won't do you any good," Heledd heard Aeron's voice from the other side of the paddock fence. He stood with his brother, both of them resting their arms on the top rail, staring at her. She knew they had not been there long enough to hear anything she might have said to the mare; she had not spoken loud enough for anyone to hear, even had they listened.

"What do you want?" Seeking comfort with Angel from the loneliness of the longhouse had not been her most brilliant idea that evening.

"The bastard has let you out at last," Aeron commented. "Or is it that he's abandoned you, this time for good?" He put his foot on the lowest rail of the fence and stepped up. The staghound straightened its legs and lowered its head. Heledd laid one hand on Bleddyn's shoulder. "Are you ill?" Aeron asked, studying her. "Or has that son of a whore done you damage?" His smile sickened her but she dropped her other hand away from her abdomen where she had held it to quell her heartache. "No damage? Then he doesn't know how to enjoy a bitch, does he? Or isn't he man enough to break you?"

Heledd lifted her chin and kept her hand on Bleddyn's shoulder. The staghound looked up at her whenever Aeron spoke. She could not see anyone she recognized in the paddock or the *buarth* beyond.

"Deal with the dog," Aeron hissed to his brother.

"You deal with the dog," Wyn replied. "It's my turn with her. You've had yours."

"There's plenty for both of us," Aeron agreed, drawing his knife as he climbed over the fence.

Bleddyn was rigid, waiting for Heledd's command. She locked her fingers in the fur of his shoulder and pulled him further back into the stables with her. Despite the dog's ferocious growling and the snap of its jaws, Aeron kept coming at her, twisting his knife in his fingers, looking for an opening.

"Don't kill my dog," Heledd begged. She gave Bleddyn the most important command she had taught him. The hound crouched and shot out of the stables, knocking Aeron out of his way and Wyn to the ground in the paddock. Aeron had lost his knife. She climbed over the stall rails and flung herself into the straw behind the colt, crawling into the corner as the young stallion screamed, rearing onto its hind legs to claw at the air in outrage. Angel joined the fracas with her own screams, kicking at the rails of her stall near Aeron's head as he searched for his knife.

"Aeron," Wyn whispered from the doorway, dusting off his clothes. "Someone's coming."

"This is just the start," Aeron hissed at her. "Down you," he shouted as if at the colt as a man ran into the paddock. "You," he called to one of the soldiers running toward him. "Get help. This colt has gone mad. He's killing her."

The soldier shouted for his comrades in the barracks. Under her breath, she calmed the colt and his mother but Aeron and Wyn had come back into the stables and were beating at the stalls and horses with whips. The colt's blood splattered over her hands and clothing as the lash cut into him. Heledd screamed at the top of her lungs for the brothers to stop but her cries fuelled their rage. The colt thrashed his hooves in the air above her head.

"He's killing her," Aeron told the soldiers, "do something. Kill the beast." One of the soldiers drew his sword and while Aeron distracted the colt, he climbed onto the rails to cut the animal's throat.

"No," Heledd cried. "Don't hurt him. Don't hurt him." She struggled to push herself up against the wall. "Don't hurt him, please," she begged, recognizing the soldier's boots. "Carwyn. Don't hurt him. It's not his fault."

Aeron grabbed the sword from Carwyn's hesitant hand and thrust at the colt. "You fool," he shouted at Carwyn. "Can't you see the animal has almost killed her? It's mad." Carwyn caught Aeron's arm and wrestled him to the floor of the stables, ripping the sword from his grasp just as Wyn came at the boy-soldier with his knife. Angel kicked her hind legs against the rails of the stall with such force one of the rails shot free at one end and hit Wyn full in the face, breaking his nose and sending him flying onto his back. Three more soldiers ran into the stables and pulled Carwyn off Aeron's chest, standing him against the post while they unarmed the elder Cenfyn.

The paddock filled with onlookers, straining to see what had happened. Carwyn was breathing heavily, nursing a cut on his shoulder, his blood dripping into the straw at his feet. Heledd pressed herself against the wall of the stables, tears streaming down her face, mixing with the colt's blood. *Someone should kill me. Someone should kill me.*

"He tried to kill me." Aeron shouted at the soldiers restraining him. "Arrest him. He wanted to kill me for helping her." The soldiers looked at Carwyn, searching his face. The boy-soldier's cheeks were pale but he met their gaze with no sign of guilt.

"What have you done?" Huw demanded, standing in the doorway, staring at his son, his hand already reaching for his knife.

Heledd threw herself at the rails of the stall, ducking when the colt screamed and reared again. "Don't touch him." She scrambled over the rails, dropping to the floor near Carwyn.

"*Pennaeth*," Aeron interrupted, "I caught this boy trying to kill your wife. You can see he's beaten her. When I intervened to help her, he tried to kill me."

"Liar." Heledd gasped. "Liar."

"This boy was intent on rape," Aeron said. "Your wife resisted."

Huw took one step forward, drawing his knife. Carwyn stood straight, away from the support of the post. Heledd reached out but the soldiers prevented her from interfering.

"It's my fault. It's all my fault," she pleaded. "Don't touch him." When Huw ignored her, his eyes full of rage and pain as he approached, ready to kill his only son, Heledd tore herself free and threw her arms around Carwyn as Huw thrust with his knife.

"*Pennaeth*," Carwyn murmured, "you're crying." His legs buckled suddenly and he fell with Heledd into the straw at Huw Bro-Dawel's feet.

"This is my fault. Blessed God. This is my fault." Heledd cried, dragging her arms free and holding Carwyn's head in her lap, soothing his brow. Huw's bloodied knife dangled from his hand and fell to the floor.

"Get the physician," he ordered. "Quick." He knelt on one knee by Heledd, searching Carwyn's body for the wound he had inflicted.

"It wasn't Carwyn," she told him, staring into his stricken face. "You know he would never do such a thing. You know he wouldn't hurt anyone. You know. You know," she sobbed. Aled ran into the stables and fell on his knees beside Huw, throwing his arm around his foster father as they both stared at Carwyn's pale face, the delicate veins in his eyelids gradually fading. Heledd bent her head over the boy. "I'm sorry," she whispered, kissing his cheek.

"Perhaps, this was a lovers' quarrel," Aeron said aloud.

"I've had enough of your poison," Nisien growled and slammed his elbow into Aeron's jaw. Aeron dropped to the ground, holding his hands over his mouth as blood spurt from between his teeth.

Meini flung herself beside Heledd, searching Carwyn's body for his wounds. "How could you do this?" she asked, looking up at her father's bloodless, soulless face, striking out at him with her fists. Aled held up his arm to defend his foster father from her rage.

"Meini," Heledd said, grasping her hand, "help your brother." She relinquished her place to Carwyn's half-sister and pushed herself to her feet. "Arrest those men," she told Nisien. "Both of them."

"Yes, *boneddiges*," he said, pulling Aeron to his feet and gesturing for the other soldier to do the same with Wyn. The brothers protested, screaming in pain as they were dragged from the stables toward the stockade. "Aled, take Huw back to the house. Send some men to carry Carwyn wherever Meini tells them and … and bring his parents."

While she waited for her orders to be obeyed, she went to the colt's stall. The young animal was terrified, his eyes rolled back. Blood oozed from the open cuts on his neck and shoulders. As soon as Heledd moved toward him, he screamed and reared. She backed away and turned her attention to Angel. The mare was still agitated but had calmed enough for Heledd to enter the stall and soothe her. She wrapped her arms around the mare's neck and sobbed aloud as Rhodri, Daf and Geraint lifted Carwyn in their arms and took him to the *pennaeth's* house. Blinded by tears, she bathed the mare's cuts, talking as quietly as she could to the two horses. When the colt was as calm as its dam, she bathed the cuts she could reach from outside the stall. When she left the stables, she went to the house and sat apart from the others of the Aled's elite command, outside the *pennaeth's* rooms, staring at the opposite wall where it rose from the flagstones.

Heledd gasped when she heard horses thunder into the *buarth* and covered her face with her bloody hands as Bleddyn galloped through the *neuadd* and down the passageway in search of her.

"I hope you're satisfied now," she heard Llinos screech. "Your whore has caused more trouble in an hour than most women cause in a lifetime. My sons need a physician. My brother has killed one of your warriors, you bastard. All because of her."

"Which one? Which warrior?" Garmon demanded. "Where is she?" His uneven gait thundered through the courtyard.

"What about my sons?" Llinos demanded, following him. "They are worth more than all of your soldiers."

Aled left Huw's room and ran to the courtyard. "Garmon, it's Carwyn. He's—"

"Where's Heledd?"

"She ... as God is my witness, Garmon—."

"Where is she?"

"She caused this," Aled said. "She admits it was her fault."

Bleddyn skidded to a stop at Heledd's knees, danced in front of her and ran back to his master. The hound barked, trotted back and forth from the courtyard to the *neuadd*, until she heard Garmon's step on the flagstones of the passageway. The warriors sitting near her got to their feet but she couldn't face him, burying her face in her lap with a sob. She could feel his eyes burning into her, she felt his rage crushing down on her.

"Garmon," Rhodri began, "it's not what you think." Garmon cursed as he shook off Rhodri's restraining hand. She waited for the blow that would kill her for what she had done, his sharp, shallow gasp prepared her for the sorrow of being killed by someone she loved more than her own self.

"Where are you hurt?" he demanded, crouching in front of her, lifting her head to examine her face. "You're bleeding. Where is the wound?"

"It's not me. It's not my blood," she said under her breath, waiting for him to strike. "It's my fault. I'm sorry. I did it. It's my fault."

"What did you do?"

"I wanted to go with you. I wanted to explain ..." Heledd met his granite-hard eyes. "They followed me and I couldn't get away. I sent Bleddyn to bring you but it was too late. I don't care what happens to me. I deserve to die," she said, throwing her arms over her head. "You should never have trusted me. It's my fault Carwyn ... is hurt. Huw. Blessed God, how can I ever repay this?"

Garmon straightened his legs, pulling her to her feet with him. Though she resisted, dragging herself down to the floor, Garmon held her against him, shielding her from the stares of the men and women in the *neuadd* who had gathered to witness the drama.

"Heledd," Garmon said, "lift your head. It's not your fault. I'm to blame," he whispered against her temple. "I failed you. I didn't protect you."

"Garmon." Geraint stepped close to them. "Garmon, she's bleeding." Rhodri and Daf pulled her out of Garmon's arms.

"It's not my blood," Heledd murmured. "It's the colt. Aeron …" Garmon's stony expression faded as she held out her hand to him. When she opened her eyes again, she stared into the blackened thatch straight above her but could only see a blur of darkness there. The fired cracked but it gave off no warm glow or light. *This must be death.* She heard a voice from a distance but could not distinguish any words or tell who spoke. *Mam? Are you here?*

"Forgive me."

*What is there to forgive? Dead is pain too.* She took a sharp breath. "*Uffern.* This is Annwn," she murmured, as a wave of nausea washed over her. She felt a soft, shallow breath near her cheek. *Garmon.* As soon as she became aware of him, his footsteps retreated from her and the door thrown open to someone else who rushed toward the bed.

"Heledd, it's Meini."

"Carwyn?" she asked, reaching out to clasp Meini's hand.

"He's at the cloister. My father had him taken there as soon as he awakened."

"He's alive?"

"Yes," Meini replied. "You are fine now. The wound wasn't deep. There will be some pain for a little while but now you're awake I can give you something that will help you."

"Where? Everything hurts," Heledd complained. "How long?"

"Since yesterday evening. It's midday now. You were only grazed but you lost blood. No one realized you were hurt until Geraint saw the fresh blood on the flagstones. Why didn't you tell someone?"

"I didn't know. I didn't feel anything. Carwyn."

"He's much stronger than you think."

"How is your father?"

"Ach, him." Meini scoffed. "He'll survive. He always does."

"Meini, you didn't see what happened," Heledd said,

clasping Meini's arm. "It may look like he meant to kill Carwyn, but he didn't, he didn't intend that."

"He has killed his children all his life. I will never forgive him for this."

"He didn't strike Carwyn. He couldn't."

"Heledd," Meini replied, getting to her feet, "my father has already made it plain, after yesterday, neither I nor my sister are welcome in his house. He blames us for what happened to you, but especially to Carwyn. Mared does not know he is our half-brother or he is Garmon's half-brother. Her only crime is lack of knowledge. I have committed no crime against my father or his son. Such a man does not deserve your sympathy. Your sympathy belongs elsewhere."

Though Heledd understood to whom Meini referred, she did not respond to the comment. "Your father blames himself," Heledd said. "He blames his own bloodline for everything. He cannot blame your mother for Aeron and Wyn, or his own sister. He cannot blame Creiddwen Owein for Carwyn. I think he believes the fault lives in his blood. That is why he turned to Carwyn first. He was looking for Creiddwen in him."

"You are fanciful," Meini laughed. "Then why did he strike?"

"He struck me, remember?"

"That blow was meant for Carwyn."

"I don't believe that, Meini. I think he saw what he hoped and was turning to strike Aeron. I got in the way. Carwyn's injury was my fault."

"That is gracious of you. Carwyn's only injury was inflicted by Wyn. My father failed."

"Meini, think. Is your father a warrior? A great hunter? A powerful and respected *pennaeth*? Hasn't he, without fail, protected, fed and clothed you and Mared all of your lives? Hasn't he loved and provided for Garmon and Carwyn? Didn't he love Creiddwen? How can a man like that *not* kill where he knows he must?"

"I don't know."

"He found what he sought in Carwyn's eyes. I know he must

have but I didn't see it soon enough. He didn't reckon on my interference. And that's why I have this," Heledd said, lifting her bandaged arm. "Look where it is, how slight, Meini." She peeled the bandage from the healing wound. "He was turning away from his son, not trying to murder him."

"It's possible."

"This is a scratch. Do you think I would be alive if he had meant to kill anyone?"

Meini sat down again and studied her hands. "Probably not," she admitted. "My father has never been half-hearted about killing, or anything else in his life."

Heledd sighed heavily. "That's what I thought. I'm glad he didn't want to kill me."

"Do you want to see Garmon now? He's been here every moment."

"I know," Heledd replied.

"He will want to see you, Heledd."

"He would do better to get some sleep." Heledd pushed herself up in the bed. "Is this your room?" Meini nodded. "It's very pretty, like you." Heledd examined her forearm for a few minutes. "Is Bleddyn all right?"

"Bleddyn?"

"My dog... Garmon's staghound."

"Yes, the dog has been outside the door since you fainted, waiting."

"Do you mind if Bleddyn comes in here?" Meini frowned. "Meini, I know. Garmon will only blame himself and I do not want that. What can I do?"

"I will tell him you will see him after you've rested."

"Is the colt all right?" Heledd asked suddenly. "Has he seen the colt?"

"I will tell him of your concern for his colt. That will give him something to do," Meini said as she went to the door and both the hound and its master leapt to their feet. Meini exchanged a brief conversation with her stepbrother and let the hound into the room.

"Good dog," Heledd whispered, calling the hound to the

side of the bed. "Good, brave, smart dog." She patted his head while he wagged his whole body. Outside the door, Garmon hesitated for a moment before turning on his heel and leaving the house through the courtyard.

Bleddyn laid his head on Heledd's hip, his eyes wide and fixed on her face. Heledd stroked behind his ears. "I hope I'm right, you know. I hope Huw didn't mean to kill his son. If he did, I'm in even more trouble. What do you think, Bleddyn?" At the sound of his name, the hound lifted his head, then leapt alert as he spun his body toward the door. The latch rose. "Bleddyn," she murmured, ready to give a command. The hound lowered his head, a snarl building in his throat.

"Heledd?"

"Bleddyn, down." The dog sat on his haunches, keeping a cautious eye on Urien Macsen as he entered the room, allowing the warrior to come halfway to the bed before he leaned forward to warn Urien from coming any closer. The warrior brought a stool and sat where the staghound determined.

"Garmon told me you had taken the best of his dogs," Urien said with a smile. "You've trained him well."

"He was already trained," Heledd admitted. "I have only taught him one thing."

"And that is?"

"The only command I need him to know." Heledd sat up straighter in the bed and studied the warrior for a moment. Heledd pressed her eyebrows together. "Why have you come to Bro-Dawel?"

"I came here for you."

"Why?" Heledd asked, her eyes widening. "What has happened? Has—. Has Huw changed his mind? Has my uncle changed his?"

"Neither, to my knowledge."

"Then why have you come?"

"Do you need to ask?" he demanded, gesturing toward her damaged arm and the still reddened scratch on her neck. "You are not safe here."

"These are no one's fault. These are my own doing."

"You beat yourself? You wounded yourself?"

"No, of course not," she replied, lowering her eyes.

"Had I known he was incapable of this simple task, I would have killed him before he ever went near you," Urien said, slamming his fist on his thigh. "He swore to me you would be safe with him, he would find you a good husband away from Talgarth. It is worse for you here than ever at the hands of your uncle."

"I've heard enough of this," Heledd said, tossing the *carthen* aside and putting her feet on the floor.

"What are you doing? You are ready to leave?"

"That depends on Huw Bro-Dawel," she said, choosing a frock from among the garments left for her and pulling the gold-colored tunic over her head, tightening the lacings.

"Why does it depend on Huw?"

"Your foster father paid my bride-price, didn't he?"

"Yes, of course."

"Then it is for him to decide what happens to me." She shook off a momentary, lightheaded sway, found her shoes and commanded Bleddyn to follow her.

"You're not fit to walk," Urien said, barring the door. "I'll bring Huw to you."

"Meini tells me you have a certain loyalty to me but your loyalty belongs with Garmon *llysfab* Huw. He truly has done everything possible to fulfill his oath to you. None of this is his doing and I'm shocked you would think for a moment Garmon could hurt me, or any woman."

"I'm relieved to be wrong," Urien said. "But how, if he has protected you, did these things happen?"

"You don't know me very well, do you?" Heledd laughed, waving him out of her way. "Now let me through so I can put an end to all this. Tell Garmon, when he has finished with the colt, I have gone to talk with his stepfather and he should come."

Huw Bro-Dawel's apartments in the house were attached to the *neuadd,* opposite the courtyard, as far from his daughters and his guests as was possible. The main room was furnished with an oak desk as long as a dining table and as wide. The chair at the desk was also oak, covered with a bear pelt and several silk brocade cushions. Along the walls were shelves of scrolled maps, leather and wood-bound books of accounts and deeds. The center of the floor was covered with a bright, purple and gold rug, fringed with braided tassels. When Heledd stepped onto the rug, her foot sank into it and she looked down to make sure it hadn't moved.

"You've recovered?"

"Yes, *pennaeth.*" Heledd had not expected either an admission of guilt or an apology. "Thank you. Meini is a splendid, skilled *meddyg.* You are right to be proud of her and to put your faith in her abilities."

"Hmmm," he said. "Possibly. What do you want, girl? I'm busy with this case, as you can understand. It is not customary for the accused," he replied, studying her, "to speak with the adjudicator before the decision is made."

"I have not come to discuss the accusations against me." Heledd said, dropping her gaze for a moment, another wave of nausea rose from the pit of her stomach.

"Sit down, girl," Huw gestured, motioning her toward a chair opposite him at the desk. "You're not concerned about this case, I see."

"I have come to discuss the contract between you and my uncle."

"What about the contract?"

"I want to know what the terms are," Heledd said.

"You know most of what is important, but here, read it for yourself," he said, handing her a thin document, tied with a purple ribbon and a cracked, gold wax seal.

"I do not read."

Huw unfolded the document, read quickly through it and asked, "Shall I read it through or do you want just the details? Garmon wrote this to disguise the real intent but I'm sure a girl of your intelligence will understand the implications."

"The details?" Heledd asked, pressing her lips together.

"The contract is between Llew Talgarth, described as your uncle and master of your bond as a prisoner of war, held against the good and rightful behavior of your father's rebellious household, and Huw Bro-Dawel, described as *pennaeth* of the Ystad Dawel, a free man and widower. Said Huw has agreed to pay the bride-price of the bondservant, Heledd *merch* Ieuan Bannawg, a virgin of good character. Said bondservant will be delivered unto her prospective husband in a timely manner and in the condition aforementioned to be wed, upon signature of this document." Huw studied the document for some time before he shook his head, closing his eyes. "Your uncle demanded a high price, even though he had reason to believe you were no longer a maiden."

"He said you drove the price down."

"There would have been no pleasure in allowing him to profit from his duplicity, my girl. For Garmon, it mattered most you came to no harm in his absence. He was prepared to pay whatever Llew asked. I knew Llew was ... eager to be rid of you."

"Why?"

"One reason was Meilor Gwesyn."

"And the other?"

"He had reason to believe Garmon would come back to take you – Urien Macsen played a role in that. Llew saw an opportunity to make a profit by selling property to a second buyer."

"He had already made a profit," Heledd said, looking at her hands. "He had rid himself of any responsibility for me."

"That is now finished," Huw said. "In the past. Once we have addressed the misery of my sister's sons, we can start afresh. Carwyn has explained all that happened yesterday and the brothers will face charges on several counts. With regard to their accusations, your witnesses were convincing. You need not worry and I will not require any further evidence of your maidenhood."

"I am as I was born."

"And you can still prove this, even after living in Garmon's house?"

"Yes. You can bring Tegwen here to examine me if you want."

"Then there should be no bar to the contract you accepted."

"What do you mean, *pennaeth*?"

"Your bride-price has been paid. I see no reason for you to delay any further in fulfilling its terms."

"I cannot."

"What?" he shouted. "You accepted this contract months ago, you have chosen."

"I did not know the terms. I was not told of any perspective husband, *pennaeth*." Heledd watched as his face narrowed and hardened, recognizing his stepson in every etched muscle. "I cannot fulfill the terms of the contract. I cannot be dishonest, *pennaeth*. I cannot give my body to a man I do not love, even in fair exchange for shelter and security for the children I may bear for him."

"Women do that all the time. Love can come … with time."

"Not for me. I have already given my heart to someone else. I have nothing to offer and that, together with my ignorance of these terms, must negate my part of the contract. I bring nothing to this union – not myself, no property, not even my body."

"Who is this man? A soldier here, someone at Talgarth?"

"I cannot tell you."

"Cannot or will not?"

"Both. I will not and, because he has never spoken, cannot."

"You are a wretched girl, Heledd *merch* Ieuan Bannawg," Huw said, half under his breath, staring at a place somewhere above her head. "You have caused nothing but trouble and given one man ten score, and many more, of sleepless nights, – for nothing, false hope."

"I do not accept any responsibility for that, *pennaeth*. No one asked me if this is what I wanted."

"You accepted the contract, Heledd."

"I did not agree to wed. I believed I was brought here as a

bondservant. When I accepted that position, I had no hope of ever seeing the man I love again. I thought I could live without him and be an obedient servant to another. I know now I cannot, not as a wife. I don't care what you do to me, Huw Bro-Dawel. I know you are a good man. I know I have caused too much trouble and you will all be well-rid of me." She stood and turned to leave the room.

"Sit down, Heledd. There is someone else who will need to hear this."

As soon as Huw shouted, the door to his office was opened and Bleddyn shot through the gap, racing across the rug, heedless of her cautioning gesture, to sit by her. Heledd laid her hand on his head, grateful for the uncritical friendship the staghound offered. She knew without looking Garmon had entered the room and stood somewhere behind her while his stepfather resumed his chair at the desk facing her. When the *pennaeth* spoke, he looked over her head, speaking only to his stepson.

"She refuses to honor the contract."

"Why?" Garmon asked. His voice was hoarse, barely above a breath.

"She will tell you herself," Huw replied, dropping his eyes for a moment to glare at Heledd. "Apparently, she has a lover."

"I did not say that," Heledd gasped. Bleddyn reacted to her distress with a growl.

"Tell this man what you have told me, girl," Huw commanded, slapping his hands flat on the desk. "And remember you are still liable to prosecution. I will not lift the charges against you until I am satisfied of your innocence."

"Prosecute me then. I do not care. I am tired of lies and intrigue, and all this secrecy," Heledd exclaimed. Bleddyn nudged her shoulder with his nose and Heledd wrapped her arms around him. "Good boy," she whispered. "Good, smart dog."

"Heledd," Garmon began but Huw lifted his hand to silence him.

"Tell him," the *pennaeth* ordered her, "or I will."

Heledd took a deep breath and pulled herself to sit erect, lifting her chin. "I cannot honor the contract between my uncle and Huw Bro-Dawel because I cannot fulfill the terms required of me. I bring nothing to the contract of any value, least of all to a husband."

"Tell him why this is so, girl."

"I have—. I had, even before I agreed to the contract, given my heart, my whole soul and being, to someone else." For a moment there was silence in the room, broken by a hiss of breath as if Garmon had been punched hard by an opponent he had not seen. Heledd met Huw's glare with her only defense, a defiant lift of her fine-boned chin.

"The girl does not even know if this 'someone else' cares for her. He has never spoken and yet she is willing to face prosecution and the threat of making restitution for his sake." Heledd could see from his expression Huw despised her. She could also see he was suffering for his stepson, trying to soften the blow for Garmon by humiliating her.

"How can I dishonor a man who has never dishonored me?" she demanded. "He has never caused me harm. I cannot accuse him of any crime against me. It is not his fault I love him. Why should I expect him to speak if he has nothing in his heart for me? If he does not, that is my misfortune and I will bear it. But I cannot compound this sorrow by inflicting pain on a man who would be my husband when he has every right to expect his full measure of me or at least to have some hope he will, in time."

"You know you will have to return to Talgarth."

"I did not think otherwise."

"Llew will not return your bride-price to me without demanding reparation from you – for the rest of your life. You know for what purpose he will use you and find most satisfactory for the dishonor you will bring on his head."

"That will not be different from my knowledge of him."

"You would rather *that* than take a husband you do not love?"

"Yes. *That* is an honest exchange between a woman and a

man."

Huw slammed his fists down on the desk, making all the objects jump. Heledd took a deep breath and squared her shoulders. Bleddyn rose from his haunches.

"Huw," Garmon said, "let me speak to her."

"Do not think she will ever see sense, my son. This kind never do."

"Just what 'kind' do you think I am?" Heledd demanded, leaping to her feet. Garmon communicated silently with his stepfather before Huw had a chance to throw the nearest thing to his hand. He let his grip on the inkpot relax.

"Sit down, girl," he said. "Garmon has asked to speak to you, I presume, in private. Will you allow that?" Heledd bowed her head once in acquiescence. "Whatever is agreed between you, if there is agreement, will be carried out. You understand? If he has been wrong about you, your uncle will see you before the end of this night. Do you understand?" Heledd nodded again.

# TWENTY

When Huw left the room, Heledd remained standing by the desk, pressing her fingertips on it, staring at the sheaves of paper scattered across its surface, searching to recognize any of the letters of the two names she had learned from Mairwen. Her ignorance and poor education undermined her defiant confidence and she hung her head.

"Heledd," Garmon said softly as he closed the door and crossed the room to stand behind her. "Sit down, will you?" Returning to the chair, she draped her arm across Bleddyn's shoulders and kept her eyes fixed on the hound's long-nosed face. For a moment, Garmon rested his hand on the back of her chair. "What can I do?" he asked, before he pulled a stool to sit facing her.

"You could start by telling me the truth," she said. Garmon clasped his hands together between his knees and bowed his head. "If that's possible."

"You know most of it," he said.

"I want to hear your version," Heledd replied, "from the beginning."

"Will the truth make a difference, Heledd?"

"That depends on the truth."

"If it is not to your liking, what then?"

"If truth is not to *your* liking, what then? I am only asking that you are honest with me. If you cannot be so, there is no reason to continue this conversation."

"Where do you want me to begin?" Garmon queried, raising his eyes to search what he could see of her face behind her flow of dark auburn hair.

"I know both Gwyn and Aled had visited Urien Macsen before you. At the time of your arrival there, last year, would be acceptable." Heledd ran her fingers through Bleddyn's rough fur, and locked her fingers in the curls on his shoulder.

Garmon took a deep breath and stared at his clasped hands for a moment. "You know Urien is my foster brother – the eldest of the three who remain." Heledd nodded. "Gwyn and Aled found opportunity to train with him at Talgarth several times over the years since he returned to his father's home. I had not. My responsibilities here and my … limitations prevented that. In the spring of last year, Urien sent word he wanted me to come. I couldn't leave Bro-Dawel until after the harvest but his messages during that interval implied his invitation was urgent." Garmon stopped for a moment, looking up at her again. Heledd had not turned her eyes away from the staghound's face. "When I did arrive, I saw no apparent reason for his impatience. I began my training under his command, as had Gwyn and Aled, to renew our friendship and commitment to one another as brothers, as warriors." Heledd heard him sigh, as though he had held his breath for a long time. "I am not surprised that your heart is given. I do not blame you, Heledd … only myself."

"Garmon," she sighed, braving a glance at him. He was not looking at her.

"Let me finish," he said. "If I had been honest from the start, neither of us would have to go through this." He straightened his back and looked at her for a few moments. "I knew nothing of you when I began training at Talgarth. Your uncle knew nothing of me – or of any of my foster brothers. He had known Huw many years before but Urien preferred to enlist us on our own merits, not necessarily in secret, but to avoid Llew's interest. I first saw you when you and Alys came to watch the training."

When he leaned toward her, she met his gaze squarely.

"I couldn't take my eyes off you. I couldn't sleep that night. The next time I saw you was the same," he said with a smile. "Urien told me everything he thought I needed to know and what your uncle had planned for you. Alys did the rest. You were," he explained in answer to her questioning glance, "a burden and stood in Alys's way. Keeping you out of Meilor Gwesyn's hands was in the interests of both Llew and Urien. Llew offered you to Urien but he knew the Bannawg would never accept his part in dishonoring you. Urien delayed accepting Llew's offer, giving him a better option – which was his reason for wanting me to arrive earlier." Garmon stroked the staghound's back for a while, careful not to touch Heledd's hand. "Urien had hoped I would be interested, if not interested, at least willing to help him protect you. I was interested. He made it sound logical, simple. And I wanted you."

Heledd turned her head to stare at the hearth on the other side of the wide room, blushing beneath her mask of freckles.

"Had I arrived at Bannawg a week later, you would have already gone to Gwesyn. With Urien's assurances of my 'suitability' as your bondmaster, Llew invited me to his table and encouraged me to court you. I signed away two years of my life to have you. When I realized you were frightened of me, I knew something was wrong. I knew Urien had not told me everything I should have known." Garmon stopped talking for a while, closing his eyes as he leaned back and took another long breath.

"I was drunk on the scent of your skin and the feel of your hand in mine. I was mad with the thought of making love to you. You were so haughty, proud, defiant. I wanted what Llew most wanted." When she swung her head to look at him, he leaned forward. "Urien's motives were good. He meant only to protect you and asked me to help him. I agreed because I wanted you to surrender your arrogance and your superiority to me. I admit," he said, studying her face, "at first, I wanted you to lower that chin."

Heledd jerked her head away again, lifting her chin firmly, turning her shoulder against him, certain he would smile.

"That night, in Llew's house, when Alys made you come to the hall dressed so meanly, and still so proud, listening to the storyteller and watching your face, I sensed your humiliation and I understood what they were doing. I heard the story they told to break your spirit. It was too late to go back. I knew the law. You were mine."

He leaned closer to her, laying his hand over hers but when she withdrew from his touch, Garmon sat back. "I knew I could not take advantage of your position despite their consent and did the only thing possible under the circumstances. Alys had the blood evidence—." Heledd gasped, staring at him. Garmon held his hand out to her, displaying the scar where she had bitten him. "From that night, I thought of you as my wife, in law." Heledd glanced at him but could not meet his eyes as before.

"And I knew that, if I went to you again, I would make love to you – because I had the legal right – and that was a crime I did not want to commit. For a few weeks, Llew was satisfied. I enlisted Goewin's help to maintain the fiction – even Urien did not know the truth. On Christmas morning, Elis heard you singing." Garmon ran his hands through his hair and let them drop onto his thighs. "It wasn't good enough for them you were my whore. They did not intend for you to be happy."

Garmon smiled briefly. "I knew I had only Goewin's unaccountable fondness for me to thank for your happiness. I had no idea what significance that purse had, but she assured me you would treasure it. Giving you anything you treasured or made your life more bearable was the least I could do after I had conspired with them to ruin you." He clasped his fingers together and stared at his hands, resting on his thighs.

"After the *Calan*, Llew told me I had to take you to the barracks, like the rest of the soldiers' whores. When I refused, he told me my contract with him was void, he would find someone else to fulfill his terms. A few days later, word came Gwyn had been killed." When Heledd glanced at him, he pressed his lips together and took a deep breath. "Before I left, I did everything I could to ensure your safety. Urien swore he would protect you. I couldn't leave without seeing you, even though I knew that would be a mistake. The moment I saw you coming from the *beudy*, I knew I was going destroy what little good you may ever have thought of me. But I had to tell you, somehow, I loved you, I wanted you and I would not leave you there. As soon as I kissed you, I realized it was the worst thing I could have done, that I had lost any hope you would forgive me."

Garmon looked at her for a long time in silence but Heledd was resolute, determined to hear the whole tale before she relented – if she relented.

"Meini was desolate with grief. Huw was in a rage and Mared's husband had also been killed. I buried myself in their pain and eased my guilt with responsibilities to my half-brother, to my command, to Aled, Huw – anyone who needed me. I told myself you would be happier without me." Though he searched her face, Heledd did not answer the unspoken question.

"Then, one morning in late spring, I awoke with you in my arms – the sense of holding you was so strong even when I opened my eyes and turned onto my back, I felt you." He rested his elbows on his knees, lowering his head. "And nothing would take away the emptiness until I convinced Huw to accept my plan. Once he agreed, I knew you would come to Bro-Dawel. Even if Urien had done as we agreed, I knew he would not keep you – if you wanted to go."

"What had you agreed with Urien Macsen?"

"That he would be your husband, if I could not find you anyone better. I know, Heledd. I know that was foolish, you were not consulted, given any say or choice. When that dawned on me, I ensured that was a stipulation in Huw's letter to Llew Talgarth – that you had to be asked if you consented to being wed."

"When did you write this letter?"

"At the beginning of April. Huw received agreement from Llew before the end of the month. Not until Aled went to Bannawg in the summer did we know you had not been consulted. Urien knew nothing and was surprised to see Aled. Mared discovered what you had endured since my departure and was delighted to share that with Meini, as you have heard. Aled demanded Llew get your consent."

"Why did that matter?" she asked, rubbing Bleddyn's muzzle

and turning his head so she could smile at him.

"As soon as Llew told Huw you had accepted, I drove them mad with orders and demands. You couldn't come here without a house waiting for you, without clothing that befit you. Only a few knew Huw was not the bridegroom, most of the orders went through him and he received the brunt of my impatience," Garmon told her.

"He was not overjoyed to see me," she said. "Why were you not here?"

"I intended to be. I thought better of it after Aled had gone. I remembered the look on your face when you ran from me that last day outside the *beudy*. I thought, if you could grow to like Bro-Dawel, Huw, my friends, there was a better chance you would not be as quick to run from me," he said, with a half laugh. "I was wrong," he said, leaning back, rubbing his eyes with the palms of his hands and scraping his fingers back through his hair. "I had only made matters worse. Aled brought you to the green wood so I could see you. Carwyn took you to the chapel – with disastrous results," he laughed. "And then, Geraint ... is he—." Heledd shook her head. "I am not surprised you wish to leave. Urien has come to take you with him – I knew as soon as I heard he was here."

Heledd stroked the hound's ears for a long time, piecing the puzzle together and sorting through her reactions to his admissions, thinking through what she needed to do. The sun had begun to set, sending long shadows over the rug and Huw's desk from the window behind her.

"You still have not kept your promise to show me a prettier, more private place," she said at last. Garmon raised his head to catch her looking at him, an uncertain frown on his brow. "He's forgotten," she pouted, cupping her hands around Bleddyn's ears and shaking his head playfully.

"You wish to go now?" he asked, still frowning.

"If it's not too much to ask and you can find this place in the dark."

Garmon stood, looking down at her. Heledd kept her gaze fixed on the hound. Garmon strode to the door and threw it open, ordering his warhorse and the mare be saddled. Heledd caught a glimpse of Geraint and Nisien as they ran from the *neuadd* to obey. Though Aled took a step toward him, Garmon shook his head and closed the door between them. When he offered Heledd his hand, she stood without accepting his help, walking to the courtyard ahead of him.

As the horses were brought, she bent over the young staghound, and whispered, "Bleddyn, home." The dog backed away and trotted toward Garmon's longhouse. Aled watched the hound go and turned to his foster brother.

"Tell Huw I am keeping my word," Garmon said while Geraint helped Heledd to mount her horse. Garmon mounted *Diawl* and followed Heledd through the gate of the *gaer*. When they were clear of the bridge over the stream and the track widened, he urged his horse forward to ride beside her but said nothing.

"I thought you were dead," Heledd said, rolling her shoulders and shaking her head to release the tension in her body.

"When?"

"When you did not come back." When he did not respond, she bit her lips together, glancing at him from behind the curtain of her hair. Garmon was watching her. "No one mentioned your name, not even Alys, as she had often done to tease me. I thought you had been killed." Though she could not see his face as clearly in the twilight, she saw the hard line of his jaw.

"Did that matter?"

"I became accustomed to it, after a while."

"Before you became accustomed, did it matter?"

"Yes," she replied. "For a long time, I was afraid you would return." She did not need to look at him to feel his sadness. "When I thought you were dead, I felt safer, but sad. When Alys told me you had left, I feared you would come back. I didn't know what I would do if you did. Still, I waited for you. I had to force myself to stop thinking about you or go mad with worry."

Garmon turned the warhorse onto a narrow track not far from the chapel in the copse. After several minutes he led her through a hidden, arched opening in a wall. Beyond the wall, he rode through several fields and dismounted. When Garmon turned to help Heledd down, she was already on the ground. She gave him Angel's reins as she slipped past him down a neat path, following the sound of falling water. A red glow filtered through the trees from the setting sun, reflecting on the smooth surface of a wide pool. Before Garmon reached the bank, Heledd had stripped out of her outer garments, pulling off her *hosan* and shoes at the water's edge.

"Are you going to swim with me?" she asked, after she had slid into the cool water, shivering until she had become used to the chill. Garmon hesitated while he tethered the horses. After a moment, he pulled his jerkin over his head and began to untie the cuffs of his shirt. He sat down on the grass verge of the bank and watched her. Heledd shrugged and swam away, diving under the water to surface near the opposite bank, swimming slowly back so she could observe his mood. "I never allowed myself to care about anyone. You already know how I felt about soldiers and why." Garmon nodded his head once, leaning back on his elbows. "At first, I didn't notice anything had changed for me. One day, I realized I had begun to think of one soldier every day. I even started to look for him. If I didn't see him, I felt empty. If I did see him, I felt frightened. I was afraid he would speak to me. I was afraid he wouldn't. He didn't."

Heledd gazed at Garmon for a moment and then swam away to explore the large pool. The fall of water from the river above was gentle, cascading over boulders and the trunks of trees for as far as she could see. When the water reached the pool, it slid beneath the surface causing only soft ripples to disturb the glass-like face. As she climbed onto one of the boulders, Garmon dove into the pool. When he surfaced, he swam toward her. She swept her hair together in her hands and wrung the water from it. Water splashed across the boulder as she twisted the plait into a knot.

Before Garmon reached her, she said, "He did kiss me

once." Changing her position on the boulder so she could bend over the water easily, trailing her fingers through the water, she continued, "I accepted the contract Huw Bro-Dawel offered because I could not stay at Bannawg. I hoped that, in time, I would forget this man." Heledd straightened her back, looking through the trees toward the sunset. "I didn't forget. I couldn't forget. Every hour of every day was worse. I was farther away from him than ever. One day, I knew I couldn't live without him – even if he never spoke. I would rather be near him and alone, than away from him and alone."

"He was a fool," Garmon said, raising his eyes to her face.

"You know him better than I do," she said. She stretched her arms above her head and lowered her gaze to his upturned face. "Tegwen Talog says I have a good back. What do you think?"

Garmon looked at her for a long moment and said, "I agree."

"Tegwen also said I have straight hips," Heledd added, rising slightly to show him. "She says I am well-built for breeding."

"Did she tell you anything else?" he asked, as he stood on the pool bed, waist deep in front of her.

"She did," Heledd answered.

"And that was?" Garmon asked, taking a step closer to her.

"She said," Heledd began, conscious her body betrayed her as her breath held of its own accord. Her eyes darkened and her breasts tightened. Between her legs, she felt a rush of longing. "She said I would need her services before summer." When Garmon lifted his arms to take her from the rock, she slid with him into the cold water, opening her lips to his kiss as their bodies sank gradually below the pool's placid surface. "If you don't like the name I have chosen for our firstborn," she said as he brought her up for air, "you had better tell me before we make him."

"What are you doing?" he asked, searching her face.

"I know you are not too drunk," Heledd murmured, leaning into his body, "and I am not angry. If you are drunk enough . . ."

"I am sober," Garmon whispered against her throat, lying back with her and wrapping his arms around her waist. "Here? Like this? In this place?"

"Exactly like this, in this place," Heledd said, lifting her hands to sweep his hair back from his forehead while he floated on his back, stroking through the water toward the riverbank. Heledd spread her fingers over his chest, tracing the definition of the muscles beneath his skin. Garmon brought them to the edge of the pool where the bank sloped into the water. Heledd fell onto her back and slid her hands down his abdomen, over his hips.

"Wait," he murmured against her ear, sliding his arm around her and holding her against him. "This will be better for you." He turned with her onto his back and lifted her shift above her hips. Heledd dragged it over her head and tossed it onto the pile of his clothes, watching his gray eyes darken and shine like coal as he gazed at her in the glow of the sunset. He raised himself on one arm, holding her with the other around her waist, staring into her wide, green eyes. "You know I am— I do not know my father, his name or station."

"I know that."

"If—."

Heledd covered his mouth with both her hands, shaking her head.

"*Menyw*," he groaned as he pulled her down to him, opening her to his kiss.

His damp skin was like silk against her as he slid his hands down her back to her thighs and spread them to either side of his hips. Heledd lifted herself to take him into her body. "Heledd," he whispered, "not yet." He pulled her hands away from him, extending her arms wide. "There is time. Let me touch you. I have waited a long time to make love to you."

"As long as I have waited?" she breathed against the soft hollow between his jaw and his throat. He pushed her to sit upright.

"Longer," he said under his breath, sliding his hands from her shoulders to her hips. "Much longer. From the moment I saw you standing above me on the wall. If not for Urien's hand on my arm, nothing could have restrained me."

"I don't believe you," Heledd whispered, caressing his arms, her eyes drifting closed. "Alys said——."

"Never trust the word of a jealous girl."

"What are you doing?" she protested, gasping as his fingers sought to touch what his eyes experienced of her pale, *brith* flesh. "You have done this before …"

"Never with you," he said, his voice husky as he pulled her head down to kiss her mouth again, "and not for a long time. I have forgotten what a woman is like."

For a long moment, they were both still. He held her injured arm, examining the scar as a wall of angry self-recrimination built between them. Heledd extended her free arm, weaving her fingers between his, leaning forward until her lips caressed his throat.

"If you have doubts, Heledd, tell me now."

For answer, she pressed the length of her torso to his body, widening her thighs to take more of him, flexing her hands over his torso as he thrust into her. Garmon laughed as he silenced her with another kiss, demanding her attention until he catch his breath. She forced him deeper inside her, gasping as he tore through her maidenhead. Garmon pressed his hands on her thighs, holding her down until he brought his need under control. "There's more to love than making a child, Heledd." He pulled her head down, opening her mouth with his kiss and held her motionless, inching his long fingers along her thighs. When he touched her, Heledd withdrew. "Let me," he whispered. "Let me touch you." He stroked her with slow, rhythmic thrusts while his thumb teased her aching flesh. At the moment she wept, his seed pulsed into her body.

"Thank you," he whispered against her temple. Heledd lifted her head, a shy smile stealing across her face. "Next time, we will have a bed."

"Are you sure? This was nice."

"Was it?" Garmon inquired, rolling with her so she was under him, taking all his weight as he pushed hard into her.

"Ouch. I see what you mean," Heledd replied, arching her back and met his gaze with a sudden recognition. "I like that too," she murmured.

"Are you cold, *gwraig*?"

"Not very. Are you?" Not until she opened her eyes to look into his face did she remember the first time he had asked the question and a blush washed over her from the core of her body. "Am I?"

"No longer," Garmon murmured, as she wrapped her calves around the backs of his legs.

"What is the name of this river?" Heledd asked, arching against him, reluctant to let him leave her body.

"Tawel." Garmon hooked his arm around the small of her back and pulled her with him to stand, hip deep, in the pool. Heledd bore down to meet his need again, embracing him with her arms around his shoulders and her legs around his back, her fingers locked in his hair. "Heledd."

"Owein Tawel *mab* Garmon," she sighed, taking his manhood fully into the depths of her body. "That's a good name for your son."


"*My* son," Garmon said, stretching his body the length of the narrow cot, "will not be as quiet as you hope."

"Why do you say that?" Heledd demanded, turning to face him from her contemplation of the cloister garden from the door of the student's hovel where they had spent the previous three days, eating the food prepared for them in the monks' kitchen and making love on the cot in which Garmon had spent most of his adolescence as a student.

They had stayed at the pool for hours, until the sun had disappeared behind the hills to the west and the last of the warmth in the air had left them both shivering. When they reached the cloister, Garmon took Heledd to the hovel, went to tell the Abbot of their arrival and to arrange a meal for them. One of the youngest of the postulates brought the meal, enough for both but set for only one. Garmon said nothing when he took the tray of food and invited Heledd to feed him from her plate, with her fingers.

Heledd wore some of the clothes she had been wearing the day they swam in the Tawel pool and some of the clothes she had found in a chest in the hovel. The autumn had swept into Bro-Dawel with a churning wind from the east. There was no hearth in the students' hovels, even those paid for by the cloister's patron in the district. The brown cloak she wrapped closely around her body was the warmest she could find and had belonged to the young scholar who, as a man, was her husband. She could imagine him, so like his half-brother, Carwyn, huddled into the cloak, studying at the desk by the window with nothing more than a candle – exactly like the candle that lit their evenings – to warm his hands while he studied and wrote his essays.

"He will be rowdy and boisterous, even bad-tempered."

"Why do you vilify him before he is born?" Heledd complained. "You don't know. He may be like me. Inquisitive, studious and serene."

Garmon had seen Carwyn once, on the morning after they had arrived at the cloister gate to seek lodging. Carwyn was returning to Bro-Dawel, the wound to his shoulder stitched and healing. Heledd had been sorry Huw had not trusted his own daughter to dress the boy's injury but she had not had an opportunity to see him for herself, only to receive Garmon's report when he returned to their bed to keep her warm for a short while longer.

"If he is like you," Garmon said, reaching across the tiny room to scoop her back to him, kicking the door shut with his foot, "he will be better loved by his father than is usual."

"In that case, he had better be like you."

"Why?" Garmon asked, sliding his hand beneath the folds of her frock, reaching toward the warmth of her thighs.

"Your hand is cold," Heledd screeched, pulling away.

"It will soon be warm," he murmured.

"A boy should be loved well by his mother," Heledd sighed, relaxing her limbs completely as he pushed her skirts above her hips and settled between her thighs for the fourth time in as many hours. "But not as well as she loves his father."

"I'm glad you said that," Garmon said, grasping the backs of her knees and lifting them toward her shoulders. "A man demands ..." he whispered, burying his passion in her body, moving in her until she groaned with pleasure and he took his own.

Heledd locked her fingers in his dark hair as she raised her chin to kiss his lips. His eyes were closed and she could see the intensity of his pleasure had taken him as far away from her as her own transported her to another world for a timeless moment. "Thank you," she whispered, both to her husband and to God, who had fashioned them for such wonderment.

"You're welcome," Garmon smiled, looking at her, all semblance of granite gone from his expression. By candlelight, on that night in the cloister hovel, his wall collapsed as they made love in the silent reverence of their trust in one another. For the first time, she had seen in his eyes every thought she would ever need to believe he loved her.

"Garmon," she began, combing his hair back from his forehead as she turned onto her side to face him. "I want to go back to Bannawg." His baffled expression gradually became a frown. "I left without any regard for them. Goewin and the others deserve better than to be abandoned and forgotten. When Urien goes, I will—." The cold rage that started somewhere in his soul brought her thoughts to a dark precipice. "Not for long," she said quickly, too late remembering his jealousy of his elder foster brother. "Just to see if there is anything I can do for them."

"There is nothing you can do," he said, turning onto his back.

"I'm not useless," Heledd replied, rising onto her elbow. "I can at least show I am grateful for their sacrifice on my behalf."

"How will you show this gratitude, *menyw*? What do you have of use to them?" Heledd stared at him for a long time. "Heledd, I didn't mean..." She rolled away from him and rose from the cot, smoothing her skirt over her legs.

"I'm going." She pulled her tunic over the linen frock and whipped the brown cloak around her shoulders.

"No, you are not." Garmon caught her around the waist before she reached the door and moved to block her path, bending his head slightly to look into her downcast eyes. "You have no weapons against your uncle or Meilor Gwesyn."

"I don't want to fight them. I want to help—."

"There is only one way to do that."

"How? How can I help them? You have already said I have nothing of use."

"You have the law. The law will take time and Urien is at Bannawg to ensure the safety of the people you love. I have made a start—." When her eyes widened, he tilted her chin to meet her surprise. "Did you think I would not? Did you believe I had no intention of seeking justice for you? Or for them?"

"Why should you? They are nothing to you and … and you have what you wanted of me."

"What might that be, Heledd Garmon? A few hours of pleasure?"

"Yes."

"I have not begun to have all the pleasure I want. A lifetime will not be enough of you. Bannawg is important to you. I knew that before you remembered how your mother died. I knew within hours of your uncle's deceit. How could I not seek justice for you after what I did?"

"Then there is no reason I should not go to Bannawg."

"You will not find them."

"Why not? What's happened?"

"Urien did not tell you?" he asked with a frown. Heledd shook her head, not resisting when he urged to her sit on the edge of the cot while he crouched in front of her. "Your uncle has driven Goewin and the other Bannawg people out of the valley."

"Where are they?" she demanded, trying to stand.

"That is why Urien came here. I thought he came to take you from me."

"Yes, I know," she said, laying her hand on his shoulder.

"On the evening Urien came, I sent Rheinallt to deal with raiders I had seen on the way back. When I realized who they must have been, I found them and knew how you would react, so I hid them."

"And how was that? How did you think I would react?"

"You had already told me you wanted to return. I thought … I knew I would lose you. I had no reason to think I could keep you when your duty was so strong." Garmon searched her face for a moment. "They are safe, Heledd, well-fed and sheltered."

"You know you will have to take me to them, don't you?" Garmon nodded. "Now." He looked at her and rose to his feet, extending his hand. "Where are they?"

"Near the place you saw Urien. Several of his command have come with Bannawg, as well as a few of the farmers."

"How many are there?" Heledd asked, lifting the hood of the cloak to cover her face as they left the hovel for the cloister stables.

"I counted between twenty-five and thirty, there may be more."

"Why did Llew do this? They have worked for him all this time, in spite of what he did to their families."

"Urien told me the harvest was poor. Llew no longer had reason to feed them. They were no longer useful."

"How is that? He used me to control them …"

"He needed them to work, not to feed them. He needed you to keep them obedient. Once he had rid himself of you, the Bannawg people were useless to him – and dangerous. Alys had secured the land through her marriage to Gwern *mab* Meilor. Talgarth, Bannawg and Gwesyn will be joined to become the largest *ystad* in that region. No one will care then how it came to be."

"What will happen to the Bannawg?"

"That will depend," Garmon said, cupping his hand under her foot to raise her onto Angel's back, "on them. And, I have to warn you, on Huw. They've come here because of you. But Huw has no duty to them."

"I know," Heledd replied, following him from the stables. Once they were beyond the cloister walls and onto the road to the north and the town, she urged Angel forward to ride beside him. "How did you hide thirty people from the warband you sent after them?"

"I knew Rheinallt commanded. He's a good soldier – he follows orders with precision. The command I gave him was specific. I knew where he would go. I went in the opposite direction."

"Did you give him that command deliberately?"

"No, but I was glad I had when I realized Urien had not come alone."

"How did you know that?" Heledd asked.

"He would never have allowed himself to be seen by Aled's men, unless he wanted to be found. He saw you with them."

"Why didn't you realize that when you were first told he was here?"

"I told you," Garmon said, glancing at her, "I thought he had come to take you away from me. If I had been thinking straight, I would have realized if he had intended to take you, he would have done so and no one would have known until after you were gone."

"He must be very good," she ventured.

"Not good enough," Garmon answered, straightening his back. "You're here, with me."

"Only because he didn't want me," she teased him.

"He's a fool." They had ridden a number of miles at a leisurely pace and, at the bend of the road leading up the hill to the market town, Garmon halted to survey the area.

"Garmon?" When he turned his head to look at her, Heledd guided Angel closer. "What will happen to us?"

"What do you mean, Heledd *gwraig* Garmon?"

"When we have seen Goewin? When Llinos Cenfyn and her sons are gone? Where will we be?"

Garmon leaned forward in the saddle to look beyond the hood of her cloak into her upturned face. "We have a son to raise, remember? Together."

"And all his sisters and brothers."

"Eight?" he queried.

"At least."

"You will be the death of me, *gwraig*."

# twenty-one

Garmon urged *Diawl* to pick up his pace to climb the slope into the town. Heledd searched in every direction around her as they rode between the houses and other buildings but could not see any face she recognized among the townspeople. No one took notice of the warrior – his face and presence were familiar to them. Besides a cursory glance at her, Heledd thought they were probably equally as familiar with the sight of a woman in his wake. They took no more notice of her than if she had been one of Aled's command. At the other end of the town, at the brow of the hill, he rode along a track through the common, nodding at some of the residents as they were grazing their sheep and goats. At the gate of an inn, he dismounted and led both horses under the stone archway into the wagon yard.

A thin man appeared at the door to the side of the archway, wiping his hands on a rag. The man jerked his head toward another building at the far end of the yard. Garmon turned toward Heledd, moving close enough to talk without being overheard.

"I will go. You go into the inn and take a room for us. The innkeeper will not ask you any question."

"Why can't I go with you?"

"He is suspicious enough. Don't give him any cause to suspect Huw may want to know what I have in storage."

"You told me you never do anything to harm him," Heledd said, "or would be against his wishes."

"Except what concerns you," he laughed. "The innkeeper will not believe you are my wife," he murmured. "Will that offend you?"

"There doesn't seem to be much difference," Heledd replied, sliding into his arms and down his body until he allowed her feet to touch the ground.

"Only a matter of the terms of the contract," Garmon said.

"I will learn how to drive a harder bargain."

"Your terms are sufficient to my needs, *gwraig*."

"Your needs are not those that concern me," she said, sweeping away to arrange a night's lodging. When she turned at the door, Garmon was still watching her and the innkeeper was grinning on one side of his mouth. Heledd lifted her chin and disappeared into the dark alehouse.

"This is a first," the innkeeper said as he came up behind her and slid past to take a large key from the rack.

"Why do you say that?"

"That one is usually more discrete when he brings his women here. The young ones of his soldiers, if they can afford it, make a show but never him." Heledd held out her hand for the key. "You're new," he said. "I haven't seen you around before. Fresh too." He leaned near and drew a breath. "Bit of advice. Don't expect too much. That way you won't be disappointed when he leaves you in the gutter like the rest of your kind."

"He's not like that."

"We're all like that, *menyw*," the innkeeper assured her. "Get what you can before he gets tired of you, aye?"

"Aye."

"Ach, you're all the same." he laughed. "Just so we all understand each other, aye?" He laid the rusty key across her palm. "Up those stairs and first door you see. The room's clean, just the way he likes it."

"I can lock the door from inside?"

"You can, but he'll only kick it down when he wants you."

"That will not be anything new," Heledd laughed, lifting her skirts above her ankles to climb the wooden stairs.

"Can't blame him if you were on the other side of the door." Heledd turned her head to look at the innkeeper, lifting her chin in her most haughty way. Her arrogance was greeted with a hearty laugh. "I'll tell the blacksmith I'm going to need a new lock. And a door."

Not surprised by both the size and furnishings of the room, Heledd unlatched the shutters over the window and looked out onto the fields and woodlands behind the inn, out of sight of the town. *Why does he come here?* She untied the neck of the cloak and draped it over the back of a chair at the long table. The room was sparsely furnished but with simplicity, not frugality. The bed, she was glad to see, was high and wide, similar to the bed in Garmon's house, with a thick, feather mattress, clean linen, cushions and a pile of *carthen* of all colors and thickness. To her delight, after the nights in the cloister, the hearth was already blazing and the aroma of the wood smoke reminded her of the day, many months ago, Garmon *llysfab* Huw had kissed her good-bye behind the *beudy* in Bannawg. *That was just one – the first – of many moments.* She rubbed her hands through the hair on the top of her head and let the hideous mop float around her shoulders.

"Thank you," she whispered, clasping her hands together, before she twirled happily in the middle of the floor until she was too dizzy to stand. With a laugh, she flung herself onto the bed and let the feeling of floating wash over her. Through the window, she could hear chirping and singing, the sounds of people at work, voices from the wagon yard. Though the air was cold, the wind was not as strong as it had been in the morning and the bright, afternoon sun warmed everything it touched. When her head had cleared, Heledd stood at the window, closing her eyes to let the light fall on her face, feeling its warmth spread through her body.

The sound of an uneven footstep on the stairs turned her immediately to face the door, a welcoming smile already making itself at home in her expression. When the door was opened, she saw a woman's muddy boot and filthy, tattered skirt. Heledd lurched forward, clasping her fists hard against her chest, biting her lips together to keep from crying out. As Goewin's familiar face appeared around the edge of the door, Heledd could not restrain a low wail, full of guilt and remorse.

"Hisht, my girl," Goewin said, gathering Heledd in her arms when Garmon's wife threw herself into them. "Had I known you'd react like this, I would have told this one to keep you away for another month." Goewin extended her arms so she could examine Heledd in more detail. "You'll do," she pronounced, giving Garmon an approving nod, allowing him to enter the room. "Has he told you what has happened?" When Heledd nodded, unable to speak, Goewin sighed. "We did not know what happened to Urien until this one came the morning after Urien left to find you."

"Are you hungry? Do you want anything? What can I do?"

"You can let me look at you for a while," Goewin laughed. "A cup of mead would be good, wine if you have no mead."

Garmon filled a tall cup for her, offering it and a chair near the hearth.

"How could you let them hide in a warehouse?" Heledd demanded of him, kneeling at Goewin's side and stroking the woman's graying hair.

"Don't blame him, Heledd," Goewin cautioned. "He's done all he could to ensure our comfort, under the circumstances. Blame your own flesh and blood."

The comment stung Heledd. She dropped her eyes and let her hands fall into her lap.

"My wife is not responsible for them," Garmon declared, standing at her side. Heledd gazed up at him and slid her hand into his, grateful for the declaration of her position in his life.

"I never said she was," Goewin replied, smiling at the two of them. "All the same, they share the same bloodline. That cannot be changed by wishing. In any case, we are well away from that evil man and his spawn."

"How many are you who have come?"

"There are eight women, a dozen little ones, three of the girls and nine of Llew's best warriors, including Urien Macsen. Talgarth has no warband, of any caliber, to protect them through the winter since your uncle has done this."

"They are not all Bannawg, are they?"

"None of the warriors but they are loyal to Urien, not to

Llew. Five of the women are of the Bannawg, including me. And three are the wives of the warriors, with their children. The girls are all of Talgarth, two are the handmaidens of Alys *gwraig* Gwern."

"Why have they come? Alys will need them when her child is born."

"Alys will not bear a child this year."

"Why? What's happened?"

"Either she was not carrying when she claimed or she lost it. You may yet have a child to inherit Bannawg before your cousin," Goewin said, patting Heledd's cheek.

"I do not want my son to inherit that place," Heledd said.

"It will be his birthright, *merch*. If he is born before any child Gwern Meilor fathers in Alys's body."

"My son will be free to win his own inheritance, just as his father has." Heledd could feel Garmon's tension coursing through his body with the sudden contraction of his fingers around her hand. "Talgarth-y-Bannawg has nothing I want my children to have. One day, I will go back to ensure my family is shown the respect a murdered people deserve. I will also ensure those women who were enslaved by Meilor Gwesyn receive justice. Beyond that, my life is with Garmon, wherever he is."

"I see you have taken time to think these matters through," Goewin commented. "I do not blame you after what you have suffered, but what of the rest of us. We have no home other than Bannawg."

"Goewin," Heledd said, throwing her arms around the woman's waist, "you are the mother I have known since I was a girl. I won't let anything happen to you while I live."

"I'm sure you mean that, my girl, but you will find it hard to achieve," Goewin said, leaning over her foster daughter and kissing the back of her head.

"I know I have been willful and arrogant toward you and all the others, but I have changed," Heledd said. "I know what you have all suffered and I will repay my debt to you, gladly. If I have to go without in order to do that, I will. I don't care about these things," she said, flicking a dismissive hand at her fine gold tunic. "I don't need another pair of shoes if it means you and all the others can live somewhere in safety and comfort." Heledd studied the woman's face. "I can do without these. I have before."

"There will be no need of that," Garmon said, encouraging her to take a chair by the table. "We will find a solution. Together." Heledd leaned her head against his chest and closed her eyes for a moment.

Goewin smiled to herself and drank from the cup. "I knew it would not take long for the two of you to come to an understanding."

Heledd's eyes flew open as she burst into laughter. "You do not know either of us very well," she exclaimed and looked up at her husband, throwing her arms around his waist. Garmon dropped his hand to the side of her head with a rueful smile.

"Well enough," Goewin replied, draining her cup.

"What can we do now to help?" Heledd asked. "Are you comfortable? Warm?"

"The warehouse is a palace compared to what I have come to know in the past years, child. We have all we need to live thanks to your husband. Until there is a better plan, we will be content. The innkeeper knows not to cheat on the provisions and we have all else we need."

"I don't want to leave you here, Goewin," Heledd said, clasping her hand.

"Tell me, when is this son of yours to be born?"

Heledd blushed deeply, the freckles on her cheeks darkening with the stain flowing upward from her breast. "If he is to be born," Heledd said.

"You are not like that silly cousin of yours," Goewin scoffed lightly. "Spring?"

"Garmon," Heledd pleaded.

"Not before summer," he answered.

"What have you been doing all these months?" Goewin laughed. "Watching the wheat?"

In time, Heledd accepted Garmon's reasoning that going to the warehouse with Goewin was a foolish gesture but she was reluctant to let her foster mother return there until she was assured Goewin was truly content. Even after she was gone and Garmon had returned, she was silent and thoughtful. Garmon coaxed her to bed but she couldn't sleep. Though the bed in the inn was much wider and more comfortable than the cot in the cloister, Heledd was not fully at ease when Garmon turned to take her in his arms.

"Did you bolt the door?" she asked.

"What is the good of that, *gwraig*? I am already in the room."

"Did you?"

Garmon got out of bed and locked the door, making certain the bolt was sound. When he returned to lie beside her, Heledd felt only a fraction more content. Despite her anxiety, she made love with him and when he fell asleep with his arm locked around her, she stared at the beams of the ceiling, her hand spread over her belly, certain she was not the only one who was lying awake in the inn.

Her sense of unease invaded her thoughts so she imagined a threat at every creak of the old structure, becoming so agitated she turned and hid in the shelter of Garmon's body with such energy he had reached for his sword before he was fully awake.

"What?" he asked in a murmur, searching the room, without moving a muscle, for the danger her fear communicated to him.

"I don't know," she whispered against his ear, tucking her head beneath his jaw, "I feel something."

Garmon stilled his breath and calmed his heart. Without a sound, he cautioned her to be silent and slid from the bed, taking a position near the door, where he could not be seen by the intruder. Heledd lay still, the *carthen* dragged over her mouth to stifle her gasps for air. With no warning, the door flew back against the wall. The room was filled with the scream of broken metal and splintering wood as an armed warrior leapt to the center of the room near the foot of the bed. Heledd's scream brought shouts from the other guests in the inn but the warrior ignored her, finding his intended target with one slow movement of his head. He raised his sword and lunged at Garmon so forcefully Heledd felt the blade in her own heart before it struck.

"I wondered how long it would take you to find me," Garmon hissed as he swung out of the path of the sword's thrust.

"I learned you had gone only this morning," Urien replied, preparing for another strike. "You would not have gotten beyond the gates if I had known what you planned."

"You are older but no wiser," Garmon said, holding his finger to his lips when Heledd drew breath to speak.

"You wasted no time finding yourself a whore," Urien commented, glancing at the figure huddled in the bed, before he slashed the air at Garmon's belly.

"What whore?" Heledd flinging herself toward her husband.

"No!" Garmon shouted, pulling her behind him before Urien had an opportunity to prepare another blow. "What were you thinking, *gwraig*?"

"What were *you* thinking?" Urien demanded of his foster brother.

"Why are you fighting?" Heledd pleaded.

Urien glared at her. "What have you done?" he demanded of Garmon, taking a threatening step closer. "Not content to ruin her in name, you must do that in deed? The innkeeper told me you had brought your whore with you. Bad enough you treat this girl like a slave in Bro-Dawel and let it be known you don't want her, you let this vermin witness your abuse?"

"Urien," Heledd began, "it's not what you think."

"The Abbot could not believe you brought a woman into the cloister."

"Where else was I supposed to take my wife?"

"Wife?" Urien scoffed. "You expect me to believe you have wed?"

"And why not?" Heledd demanded, stepping out from behind her husband. "Do you think I am unworthy of a good husband?"

"*Boneddiges*," Urien said, "if I thought you unworthy or

Garmon a good husband, I would not be here."

"I was good enough to stand in for you," Garmon said, stung by his brother's criticism.

"I had no choice then," Urien answered, lowering his weapon. "Your commission was to find her a good husband, not allow her to be assaulted and her good name destroyed."

Heledd turned her back on Urien and looked into Garmon's eyes. "Do you want to hit him or shall I?" Garmon looked back at her, some warmth returning to his expression as he extended his arm to draw her to him.

"You had better," he murmured, "it is unlikely he will let me near him."

"Urien, we appreciate," Heledd said, turning in Garmon's embrace to address the warrior, "you have the best of intentions but that does not give you the right to insult us." She raised her hand to caress her husband's cheek and was glad when he returned the gesture of affection by kissing the palm of her hand, and tightening his arm around her. Urien stepped back and sat on the edge of the bed.

"Why didn't you say something?" he demanded of Garmon.

"I had no right to say until Heledd chose. I didn't know myself what she wanted. Until she gave her consent, I could not exert my rights as her husband, though I have considered her my wife from the moment I held her in my arms."

"You could have told me," Heledd complained.

"I did," Garmon replied. "You refused to hear me." When she frowned at him quizzically, he said, "*Gwraig.*"

"Ach, how am I supposed to understand such a meager attempt? You know I'm not as clever as you are. In fact, that is a very sorry answer, Garmon. I don't know why I have wasted all these months on such thin evidence. I must be simple." She turned away from him and fixed her gaze on Urien. "You are no better. How did you think this would end when you put your plan in the hands of someone so ... subtle? Why didn't you just tell me from the first what you knew and how you thought to prevent it?" Urien raised his eyebrows and exchanged a glance with his foster brother. "Ach, you're as bad as each other. Don't think I will forget this, either of you. Now, if you don't mind, I am tired and I will need all the sleep I can get." Heledd dismissed Urien with a wave of her hand and crawled back under the *carthen*. "If you are going to talk, find somewhere I cannot hear you."

Two days later, Heledd was not surprised Urien chose to stay with his command and the people from Bannawg for whom he had accepted responsibility. For herself, she did not want to return to Bro-Dawel, but understood Garmon could not stay away any longer. Urien had brought the news the Cenfyn family were preparing to leave after the brothers had received treatment for their injuries. Aeron had lost only one of his teeth but Wyn's nose would never be straight again. Heledd thought this was less punishment than they deserved for the trouble they had caused but she did not want a protracted vengeance any more than she wanted compensation from Meilor Gwesyn and Llew Talgarth for the murder of her family.

The week of love making and indulgence had made her too tired to want much more than a long night of undisturbed sleep, to get back to a routine of usefulness and to settle into her new life as the wife of the commander of Huw Bro-Dawel's warriors and their warbands. She was not surprised by the change in her attitude toward soldiers, at least not the soldiers trained by her husband. Though she had brief opportunities to see those trained by Urien at work during the days she became reacquainted with Goewin and the others, she did not feel the same security in their presence as she did with Aled's command.

She was not certain how Huw would react to her return with his stepson. She had never been sure of his opinion of her, even before she had stood her ground against the contract offered to her. Her reluctance to return grew through the day, as soon as Garmon had told her it was time to do so. That night, she went to bed early and was asleep by the time he returned from his conversation with Urien and Goewin.

Though she did not experience the same unease as on the

first night at the inn, Garmon's restless attempts to make himself comfortable woke her with a scream and a pounding heart. She bolted upright in the bed. Garmon laid his hand on her shoulder. "I didn't intend to wake you," he said, sliding his arm around her waist and pulling her back to lie with him. "You're all right," he murmured. Heledd was confused but accepted his caresses without protest and opened her body to him the moment he sought her.

In the morning, Heledd was languid and put no energy into her preparations to return. Garmon watched her brushing her hair for such a long time he was lulled into the sleep he had lost the night before. Heledd was amazed to see him stretched out on the bed in the late morning, sleeping more soundly than she knew he slept most nights. Conscientious she might wake him if she tried to join him on the bed, she busied herself with small tasks, as silent as a breeze across distant wheat fields. The most interesting task she found was to search for the letters she could recognize among those that had been carved into the oak planks of the table by previous guests. She could recognize some but could not complete all the letters she knew were needed for Garmon's name or her own.

In frustration, Heledd dismissed the scratches with a wave of her hand and left the room in search of an activity that was not so constantly proving her ignorance. At the bottom of the wooden staircase, she entered a room full of farmers and townspeople, some of whom she recognized from the *gaer* and the harvest. She hesitated for only a moment before the friendly smile of one of the men caught her attention. She returned Martyn the Shoemaker's smile with a warm grin before descending the remaining stairs to join him at the table.

"I am surprised to see you," the shoemaker said. "Are you well?"

"What you doing here, Martyn?" Heledd asked, accepting the flagon of ale he offered.

"It is market today, *boneddiges*. I've come from the *gaer* to trade and to buy good leather."

"May I join you? My husband is asleep and I have never been to market."

"Of course. There are a few here from Bro-Dawel. You'll be in good company," Martyn assured her.

When none of them raised an eyebrow at her use of the term 'husband', Heledd was more confident and joined in their laughter, sharing some of their meal with them. When the group of farmers had finished their refreshment, Heledd walked out of the inn and its wagon yard with them into the bright autumn sunshine, barely able to restrain herself from running into the festooned street of stalls and carts selling the wares of merchants from far-flung countries.

The sights and the smells of the market street were unlike anything she had ever experienced. In a short distance, she could find cloth for a fine garment and a simple frock, silks and damasks, flax, linen and cotton, some dyed in vibrant colors and some in their natural variations. Despite her determination to find an activity that did not prove her ignorance, Heledd found she had far more questions for the merchants than she could possibly ever have the answers. They answered with patience and some with genuine interest to inform her.

Although she looked at the finer fabrics, she was draw to the cotton – a fabric that felt strong and soft to the touch. "What would you use this fabric for?" she asked the merchant, holding up a length from the bolt of natural-hued material.

"This cloth has many uses, *boneddiges*," the tall merchant said. "It can be used for garments, bedding. It is sturdy and delicate, soft to the touch as you can feel. Many of my customers use it for undergarments."

"Do they use it for children, very small children?"

"It is particularly suitable for children, *boneddiges*," he replied, "especially infants." He offered to cut her a length but Heledd shook her head.

"I cannot buy it now. Perhaps when you are next here."

"That will not be until the spring," he said, taking the bolt from her and laying it onto the pile of others.

"I will come back in the spring. That will be in plenty of time."

She moved away from the stall and toward a soap merchant, being careful not to arouse his hopes she would buy from him. She filled her lungs with the scents of the herbal soaps to decide which one Garmon preferred. Before she made a decision, her attention was diverted to examine the merchandise of a haberdasher's stall. Although there was nothing she had money to buy, she spent a long time examining each item that caught her attention, holding it in her hands and up to the light, feeling its quality, testing its strength. The haberdasher remained silent, offering similar objects for her scrutiny until she clasped a thimble in her fingers that fit her as though it had been made to her measurement and with her exact taste. It was silver with etched circles and knots around the turned collar. Each indentation was spaced precisely and the workmanship was perfect.

"I have never had one of these," she said, half aloud.

"It is one of the best," the haberdasher commented, stepping closer.

"Who made it?"

"A silversmith living in the north. Her work is very fine."

Heledd gazed at the thimble on her middle finger for several moments before slowly slipping it off and putting it back into its small, silk-lined box.

"Shall I wrap it for you?" the haberdasher asked, picking up the box. When Heledd shook her head, he frowned at her.

"There is no need for that. My wife will take it as it is."

Heledd glanced over her shoulder and turned a joyous smile on the haberdasher as she held out her hand. When he placed it into her hand, she clasped the box to her heart and then carefully placed the box in her purse.

"That is a fine purse," the haberdasher commented. "There are not many of that quality these days."

"This belonged to my mother," Heledd said, "and was a gift from my husband." Though this information confused the haberdasher, Garmon's thoughtful smile was enough.

"If you ever wish to sell it," the haberdasher offered, "I am a ready buyer."

"Thank you, but I will keep this with me always." The haberdasher nodded, took Garmon's coins and wished them well. "I have not had opportunity, until now," Heledd said, meeting her husband's gaze, "to thank you for returning this to me. I meant to do so soon after you gave it. Even before I recognized it, I valued this gift and I was grateful to you for it – I did want to thank you."

"I cannot take any credit for its value to you," he said. "I wanted to give you something useful. Goewin saved me from making such a paltry gesture." Heledd threw her arms around him briefly then turned back to the inn. "I saw Mared. Ceinwen and Rhian, as well. They are here in the market. I didn't speak to them, I was looking for you," Garmon said, meeting her eyes. "We can't put off returning to Bro-Dawel," he said after a pause. "Huw will hear we are in the town and wonder why we have stayed away so long."

"I know," Heledd replied, "but I'm so happy here."

"You will be happy in Bro-Dawel," Garmon assured her as they climbed the stairs to their room. "And if you are not, we will leave."

# cwency-cwo

The gates of the *gaer* were closed as Garmon approached but the soldier on duty acknowledged his commander's call for admittance. While they waited for the bolt to slide away, Heledd dropped from Angel's back and handed the reins to Garmon. She moved to the side of the opening and, as Garmon was greeted by some of the men in his command, she walked behind them toward the longhouse, too weary to feign interest in a homecoming. As she had suspected, Garmon was caught up in his duties and responsibilities before his foot touched the soil of the *buarth*. She heard Huw's bellow for torches and his cheerful greeting when Garmon reached the courtyard. As she opened the door of the longhouse, she called Bleddyn to her to silence the other hounds. Heledd slipped through the door and bent to hug the young hound's neck before going straight into the bedroom, leaving two of the hounds in the outer room.

She was grateful for the fire that had been kindled in the hearth. The journey from the town had been arduous. She was cold and listless. She picked from the food laid out on the table, wondering how anyone had known they would be returning that night. The bed was prepared, with the linen and *carthen* turned down – all fresh and clean-smelling. She bathed and slid into the softness of the featherbed as though she had been sleeping on hard ground for a week. Bleddyn curled up on the flagstones at the side of the bed, in front of the fire. The other hounds paced between the bedroom and the front door, but after a while, they, like Heledd, gave up waiting for Garmon to come home.

Although her dreams had been less violent in the week that

had passed, she was plagued by other concerns and tasks. These flew at her like wind-severed leaves and she felt her heart racing often, waking through the night to see Garmon had not returned, even though the dawn was near. With a deep sigh, Heledd resigned herself to sleeping alone more often, pouting and taking over the middle of the bed. Until she returned to her dreams, she listened for his uneven footstep at the door of the room.

When he eventually entered the longhouse, announced by the panting of his hounds and Bleddyn's alert, soft bark of welcome, Heledd heard his sharp gasp as he stripped out of the clothes he had worn for a week, dropping them carelessly onto the floor where they fell. He limped across the room to the bed, sitting beside her while he watched her sleep by the light of the fire. Heledd opened her eyes to meet his gaze, inviting him into the bed with her. She slid into his embrace and pressed her body against him, tilting her chin to entice his kiss. Sighing as his hands glided over her body, she released her languid desire to his demands, encouraging him to take his pleasure in her in whatever way he craved.

With several more hours of sleep than Garmon, Heledd woke to the first sounds of the day in the *gaer*. Jealous of their time alone, although she woke from hunger, Heledd decided against rising. Instead, she lay next to Garmon, studying his sleeping face, remarking the signs of stress and pain, fatigue that brought lines to his brow above his straight nose. Beneath his eyes, dark smudges proved he needed sleep and she sacrificed her hunger to his greater need, leaving him to sleep as long as he required.

She heard voices and footsteps outside and, once, a servant entered the longhouse but Heledd did not disturb her husband by rising. Despite her wakeful listening, she slept again for short periods during the early morning, waking fitfully to find Garmon still in slumber. By mid-morning her need for food faded as she slept and when she awakened shortly before midday, she was alone.

Throwing off the bedclothes, she darted into the outer room

but that too was empty. A platter of fruit and bread awaited her at the table as well as a jug of ale. Heledd ate in the chair by the hearth, pouting when she saw the hearthstone had been scrubbed clean, leaving no trace of her name. *If he thinks I will care … why would he do that? I —*. Heledd leaned to look around the large room and then stood to search the bedroom. *Where are my clothes?*

All three of the staghounds were gone and when she searched through the chests in the bedroom, she could find nothing belonging to her, except what she had been wearing for a week and her black purse. She opened it to ensure the silver thimble was still there as well as her needle, pins and skeins of thread. Puzzled by the disappearance of all the garments Garmon had given to her, Heledd made a thorough search of the bedroom and the house. In the process, she saw Garmon's clothing was carefully tailored, pressed and arranged on shelves in the tall chest by the door. When she had finished searching for anything belonging to her, she had left his clothing in chaos.

Her search extended to his desk and the stacks of documents and boxes of papers, inks and quills standing in ordered areas along its top edge. For a while, she entertained herself by studying the documents to find the letters she could recognize and was delighted when she saw all of the letters of her own name several times in one document, as well as the letters she knew were Garmon's name all together at the bottom of the same document. She laid the document carefully away to be studied later.

She found a small sheet of paper without any marks on it and practiced making the letters of her name with her finger before she gathered enough courage to attempt to use one of the quills. With a deep breath she chose the smallest, cleanest of them and held it between her fingers, trying to remember how Mairwen had held the small piece of charcoal. *Ach, this is no good.* She threw the quill down. *I will never learn this.*

She returned her attention to her exploration of the longhouse and its contents, unmindful of the disorder she left in her wake in her delight at finding some of Garmon's childhood toys in a small box in the storeroom at the far end of the house. When she heard the three dogs bounding into the house and the hissed, "*Uffern*," Heledd surveyed the muddle she had created with dismay.

"Look what I have found," she exclaimed from the depths of the dim storeroom. "Our son can play with this," she said, emerging with a carved figure held high.

"And who will put all this in order after you have played enough?" Garmon asked, standing at the door with the staghounds.

"Oh, I will," she replied, diving back into the small, shelf-lined room.

"I do not need to ask what you have been doing while I worked," he commented.

"Neither do I need ask why you left me, without so much as a single word of explanation, although I had waited – *patiently* – for hours for *you* to wake though I was faint with hunger," Heledd said, planting her hands on her hips as she turned to glare at him from the door. "No need for you to think of me – alone all day – while you are 'working'."

Garmon stood silent for several moments, looking at the evidence of her activity in his absence. When he cleared his throat to speak, she pressed her lips together and cocked her head. "You were asleep. I didn't want to wake you."

"You did not, even for a moment, think I might want breakfast," she accused him. "You were only too happy to be rid of me, to be with your friends and family. You did not care you left me here to wake alone."

"You have had sufficient occupation," he replied.

"Only because I could not find anything to wear." She took a few steps through the jumble of his belongings. Garmon glanced at the empty platter and the drained flagon of ale lying on its side. Heledd followed his gaze and tossed her head to shake her hair from her shoulders, leaning against the wall with her head bowed. "Are you angry with me, Garmon?"

"No," he replied. "Are you angry with me?"

"I cannot stay angry with you," she laughed, raising her chin.

"Heledd," he whispered, "come to me. I cannot cross the floor to you." She leapt at his command, flying into his arms amid the clutter strewn at his feet. "Do you forgive my neglect," he asked, lifting a wisp of red from her brow, "or are you only bored with my meager possessions."

"I forgive you," she said, "but I am bored too. I want to learn writing."

"Writing leads to reading," Garmon replied, glancing at the documents abandoned on his desk.

"Do you write what I should not read?"

"Not often," he admitted. "You will need to read when you—."

"When I what?" she inquired, sweeping his hair back from his forehead with her hands and peering into his granite-hued eyes, aware she could not read all of his moods. "Garmon, tell me what troubles you now. Are you angry I have touched your property?"

"All I have is yours."

"I am very stupid," she said, "you must be worried I will be useless. I will disappoint you," Heledd sighed, slipping from his arms and returning to the bedchamber.

"Never," he said, following her to the door of the bedroom.

"Were your expectations so low?" she asked, dropping listlessly to the bed and dragging the bedclothes over her head.

"What has happened? What has changed your mood?" He cleared a narrow path to the bed and sat on the edge, coaxing her to look at him but she refused to let him see her face. "I cannot read your mind, Heledd," he complained. Heledd cried aloud for some time before he pushed himself to his feet. At the door, he said, "I have asked for a meal to be served here for us. Join me when you wish."

When he had closed the door, Heledd forced herself to calm her weeping and listened for every sound coming from the outer room. She was ashamed she had left such a mess for him to straighten but refused to give in. After a while, he exhaled deeply as he sat in front of the hearth. The dogs sniffed at the bedroom door and returned to their master's side when he snapped his fingers. Heledd burst into loud tears again but Garmon did not return to the bedroom to comfort her. After a while, she heard several people enter. She listened to voices and thought she heard the clatter of wooden bowls and cutlery. Garmon spoke several times but she could not hear what he said and when the visitors finally left, Heledd threw off the *carthen* and opened the door to the outer room, prepared to offer an apology.

Except for the staghounds, the outer room was empty. The remains of the *cawl* was cold and the cheese dry but she was too hungry to reject what he had left for her. For some time, she sat in his armed chair in front of the hearth, holding her knees to her chest and staring at the flames. The dogs ignored her. The wind stirred the embers in the grate and the flames of the two candles on the table flickered.

Heledd resigned herself to the choice between waiting for Garmon to return or joining him, wherever he was. *It is always better to face what will come.* In all the clutter of the bedroom, she could not find her shoes. The frock and tunic she had worn all the previous week were lying where she had left them in the corner of the room. She huffed and made the best she could of them before wrapping the brown cloak she had found in the cloister around her. The *buarth* was lit by torches standing in stone carn at intervals. Most of the residents of the *gaer* were in their homes. She thought first of going to Aled's house but there was no light in the narrow window by the door.

With reluctance, she walked toward Huw's house. She entered through the door leading to the *buarth* away from the courtyard, thinking her clothes had been moved back into her room in the *pennaeth's* house. The door to the room was ajar. The mattress on the cot was turned and folded but there was nothing else in the room. Her other, older tunic and linen frock were also gone, as well as her old boots. Perplexed, she started toward the dining hall through the smaller passageway, deciding her belongings may have left in the *pennaeth's* care. As she neared the doors of the *neuadd*, one of the younger girls caught her eye. "That's mine," she gasped. The girl stopped in her tracks, gasping in her own right. "Who gave you my clothes to wear?" Heledd demanded, staring at the mulberry tunic.

"The *pennaeth*," the girl answered, stepping back. "Mared said I could have it."

"But it's mine," Heledd complained, feeling her sense of injustice welling, lifting her chin to stem the flow of tears that threatened.

"What is the delay?" Ceinwen asked as she opened one of the doors. She stepped out and snapped the door closed behind her. "What are you doing here?"

"This girl is wearing my clothes," Heledd said, stung by Ceinwen's cold tone.

"You left them here, Heledd. We do not let good clothing go to waste."

"But I have only been gone a week."

"Lower your voice," Ceinwen scolded, "or the *pennaeth* will know you are here."

"Why does that matter?" Heledd demanded, stepping toward the door. Ceinwen barred her way as the door opened again and Mared stood in the gap.

"I want to see the *pennaeth*," Heledd answered, scowling at the two women.

"How do you dare come here?" Mared demanded, turning to Ceinwen. "The little whore has come crawling back," she laughed, "and she's barefoot. Are you one of the dusty footed wanderers now?"

"I should have known you would not change," Heledd retorted. Aled and Huw reached the door just as Mared pulled back her arm to strike. Heledd pulled herself to her full height, raised her chin to its highest and spun away.

"Heledd," Garmon called from the doorway, shouldering past Aled and Huw. "What are you doing here?" he asked as he caught her wrist.

"I could ask you the same," she answered, turning on him, "but since you have asked, you *told* me to join you when I so wished."

"I did not command you," Garmon replied, lowering his

voice.

"Tell. Command. Order. It is all the same and when I do as you command, you are not there." She turned away again. Aled laid his hand on Garmon's arm but his gesture was shrugged away.

"Where are your shoes?"

"I couldn't find them in the dark and," Heledd took a deep breath, raising her arm and pointing to her left, "this girl is wearing my tunic."

Garmon glanced at the girl and dismissed her. The girl darted away along the passage.

"So," Heledd snapped, whirling to face her husband as if there was no one else near them, "this is what I can expect. My belongings are stolen from me and you condone it, just because I have dared to— to—." Garmon raised his hands in protest, taking another step toward her.

"Garmon," Huw intervened, "I will deal with this creature."

"Heledd," Garmon murmured, reaching his hand toward her, "how am I to know what happens when I am not here. The girl was frightened."

"That is no excuse," Heledd said, "theft is theft and," she took another deep breath, "how are you to know when you cannot be troubled to ask when you know you have hurt me and then seek the company of your friends when it suits you." She felt a hand on her shoulder and turned to look into Geraint's eyes.

"Heledd," he whispered close to her ear, "...but not unkind."

When she turned her head to look at Garmon, she could see his jaw was turning to stone and his gaze was as hard as she had seen it whenever uncertainty overtook him.

"I cannot read your mind," he said.

"You could ask," Heledd replied, taking a step toward him. "I cannot read your mind either and I cannot ask the wall for an answer when you are not there."

"Garmon," Mared said, "slap this whore and let us get on with our meal."

"I'll slap you, you hateful—."

Garmon stepped between the two women before Heledd's hand could find its target, taking the blow on his shoulder. "You are right," he said, clasping her hand in his.

Garmon lifted her in his arms. "You will be the death of me, Heledd *gwraig* Garmon."

"You should not have left me alone."

"I know."

"Then don't do so."

"I won't."

"And—," Heledd began.

"Another command?" he asked, lowering her feet to the floor when they had reached the longhouse and crossed the threshold.

"Just so you know and need not ask," Heledd said, "I do not cry often but when I do, it is because I am hurt or frightened."

"Which caused these recent tears?" Garmon lifted her chin on the crook of his finger.

"If I knew I would tell you," Heledd replied, raising her arms to encircle his neck. Garmon shook his head, kicking the door shut behind him.


Heledd clasped the quill in her fingers again, struggling to position it exactly as Garmon had shown her. "I didn't realize this would be so difficult," Heledd lamented, rubbing the side of her head. The quill seemed to have an obstinate streak of its own will and wavered from left to right as soon as she touched the nib to the scrap of paper. Despite her growling, the writing refused to come from the ink as it did for Garmon. "There is something wrong with this quill."

"A poor craftsman blames his tools," Garmon reminded her. "It will be easier if I help," he ventured.

"I want to do this myself," Heledd declared, dropping the quill and pushing the paper to the side. She propped her head on her hands and stared at the opposite wall. "I'll never do this. I'm too stupid." Garmon pulled her onto his lap, positioned the quill in her hand again and brought the paper in front of her. "How will this help?" she asked, half turning to offer him a kiss.

"Concentrate on your work, *gwraig*," he said, laying his hand over hers. "Dip the nib in the ink. Not so much," he instructed, tapping the nib on the edge of the inkpot. "Nib on the paper and one stroke down, one to the right. Like so."

"It's easy when you do it," she sighed. He released her hand and gestured for her to make the same line to the right of the first. Her mark wavered and the nib bent. "See?"

"Heledd, my love, you're making it hard work. Loosen your hand. The quill is not a butter churn. You don't need all your strength to make it do as you want. Do it again." Heledd wiggled her fingers to relax them but when she took the quill between them, her tense effort bent the nib so it could not be used. "Maybe I am not the right teacher for you."

"A poor teacher blames his pupil," Heledd chided.

"Ceinwen is a teacher. Or Meleri," he offered again. "They have more experience than I do."

"No," she said with such force he looked at her for a long time. "Who taught you?" she asked in a softer tone, turning her head away.

"My mother and the monks."

"My mother is dead and I am too old to be tutored by monks," Heledd said. Garmon sighed, dropping his chin on her shoulder to watch as she took another quill. She took a deep breath as though she was about to undertake a mighty effort. When she let it out, she touched the nib to the inkpot with a shaking hand. Garmon pulled her hair away from her neck and kissed her throat. "Don't," she whispered, biting her lips together. As she touched the nib to the paper, he plunged his hands between her thighs and gathered her shift in his fingers until he could reach her bare skin. "Don't," Heledd murmured again, pressing her knees together.

"You work," he said, "I'll play."


Nine days after their return from the town, Heledd opened the door of the longhouse and restrained Bleddyn from running past her until she had fastened the scarf around her hair. "You won't be welcome in the *beudy*," she told the hound. "Find your master." She gave the dog the hand command she had taught him and filled her lungs with the fresh, late autumn, sun-warmed air. Straightening her back and tilting her chin, she opened the low gate and walked through the *buarth* into the shadowed milking shed. Without hesitation, she took a place in the next empty stall, positioned her stool and bent her head to the task, aware several of the women near her had stopped their milking to stare. After a short time, their chatter resumed and Heledd relaxed to the rhythmic sound of the milk clattering into the pails.

Though her head was swimming and she had had a queasy feeling in her belly all morning, she was happy to be where she knew she was useful. She had mastered the marks for the letters of her name and, from there, she had taught herself, in a fashion, to make the marks for Garmon's name. She practiced these and learned to salvage the scraps of paper she used by scraping the ink away with the blade of the small knife he had given her but, too often, her head began to hurt and she wanted most of all to sleep – undisturbed.

Heledd pressed her cheek against the cow's rough haunches, unmindful of the mud smudging her already brown-dappled face. The monotony of the milking was soothing and gave her time to think. Garmon had not wanted her to leave the house to work in the *beudy*. Their argument was ferocious that morning and neither had won – they simply gave up the effort to win. He had finished his breakfast in silence. She had dressed in her work clothes in silence. When he walked out the door to go to the stables, he kissed her lightly on the lips and she responded with the same acceptance.

The idyllic days and nights of playing at love had come to an end. Heledd could not remember what she had said and she had soon forgotten the words he shouted at her but the result was a defeat for both. She thought it was unlikely he would have forgotten the insults she had hurled at him in her own cause.

Many long hours of toil were to pass before she saw him again.

When the other women took short breaks as the cowherds took the first cows out to be replaced with a second group and then a third, Heledd found a sunny spot near the open shed doors to breathe fresher air and to warm herself. Across the *buarth*, beyond the barracks, she could see the soldiers near the stables, gathered around the paddock as they had done so many weeks before to watch Garmon *gŵr* Heledd *llysfab* Huw train his colt. Though she was tempted to join the women as before, she thought Garmon would not welcome her.

When all the cows were milked and driven back into the grazing fields, Heledd washed her hands and face and followed some of the older women to the work at the cheese press until their day's work was finished. When the cheese mistress saw Heledd at the door, she frowned but relented, giving the new wife the least skilled task. Heledd's hands had softened over the few weeks she had been absent from the *beudy* and she found them too tender to be useful. By mid-afternoon, she was nearly in tears because she was not as capable in making cheese as she had always hoped to be.

"Is your work finished for today?" Garmon stood in the doorway, watching as she struggled to bring the cheese press under her control.

"Yes," Heledd said with relief. "I cannot learn it all in one day. How was the colt today?"

"He has gone wild since I have neglected him these past weeks. Aled claimed they had given him attention but the little brute wouldn't let anyone near him. He's still skittish."

"I don't blame him. If he were not intended to be a warhorse, I would call him *Nefwy*."

"I think my friends would rather call him *Uffern*," Garmon laughed. "He's caused some damage to them in the past weeks, but *Nefwy* is a good name for a warhorse – he will send a few men to their Maker during his lifetime."

"What shall we do tonight?" Heledd asked, crossing the threshold and dropping her shawl onto the table as she went through to the bedroom. She had already stripped out of her tunic and frock when he reached the door of the room, carrying her shawl to be put on the peg behind the door. Pouring water into the basin, she bathed her face and arms, drying herself with a flannel cloth. Garmon watched her from the doorway, a slight frown finding its way to settle between his eyes.

"A meal will be here soon. I have some work," he said, nodding toward the documents on his desk.

"Something about the law?" Heledd asked without looking at him.

"I have no more to do with that since Hywel ordered them written. Why?"

Heledd turned partly away and wrapped a robe around her shoulders. "What laws should I know?"

"Those that govern your property, the rights of your children by marriage, divorce, any crime you commit," he said, laying his hands on her shoulders.

"Are you my husband?"

"Yes, you know I am," he replied, peering at her profile.

"How? How are we wed? In law."

"By consent," he said, "as a free woman and a free man. As equals."

"Is that good?" she asked, turning to face him, laying her head on his shoulder. Garmon stroked her hair for a moment and lifted her chin, kissing her softly.

"That is good," he whispered against her mouth.

# twenty-three

After they had finished their meal, one of the household stewards came to the door of the longhouse with the message Huw Bro-Dawel wanted to see them in an hour's time.

"Is there anything I should know before we enter?" Garmon asked his wife as they walked together through the courtyard.

"I have done nothing wrong ... today," Heledd replied, pulling the hood of the brown cloak from her head as she walked through the door of the house and into the smaller, private dining hall for the *pennaeth*'s family. Though there were several members of the household and other residents of the *gaer* in the room, Huw was not there. The steward who had brought the message came to greet them and led the way to Huw's private office. When Heledd walked past Ceinwen and Mared, she was surprised they smiled. Their reaction to her when she returned with Garmon was still in her mind and she did not respond with more than a nod of her head. Meini also smiled. Heledd hesitated for a moment near her, extending her hand out of sight of the others to which Meini responded with the same quiet gesture.

The door to the *pennaeth's* office was opened to the commander and his wife before they reached the threshold and was closed behind them. Huw sat at his desk, facing the wall away from them. A small oil lamp illuminated the desk. The only other light in the room came from the hearth. Huw waved his hand toward two chairs placed in front of his desk, exactly as they had been when he had questioned Heledd about their contract. Hesitating before taking the seat he offered to her, Heledd glanced at Garmon who held the back of her chair and, from inside his hooded cloak, was removing a tied scroll of documents. He lifted his eyes to meet her gaze, smiling briefly before he took his own chair.

"I see you have learned to communicate with one another at last," Huw Bro-Dawel said, turning his head to study his stepson and stepdaughter-in-law. "Have you brought what I asked?"

Garmon handed the scroll to the *pennaeth* and leaned forward in his chair, his elbows across his knees.

"Is this everything?"

"Everything I could find."

"What is it?" Heledd asked. "Something I should have known about before we entered?"

"I spoke too soon," Huw said, turning a cold stare on both of his guests.

"I have been distracted," Garmon replied to the stare with another brief smile. "These are the documents detailing the property that will dictate the terms of our marriage contract," he told Heledd.

"I'm not surprised you never told me," Heledd said, "since I have no property to detail."

"That is untrue," Huw told her. "As the sole surviving member of your father's descendants, you are entitled to all he owned until his death – or compensation for it."

"What does that mean?" she scoffed. "Everything now belongs to my uncle."

"Under false pretexts, as the so-called victim of your father's betrayal," Huw told her. "That, we all know, is a lie he and Meilor Gwesyn have perpetrated to protect their unlawful gains and to hide their conspiracy. Garmon has studied the evidence they presented—."

"You should have told me," Heledd said as she leapt to her feet and strode toward the door.

"You should have told her," Huw agreed with a laugh.

"Heledd, come back and listen," Garmon commanded. "There was no point in telling you when the evidence was not there. I did not want to give you any false hope you could inherit Bannawg."

"Is that the real reason or a convenient excuse?"

"Why would I need an excuse?" he demanded.

"To trick me into signing a contract I could not read and steal everything I did not even know I had?"

"You think I am capable of that?"

"You wouldn't be the first to tell lies to me," Heledd said, turning to face him. "Nor the first time *you* lied."

"Sit down, Heledd," Huw said. "No one in this room has conspired to cheat you, least of all your husband." When she turned her face away, tilting her chin, Huw continued, "If anyone is to blame, *menyw*, it is me. When Garmon told me what he had learned about your family from Urien and the woman, Goewin, I was curious. He also told me what you remembered. I know enough of these kinship laws to seize an opportunity for your sake and that of any child you may have." Huw stopped for a moment and pointed to the chair she had vacated. Heledd complied but sat on its edge, ready to flee. "As you know, your uncle claims to be the victim but there is now certain evidence – not just the word of a few surviving women – Meilor and Llew conspired to attack your father, to steal his land and kill his family."

"What evidence?" Heledd asked.

"When Gwyn was killed, Garmon returned here. Initially, I thought his melancholy was grief for the loss of his foster brother, but when it did not lift, I discovered what he had been keeping to himself while we grieved for Gwyn." Huw glanced at Garmon, receiving a curt nod in return. "Neither Urien nor Garmon meant any harm to you but mistakes were made by both, and, consequently, by me. Until Garmon found these documents," Huw said, laying his hand on the scroll, "you were, in law, a prisoner of war and, by sufferance, to the status of bondservant. Llew claimed the right to dispose of your bond as he saw fit. I purchased your bond for Garmon's sake and brought you here so you would have an opportunity to know him as a man worthy of your esteem. He wanted you to have choice, since he had denied you that right at Talgarth-y-

Bannawg. All this you know."

Heledd nodded, glancing at Garmon.

"Perhaps," Huw continued, "you do not know that, since your uncle consented to Garmon's having intercourse with you, in law, you became his wife, if he agreed – which, so he tells me, he did. Although your uncle had denied you the right to wed, his action contradicted that decree. Though you were not aware of it, you had a husband by your uncle's consent, against your own will."

"Is that lawful?" Heledd queried, staring at her tightly entwined her fingers.

"It is," Huw told her, "but, as I said, Garmon was not content. You know all this as well." He dismissed the details with a wave of his hand, picking up the scroll. "This is your future, my girl. I am a practical man, much more practical than this man or my daughters. I insisted your husband investigate your family's history for the sake of your children together." He opened the scroll and read for a short time. "In any case, this is the position, Heledd. You have a right to claim your father's property or to claim compensation."

"I do not want Bannawg," Heledd answered.

Huw Bro-Dawel lowered his brow in a deep frown. "Garmon told me you wanted to return there."

"I believe it is my duty to ensure the people who live there, and were faithful to my family, do not suffer any longer. I know there are seventeen children who were taken as slaves to Gwesyn. I also know there are nearly thirty who…will be without homes. My life and future are here, with Garmon, but I will not abandon those who have sacrificed for my sake."

"What can you do?" Huw asked. "Without land to shelter and feed them, you do not have much to offer."

"You said I can claim compensation," Heledd replied. "That would be a start."

"That is a lengthy process," Huw told her.

"The alternative is war," Heledd said, "and I will not send any man or woman to their deaths on the chance I could win back land stolen before some of them were born."

"The quest for compensation may also lead to war," Garmon interjected.

"Possibly, months or years in the future, if the law cannot put right what my uncle and Meilor Gwesyn have done."

"How many of your friends do you intend to bring here to Bro-Dawel to live?" Huw demanded.

"None if they are not welcome, *pennaeth*," Heledd said, looking into his blue-haloed brown eyes. "I know you believe I should claim Bannawg for my son—."

"What son?"

"Garmon's son, the son I will bear him."

"What do you know about this?" Huw asked his stepson.

"We have discussed the possibility," Garmon said, smiling at Heledd.

Huw turned his attention to the scroll and another document on his desk. "Bannawg is worthless, always has been, fit only for grazing and scratching a pauper's living from its rocks. One day it will disappear beneath the river from which it drinks," Huw commented, pushing a document toward her. "Sign this."

"What is it?"

"Your contract of marriage to my stepson. Garmon will read it to you, then you will sign." Heledd studied the *pennaeth's* face for some time. "You have no cause for your distrust, *menyw*. I would not disadvantage my grandson any more than I would disadvantage one of my daughters. This is no different to the contract proposed by the man who will be Meini's husband."

"Meini is to wed?" Heledd exclaimed, "but you said she would not have another husband."

"The man made an offer I could not justify refusing, though it is against my better judgment," the *pennaeth* replied with a broad grin. "The man is a fool, obviously. My meddling daughters have a great deal to do with recent events. They are both far too clever for their own good." Heledd noted there was an element of pride in his tone in equal measure to his aggravation. "Meini at least has the good sense to keep her thoughts to herself. Mared is motivated largely by passion –

thought comes too late."

"Does this mean you will let Meini raise her daughter, Angharad?"

"You are well-informed," the *pennaeth* said in a tone that told Heledd he was irritated as well as gratified by her powers of observation. "The man has indicated his willingness to raise the child as his own."

"Who is to be her husband?" Garmon asked.

Huw touched his nose and winked. "He is known here and I have no doubt of his character but, as he has not yet spoken to Meini, you *will not* spoil the surprise. Understood?" Garmon creased his brow in thought. Heledd hid her smile behind the curtain of her red hair and listened carefully to the terms of her contract with Garmon.

She was described as a free woman of property, a *gwraig briod*, and he as a free man of property to be married by consent, as equals in partnership. Her property, brought to the marriage, included a black damask purse containing items of value to the household, a gray-dappled mare and an equal share in its future offspring, clothing and bedding, a fine-crafted, etched silver thimble, as well as proceeds from any lawsuit undertaken for compensation for the loss of land and the lives of her family.

Garmon's property included a ruddy-hued warhorse, one colt and an equal share of other offspring proceeding from the mating of his warhorse to his wife's mare, a catalogue of weaponry, a house and its contents, two dairy cows and a bullock, clothing and other household items as well as books and maps, jewelry and other personal items which had belonged to his mother and two fields of the Bro-Dawel *ystad* as a wedding gift from his stepfather.

"Will you sign, Heledd?" Garmon asked her when he had finished reading.

"It is very generous," she murmured, touching his wrist, lifting her gaze to look into his gray eyes, sorry to see uncertainty reflected in them. "I am honored to be your wife, Garmon *mab* Creiddwen Owein *llysfab* Huw," she said taking the quill Huw held out to her and signing her name with the confidence of a woman who had learned to write. Garmon signed his name to the side of hers and Huw witnessed both.

"You've taken enough of my time," the *pennaeth* said, "Back to your house and whatever you have found to do there these passed days."

"Will you go to the *beudy* tomorrow?"

"Yes," Heledd said, "I want to see which of the cows belong to us and to ensure they receive the best treatment. That will make the cheese mistress take notice of me. I won't give her any milk from our excellent cows if she refuses to teach me."

"You will make an excellent *gwraig briod* I see," Garmon laughed.

"Don't think you can breed my mare again soon. I want to see how well you train this colt before I entrust you with the expansion of our investment."

"If I thought you knew what you were talking about, I would be worried."

Heledd stepped close to him, laying her hands on his arm. "Garmon, what should I do about Bannawg?"

"The land or the people, *gwraig*?"

"The people are more important to me, but I think everyone else believes the land should be, for our children's sakes."

"I can provide for our children. All eight of them."

"Ten."

"How did that happen?" he laughed.

"While you were sleeping," Heledd said, turning toward the others in the room with an expression of confidence that did not require an extreme angle of her chin. When she sat down at the table opposite her stepsister-in-law, Heledd smiled at Mared without any semblance of guile. Mared glanced up at her for a moment, frowned for a time and then shrugged, returning her attention to the small trout on her plate. Heledd leaned forward, peering at the fish and wrinkled her nose. "Does that taste as bad as it smells?"

"It is quite good," Mared said.

"What's that?" Heledd asked, pointing to a lump of yellow mixture at the side of the trout on Mared's plate.

"Turnip, of course." Mared pushed a bowl of the mashed root under Heledd's nose. "It's all I can bare to eat now. With honey. Take some, if you want. I can't eat all this."

Heledd scooped a small amount of the turnip onto a plate and lowered her nose to sniff at it. Though it had a strong odor, her stomach didn't turn immediately and she took a small amount onto a wooden spoon. Mared pushed a pot of honey toward her but Heledd shook her head, slowly opening her mouth to taste the vegetable, keeping her eyes closed.

"Let's not pretend we are or can be friends," Mared said.

"We can at least not be enemies," Heledd offered, accepting the pot of honey. "I will stay out of your way, as much as possible."

"That much, I will appreciate. If you will excuse me, Heledd *gwraig* Garmon, I see my husband has returned from his patrol and will want to bathe before he has his meal." Mared rushed into Rheinallt's waiting arms and was swept from sight.

"What did she say to you?" Meini asked, taking the seat Mared had vacated. "She has been in a bad mood since Tegwen told her she was pregnant."

"Why?" Heledd asked.

"She's already past twenty-three and this is her first pregnancy. She's worried something will go wrong."

"Why should it? She's strong."

"Whenever she has thought she was pregnant before, her bleed has returned. Tegwen has told her she needs to be cautious," Meini said. "Rheinallt loves her. I don't think he will care but her first husband wanted a child. Mared does not want to disappoint Rheinallt. If she cannot carry this child, she believes he will divorce her."

"He isn't likely to do that," Heledd said, glancing in the direction the pair went when they left the family hall.

"Rheinallt already has a child," Meini commented, "and has recognized the boy as his. Mared wants to give our father his first grandson as well as carry a child for Rheinallt — she does love him very much."

"Who is the mother of his son?"

"A woman from his district. Rheinallt was very honest with my father. He told Dada he had been sleeping with Mared since a month after Pryderi's death. Dada could hardly refuse him the right to marry her after that," Meini said with a shy smile.

"Is that true?"

"Mared was devastated when Pryderi was killed. Rheinallt was very kind – perhaps that did lead to more but he demanded to marry her."

"Your father seems to prefer men who demand," Heledd said, stopping herself from telling Meini what she had learned only a few minutes before. "Perhaps …"

"Don't say anything, Heledd. My father will not change his mind where I am concerned. He did not want me to marry Gwyn and he does not want me to have Gwyn's daughter with me. And I don't believe Urien is the kind of man who would use abduction as a means of acquiring a wife – not his own foster father's daughter in any case."

"He may … insist, as Rheinallt did."

"By now, I do not think he will even ask. He has always been much more concerned with you than ever with me. When he left here to find you, he said nothing at all to me. Not even good-bye." Meini sighed and gave Heledd a weak smile. "I'm not the kind of woman who inspires great passion as you and Mared do."

"Someone wants you, Meini," Heledd said, "I'm sure of it. One day, when you least expect it, he will be standing before you. And your father will not be able to refuse him."

"I'm quite content, you know," Meini said, lifting her eyes to look around the room. "I have friends and many people to care about. And I have a daughter. Now Dada is happier, I have hope Garmon can persuade him to give Angharad back to me."

"I know he will," Heledd said, reaching across the table to clasp Meini's hand.

"So you have decided to make an appearance at last," Geraint said, taking a seat next to Heledd. "What's this?" he asked, picking up the pot of honey. "This stuff is best served fermented."

"You would know," Meini said. "Shall I prepare a remedy for your head to be ready for you in the morning?"

"You know best, *meddyg*," Geraint laughed, turning his head to peer at Heledd. "Garmon has said you will want to ride sometime in the next few days."

"Did he?" Heledd asked. After a moment, she said, "Yes, I will. Will you come?"

"At your service, Heledd Garmon, as always."


Heledd's new found confidence thrived over the following three days and came from the certainty that, whatever her circumstances or the decisions she made regarding them, she had value as a person as well as owning property in her own right that could not be taken from her. She was protected by the law. The mare she rode belonged to her. The clothes she wore belonged to her. Her future belonged to her and she had chosen, as a free woman, to wed a man she loved. In exchange for her freedom, she had accepted responsibilities to her husband and to her society she found no heavier to bear than the cloak shielding her from the wind from the north as she rode with Meini, Geraint and Carwyn along the road toward the market town.

Huw Bro-Dawel had agreed she had responsibilities to the Bannawg people. Although he had been angry with Garmon and had shouted at his stepson for a full hour before Heledd was allowed to put her case before him, the *pennaeth* gave her permission to pursue her case.

Though the sky was heavy with the threat of storms, Heledd had another, even more heart-felt, reason for wanting to travel to the town. Meini had not been away from Bro-Dawel for weeks. In her usual way, she carried her sorrow in silence – a day in the market and away from her father was due.

Garmon anticipated no serious threat to their safety and only cautioned Heledd to stay always within sight of their escorts. She had promised to do so but was so eager for the journey she woke far earlier than any of those who would be traveling with her and, toward the time for breakfast, suffered for her excitement when everything set before her, with the exception of the bread and ale, made her feel ill even to look at it.

"Have you brought your remedies?" Heledd asked, as the town came into view.

"I always carry a few treatments," Meini said, gesturing toward the leather satchel draped over the shoulder of her young, brown gelding.

"Do you have anything for an aching head? And it's not what *you* think," Heledd added with a laugh, glancing back at Carwyn.

Meini smiled and also looked at the boy-soldier. "I always carry something for bad heads when I am around warriors," Meini said.

"Do not include me in your denigration of the character of warriors, *menyw*," Geraint said, turning a broad grin on them.

"Ach, I have given you plenty of doses of this drink, Geraint," Meini chided.

"Not recently," he said.

"No, not for some time, I suppose."

"I am a reformed man," he said, turning his head back to scout the area around them as they rode into the lower end of the town, squaring his broad shoulders.

Heledd had not been in the town since the day of the market and was disappointed by the lack of color and activity. People crossed the road in front of their horses and a few others walked beside them toward the inn or away from them toward their houses. No one took notice of them and they dismounted in the wagon yard of the inn to no more interest than that of a few geese scurrying under the horses' hooves toward the shelter of a bale of hay.

Heledd and Meini led the way into the inn while Geraint and Carwyn secured the horses and gave them water. The horses nudged the geese out of the way to rip at the hay. The protests of the geese brought the innkeeper from a backroom and he smiled at the two women.

"You have brought reinforcements, I see," he said to

Heledd, appraising Meini before recognizing her as the *pennaeth's* daughter. "What can I do for you, *boneddiges*?"

"We will have a jug of ale, please," Meini replied, "with bread and cheese." Their warrior escorts entered the inn and stood to the side of the door, studying the room and its occupants. "Also for our friends. Not so much for the tall one," she said with a glance at Geraint. "He has renounced his bad habits," Meini told the innkeeper with a smile. When the two women took seats at the table, Meini searched her satchel for the pot of the remedy for Heledd's head. Before pouring ale into the cup, Meini gave Heledd a small amount of the drink and thanked the innkeeper for the ale. She leaned toward Heledd and said, "Garmon is happy."

"He should be," Heledd laughed in reply.

"I'm glad for you," Meini murmured, digging into her satchel again and removing a variety of pots and tools, then putting them all back again with a quiet laugh.

Heledd reached across the table and patted Meini's hand.

"I am concerned about my daughter. Every day, I know she grows more fond of Carwyn's foster mother and is less happy to see me. I have asked my father countless times, but he will not relent." Meini glanced at the two warriors sitting at another table and lowered her voice further. "Dada said I must have a husband before he will let me raise my own daughter," she said, "but he will not accept any man who shows such poor judgment."

"But—," Heledd bit her lips together. "Why did he say such a thing? That's cruel. What have you done to deserve that? When did he say that to you?"

"Before Urien left to find Garmon. My father was angry Garmon had gone for so long and sent no message ... we all thought he had taken you back to Talgarth-y-Bannawg. Urien was so angry when he heard that, he told my father he would kill Garmon if it was true. When Urien did not return ... I did not know what to think," she said, "I don't understand why he has not come back to the *gaer* ..."

"I'm sure he has good reasons," Heledd offered, tearing off

a small amount of bread and nibbling at an edge. The taste of it in her mouth was like mud and she dropped the bread on her platter. "I'm sure he will return," she said, unable to tell her friend Urien Macsen's responsibility to Bannawg was stronger than Meini's love or need for him.

"No, Heledd. My father must have told him to go. He does not want another of his sons to die because of me."

Heledd met Meini's eyes. Though she wore a smile on her lips for Carwyn's jubilant boasting and Geraint's indulgent good humor toward the boy-soldier, her pale blue eyes were bleak. Heledd slid onto the bench beside her and put an arm around Meini's waist, laying her head on her shoulder. "I know," she whispered.

"Don't be kind," Meini murmured. "I cannot bear it when people are kind."

"Urien Macsen is coming now," Heledd said, giving Meini a hug. "You will feel better after you've spoken to him." She motioned to Geraint and Carwyn to come with her. Geraint spoke to Carwyn, ordering him to stay with the *pennaeth's* daughter, and followed Heledd. "Garmon and the *pennaeth* know what you will soon see," she said to him, "but no one else should know, at least not for a while, do you understand?"

"If Garmon knows and has agreed, you can depend on my discretion," Geraint replied. "Does Meini Gwyn also know?"

"No. And she should not, at least for a time." Geraint frowned but eventually agreed and Heledd knocked on the door of the warehouse. She could see one of Urien's men behind the door and the movement of others, before the wide door was opened a crack. "I have come to see Goewin," Heledd said. "This man is with me." The soldier, whom she should have recognized from Talgarth-y-Bannawg but could not, nodded once and stepped backward. When Geraint entered, he was studied before allowed to proceed further into the cavernous building with his weapons. Heledd saw Urien's men and Aled's command all wore their hair in the same short-cropped style – a mark of their status as warriors of an elite rank. Their mutual recognition eased the tension as Urien Macsen came forward.

"You have brought good news?"

"Not the news you have been expecting, not yet in any case," Heledd replied in a lowered voice. "Meini Gwyn is here to speak with you," Heledd said. When he frowned and glanced at Geraint, Heledd cocked her head at him, puzzled. Urien gave her a curt nod. "She is waiting for you in the lower room of the inn." Urien inclined his head and walked out into the sunlight. Heledd saw him hesitate and take a deep breath before walking the distance across the yard to enter the inn through the heavy, planked door. "Where is Goewin?" she asked one of the Talgarth warriors. He pointed to a far corner.

Heledd crossed the floor of the large, empty warehouse and peered behind the makeshift wall separating the women from the rest of the group of refugees. Goewin sat on a stool by a small window, using the light shining through it to make repairs to a child's garment. When she looked up to see Heledd, she smiled and beckoned her foster daughter to sit with her. Heledd greeted her with an embrace and laid her head in Goewin's lap.

"You have been gone a long time," Goewin said.

"I'm sorry, I should have sent word."

"You have had other matters on your mind, I'm sure." Goewin patted her head and said, "Look up, my girl. I want to see for myself how you are." Heledd lifted her head and allowed Goewin to study her for a while.

"We will have our rightful heir to Bannawg long before that pasty girl conceives a child by her boy-mate," Goewin told the other women nearby. Heledd sat upright and stared at her foster mother. "We will have no need for Bro-Dawel now," Goewin said. "We will chase the dogs from our home and take back what is ours. Your son will be born on the land that has belonged to his forefathers for nine generations."

Heledd stayed with Goewin, renewing her friendship with Heulwen and her *baban*, Elain and the other Bannawg women for a while longer. When she said she must go, Garmon was expecting her, Goewin kissed her cheek and sent her back to her husband with a grin. As she emerged from behind the temporary wall of sacking and horse blankets, she smiled at

Geraint, who stood when she reappeared.

"Are you ready to go home now, Heledd?" Geraint asked her in a low voice as she reached his side. Heledd only gave him a slight nod as he opened the door of the warehouse for her. Across the yard, she saw Urien Macsen at the door of the inn, talking with the innkeeper. Carwyn stood at the door of the inn, greeted Geraint with a nod and darted back into the tavern room. They had walked halfway across the yard before Geraint stopped and searched her face. "Will you return to Bannawg?"

Heledd stood for a moment in the sun, wrapped her cloak more closely around her, secretly embracing her unborn child. "You heard?" When he nodded, she asked, "Everything?"

"Enough, Heledd, to know you have good news and bad news for Garmon."

"I would like to tell Garmon this good news. Will you let me tell him first?"

"Yes," Geraint replied. "And the other?"

"Also the other. Garmon will know what to do," she assured him. "What did Meini say?" Heledd asked of Urien Macsen when they met in the yard. Her broad smile brought a smile from him in return.

"You have grown, Geraint Padarn," he said, glancing at the younger warrior. "You will be welcome in my command, should you seek better employment."

"He won't," Heledd hissed, excusing his bad humor for reluctance to speak in front of Geraint. She glanced beyond Urien, toward the interior of the room.

"The offer stands," Urien said, slapping the side of Geraint's belly. The younger man excused himself and joined Carwyn in the tavern.

Baffled by Urien's response, she asked, "But, didn't you have reason to speak to Meini?"

"Why should I?" he asked, a frown on his face.

"No, of course not," Heledd said. "I have such a bad head, I imagine things."

"You have seen Goewin," he commented. "All is well?"

"Yes. That is, it will be soon."

"What news have you given her?"

"I will come back or send someone to let you know what will happen in the next few weeks. Garmon has been considering – making preparations."

"Good. He is good at tactics in war. Not so good with women, eh?" Urien laid his hand on her shoulder for a moment then returned to the warehouse.

"I could say the same for you, Urien Macsen."

# TWENTY-FOUR

Huw was in his office at the beginning of an evening's feasting. When his steward came into the *neuadd*, he spoke in turn to Mared who went immediately into the office with Rheinallt at her heels. Meini followed, with Garmon and Heledd close after. Mared paced the long room between the hearth and the desk. Rheinallt watched her from the long bench against the opposite wall, leaning his back comfortably among the cushions, occasionally rubbing his newly cropped black hair. Meini sat beside him. Heledd, who felt the fatigue of the day's preparations more acutely now her pregnancy had taken hold of her body, sat with them. How Mared could have so much energy to fly about the room was incomprehensible to Heledd who was content to watch Garmon taking a chair at the hearth.

"You have been working in the apothecary for long hours," Heledd commented in a low voice.

"I am useful there," Meini replied, staring at her herb-stained fingers. "And it is the only place I am free to think."

"What do you think about?" Heledd asked, touching Meini's arm.

"My daughter." Meini met Heledd's gaze for a few moments and sighed. "It is hard to think about anything else. Has my father said anything to you?"

"About what?" Heledd asked, cautious.

"Now, he has told me I may wed with his blessing, if there is a man foolish enough to want me."

"Why does he say such things to you?" Heledd cried under her breath, glaring at Huw.

"He does not mean to be cruel. He says as he thinks."

"You are too kind to him, Meini. Especially when you have been … disappointed. Does your father know you love Urien?"

"No, and I don't know why I do," Meini said. "He has never loved me."

"Perhaps he waits for a better time … when he has more to offer you."

"Perhaps," Meini replied, smiling slightly as the door from the *neuadd* opened again.

Only Huw was not surprised to see Carwyn enter the room, followed by his foster parents and Geraint.

Heledd watched the door for a while for the rest of Aled's command as well as Aled and Ceinwen to enter but the steward did not return and Huw sat in silence at his desk for several moments, staring at a pile of documents and a small wooden casket. Heledd watched his face for a time then turned her eyes on Garmon, to see if he had any knowledge of what the *pennaeth* was thinking. When Huw lifted his eyes, he sought first to call Carwyn's foster parents forward.

"Bring your son," he said to the steward, who in turn placed his hand on Carwyn's shoulder. "I am grateful – I can never express and you will never comprehend how deeply grateful – for the years of faithful care you have given." Huw dismissed their response with a small gesture of his hand. "Mared, Meini, Garmon, come here." The three gathered at the end of the long desk as he indicated. "There is no soft way to do this. Carwyn, this woman, who has been your mother for many years, has told me you are aware she is not your true mother but has cared for you as her child because your mother is dead. It is time for you to know Garmon is your mother's other son."

Carwyn reeled back as though he had been hit in the chest.

"Mared and Meini are your half-sisters through your father."

Mared gasped, her knees buckling slightly. Rheinallt leapt to support her, leading her to the bench to sit with him.

"I will answer all your questions. You are my lawful son and I have always regretted the necessity of keeping you ignorant of my love for you and for your mother. These belonged to her and she would have wanted you to have them." Huw placed the casket at the edge of the desk and leaned back in his chair, his eyes fixed on Carwyn's face. In the silence, Heledd searched the faces of all the people in the room, realizing she had come to think of them as her family. Mared, whose shocked expression was not founded in rage but sudden comprehension, stared at her younger half-brother with amazement and something akin to familial pride, if not love. Heledd ventured a smile in her stepsister-in-law's direction but turned her head away when she heard Huw call for his steward to enter again.

The door opened but the steward waited outside while someone else was brought through the door in the arms of one of the youngest maidservants. Meini turned as if she had been tied with a cord to the infant and rushed toward the door only to stop, turning back to ask her father's permission to take her daughter from the young girl.

"My granddaughter will be raised in my house, as she should always have been," Huw said to Carwyn and Angharad's foster parents. "Again, I am grateful to you." He made a motion of his hand to release Meini from her waiting and his youngest daughter scooped her baby into her arms, burying her face in the infant's neck uttering a joy-filled sob. Angharad squealed with delight, patting her mother's hair with fat hands.

Carwyn had not said a word or moved since his father had placed his mother's possessions in front of him. Behind him, his foster parents, standing together with their arms around each other, watched with trepidation as their foster child of thirteen years began to understand what had happened. Besides Carwyn, Garmon and Geraint stood with equal watchfulness. Huw made another gesture and Geraint took several steps backward, to stand near Meini who was playing with her daughter in complete abandon.

Garmon laid his hand on his half-brother's shoulder. Carwyn looked at Garmon's hand for a moment, and then turned his face toward him. In a tone too low for Heledd to hear, the two brothers began to talk and Heledd returned her attention to Meini whose happiness was wonderful to see after her grief and disappointment. Heledd stood and took a few steps toward her friend to share her happiness but hesitated when she saw Angharad straining away from her mother, stretching her arms toward Geraint.

The baby was so insistent Meini released her as Geraint extended his hands to take her. He settled Angharad on one arm and the baby nestled against his shoulder while the warrior met Meini's searching look. Heledd held her breath when Geraint lifted his free hand to stroke Meini's cheek. He leaned toward her and whispered to her for some time. Meini kept her head bowed, listening to the young warrior while her daughter patted his face.

When Meini did look up to meet Geraint's eyes, her expression was full of doubt. Geraint slid his hand to the back of Meini's head and drew her closer to him, bowing his head to kiss her mouth. Heledd glanced at Huw to see what he would do about Geraint's assault on his daughter – in full view of her family – but, if the *pennaeth* had seen what had happened, he was too concerned with Carwyn to interfere. The boy-soldier had sunk into a chair facing his father, staring at his mother's casket of possessions. Garmon was standing over him, still with his hand on Carwyn's shoulder.

Heledd returned her attention to Meini and Geraint. Mared had also become aware of the couple and both of them watched in amazement as Meini lifted her arms to embrace Geraint and her daughter. Geraint's hold on both of them tightened visibly as Meini returned his kiss.

"Between myself and God, I never imagined he was the one," Mared said under her breath.

"Neither did I," Heledd admitted. "I thought she loved…someone else."

"I thought he loved … someone else," Mared agreed with a quiet laugh. "How funny." She glanced at her sister for a moment. "Rheinallt thought it was strange Geraint was here, but not Aled as a foster brother."

"I thought he was here for Carwyn's sake."

"Did you know about this?" Mared asked, her expression hardening as she glanced at her half-brother.

"I guessed."

"How? I have known Carwyn all his life and I never imagined."

"I saw the likeness between him and Garmon. Once I saw that, I had only a few questions."

"Hmmm. I knew you were dangerous," Mared said, turning her back for a moment. When she turned back, she said, "Your child will only be a step-grandchild, you realize."

"I realize that, Mared. You need not be concerned."

"Good, at least we understand one another." She turned her attention to her newly-promoted husband and slipped luxuriously into his ready arms. Before they had a chance to settle on the bench, Huw began to dismiss everyone from the room, beginning with Carwyn's foster parents and the maidservant. Geraint and Meini were the first of the family to go and Heledd urged Garmon to come with her in their wake. She was not surprised when Rhodri, Daf, Nisien and Aled greeted their friend and fellow warrior with a cheer. Geraint kissed his stepdaughter and, with Meini's permission, handed her into the care of her foster mother once again.

Geraint's comrades and their wives swarmed to the couple. To Heledd's complete amazement, Meini had not taken her eyes off the handsome, vigorous and obviously passionately in love Geraint – the foolish man her father had commended to his daughter. Though how *she* felt was not apparent, Heledd wondered how long he had been in love with Meini and how, if his feelings for her were so strong, he had kept them so quietly to himself.

"What is this all about?" Garmon asked Heledd, watching the joyous celebration among Aled's command. He had seen nothing that happened between Geraint and Meini in the *pennaeth's* office.

"Did *you* know?" Heledd asked Ceinwen.

"No," she answered. "I thought it was odd when Geraint was called into the *pennaeth's* office with Carwyn. And then these four kept their eyes on that door as if their lives were linked to it. I still don't know what it means."

"I believe Meini has accepted Geraint as her husband," Heledd replied, watching Ceinwen's reaction.

"He has kept quiet," was Ceinwen's only comment, apart from a broad smile.

"Even Garmon didn't know."

Angharad fussed at the confusion around her and threw herself out of her foster mother's arms. Geraint caught her with a laugh and handed her to Meini, wrapping his arms around both his women until his friends brought him flagons of ale and mead. Geraint took one, grinning into Meini's upturned face. "I am a reformed man," he told his comrades. "One will be enough." When he drained the flagon, he thrust it into Nisien's hand and claimed another kiss from his wife, receiving cheers and encouragement from the rest of the warband gathered in the *neuadd*. Garmon managed to wrest Meini away from Geraint for a brief exchange before she returned to her husband's possessive embrace and passed Angharad to her foster mother to be taken to her bed.

When, after she had been kissed by Aled and all of Geraint's friends, a momentary startled look filled Meini's pale blue eyes. As another warrior came forward, Meini turned toward her husband and lifted her eyes to meet his searching gaze. *Geraint knows she loves Urien,* Heledd lamented to herself, pressing her lips together, *and Meini knows he knows.*

Geraint touched Meini's cheek. "You will be content?"

"I will be happy," Meini replied, pulling his head down to her, demanding his kiss. Geraint cupped her face in his hands, replacing every thought of Urien Macsen in his wife's heart with a lingering caress. Meini slid her arms around his waist, pressing her body against him and smiling when he responded with a passionate, searing kiss. The other warrior waited a moment, then pushed Geraint out of his way and took his kiss from the bride. Meini kissed the man lightly and laughed. She laid her hand on Geraint's arm and he kissed the top of her head, before leading her by the hand to a more private place.

"It seems you were wrong," Garmon told Heledd, watching the couple run the gauntlet of lusty well-wishers.

"I wasn't," she said. "But I'm glad she has chosen Geraint." Heledd turned to look at her husband. "If you knew, why didn't you tell me?"

"I had even less information than you, *menyw*," Garmon said. "Aled has just told me he knew nothing until this morning but Geraint has planned this since Meini was in mourning for Gwyn. Geraint made his intentions clear to Huw only hours before Huw announced it to us. Meini claims she knew nothing of his feeling for her until he told her this evening."

"I wonder what he said to her," Heledd said.

"Enough," Garmon replied, putting his arm around her waist.

"She will be happy with Geraint."

"No doubt," Garmon agreed with a laugh as another cheer was raised in the *neuadd* when one of the wives ran in.

"They've bolted themselves in Meini's room," she announced, laughing. "Those two were on each other before the door was closed."

"It's about time Meini showed she has her father's blood in her veins and not just noxious remedies," Mared said as they began to find places at the table while they waited for the *pennaeth* to emerge from his office with Carwyn. "She's been a nun far too long."

"And you aren't?" Rheinallt asked, pouring cups of mead and flagons of ale for everyone near him at the *pennaeth's* table. "Geraint has kept his eye on her for months."

"How do you know?" Mared asked, staring at him in her most superior manner. "I never saw anything at all between them."

"Neither did I," Heledd added. "In fact, I thought she loved someone else."

"You women think it's all about agonizing and swooning," Rheinallt laughed. "Geraint decided he wanted Meini and worked through what he had to do to get her. He's been visiting Carwyn's foster parents every day for weeks – long enough to know Angharad was the key to Meini's heart," Rheinallt said. "Once he had the key, the rest was straightforward."

"What was that?" Heledd jumped. Two of the stewards ran toward the door of the office at the sound of a shout and an object hitting the door, followed by another angry shout. There was a long flow of swearing, a few calmer words and another shout.

"He will never change," Mared said. "This is how he was with Meini and me. Even Creiddwen Owein heard this ranting." She rejected the portion of the meat Rheinallt cut for her and took instead a spoonful of honey. Rheinallt frowned before devouring the meat.

"Carwyn is also shouting," Heledd observed.

"Carwyn shouts louder," Mared laughed.

The stewards stood at the door for a time. Huw did not call them to enter and they turned away to other duties.

"I thought you would have taken this news differently," Heledd commented.

"Why?" Mared demanded. "I'm not an idiot. Now I know he is my brother – half-brother – we will learn to understand one another. We have my father's blood, after all."

"You had very strong objections to me, when you thought I was to wed your father."

"This is different," Mared said. "Carwyn has been a member of this household, of a sort, since he was born. He's not a stranger or any sort of threat to my position as the eldest. When my son is born, he will still be the first grandson and his part of Bro-Dawel will be secure. With someone like you, who knows what sort of ideas you might put in my father's head." Mared picked up her cup and tilted it to her lips. "And we did have a rather gruesome picture of your background and character. How was I to know your uncle and cousins were such liars? Garmon has never included me in his circle of friends. It's my part to be the skeptic, to put everything to the test."

"You are very good," Heledd said. "I was assaulted and your half-brother almost killed."

"Ach, most of that was your own stupidity. Anyone but an imbecile sees what sort the Cenfyn are. You did fairly well to avoid them but you could have avoided trouble completely if you had left Aeron to his games with Rhian. He would have been dispatched very quickly had he even looked at her after that first evening."

"So I have been told," Heledd admitted.

"And, you were so slow to realize how it was with Garmon. If he had written your name on his sleeve, he could not have been more obviously in love with you."

"That was more complicated than you think."

"Oh, you think so?" Mared laughed. "It is embarrassing how you persisted in not seeing when he gave you so many clues — even my ridiculous aunt could see he adored you. Never mind, Heledd, it was cruel to bring you here on false pretenses. Oh, look," Mared exclaimed, "they've reconciled their differences."

Huw had opened the door to the office and brought Carwyn into the *neuadd* with his arm around his son's shoulders. Carwyn was still dazed and his eyes were red-rimmed. Once inside the long room, Carwyn nodded once to his father and went to sit with his friends, accepting a flagon from Nisien. Carwyn looked around the *neuadd* and asked "Where's Geraint?"

"He's taken Meini to bed," came the answer from several warriors and their wives near him. Carwyn's expression made them laugh. Nisien leaned to whisper the story.

"I would like to have a quiet meal," Huw declared when he took his place between Mared and Heledd. "Is that possible with you two near me?" As if one, Heledd and Mared turned their shoulders to the *pennaeth* and ate their meals with their husbands.

The mead flowed through the evening and for the first time since Heledd's arrival at Bro-Dawel, Huw called his *bardd* to entertain him. Tegwen Talog's husband entered the *neuadd* from the area of the house designated for the most important dignitaries and guests. Talog Bardd sat by the hearth, in a chair carved from the trunk of an oak, brought in by four of the stewards ahead of his entrance. Another man entered, cradling a harp. He sat to the side of the *bardd's* chair, stroking the strings lightly, twisting the ash wood pegs as he plucked.

Talog Bardd was dressed in a long purple, silk brocade coat, embroidered with gold and trimmed with black velvet. Beneath the coat, he wore a black tunic that reached the floor, covering a linen shirt with deep lace cuffs and collar. He wore gold rings on the four middle fingers of his hands and a gold torque encircled his neck. Talog thanked the stewards for positioning his chair, lifted his hands in greeting to the *pennaeth* and, having received permission from Huw Bro-Dawel, he stepped forward to begin his song.

"Long ago, before the birth of many, Bro-Dawel was a blessed place. So blessed was this land, that an angel decreed the land would be fruitful and the *pennaeth* would be happy."

Huw sat back with his goblet of mead, listening to the song he had commissioned for the occasion. At the end of each phrase of the song, the harpist played his music.

"It is the way of men that all decrees, however high their beginning, are tested and despoiled. So it was for Bro-Dawel. Many years passed before the land was cleared of the curse of the avenging angel whose first blessing was so ill-received. The land was again blessed and to prove this, the angel caused Bro-Dawel to be visited by a woman to fill the heart of the *pennaeth*. For many years, this woman, his wife, remained with this man, loving him and his children, giving him more children to love in return."

Heledd glanced momentarily at Garmon. He, like his stepfather and his half-brother, sat with his head bowed. A quick look to her left confirmed Mared was also listening in silence.

"And men destroy what they most love," the *bardd* lamented. "What is good and kind, what is beautiful and loving in their eyes, they seek to maim for fear they will be outshone by its light. Love was killed. Beauty destroyed. Honor and grace driven away. His wife fled his arms, though he held her with all his might and all his love, he could not keep her with him.

"But his wife did not leave him alone. For his love of her she left her sons and the love she had given his daughters.

"Bitter and angry, the man rejected his wife's gift. Turning against his own flesh because it was not hers, loving wholly that which came from her body. He had not protected his wife from the worst in him. His own flesh blossomed without his tending, because she had loved them as her own.

"Before his life was at an end, the daughters of his flesh bore their own cherished fruit and the sons his wife had entrusted to him were better men than he could hope to be.

"On this eve of reconciliation, the *pennaeth* of Bro-Dawel proclaims the youngest son of Creiddwen Owein, his beloved wife and most cherished memory, Carwyn *mab* Creiddwen Owein, *mab* Huw Bro-Dawel.

"May all Huw Bro-Dawel's sons and daughters and all their many children and all their loving spouses, live long, joyful lives between themselves and God."

Talog Bardd bowed to Huw Bro-Dawel and sat in his chair. The *neuadd* was silent for several moments. When Aled and the three men of his command sitting by Carwyn understood what the proclamation meant, they turned on the youngest member of the command and pulled him from the bench, giving him a rough show of their affection for him as their comrade as well as the son of their *pennaeth*.

"No one can ever say, Dada," Mared said to her father, "you do not know how to delight and entertain. Talog Bardd has earned all the gold you pay him."

"I trust you have not been disappointed," he commented, raising his goblet in salute to his eldest daughter.

"Never."

# twenty-five

On the evening marking the end of the ninth day of Geraint and Meini's wedding, a warband of twenty prepared for their journey at dawn. Some went to their beds for a few hours rest. Some found company. Carwyn went first to his father's rooms and then to the barracks. Garmon and Heledd, and other husbands and wives, spent the remaining hours of the darkness in one another's arms. When the first call from the horns came, Heledd lifted her arms around her husband's neck and kissed him awake.

"You will see," Garmon told her as if he could read her thoughts from the way she clung to him, "we will all return successful before Advent."

"You are already successful," she replied, slipping from the bed.

"Where are you going? There's no need for you to watch us go, it is too cold, stay in bed, *gwraig*, so I may think of you thus," he laughed, pulling her back and pressing her body beneath him into the mattress.

"You will remember me thus whether I stand or lie," she commented, throwing her legs around his hips. "And I'm going with you, remember?"

"No," he said, "you are not. We have discussed this."

"You have discussed this. I have decided."

"Do I have to tie you down?" Garmon asked, clasping her hands together.

"You can try but I will free myself eventually, or be freed, and I will follow you."

"Hisht, *menyw*. Allow me to make love with you now and fix

this in my mind to keep me content while we are apart."

"Garmon—."

He pressed his fingers to her lips and said, "Hywel's word carries weight, even in Gwesyn. You will not have long to wait before we make love again," he whispered, sliding his hands under her thighs.

Even so, Heledd's horse was waiting for her when she emerged from the longhouse before the warband was ready to leave the *gaer*, carrying a satchel of her clothes, wearing the brown cloak over a quilted woolen coat, pulling her leather gloves over her fingers with her teeth. Garmon frowned when he saw her approaching the stables but did not interfere when Carwyn offered to lift her onto the mare's back. Heledd took the reins, relaxed her shoulders and, with a deep breath, shook her head.

Ceinwen and many of the other wives stood in a quiet corner of the *buarth* where they were not in the way but could see their husbands before they left for what many of them believed would be a longer journey than the warriors admitted. None of the women expected their husbands to notice them or to interrupt the preparations to allay their concerns.

The thin mauve line distinguishing the hilltops from the black sky brought a blast of wind from the north. Garmon led his warhorse from the stables to head the column of warriors under his command. Urien had already mounted with his four-strong warband waiting at the gates. Huw, clothed in wool and furs, entered the courtyard with his sons-in-law, Rheinallt and Geraint, who mounted their own warhorses, waiting for their *pennaeth* to do the same. Mared did not appear, but Meini, once Geraint was on his horse, rushed forward from the door of the house and lifted her arms to her husband. Geraint bowed over her to receive her embrace, lifting her with one arm from the ground to kiss her as though they had never kissed before and would never kiss again.

Heledd turned her attention to Urien and saw he watched the wedded pair as well, but in the dawn light, she could not read his expression. Though she wanted to speak to Garmon she knew better than distract him with her concerns for Geraint's safety. If there was a warrior who could defend himself from his wife's former 'beloved', Geraint was that man. When she again looked in the direction of the house, Meini had brought her daughter and held her up to Geraint. Angharad's stepfather clasped her to him and kissed her round cheeks. When he passed his stepdaughter back to Meini, he caressed the cheeks of both before urging his mount forward and away from his new family.

Heledd became aware the warband had now all mounted and she turned her attention to her own husband at the same moment he looked in her direction. Their eyes met and held for a long moment. When he raised his hand the whole of the company moved forward through the gates of the *gaer*, riding in pairs behind the *pennaeth's* banner. Heledd urged Angel forward and took her place beside Garmon, glancing at the courtyard to see Meini waving her daughter's hand in farewell to Geraint. She also saw Geraint watch his wife for a moment as Urien Macsen came into her line of sight. Meini's eyes followed her husband until she turned to join the other wives waving farewell. Heledd felt Garmon's stern gray eyes fixed on her and she met his gaze with a reassuring smile.

"You will tell me if you are fatigued," he commanded and turned his eyes away.

"Of course," she replied. "What is the name of the new soldier in Aled's command?"

"Another soldier has caught your eye?" Garmon asked, grinning in spite of himself.

"I have acquired a certain preference."

"You will come to know him soon enough, *menyw*," Garmon answered. "He has been trained especially for you."

"I know what that means, Garmon," Heledd said. "It won't make any difference. What is his name and where is he from?"

"He is Arwel *mab* Elain Casnar. He was born at Bannawg." When Heledd turned her head to look back at the warrior, Garmon said, "You know his mother. He was among the few who were not killed or taken to Gwesyn. Arwel requested to be transferred to Aled's command, to protect you. His father was one of Gwesyn's soldiers, when Meilor visited your father as a friend, five years before he betrayed that friendship."

"You trust him?"

"As much as I trust any man with your life," Garmon replied. "And, I have overseen his training. He knows what to expect from you," he laughed, "and Arwel was keeping an eye on you before either Urien or I took notice."

"That's reassuring," she said. "I don't recognize him from Bannawg, only from the warehouse," she admitted.

"That's reassuring," Garmon said. "If you did know him, I would be jealous."

"He is quite handsome—."

"Do not test me, Heledd," Garmon warned. "You do not know where that will lead."


The journey beyond the boundary of the Bro-Dawel *ystad* was a welcome adventure for Heledd. When she had first traveled to the west, she had not taken much interest in the land through which she passed. Her attention had been engaged by fear and the prospects awaiting her. Though she had good reason to be engaged by the prospects awaiting her in Gwesyn, fear was not present to distract her from her surroundings. By the time the sun had climbed far enough into the sky to show every detail of the territory into which they had ridden, they had traveled for two hours and had reached the crossroads beyond the Abbey *ystad*.

Once they left Bro-Dawel, they rode the smaller tracks farmers and hunters used. A twenty-strong warband attracted attention on the drovers' routes and they avoided the towns and villages. To cross the Taf, they rode northeast for another hour, crossing at the narrowest bend before the river widened and flowed into the Tywi estuary. Though the trek had been explained to her, Heledd regretted she had not listened carefully, trusting Garmon and his stepfather knew the best route and the safest. She could not have said where she was or how to return to Bro-Dawel.

The Taf was at low tide, Garmon told her as he lifted her from her horse onto *Diawl's* back for the crossing. "You will not get your feet wet this time," he said, holding her with one arm and guiding *Diawl* with his other hand.

"It's too cold for swimming," she said, "and it would be pointless."

"Pointless?" he asked, spurring the warhorse up the embankment on the other side.

"I have all I wanted from that adventure."

"All?"

"All," Heledd repeated, sliding from the back of the horse to rest while the others crossed out of sight of the nearby river port. "We needn't do such a thing again for a long time. In fact, now we know we are having a child, we can sleep separately if you like."

"I do not like," Garmon said, striding toward her. "But if you like, I can arrange it." He lifted her chin and stared into her eyes. "Unless you have some reason for making that suggestion, do not do so again, Heledd. I do not like games or tests."

"I will remember," she replied, pushing his hand from beneath her chin to her waist. "Will they be a long time crossing?"

"Not long enough for my needs," Garmon said, "but I can take care of yours now." He clenched his arm around her and pulled her hard against his thigh. Though his movements were imperceptible to anyone coming toward them, and shielded by the bodies of the two horses he held with his left hand, Garmon stared into her green eyes until they drifted closed with the first convulsions of her body. "You have not had enough of riding," he murmured as he lowered his head to take her mouth.

"Neither have you," she replied, sliding her arms around his neck to savor the sensation of loving him with all she had to offer. The blush had not faded from her cheeks when she glimpsed riders coming up from the river bank.

"I would not have considered you cruel until now," Geraint laughed. "I have only begun to become acquainted with my wife and you two flaunt your familiarity at every opportunity."

Garmon smiled at Heledd for a moment before releasing her and turning on the bridegroom. "You will have ample opportunity, Geraint, to practice your skills," Garmon told him, "in many areas of combat. You will not be long in discerning your opponent has greater capacity than you imagined."

"You forget under whose tuition I have spent these four years past," Geraint replied, leaning on the neck of his warhorse, grinning as Heledd slipped to the side of her mare and dropped her forehead onto the animal's shoulder to recover her composure.

Huw took the opportunity to call for a rest and dismounted. When he walked toward his stepson, he looked askance at Heledd and frowned at Garmon. "She should not be here if she is ill."

"She is not ill," Garmon replied without looking at his wife. "We will be stopping for the night in three or four hours, in any case."

Heledd shielded her eyes as she looked up at the sky. The sun was already moving into the west.

"At this pace, we will not reach the Gwili *ystad* before nightfall," Huw complained.

"We cannot go any faster in this terrain," Garmon answered with equal irritation. "If you are concerned, ride ahead."

"Your brothers have all had the good sense to leave their wives at home where they belong," Huw grumbled, glaring at Heledd.

"None of them are concerned with this," Garmon replied, "Heledd is."

"Even as she jeopardizes our success?"

"You can turn back if you are worried," Heledd said, taking the reins of her horse from Garmon. "You forget you agreed I have something to offer in this venture."

"Just how far do you think you will get inside Gwesyn's territory if I did turn back, *menyw*?"

"Garmon will find a way," she said, planting her hands on her hips and facing him straight on.

To the side of Huw, Carwyn was gazing at his father, his mouth in a hard line. In the space of a few days, he had become Carwyn *mab* Huw in more than name. His mannerisms and passions had surfaced; he was as stubborn as his half-brother and as forthright as his father. "Why are you turning your wrath on her? Garmon is right. This concerns Heledd's family – as her friends, we have a duty to help her."

Huw narrowed his eyes at his son but said nothing further. When he turned his gaze on Heledd again, he was less angry, gesturing for her to mount. She grabbed the crown of the saddle and put her foot into the stirrup but did not have the momentum to pull herself up. Garmon stepped forward but she said, "I can do it."

Huw strode over and lifted her by the waist enough for her to throw her leg over Angel's back. "No one expects you to be a man," he growled, striding to his own warhorse and mounting with the ease and vigor of a man half his age. "Ride with me," he commanded her and set a pace that took them ahead of the others. When he had put distance between them and his warband, he slowed and studied her for a moment. "Do you understand what you will encounter?"

"Gwesyn killed my family. I watched them die. Do you think anything can be worse than that?"

"How much do you love my son?" Huw pulled up his warhorse and raised his hand to stop the warband from coming any closer while he spoke to her. "Garmon is as much my son as any child of my own flesh. He would give his life for you. I would give mine for him – as well as Carwyn and my daughters. If you love him as I believe you do, you will listen to my counsel, Daughter." He swung his horse around and faced her, moving alongside, coming between her and the others, blocking her view of Garmon. "Let me deal with Gwesyn. He will eat you alive and delight in your agony. Show him any weakness and he will exploit it. What do you fear most?" he asked, studying her face.

"I do not want to see what I have seen before," Heledd said without hesitation, "the deaths of those I love."

"That will happen," Huw said, "or they will see you die. Accept it. The same fear is in us all. I killed my own son to prevent him from killing another. I live with the fear of my children's deaths. Garmon fears for you. You for him. Geraint for Meini and she will for him, one day." Huw cupped her chin in his hand. "Meilor Gwesyn loves no one, is faithful to no one. He is ruthless in his pursuit of power. He will torment you with glee and delight in the sound of your heart breaking."

"How did you ever call this man a friend?"

"I was young once. Your father also called him friend and brother. Your uncle too. We were schooled in the same cloister and learned warcraft under the same *pennaeth*. Aled, Garmon, Urien, Gwyn and Rhydderch had the same experience. Only Rhydderch turned against his brothers, in he was like Meilor."

"What should I do?"

"Meilor must be stopped. I had no reason to concern myself before," he admitted, "but for the sake of my grandson, Gwesyn will reap what he has sown."

"You mean to kill him?"

"Only after he has paid compensation," Huw laughed.

"That will only lead to more bloodshed," Heledd said, grasping his arm. Huw Bro-Dawel looked down at her hand for a moment and smiled, covering her hand with his own. "And what if you are killed? That will be my fault and your children will seek revenge."

"I do not intend to be killed. I have more grandchildren to welcome into the world."

"Does that matter to you?" Heledd asked, doubtful.

"Why do you think I granted Rheinallt permission to wed Mared? Why is Geraint with Meini?"

"You told Meini she would not have another husband, so everyone could hear."

"Only a man who wanted her enough would have defied me," Huw said, glancing over his shoulder at Geraint.

"Did you know he loved her?"

"Not until he demanded permission to ask her."

"Even though she loved Urien?"

"If he had asked me, I would have sent him out on his chin. I should not have given her to Gwyn – he took no for answer and sent Garmon to plead for him. Ah well, if I had not, I would be one granddaughter less. Meini deserves better than both Gwyn and Urien – Geraint has passion enough to awaken hers."

"I think he has done that," Heledd laughed.

"She will forget this girl's infatuation for Urien in Geraint's bed," Huw agreed.

"I think she already has."

"Well then, I will need to live long enough to see what sort of offspring they produce."

"There will be a lot of babies born in the summer," Heledd said, "all of them your own grandchildren."

"All the more reason for you to let me deal with Gwesyn," Huw said, frowning at her. "And you should not have come. If Gwesyn suspects you are carrying a child, he will rip it from your belly."

"I am well-protected, Father."

The following two nights, the warband spent sleeping in the travelers' dormitories of the two *ystad* belonging to Huw's closest allies between the market towns of Caerfyrddin and Llanymddyfri. While the men all slept together in the *ystad* hall, Heledd slept in a room in another part of the house. Although she would have preferred to be with her husband, the men slept on stone shelves with straw mattresses in the same *neuadd* in which they had eaten. She had a narrow cot and a door that bolted. Although she was well aware if a warrior was determined to enter, no bolt would prevent him, she was glad of the solitude in order to prepare herself for the ordeal facing Gwesyn presented.

Huw had filled her head with gruesome tales to illustrate Meilor Gwesyn's character, much of which she wanted to discount as an attempt to scare her into staying behind, but she could not discount what she already knew about him. She expected Meilor to be the same loud, demanding, and arrogant man she had seen from the safety of her place in the kitchen when she was ten years of age and still believed her father was the traitor. As she lay down on the cot, using Garmon's monastery boy's cloak as an extra covering to ward off the chill, she was glad she had not known the truth then. Heledd had no delusions about what her life would have been had she discovered the truth while she lived in Talgarth-y-Bannawg. She would have accused her uncle and had no friends of any strength to prevent him from punishing her. If he could contemplate turning her out of his house to a life of depravity when she still believed his lies, Llew Talgarth would have done much worse to keep her quiet as a young girl.

She had grown fond of her life since her journey to Bro-Dawel and all that led up to the moment when Garmon *mab* Creiddwen Owein had taken an interest in her was necessary to make her what she was for him to love. And all that had happened to him made him the man she could love – despite his insistence on being a soldier.

To help her to quell her anxiety about the end of her journey to Gwesyn, Heledd turned her thoughts to the future months – to the time when her baby was to be born. She did not care much about the suit for compensation except she believed Meilor Gwesyn and Llew Talgarth had to be punished for their actions. She did not want their deaths, only justice and acknowledgement of their wrong-doing. Her children, she knew, would be born in safety and security, with a father who could provide for them – all ten of them – for as long as necessary. What had happened to her father, Heledd had faith, could not happen to Garmon. She had no reason to doubt her belief she had seen the worst life could do and would not, again in her life time, have to watch her loved ones die – at least not as her family had died. Despite Huw's admonition to accept the inevitable, Heledd knew in her heart Garmon would live to be an old man with grandchildren, just as Huw had, and she would be with him.

When Huw Bro-Dawel crossed the mountain into the Gwesyn *ystad*, only Heledd, Geraint and Aled were with him. The road they traveled led directly to the great house and would take them a little more than an hour. During this final leg of the journey, Huw reviewed every detail of the plan they had discussed since leaving Bro-Dawel to ensure they all knew exactly what they were expected to do, every possible variation and obstacle they could imagine might be in Meilor Gwesyn's mind.

"No matter how well we plan, Meilor will astound us with his craft. Think as he thinks," Huw enjoined them.

Heledd shivered though she was warm beneath the layers of fur, quilted wool, silk and leather she wore. Despite the preparations they had made and the assurances Garmon had given her he would be near at hand under all circumstances, the wind seemed colder on the eastern side of the Bannau Hills. The snow seemed gray. The trees were stark in the morning fog, their branches dragging toward the colorless earth with the weight of the ice that had frozen overnight. She hunched her shoulders to bring the fur collar of the cape closer to her neck.

The heavy leather jerkin beneath her gold brocade coat did not hold the warmth as surely as silk but it gave her a sense of the protection of body armor and Huw had insisted she wear it at all times to protect her unborn child. Aled and Geraint were also wearing leather jerkins under their quilted coats but Huw wore only velvet and silk beneath his cloak.

"If this is too hard for you, Heledd," Huw said, "Aled will take you back to Talhaearn, agreed?"

"I have prepared for the worst I can imagine," Heledd replied.

"Preparing and seeing are very different, my daughter," Huw reminded her, nodding in the direction of a pile of fallen branches at the side of the road. As they rode forward, a woman and children raised their heads from it, ragged and starved. The first of Gwesyn's inhabitants to greet Heledd swarmed around the four horses, clutching at the riders' feet and begging for food. "No," Huw told her when Heledd reached for her sack of provisions. "Go away, woman. We have nothing to offer you."

"Take my daughter," the woman said. "She will do whatever you want, or one of my sons. A loaf or even a crust of bread and you can have them, beat them, work them hard, use them in any way you want, please," she rasped.

"Take your children away, woman," Huw said, spurring his warhorse. "They are of no use to us."

"Beat me instead. I will do anything you want, give my children some bread."

"No. We are here to see your *pennaeth*. We have no time for you."

"When you see Meilor Gwesyn, tell him you saw a woman with three children begging at the side of this road. He will be glad to know one of the children is dead."

"Woman, I will tell him. Now, let us pass."

The woman pulled her children into the ditch by her shelter and watched the four riders go past. Heledd could feel their eyes on her back but she did not turn to look at them again. When they had gone a few hundred yards further, she said, "Huw, why didn't you let me give her bread?"

"You do not know why she is being punished and Meilor Gwesyn will not forget your interference. Keep your mind on why we are here, Heledd."

"Yes, Father," she replied, sighing heavily.

"Heledd, become accustomed to using my title," he urged her quietly. "Until we leave Gwesyn, I am not your father-in-law, remember? I own your bond – let them think as they like."

"Yes, *pennaeth*."

"Better."

"I will do my best, *pennaeth*."

All along the road and across the landscape of rugged hills, Heledd saw desolation and poverty. The few people who came close enough for her to study wore filthy rags. As they came nearer to the great house, they saw soldiers who did not challenge them or even stop to look at the four strangers to their *pennaeth's* land. They were not curious or cautious. Many were drunk or hard at soon to be. The workers and tradesmen were cautious of the soldiers, giving them wide berth when their paths crossed.

Heledd's heart clenched and choked her when they reached the village that had grown outside the stone walls of the *gaer*. The soldiers were everywhere she turned her eyes. Some of them had been at Bannawg. Some of them had raped and murdered her sisters as well as many of the other girls and women. One of them was Arwel's father. Heledd forced herself to take no notice of the soldiers lest her interest be questioned. She made note of the threat they posed to her and her friends.

They enforced their *pennaeth's* rule with fear and were themselves undisciplined and lazy. She believed Huw had foreseen this as one part of his plan to force Meilor Gwesyn into accepting her claim. A twenty-strong, well trained and thoroughly disciplined warband could out-maneuver men who strutted down the streets and pushed women and tradesmen into the gutter as they passed. Even drunk, they exuded their power, lying against the walls of the Gwesyn *caer* and abusing anyone who came close to them. The first challenge to Huw Bro-Dawel's presence came at the gates.

"I am here to see the *pennaeth* of this *ystad*," he told the commander of the household guard. "This is my son-in-law, Geraint Padarn and my foster son, Aled Mathonwy." The commander glanced at Heledd and shrugged. He sent one of his command to speak with Meilor Gwesyn. "Do not be complacent about their lack of interest in you," Huw told Heledd under his breath. "If they believe you are of consequence, you are in less danger."

"I understand, *pennaeth*," she said, lifting her chin a little higher.

"As haughty as you please," Huw laughed, "it suits you well, *menyw*."

When the soldier returned, the commander said, "You and your company may enter. The *pennaeth* will see you in his *llys* once he is available. Follow this man." He indicated another soldier who also glanced at Heledd and turned to walk across the cobbled courtyard.

"They are appraising your value to me," Huw told her. "Garmon tells me you are skilled at hiding your fear. Now is a good time to demonstrate this skill."

Heledd smiled to herself but let her face show only her distain for her surroundings. They were guided through a wide, arched *porth* into another cobbled courtyard. The courtyard widened as it swept to the right around a lime-rendered wall and opened into a square. More than fifteen joined buildings, each constructed of a different material from its neighbor, opened their doors into the square. The *pennaeth's* house was at the farthest end of the square.

Huw dismounted and lifted Heledd from Angel's back, pulling her hand through his arm. He handed the reins of their horses to Geraint. Aled did the same and followed his *pennaeth* across the courtyard on foot. Geraint walked behind them. At the wooden doors of the house, a groom took the horses and led them through to the stables. The four visitors entered another arched *porth* leading to a reception hall. There, they were greeted by one of the stewards who dismissed the soldier with a sharp wave of his hand.

The reception hall was long and wide, furnished with a table down its center and lined with benches, occupied by men of various ranks – landowners, tradesmen, monks and warriors. Heledd walked past them with her chin at a severe angle and her hand firmly grasping Huw's arm beneath the thick purple velvet of his coat. Though she did not turn her head to look at the waiting men, she sensed their apprehension. The steward opened the door at the end of the long hall and stood aside for them to enter.

# TWENTY-SIX

Heledd held her breath as she entered the room. Nothing she had imagined about Meilor Gwesyn prepared her for the opulence and grandeur of his *castell*. The walls were hung with tapestries and crimson damask. They stood on a red and yellow carpet as thick as the one in Huw's office but covered the floor from wall to wall and was edged by white silk tassels. At the center of the room, a square table, large enough to be the size of a room, was topped by a candleholder standing as tall as a half-grown child. It held one hundred unlit candles. On one wall of the square room, the hearth stood cold and empty except for two great irons that could hold a log as long as Heledd was tall. The mantel, made from the trunk of an oak, was the same height as the top of Geraint's head and as thick as the full length of a man's arm. On either side of the irons, there were stone benches and Heledd could easily walk into the hearth, without ducking.

Despite the tapestries, the room was frosty with a gusty draft from the chimney that swept around the room, shaking the crimson drapes so they looked like rivers of blood. Heledd shivered, looking around her for a place less exposed. Garmon would have taken her in his arms but she could not ask that of her companions – her intimacy with her husband allowed her privileges she had not considered before and new ones she discovered on a daily basis. She had only to meet his eyes for him to understand her. She had only to touch him for him to turn to her. She had only to—.

"When they told me Huw Bro-Dawel was here, I wondered if you would be with him," Alys said as soon as she had opened the door.

Heledd looked at Huw for a moment before turning to greet her cousin. She bowed her head slightly as she walked across the thick carpet. "Alys, I did not expect to see you here."

"I didn't expect to see you again, anywhere," Alys replied, ignoring Heledd's outstretched hands.

Heledd let her hands fall slowly to her sides, her chin rising perceptibly. "May I introduce you to the *pennaeth* of Bro-Dawel, and his sons?" Heledd turned toward the three men who bowed at the waist to Meilor Gwesyn's daughter-in-law. Alys greeted Huw Bro-Dawel and accepted his greeting before turning to the others.

"We have met," she remarked to Aled as she accepted his hand.

"Yes, *boneddiges*," he replied, bowing again.

"How are you, Aled Mathonwy? And your wife?"

"I am well, as is my wife."

"Have you also brought your daughters?" she asked Huw.

"Not this time, *boneddiges*. This is my youngest daughter's husband, my son-in-law, Geraint Padarn."

Alys extended her hand to Geraint, looking up into his deep blue eyes, a slight blush bringing color to her cheeks as he bowed over her hand. He neither kissed it nor held it against his heart but his smile had a similar effect on Alys *gwraig* Gwern. She withdrew her hand from his grasp slowly and returned her attention to her auburn-haired cousin. "What a happy coincidence this is. I am here with my husband … and here you are as well with …. We will have ample time to talk while the men discuss their business." She approached Heledd, blocking her from the men. "You look exhausted, haggard."

Heledd dropped her eyes for a moment, remembering Huw's warning to her about her unborn child. "We have been staying in basic accommodation for two nights," she replied, meeting Alys's searching gaze.

"Oh really? They allow wh— women to stay in cloisters, do they?"

"We stayed with friends of the *pennaeth*."

"Oh, I see. Special accommodation," Alys laughed. "Well, come with me and we'll find you a suitable room," she said, grasping Heledd's arm.

"With respect, *boneddiges*," Huw interrupted Alys, as Aled and Geraint stepped forward to block her exit, "Heledd will stay with me."

"Oh, I *see*," she simpered, giggling at the show of dominance. "Very interesting," she whispered to Heledd. "You obviously give the old man cause for concern." She turned toward the three men. "How delightful my cousin has found such good friends. And I am delighted to see her again. We did not believe we would ever see her *here*." To Heledd, she said, "We will have opportunity to talk this evening," as she swept out of the room.

Huw contemplated the floor for a moment before he gestured to Heledd and brought her into the circle of his arm. "You will have to bear this for some time," he said.

"I have had to bear this most of my life, *pennaeth*. Another few days will not hurt me." He kissed the side of her head and dropped his arm.

"Tell me if she says anything of importance."

"I will."

"And remember your husband is close."

"I know," Heledd replied, smiling into his haloed eyes. "You are very kind, *pennaeth*. I am grateful to you."

"There is no need for that," Huw smiled and turned his attention to his sons.

No refreshments were brought while they waited and no messages came from Meilor Gwesyn during the several hours the four visitors were left alone. During their wait, they had ample time to discuss but kept their conversation to the general observations of friendly guests in the home of a respected man of high status. Heledd finally succumbed to the fatigue of the journey and the demands of her *baban's* early growth. She sat in one of the large armchairs by the hearth, where the draft from the chimney swept away from her, and was nearly asleep when the steward came back into the room with a taper to give them some light. Though he only lit four of the candles, there was enough warmth from their glow to take the chill from her hands.

As he left the room, the steward said, "The *pennaeth* will be with you in a short time. He has had many disputes to settle today and begs your forgiveness for his inhospitality. He will be available later this evening but, in the meantime, he begs your indulgence."

Huw made a similarly courteous reply and stood by the hearth, near Heledd. When the steward had gone, he said, "Meilor Gwesyn is renown throughout this region for his hospitality." His three companions understood his meaning and smiled quietly amongst themselves. Shortly before another hour had passed, the steward returned, leading a small group of servants who were carrying jugs of warmed mead and cups. "Please thank our host for his kindness," Huw told the steward as the servants left the room. The steward inclined his head and left the room. Less than a minute later, the door burst open and the *pennaeth* of Gwesyn bounded across the room toward his long-time friend.

"Huw," he shouted. "You old wolf, I have missed your company these past years. It is good to see you, old friend."

"I have been where I have always been, Meilor. You know the road as well as I know this."

"Ach, a man becomes embroiled in business and politics – time passes. As it has for both of us," Meilor Gwesyn concluded, appraising his former ally with critical eyes. "You are older and, I hope, wiser."

"As are you, no doubt." Huw clasped the hand offered to him and received the embrace of a comrade-in-arms. "Allow me to present my son-in-law and my foster son." Meilor furrowed his brow. "I believe you have also met this woman," Huw said, extending his hand to Heledd who stood at his behest and came forward to stand at his side.

"Her face is familiar," Meilor replied, bowing as he showed Heledd a smile no warmer than a grimace, studying her face before his eyes shifted to take in the rest of her body. "If we have not met formally, the fault, I'm sure, can be redressed, *boneddiges*. You are welcome in my house, Heledd *merch* Ieuan Bannawg. I hope you will accept my hospitality with the open-heartedness with which I offer it." Heledd inclined her head briefly but did not return his smile nor open her mouth to speak. "By coincidence, your lovely cousin is also here. The two of you will have occasion to hear each other's news," Meilor said. "I will have you taken to her apartment."

"If you have no objection," Huw said, "I prefer Heledd to stay where I can see her." To emphasize his meaning, he clasped her wrist and pulled her to stand nearer to him.

Meilor grinned, and nodded once to acknowledge his friend's possessive nature. "I do not blame you, Bro-Dawel. Such a beautiful creature can easily escape the limited reach of men our age. It pleases me to see you have found her of some comfort to your later years."

"Would that you could find such comfort," Huw replied.

"Ach, you know me better than that, old friend. Women provide only one service of any value to me and there are plenty here who excel at that. You no doubt met one of them on the road from Talhaearn."

"She has sent a message to you," Huw said. Meilor encouraged him to speak further. "She said you would be happy to know one of her children is dead. We met three of them, the girl and two sons."

"Thank you for bringing that news. One less mouth to feed, eh?"

"What was the woman's crime?" Huw asked, cocking his head slightly.

"Not hers, her husband. One of my soldiers caught the man trying to steal from me. He's in prison and she's begging." Meilor glanced at Heledd but she gave him no sign of what her thoughts might have been on the matter. Her chin was high and her eyes were focused on the tapestry to her right. "I may grant the woman parole if she provides me with the death of another of her brats."

"What did the man steal?" Huw inquired, taking a sip of his

mead.

"Bread." Meilor chuckled. "I've told the woman she must beg for bread until either her children die or her husband. He's dead but I will not tell her until she kills another child." Heledd closed her eyes for a moment. "Does that disturb you, *boneddiges*? Do you have some sympathy for thieves and whores?"

"You are *pennaeth*," she said. "I do not know the circumstances and would not presume an opinion."

"You have trained her well, Huw," Meilor said, appraising his guest once more. "Her uncle assured me she was beyond redemption or I would have had her years ago."

"Your own knowledge of Llew Talgarth will give you the truth of the matter."

"Ach, I know he cheated me, on several occasions, but has proved useful on others. Justice will prevail, eh?"

"Justice usually does, my friend," Huw agreed, saluting Meilor Gwesyn with his own excellent mead.

"My steward will show you and your sons to suitable rooms – the best I have to offer such good friends – and then we will have our meal. Bring the woman with you, if you so choose. She will find our entertainment this evening most enlightening."


As they were shown to the *neuadd*, Heledd scanned the many faces of stewards, warriors and servants but saw no one she recognized. Huw assured her Garmon and the others were near, but she could not imagine where or how they could be close enough to help her if she needed them. Huw had attempted to bolster her courage while they were in the room Meilor had assigned but only Garmon's physical presence would be enough for her. Although Aled was in his place, no one could stand in Garmon's place to protect her in the huge, cold great hall of the man she most feared. Huw laid his hand on her arm as they walked between the rows of tables toward the *pennaeth's* raised platform.

Meilor watched their approach with narrowed eyes though

his lips were smiling. He stood when Huw reached the dais. The two *pennaeth* bowed to one another and Meilor gestured for Huw to take the seat beside him. He requested Heledd sit on his left, next to Alys, so they could talk freely, he told her. When Heledd took the seat, a servant handed her a damp cloth to wash her hands. As she unfolded it, a sprig of lavender fell into her hand.

Heledd crushed it in her palm and handed the cloth back to the servant without making eye contact, without showing any outward sign her husband was close enough to protect her. After a moment, she secreted the sprig in the black brocade purse on her hip as she turned to acknowledge Alys's greeting. Armed with this evidence Garmon had found a way into Meilor Gwesyn's fortress, Heledd's confidence returned despite the expression of pity on Alys's face.

"What is wrong?" she asked.

"You still have that tattered purse," Alys said.

"Yes."

"But why? Bro-Dawel has obviously given you some very fine garments. Why would you want to keep a rag like that from a man who so mistreated you?"

"As a reminder," Heledd said, "of how much my life has changed because of him."

"I hope you don't believe I had anything to do with what happened to you. I was horrified when my father ordered him to take you to the barracks."

"Were you?" Heledd asked, tilting her head.

"Heledd, how could you think I wished that on you? I know now it is bad enough to be at the mercy of a man who is your husband but that … I truly believed he was to be your protector, not your—."

"Not my what?" Heledd asked. "Never mind, Alys, I cannot blame you. I'm sure you had no idea what your father and brothers planned for me. You were so full of happiness for your own future, how could you possible wish me ill?"

"You are generous," Alys commented, "considering the life you have been forced to accept."

"Huw Bro-Dawel is a good man, just as your father told me he was," Heledd replied. "I have no complaint of him. I have food and shelter, good clothing and plenty of work to keep me busy. I have even learned to write and read a little."

"He has taught you to write?"

"For writing, I have a special teacher, one who was at a cloister school."

"Why do you need to know writing for what you do?"

"So I know what concerns me, if it is written," Heledd replied with a merry laugh, drawing the attention of her host as well as her companions and others in the *neuadd*. "There is more," she said in a lowered voice, "to pleasing a man than being pretty."

"Tell me about your life there. Where do you live? You said you have work."

"I work in the *beudy*, of course, every day. I live in a house of my own with a *neuadd* and a bedroom. My life is better than I could ever have expected."

"That was never much," Alys commented, "considering you have been a bondservant since your father ... was executed."

"No, but the *pennaeth* of Bro-Dawel has shown mercy."

"I couldn't bear that kind of life. Marriage is bad enough," Alys whispered, glancing at Gwern on her left who was deep in conversation with his older brother, "but to be forced to the bed of such an old man would be intolerable."

"Age is the least of my concerns," Heledd replied.

"Does he strike you?" Alys murmured, pushing the sleeve of her frock up her arm to show Heledd a fresh bruise.

Heledd stared at her cousin's arm for a few moments after Alys had covered the bruise and turned to take a sip from her cup of mead. "Your husband did that?"

"That is nothing," Alys said aloud, with a smile, glancing at the tip of the scar on Heledd's arm. "Tell me about the work you do in the *beudy*. Do you also milk the cows?" Her tone attracted her father-in-law's attention and Meilor studied the two women with narrowed eyes as Heledd answered.

"It is the same work I did at Bannawg," Heledd replied,

deliberately using only the name of her father's land. "I also milk, at least ten cows in the morning and the same at night. Last week, I made over one hundred rounds of cheese, with the other women's help, of course."

"I'm surprised you make this creature work as well," Meilor said to Huw Bro-Dawel. "Are you so old you cannot keep her occupied?" He turned toward Heledd. "I will show the old man how to occupy a spirited animal," he laughed, leaning toward her.

Heledd leaned away as far as she could just as one of the servants bent over the front of the table to fill the *pennaeth's* cup with wine, knocking the cup over as Meilor reached for Heledd's wrist. Wine cascaded across the table and Heledd jumped from her chair to avoid the dark liquid, escaping Meilor's grasp. The *pennaeth* struck out with his fist and the servant reeled back, clutching his jaw. Heledd sought the shelter of Huw's side, hiding her face in his sleeve as she watched Arwel dart out of sight. Though Meilor shouted for the servant to be caught, he was gone before anyone had seen which one had angered the *pennaeth*.

"Skittish as a colt as well," Meilor observed, casting a dark look in Heledd's direction. "Come back, girl," he murmured though Heledd recognized the threat in his tone. Huw patted her arm and encouraged her to return to her chair. "You have no cause for alarm," he said for her ears alone.

"I would not disgrace my friend by soiling my hands on the likes of you." Meilor beckoned a steward to bring a cloth and more wine before he said, "Your bondmaster obviously finds you more useful as a char than for bedding."

Heledd raised her chin slightly but did not refute the comment. Though she kept a watch for Arwel, he did not reappear – at least not in any guise she recognized. By the time most of the company in the great *neuadd* were fed and drunk, Meilor had turned his attention to Huw Bro-Dawel and his reasons for the journey after so many years. Though Heledd listened, she heard little of their conversation. She was distracted by Alys's inexhaustible chatter until Meilor Gwesyn slammed his flagon on the table.

"And now, we will have the entertainment," he shouted, raising a hand and gesturing for a troupe of actors to come forward from the rear of the hall. "This will enlighten you, *menyw*," Meilor said, "and delight many. The actors have worked hard to bring this piece to us this evening. Let us show our appreciation before they begin," he commanded, clapping his hands together until everyone in the hall did the same. He sat back in his cushioned chair, folded his hands across his chest and smiled at the actors.

Heledd's heart filled with dread as the troupe of five cleared a space before the dais and set up their simple scenery of a few chairs and two benches side by side. One of the actors, a woman with her hair braided with red ribbons down her back, laid down on the bench and pretended to sleep, then woke suddenly at the sound of another actor pretending to climb into the bed with her.

"Ah, my love. My husband will catch you, if we are not careful."

"Your invitation is too clear and too hot for me to ignore. Open but the slightest and we will love for all the night without that old man waking." The two actors embraced, making a show of laughing and teasing one another for several minutes while their audience encouraged a more realistic demonstration of their passion. A third actor, as a bent old man, stumbled into the scene and seemed oblivious to the activity on the bed.

"Ach, it is a cold night for any man to be alone but my pretty young wife is sleeping sound. She does not like when I wake her." The actor stumbled from one side of the scene to another, making the audience laugh with his bumbling antics. The two on the bed slipped out of sight for a short time and when they returned, the woman had a big belly, making a spectacle of her condition. "But how can this be?" her old husband asked the audience. "Six times have I slept with her and six children has she borne me. Who has planted this seventh seed that grows so strong and willful?"

Heledd watched the players and did not have to stretch her

imagination to guess who the three characters were intended to represent. Although she resented the portrayal of her parents, she refused to give Meilor Gwesyn the satisfaction of a reaction. She sipped her wine, watched and listened to the actors only to learn how she could use the insult to herself and her parents to hurt Gwesyn.

In the second part of the performance, the actor playing her mother gave birth in a comedic and noisy way to a daughter who immediately strutted around the stage, holding her chin so high she couldn't see where she was going. Heledd smiled at the caricature of herself as the actor flounced about and covered her face with her apron every time one of the other actors appeared as a soldier. The worst moment came when an actor limped toward the daughter who stood with her head thrown back and her tunic over her face while the limping actor kissed her hand and held it to his heart before cackling and carrying her off over his shoulder, delighting the audience with the haughty girl's downfall.

Heledd had rested her head on her hand halfway through the second act and yawned several times despite the blatant attempt to humiliate her. Only Alys could have written the end of the play but Heledd did not acknowledge her cousin's contribution. She was disappointed with Meilor Gwesyn's lack of imagination. The single truly inventive event in the productions was the suggestion her uncle had been her mother's lover and consequently her father. While the rest of the audience showed their appreciation, Heledd yawned again, tracing the shapes in the grain of the table, finding letters cut into the wood.

When the audience quieted, she lifted her head from her study of the table and met Meilor Gwesyn's gaze with a stifled yawn. "Excuse me, *pennaeth*. Our journey today was tiring." She sat back in her chair, drinking from her cup. "Thank your actors, on my behalf, for their effort, of course, but with your permission, I would like to retire." As she stood, her three companions pushed their chairs from the table and rose to their feet. Huw extended his hand to her and Heledd slipped comfortably into the embrace of his arm, glancing up into his kind eyes with a smile.

"We will talk in the morning," Meilor told Huw Bro-Dawel, "alone."

As the four visitors left the hall, Gwesyn turned his wrath on the actors, whose performance failed to humiliate Ieuan Bannawg's daughter.

As they reached the stairs leading to their rooms on the floor above the hall, Huw patted her hand. Heledd trembled with rage as she looked into her father-in-law's face. "I know, child, but hush," Huw said, pressing a finger to his lips. When they reached the room and had ensured it was empty, he opened his mouth to speak.

"I felt sorry for her," Heledd exclaimed.

"Who?" Huw asked, dropping into a chair to watch her pace the room.

"Alys. I should have known – I did know. If I had had a weapon... How dare she drag Garmon into such a poor, disgraceful attempt to insult me?"

"I doubt Garmon would find that any more insulting than you did."

"Fiction. Worse than that. Lies. They must think I still believe that ridiculous fabrication." Heledd sank into another chair with a heavy sigh. "Do you still think you can win?"

"I know it, child."

"Well, I know one thing. The soldiers have no discipline and lack any real loyalty."

"So you've become a military observer?"

"Even I can see that," she laughed. "Arwel got into the house. Garmon is here as well. As skilled as he is, I don't think that would have been as easy as it seems to have been, if Meilor had any real commitment from his army."

"Well understood, *merch*. We'll make a commander of you yet."

"Have you seen Garmon?"

"Yes. It wasn't easy, mind. I doubt even Aled recognized him. How did you know he was in the house?"

"He sent me a message," Heledd replied with a smile, "but I didn't see him. Is he well?"

"Hard to tell," Huw laughed. "Go to bed, Heledd. Garmon won't want you to see him. Don't look for him among the throng in the hall. Know he's there and be at peace. He will make himself known if needs be."

"I only caught a glimpse of Arwel when Meilor tried to touch me. If he does that again, I will defend myself."

The bed into which Heledd crawled that night was against the wall and enclosed within a cupboard. She slid the door shut and settled into the feather mattress, aware Huw had left the room and Geraint struggled to make himself comfortable on the bench. Her growing infant demanded the last of her energy and she fell asleep, despite her anxiety for Garmon and the child in her womb. Although she had not publicly reacted to the play, scenes from it stirred her memories of her mother's death. Her dreams were agitated and violent through the night and she woke frequently, gasping for breath and staring into the dark cavern of the cupboard bed.

Though she could see a flicker of light through the pattern of holes carved in the upper portion of the oak panels, until she woke the following morning, she did not open the narrow doors. When she did, she was surprised to discover the hour was late and she was alone in the room. Confident she would not be left without protection, Heledd sat in the opening, at the edge of the bed and dropped her feet to the floor. From her loosened hair, something dropped to the bare planks of the floor. Heledd found the blue cord, a delicate gold ring tied in the middle of it.

She held the cord and the ring close to her heart for a long time, wondering at the ability of her husband to show his love for her in ways that were intimate only to them. How Garmon knew she had fallen so completely in love with him on the night her uncle had intended her destruction, Heledd could only guess. That she knew she would fall in love with him, over and over, from one day to the next was without question. She slid the gold ring with its emerald stone on the finger of her right hand and admired its perfection for several moments before she leapt from the bed and whirled around the center of the room. As she chose her garments for the day, she hummed tunes to herself and danced with each piece of clothing that came from her satchel.

After she had chosen her garments and was considering what to do about her breakfast, she was disturbed by a timid knock at the door. Heledd walked to the door making as little sound as possible and peered through a small crack between the planks. She could not see much in either direction but recognized the servant girl as the one who had come up with them to show the way to the room. The girl held a tray of food in front of her and did not seem apprehensive.

"Who is there?" Heledd inquired when she had stepped a few feet away from the door.

"I have brought your breakfast, *boneddiges*."

"Is there anyone with you?"

"No, *boneddiges*, I am alone," the girl said under her breath. Heledd opened the door, bracing herself against it, in case anyone attempted to push his way in through the small gap she left for the servant. Once the girl was through, Heledd slammed the door shut and shot the bolt into its bracket.

"Thank you," Heledd said, clearing a space on the small, square table for the tray. "I was just thinking about breakfast."

"Your *pennaeth* said you would be."

"Do you know where Huw Bro-Dawel is?"

"He is with Meilor Gwesyn, *boneddiges*. They have been in the *pennaeth's* office for several hours."

"What is your name?"

"I am called Branwedd," the girl answered, setting the tray on the table.

"Have you always lived in this *caer*?"

"No, *boneddiges*. I come from a village to the south."

"Which one is that?"

"I do not know its name. I have lived here since I was a

child. Will you require help to dress?"

"Thank you, but I can usually manage on my own," Heledd said with a shiver.

"There are no fires in any of these rooms," the servant told her. "The *pennaeth* keeps only one fire, in the *neuadd.*"

"I will wear a coat as well as my tunic then." Heledd sat near the table and poured a flagon of ale. "Have you eaten, Branwedd?"

"Earlier, *boneddiges.* Before my work began."

"Sit down and keep me company," Heledd urged, patting the seat of the other chair. "I cannot possibly eat all of this," she added, pushing the platter of bread and cheese toward the girl, careful not to show her distaste for the strong odor of the food. Branwedd took a piece of the cheese and stuffed it into her mouth, swallowing before she had chewed. "Do your parents also work in the *gaer?*"

"My parents are not here. I don't remember much about them, except their names."

"What are their names?"

"My father was Custen and my mother was Branwen."

Though the names meant nothing to Heledd, she thought it was possible the girl was one of the seventeen who had come from Bannawg to be bondservants to Gwesyn. "Are there any others in the household who don't remember their villages or anything about their parents?"

"I don't know, *boneddiges.* I have never spoken to anyone about it. There are a few in the house who are near to me in age."

"I am about your age," Heledd said. "I come from Bannawg which is a small *ystad* in the south. My parents died when I was small."

"Alys *gwraig* Gwern has come from Talgarth-y-Bannawg," Branwedd said.

"It was my home too," Heledd answered. "Alys is my cousin. Her father is my uncle."

"Yes, *boneddiges*, everyone knows who you are."

"Have another piece of this cheese," Heledd offered,

holding out the plate.

"No, thank you, *boneddiges*," she replied. "The cook will know I have eaten."

"What's wrong with that?"

"The cook is very strict about when we eat – so he can control his stores and report to the *pennaeth* at the end of the week. He likes to have surplus, just in case."

"In case?"

"In case the *pennaeth* thinks the cook should have more."

"What happens if the *pennaeth* wants more?"

"Someone gets punished."

"Do you know the woman who is on the road with her children?"

"No, but I know about her. Her husband is dead." Branwedd shrugged and added, "We were told yesterday."

"Perhaps now the woman and her children will be released," Heledd suggested.

"Perhaps," Branwedd answered, beginning to clear away the tray. "I must go, if you don't need me, *boneddiges*." When Branwedd left the room, Aled was standing outside the door and entered as the girl turned at the stairs, holding his finger to his lips until the door was closed behind him.

"What did you tell her?"

"Nothing useful. I think she may be one of the Bannawg children."

"They are not children, Heledd," Aled reminded her. "Do not expect they will all run to your banner. Most are settled in their lives here and will not seek change."

"At least, I can offer choice," Heledd replied, sinking back.

"Huw has been with Meilor Gwesyn all morning. He wants you to come now," Aled told her. "Prepare yourself, Heledd. Meilor is in no mood to negotiate."

When Heledd entered the *pennaeth's* office, she took time to become familiar with her surroundings so her eyes could adjust to the darkness. The room was not lit by any lamp or candle other than a small brazier by the table he used for a desk.

"Come in, *boneddiges*," Meilor invited, his voice like crusty syrup. He extended his hand to her but she walked across the room toward Huw Bro-Dawel instead, greeting Meilor Gwesyn with a gracious nod of her head and a fixed expression she hoped conveyed civility. She did not bother to express any other courtesy – the man had slaughtered her entire family and she did not believe even he thought she should show him warmth or interest. "Huw and I have been discussing our younger days and the many exploits we have shared. Now, I believe you also have some history to discuss."

Heledd swallowed hard. All the planning for this moment had not prepared her for facing the *pennaeth* of Gwesyn, the murderer of her family, with a claim for justice for his crime. She tilted her chin, turning her head a fraction to the side so she could see Huw out of the corner of her eye.

"I have been informed by others more learned than I am I have good cause to ask for justice."

"Do you?" Meilor inquired, smiling broadly. "Have they?" He leaned back in his high, cushioned chair and tapped his fingers on the papers strewn before him. "What evidence, what testimony, do you have to support this claim?" Before she could answer, he continued, "You realize I do not accept these charges. Unless you have witnesses – other than women, of course – there is no proof any wrong was done, but a great wrong – committed by your own father – was put right."

"My father committed no crime against you or his brother. I have witnesses, eye witnesses, who have sworn to a high court of judges and *pennaeth*, my uncle was the aggressor and you supported his crime against my family."

"Bring your witnesses, *boneddiges*," Meilor said. "I will prove they lie. I will not waste my time further with this fabrication, this rewriting of established fact."

"I am not required to bring my witnesses before you, *pennaeth*," Heledd said, recalling all Garmon had tutored her to say. "Their testimony has been given, and tested, in a court of law. The king has brought this case to the attention of the other *pennaeth* of Powys."

"And my friends have exonerated me. Therefore—."

"The king has signed this document," Heledd interrupted him, pointing to the sheaf of papers Huw had brought with him on Meilor Gwesyn's desk, under his fingers.

"Show me where it says I am guilty, *boneddiges*," Meilor demanded.

"Here," she told him, laying her finger on a paragraph on the first page. "And here," Heledd turned to another page and slapped her hand down on the second paragraph, "and here – the whole catalog of your crimes against my family, including the rape and murder of my sisters," she jabbed her finger at the words, "and the beheading and desecration of my brothers' bodies."

"And your mother?" Meilor asked, a flat smile stretched across his jaw.

"My mother was murdered by Llew Talgarth. This I saw with my own eyes. And for that act of murder, he will pay her honor-price directly to me."

"You expect me to accept this testimony? To admit guilt?"

"I claim what is my right to claim – compensation for the unlawful killing of members of my family by soldiers who were under your command."

"This was all a long time ago, child," Gwesyn said. "No one can remember exactly what happened, what orders were given. In the heat of battle, under circumstances of war, all is justified. Even Hywel understands that."

"I understand that," Heledd said. "I have lived with soldiers all of my life. The *pennaeth* of Bro-Dawel is a soldier – he has an army of immeasurable strength – a disciplined, powerful army," she added.

"What are we talking about here?" Meilor asked of Huw, with a laugh. "Is she threatening me with your warband?"

"Not directly," Huw replied, smiling in return.

"Seventeen children were stolen from Bannawg," Heledd continued. "Forty men were killed, eighteen women were raped and all were made widows. On their behalf, as it is made plain in that document, I demand their honor-prices be paid, to each as is due them for their suffering, unlawfully inflicted."

Meilor rose to his feet, laying his hands flat on the desk and leaned toward Heledd *merch* Ieuan Bannawg. His face was reddening and his jaw had hardened – like granite – a thought that brought an unbidden smile to Heledd's lips. Her smile enraged him even more and his eyes bulged from his head. Suddenly, he cocked his head and a smile returned to his expression.

"As I said, all this was a long time ago. Men act in battle in ways that cannot be predicted or controlled. I will ponder this claim for a few days. While you are here, you will have time to renew your friendship with Alys, who, I must tell you, has looked forward to your visit here with the joyful anticipation of a child."

# twenty-seven

Heledd walked into the garden of the *pennaeth's* great house, aware at every turn one of his minions was watching her. More comforting to her was the assurance Garmon also had placed men to watch her and she approached her fair-haired cousin with confidence. Alys was seated at the end of a stone-paved walk, her hooded woolen cloak wrapped loosely against a mild breeze that seemed to bring the warmth of the sun into the long garden.

"I'm so glad you have come," Alys said. "I thought you might blame me for that despicable performance – how they ever came to write such lies, I will never understand. Did you sleep well?"

"Yes, very well," Heledd said, laying her hand over the ring her husband had secreted into her bed. "I always do."

"Really? I wish I could say the same. I have such difficult, troublesome nights – even when I am alone."

"I am rarely alone ... now," Heledd said, inviting Alys's likely curiosity, in hope of learning more from her cousin's questions than she gave herself in answers.

"Your ... *pennaeth* is quite old," Alys observed.

"I have found him to be ... vigorous," Heledd replied.

"Knowledgeable as well," Alys said. "He has had more experience than most."

"I do not know that."

"He is as old as Meilor," Alys said, "and Meilor has had many opportunities to gain experience of women. I would think, anyway," she added, looking away from Heledd for a moment, a slight glow fading from her cheek as she turned back to study her cousin. "I did feel so sorry for you, Heledd, when my father sold you to such an old man. I thought you would be unhappy … but I can see you aren't. You are glowing … is it just good health or are you happy?"

"Happy is not a word I know," Heledd confessed. "I do not know what it means."

"I understand it less now," Alys replied, "than I did when I was younger. You know, don't you, I lost the child I was carrying when you left Talgarth-y-Bannawg."

"No, I didn't know that," Heledd answered.

"An accident … I fell from my horse … Gwern was very angry," Alys told her. "He has forgiven me, of course," she added.

"Is that why he beats you?" Heledd asked, unable to curb her anger.

"You didn't believe that, did you?" Alys laughed. "You really are an innocent, aren't you? This," Alys said, pulling back her sleeve, "is passion."

"My—." Heledd bit her lips together. "I do not bear the cuts and bruises of any man's 'passion'," she said, lifting her chin.

"Then what is that?" Alys ripped Heledd's sleeve above her elbow, dragging her red-painted nail along the scar.

"Nothing. An accident, in the stables."

"Do you bear anything?"

"What do you mean?"

"You have been a whore for one man and the consort of another – where is your child by either man? Are you barren? Or do you rid yourself of these brats before their growth disfigures you?"

"I would not know how to do that."

"There must be women near you who can perform such mysteries," Alys ventured.

"If so, no one has offered that service and I have not sought it."

"Then it is the men who are not man enough to fill your belly."

"Think as you like, Alys. What happens between me and the

man with whom I share a bed, is not for you to know."

"Ach. You have not changed. So secretive, so private," she sneered. "I know more now than you will ever know. I have had a man in ways you will never experience – ways that give a woman pleasure beyond endurance. Ways that leave a woman enslaved ...."

"I prefer my freedom," Heledd answered, suppressing a smile. Gwern *mab* Meilor was not the lover her cousin described. He was the boy-mate Goewin called him. "Alys, can we not be friends, after all that has happened? I have never meant you harm in any way. I know you are angry I have come here to seek justice from Meilor but that should not affect you. You will still have more than it will ever be possible for you to use. You will still have your husband who so delights you. Nothing I can do will change your life for the worse."

"You have accused my father of a hideous act against his sister-in-law. That is a shame that will cast a stain over me as well. How can you suggest we be friends?"

"You did not mind casting shame upon me and I do not carry a grudge against you. Can you not show me some kindness?"

"Kindness? You think you deserve kindness?"

"I believe everyone deserves that much, no matter what they have done."

"You did not feel that way when my father let that wretched soldier have you. This is all vengeance against my father for selling you to a dirty brute and an old, old man."

"Huw Bro-Dawel is not old and — I have never known a 'dirty brute'."

"No? I suppose you like to think Garmon Dolwyddlan was kind, a perfect lover."

"He was kind," Heledd replied.

"But not a perfect lover." Alys laughed again.

"There is no way to resolve our differences, Alys. That causes me some sadness but it is not something that will ruin my life. I have many kind friends. I can depend on their support. I do not need you to be generous toward me, any more than you need me to be kind to you." Heledd rose to her feet and extended her hand, forgetting she wore Garmon's ring. "I wish you the life you deserve."

Alys grasped Heledd's hand, holding her fast. "You have done well for yourself, whore." Alys ran her finger over the stone fastened in the gold band. "But you will never have a husband to complete your happiness." With a dismissive gesture, she shoved Heledd's hand away from her and turned her back.

As she walked down the path, Heledd felt the jab of pain the pressure of Alys's grasp had put on her ringed finger. She looked down at her hand and saw the gold band had left a mark and Alys had scratched her deep enough for her finger to bleed. Leaving a scar to remind Heledd of her 'passion' was her cousin's way. Heledd purposefully moved the ring to her left hand.

Though she longed to see Garmon and to tell him everything she felt, Heledd knew he was informed. She did not have to endure another performance or another interview with Meilor. Neither did she have to spend any free moments with Alys. She had begun to suffer with sickness and fatigue, taking longer to dress in the mornings and enjoying a languor in the afternoons that allowed her to pretend an interest in embroidery. While some of the women of Meilor's household gossiped around her, Heledd concentrated hard on the simple chain stitches she had been shown, striving to make them even.

When Huw Bro-Dawel called her away from the company of the Gwesyn women, she secreted her small embroidered cloth in her black purse and followed him to the room at the top of the house in which he had been sleeping. "There is less chance we will be overheard here," he told her.

"Someone has spied on me?"

"Not that I know. Garmon would have said."

"Where is he now?" Heledd asked, in a forlorn tone that made Huw looked at her with a frown.

"He is here, child, in the house. Near enough." He sat by her and took her hand. "Meilor has made an offer at last."

"I—. No. I will not accept any offer other than what I claim."

"Listen, Heledd. You must consider carefully. Meilor will never admit responsibility for the deaths of your family – that is too close to admitting guilt. He will not put his honor in question. He proposes, instead, he will settle all the compensation you seek, as a bride-price, if you accept his eldest son as your husband."

"No."

"Shush, Heledd. Let me finish," Huw urged her. "Hear what I say."

"I cannot and will not do that," she told him. "I already have a husband."

"Divorce is possible."

"You are making sport of me," she said, unsure he was.

"Elgan is also married and Meilor will arrange a divorce for him."

"Never. I will not consider it, even for a moment."

"Heledd, it is a matter of expedience. If you want compensation for yourself and your people, this may be the safest, most efficient way of achieving that aim."

"And what do you suggest I tell Garmon, my husband?"

"He is a soldier and a lawyer – he will understand."

"If he understands, I do not." Heledd exclaimed. "I will not divorce him."

"Garmon already knows what Meilor has offered," Huw told her, pulling her left hand toward him. "It is no more than you have already done by switching your ring to this hand. He will accept your decision. You can take Elgan as your husband—."

"I have told you, I will not. The thought sickens me."

"—And keep Garmon as your lover."

"Huw, what are you thinking?"

"I am thinking. You are feeling. Think of Goewin, Heulwen, Elain – you are fond of them, and all the others like them you want to be safe. Getting justice for them from Meilor requires sacrifice …" Huw told her, laying his hand on her shoulder with a sad smile on his face.

"I have already made my sacrifice," Heledd replied. "I do not owe him anything else and I will not trade myself, even if it means there will be no justice for others. I will stay with my husband. I know it is selfish and ignoble but I cannot leave Garmon. I love him and I would rather die than be separated from him like this."

"You have responsibilities—."

"I have a responsibility, first of all to my child—."

"That is exactly my point, Heledd. Meilor's son will never know your child is not his and your child – Garmon's child – will hold all this."

"You are mad," Heledd laughed. "My child will be raised in a decent home by his true father. I want a life and I want to die of old age. Nothing you say, no argument, no thinking, no sensible reasoning will change my mind. I have seen what has happened to Alys here – she is her father-in-law's mistress and her husband beats her for pleasure. I will not, for anyone's sake, subject myself or my child to that. My child and I deserve better and if you are not prepared to help me—."

Huw rose to his feet, still holding her hand, an angry frown in his eyes. "You have no strong opinion on this matter, I see."

Heledd opened her mouth to answer, a pout coming to her face. "Isn't it dangerous to make such a suggestion when you are not sure of the answer?" she demanded. "Suppose I had agreed to Meilor's proposal?"

"I was sure of your answer, *merch*," Huw answered. "But I knew you were not, nor was Garmon. He felt you had a right to choose."

"His sense of equality will get us both into trouble," Heledd sighed.

"Your first duty is to yourself. He knows that, Heledd. If you believed you have a duty beyond that, Garmon would not stand in your way – he would commit himself to helping you. I am grateful you love him more than any absurdity such as duty. Your cousin has chosen her fate and many of your father's people have done the same. Meilor has no choice other than war – a war he knows he cannot win. Making this proposal was a desperate effort to save face. Unless you have good reason to do so, I suggest you take the compensation in a way that will allow him some semblance of honor."

When Heledd next saw Meilor Gwesyn she discovered that refusing his proposal gave her great pleasure. Despite his outrage that a dapple-faced girl had the audacity to stand in his way, he chose instead to accept a compromise proposal that gave her the justice she wanted and allowed him to appear an honorable man. To celebrate the treaty between Gwesyn and the newly formed *ystad* of Bro-Heledd, Meilor Gwesyn ordered a feast.

Bro-Heledd consisted of a patch of land between Gwesyn and Bannawg upon which a carn was to be erected and each stone was to bear the name of one of her family, marking their final memorial place and a testament to their lives, cut short by war. For each of their lives, Meilor Gwesyn agreed to add a sum equal to their honor-price to Heledd's property which she would hold in her own right – Meilor presented this to her as a wedding gift, rather than compensation and the fiction did not go beyond the ears of those in the room who signed the documents. Similar arrangements were made for the widows and injured women. All of the stolen children were offered their freedom and a home in Bro-Dawel, along with a portion of their honor-price whatever they chose to do with their freedom.

On the night of the feast, Heledd sat next to Meilor and was not afraid he would touch her as she had been on the first night she sat at his table. Before the feast had progressed far and before the company had begun to drink, the chief steward presented himself at Meilor's dais and announced there were visitors at the gate, asking for hospitality. Meilor shrugged and gestured his acceptance of their request with his hand, turning toward Heledd for her agreement.

"This is your home, *pennaeth*. The honor of showing graciousness to your guests is always yours," she said.

As the guests begun to arrive, Alys at first clenched her jaw then turned wide eyes on her cousin. "Did you know he was here?" she demanded.

"Who?" Heledd asked, glancing at the door as Urien Macsen entered. "Oh, I see. I did not know he intended to be here."

"You know him? You have given shelter to him after what he did to my father?"

"Alys, your father is not my friend, Urien is." Heledd said plainly, leaping to her feet when the next guest entered and smiled across the long expanse of the room at her.

"Ha. Now we will see who feels shame." Alys said, turning to her father-in-law. "That is the hireling I told you about, the one who bought Heledd for a few meals at my father's table."

Garmon turned his eyes on Huw who, before Heledd could leave the dais, caught her in his arms, saying "You have no reason to fear that man, Heledd. Stay where you are."

Heledd searched his eyes to understand why he did not want her to go to her husband. She glanced again in Garmon's direction and saw the whole of Huw Bro-Dawel's warband had entered the room, without weapons, and were finding places to sit among Meilor Gwesyn's household guards and stewards. Heledd studied Huw's face for a moment longer until he stroked her cheek – an intimate gesture unlike him and she sank back into her chair between Alys and Meilor in time to see Garmon pull one of the serving women into his lap. Without her knowing, something had happened other than what she had understood was the plan and the sense of uncertainty bewildered her.

"He hasn't changed," Alys said to her in a low voice, "just as handsome and as lusty as he was when he played with you. No wonder you didn't complain. I think even I could have become accustomed to his needs. You must have been disappointed to find yourself with an old stick after that one."

"My men and I are grateful for your hospitality, Meilor Gwesyn," Heledd heard Urien Macsen say as he bowed his head slightly. He stood in front of the *pennaeth*.

"I should not have done so," Meilor replied with a laugh. "As you can see, Alys *merch* Llew is among my guests tonight.

You have done harm to her father's *ystad* with your rebellion."

"Llew Talgarth chose to rid himself of his Bannawg connection, some of whom were men in my command or the wives of my men. I had a duty to them."

"Are these your rebellious troops?"

"Only three of them are Talgarth men. The others are from districts to the west and north."

"Why have you come here? I have a full complement of warriors. I do not need mouths to feed."

"We are not here to beg," Urien declared, pulling himself to his full height, towering over all of the soldiers near him. "We are travelling to the southwest of the country to join Hywel's army."

"The king of the South changes our laws. I'm not surprised he builds his army to enforce them," Meilor commented. "You will want to meet my other guest – the *pennaeth* of Bro-Dawel. He is a great friend of this Hywel. Perhaps he will put in a good word for you. And you already know Heledd *merch* Ieuan Bannawg, a very special guest in my house tonight."

"I know her," Urien said, bowing his head once in Heledd's direction and turning his attention to Huw. "*Pennaeth*," he said in greeting. Heledd saw no other exchange of communication between them and thought they must have decided their plan well in advance of this 'chance' meeting.

"Sit and feast with us, Urien Macsen. My daughter-in-law will forgive this transgression since you have not come to do her an injury." Meilor leaned forward for a moment and then said, "Although, from the way she stares at your friend, I think she might welcome whatever he chose to inflict upon her."

Alys glanced at her father-in-law but did not rise to his baiting. Instead, she rolled her shoulder and turned her body to face him. Meilor responded with a narrow smile. Heledd recognized the pangs of possessive jealousy Meilor's smile conveyed and wondered if her expression was as apparent when she had seen Garmon take the girl in his lap or when she had seen Alys's eyes fall so speculatively on his body – the needs of which Heledd herself had come to know. Alys's assumptions about her relationship with Garmon, Heledd trusted, would blind her cousin to the truth and she turned her attention away from her husband's activities to discover what had brought this change of plan.

Elgan, Meilor's eldest son, was with a group of men only a few feet away instead of seated at the table on the dais as he had been on the first night they had been at Gwesyn. If he meant to be secretive about his activity, he did not disguise his interest in her. Though she was reluctant to do so, Heledd allowed Elgan *mab* Meilor to make eye contact with her. The moment she did so, she felt uneasy but could not then disengage from the contact despite the danger she sensed. Her rescue came from Elgan's brother. Gwern grabbed his wife's hand and held it above the tip of his knife, threatening to push her palm onto the blade. Heledd watched, afraid to make a move, as Alys fought to drag her hand free and her husband fought to impale her.

"Gwern," Meilor said, "if you damage her, you will pay reparation from your own resources."

"Wanton," Gwern hissed under his breath as he discarded Alys's hand as he would a rag and laid his knife at the edge of his plate.

Heledd wondered how long he had known his wife was unfaithful to him. When she next searched the room for Gwern's older brother, he and his group of men had left. She understood Elgan plotted against her but she had faith someone she trusted would tell her what she had to do. Aled and Geraint were in conversation at the end of the table. Huw spoke easily with Meilor. None of Urien's warband had moved from their seats at the tables and Garmon had turned his back to her to play a game of *gwyddbwyll*.

"I've had enough of this, haven't you?" Alys said, leaning close to Heledd. "I have something to show you." When Alys stood, Heledd glanced around her but none of the men she trusted took any notice when she also stood to follow her cousin. As they climbed the stairs and turned toward her own room, she thought she had been mistaken and had allowed her imagination to get in the way of her better judgment. "You will find this amusing," Alys said, opening the door and walking into the room. Heledd hesitated a moment but had no sense anyone else was in the room. "What is the matter with you? You've slept in this room since you arrived – nothing has happened to you. Look," Alys said, sweeping her arms out to her sides, "it's completely empty, just the way you left it."

"I'm sorry," Heledd said. "I'm …"

"I don't blame you. I was shocked when I saw Garmon Dolwyddlan too. What do you suppose brought him here? I wonder if he knew you were here."

"I don't see how he could know that," Heledd lied, running her hand over the back of the chair by the small table.

"Urien might have told him – they were great friends, remember? Urien did encourage my father to let that hireling have you."

"Then Urien would have to know I was here – what could it possibly matter to either of them? Garmon lost interest in me months before he left Bannawg – he didn't even tell me he was going, remember?"

"That's true," Alys admitted. "Oh well, it's pointless to speculate, isn't it?" Heledd nodded and walked over to the small window overlooking the innermost courtyard of Meilor's house. "This is sometimes my room, you know. When Gwern has better things to do than be with me."

"When is that?"

"When his father sends him on errands or to hunt some mysterious creature tormenting the villagers." Alys sauntered across the wooden floor and ran her hand over the panels of the cupboard bed. "The bed is very comfortable, don't you think?"

"Yes," Heledd agreed. "It is good quality…."

"Clean, too. When you are in this bed, the whole world seems far away, don't you think?" Alys sat in the opening of the cupboard and leaned back, supporting herself on her outstretched arms. "The first time I slept here, I knew I would never willingly sleep in another bed. You must feel that way about …well, tell me, is it Huw Bro-Dawel's bed – he doesn't behave like your lover. Tonight was the first time I have ever seen him touch you and that was not the caress of a man who has made love to you. In fact, that hireling looked at you – just for a moment – and he had the look of a man who knows a woman."

"Wishful," Heledd said.

"You haven't answered my question," Alys said, lying back on the mattress. "Who is your lover at Bro-Dawel? And don't tell me you do not have one – I see it in your eyes. Your lover satisfies you very well."

"Now you are being wishful," Heledd laughed. "You have seen yourself Huw is not interested in me – nor are any of his soldiers. You know very well I am not the kind of woman who is attractive to men – I'm too tall, too freckled, too rough. Look at my fingers," Heledd said, holding out her hands, palms down. "I cannot even keep my nails trimmed, let alone clean."

"I didn't say you were beautiful," Alys admitted. She drew up her legs and turned into the cupboard, lying lengthwise, so Heledd could only see the middle of her body. "But I would like to know what Meilor sees in you."

"That is silly," Heledd exclaimed. "If anything, he sees a threat."

"You a threat to him? Now, who is wishful? He wants you. He wanted you from the first time he came to Talgarth. He took me for Gwern when my father tricked him and gave you to that northerner." Alys played with the door of the cupboard, pushing it to and fro. "He knows you have been a whore and he wants to find out if you've learned enough to satisfy his needs. I would be jealous…but I know you. He will play with you for a while and soon be bored – like Garmon was bored, after just one night." With a flourish, Alys slammed the door of the cupboard, laughing.

Heledd turned to look at the cupboard. She could still hear Alys's laughter but there was something strange about the sound. For a moment, she thought about opening the cupboard to see what her cousin was doing in her bed. While she hesitated, she felt a sudden wave of nausea and grabbed the window sill to keep from crumpling to the ground. Not wanting

Alys to question her about her health, Heledd turned back to the window, drawing deep breaths of the wintry air into her lungs, shaking off the sickness.

"There's a pretty sight."

Heledd held her breath, stiffening as though she had been frozen by a sudden pall of icy breath. She did not know the man's voice. She had not seen him enter the room. She had not even heard the door open or the boards of the floor creak under his weight. Her fingers dug into the frame of the window, holding fast to the only solid object she had near her and her only thought was if this man touched her, her child was in danger. Wherever Alys was, she made no sound. Heledd blocked everything from her mind but what she needed to know to protect her *baban*.

His voice told her he was still some distance away. Out of the corner of her eye she tried to judge whether she could reach the door to the corridor. Her only weapon was deep in her damask purse and to reach it, she would have to move. If the man had a weapon, nothing she could do would stop him. If she did nothing, he would kill her easily, even without a weapon. She edged slightly away, turning her body to the side to hide her left hand as she slid it down the wall to her purse, keeping the silver thimble from clinking while her fingers hunted for the tiny pair of shearing tongs. When she felt them in their leather sheath, she worked them free. Alys's muffled laugh came through the oak panels of the bed and Heledd heard the door whisper. *He's in my bed.* She held the tongs tight in her hand as she would a paring knife.

"What are you waiting for?" someone hissed. "She's alone and the door is bolted."

"What are you doing there?" the man she first heard asked. Heledd sensed the cupboard was open and he was coming through the sliding door.

"Who are you?" she asked, her voice breaking.

"Are you frightened, *menyw*?"

"What do you want?" she asked, trying to put strength in her voice. "Who are you?"

"Call me 'husband' for that is who I will be before dawn." Heledd turned her head slightly to catch a glimpse of the man who now stood in the room. Another man was half way out and put his foot on the floor. "By right of the eighth form of marriage – as Hywel has determined."

"I don't know that law," Heledd said.

"No? You only know the laws that suit you, is that it? The laws you can manipulate to steal from your betters?"

"Don't talk." Heledd heard a woman whisper. "Take her. Get it over with."

"I'll explain to you after it's done," the man growled at her as he lunged forward in the darkness. The other man came at her from the side of the room nearest the door. Heledd screamed and, as they grabbed her by the arms, lashed out at the first man with the tongs, stabbing into his gut. "Bitch." he gasped and pulled his arm back to punch her. Heledd lashed at the other man and dropped to the floor, dragging her arms out of their grasp. Behind the men, a woman screamed and the sides of the cupboard exploded, showering Heledd's assailants with splintered wood. She curled herself into a tight ball to protect her unborn child and covered her head with her arms, clenching the tongs in her fist.

"Threaten my wife again, Elgan, and I will kill you," Garmon said as he threw the *pennaeth's* eldest son against the wall and kicked the second man to the other side of the room.

"The others are out of the way," Geraint said, as he dropped to the floor of the room from the ruined cupboard.

Heledd pressed her back against the wall and pushed herself halfway into a sitting position as Garmon bent on one knee and pulled her against him. Heledd wrapped her arms around him and finally let out the breath she had held the moment Elgan spoke. "Are you hurt?" She shook her head against his chest. "We knew they were plotting but, until Alys brought you to this room, we weren't sure. Are you all right?"

"I bolted the door," Heledd said.

"I noticed. It is more robust than the doors at Bro-Dawel."

"How did you get in?"

"Meilor's secret passageway. Arwel told us about it as soon as we arrived."

"I didn't know," Heledd murmured, a shiver running through her body.

"Alys did, but you were in no danger until tonight," Garmon said, stroking her hair and bending his head to kiss her temple. "I'm sorry we weren't here sooner. Are you sure you're all right?" he asked a third time. When she nodded, he whispered, "And the *baban*?"

"Yes, we're fine."

"Get rid of those two and clean up this disorder. Do something about that door to the passageway, will you?" he said to Aled and Geraint, rising to his feet and lifting Heledd with him. "Put Alys in her husband's bed for now. Let her sleep off the drug there. She may enjoy his attentions better in that condition."

"Garmon," Heledd asked, curling into his arms as he carried her from the room, "what's the eighth form of marriage?"

"The acquisition of a wife by abduction and rape," he answered. "It's only legally binding if the woman is not already married."

"Which I am," she said, sliding her arms around his neck.

"Yes, in the first instance by the third law – when I slept with you with your uncle's consent – and most importantly, by the first: by mutual agreement, as equals."

"We have been married for a long time," Heledd pondered.

"More than a year, *gwraig*."

"I still think you should have told me sooner."

# tuuentʒ-eight

Garmon stretched his body, wondering how it had happened that sharing his bed with this woman resulted in such a narrow space for him and so wide for her. If not for his training to sleep wherever there was opportunity, he would not have been able to endure all the many, long months of restlessness and bad temper flung at him.

"What are you doing?" Heledd whimpered. "I was comfortable."

"I am not," Garmon replied, easing the cramp in his leg.

"Making me miserable eases your discomfort?" The infant in her womb gave its father a vicious kick in its mother's cause. Garmon winced and rubbed his side for a moment. "You deserved that," Heledd said, shifting laboriously onto her back. "Now, I cannot breathe."

"Take the bed," Garmon said, "I cannot sleep any longer."

"You think I have slept at all?"

Garmon knew better than to detail the number of times she had woken him while she slumbered on. "You will sleep better without me."

"How can you say that? I must have some support for my back."

He gazed at the mound beneath the *carthen* that had once been her soft, inviting belly and wondered if he would ever again entertain the idea of pleasure.

"Don't look at me like that. I know I'm ugly," was followed by a valiant effort to turn her back to him in tears. Garmon moved against her, lifting her side just enough to start the momentum of movement, positioned himself as her back rest and contented himself with another hour of providing Heledd with comfort and warmth. She sighed deeply, snuggling against him and was soon asleep again. Garmon stared at the wall, resting his chin on the top of her head. *How much longer?* First there were months of sickness and fatigue; then jubilation and tireless preparation; and finally months and months and months of complaints. This was that and that was this. Closing his eyes, Garmon tried to sleep but somehow his unborn child found yet another way to torment him. No matter where or how he draped his arm around his wife, the infant lashed out. Only by throwing the offending arm behind his own back and perching precariously at the edge of the bed could Garmon avoid the abuse.

"Can you not be still?" Heledd sighed.

"I am only a man," Garmon answered, "not a wall." He knew the moment he spoke that any contentment in life was over for a long time to come. "I will bring your breakfast," he offered as he left the warmth of the bed and dressed in the darkness.

Heledd listened while he stumbled around the furnishings in the room, holding her breath so he could not know she was angry and would not question her. *Go. Just go.*

Branwedd was the first of her friends to come into the longhouse while Heledd was eating the breakfast Garmon had left for her. Had she known he went hunting with Huw so early in the season, she might have been less sullen with her words of thanks. Her belly had grown so large she could not sit at the table and rested the small platter on the crest of the mound, balancing it precariously and righting it when the *baban* chose to kick out.

"Ach, I am tired of this," she said, running her hands down her swollen sides and under the protrusion to lift it off her thighs for a moment. "What are you doing today? It is so hot, I feel like a loaf in the oven."

"This house is cool," Branwedd said. "You should work in

the kitchen if you want to feel what it is to be hot."

"I know the perfect place," Heledd sighed, setting the platter on the stool beside her, "but I could never get there like this."

"Where is the perfect place?"

"On the Abbey *ystad*. Where the Tawel falls into a deep pool and trees dip their leaves in clear, fresh, cool water."

"Stop," Branwedd laughed. "I want to be there."

"Could we?" Heledd pleaded, pushing herself forward to the edge of the chair.

"You know you can't, Heledd. Goewin and Tegwen have told you."

"I am all swollen with heat. Look at me. Garmon can't stand to be near me. And he never makes love to me – not like he once did."

"That's not true."

"Then where is he? Why did he go hunting?"

"Is that what he told you?" Branwedd asked, pressing her lips hard together when Heledd turned a glare on her.

"He said Huw was going…and he had a mind to join him. Where is he?"

"He has taken some of his new men into the woodlands, to train them."

"He could have told me," Heledd pouted. "Ach, I wouldn't have heard him if he did. I can't stay in this house another minute, Branwedd. Let's go for a walk."

Branwedd found Heledd's shoes in the bedroom, pulled her friend from the chair and helped her put a loose fitting tunic over her summer frock. Bleddyn leapt to the door, wagging his hind quarters. Once outside, Heledd took a deep breath of the midsummer air and released it slowly, savoring its fragrance. The garden Meini had helped her plant was now in full bloom and the lavender flower heads shot up above the gray-green foliage, waving their purple tufts like Huw Bro-Dawel's deep violet banner above the *gaer* walls. Heledd had not developed any more interest in herbs or remedies but had enjoyed the cultivation of useful plants. While she dirtied her hands and toiled on her knees, Meini snipped and pruned what she needed from Heledd's garden as well as her own. To Heledd, the flowers and plants were their own reward. To Meini, they were just the beginning of their usefulness.

With Branwedd's help, she lowered her cumbersome body onto the stone bench Garmon had built for her so she could sit in her garden in the afternoons and evenings, after her work in the cheese vault or the *beudy*, her hands finally idle at the end of the day. The morning sun poured over the wall onto the long beds of comfrey and chamomile, evaporating the dew from the tips of the leaves and forcing the sunflowers to turn their heads to watch as the sun climbed higher above the copse between two rivers. Sitting beside her, Branwedd plucked a length of cloth from the pocket of her apron upon which she was embroidering an intricate pattern of circles and knots for her husband's padded jerkin.

Since Arwel had returned from Gwesyn, he had been promoted to command his own band of soldiers – two of whom had chosen to leave Meilor Gwesyn's service and their home district to accept service in Bro-Dawel. Branwedd and these two warriors were the only three of the seventeen Bannawg children who chose to leave Gwesyn.

The winter and spring had been hard in every district. Snow had fallen from the moment they had returned to celebrate the Nativity. When the snow stopped falling, the rivers began to swell. The chapel in the copse was flooded for weeks and had to be repainted once the water subsided. The *gaer* was above the flood plain when the snow melted and, for its inhabitants, the spring had been easier.

They had heard from the traders parts of Talgarth-y-Bannawg had fallen away in mudslides, taking much of Llew Talgarth's *gaer* with them. So many of Gwesyn's people had died over the winter the farmers were struggling to plough the fields.

"That's very pretty, Branwedd. Where did you learn needlework as fine as that?" Heledd asked, extending her hand to take the cloth.

"There was a needlewoman in Gwesyn's employ. We all had to learn another skill in addition to our work in the house."

"That is a worthy skill. Arwel will be proud to wear it."

"I hope so," Branwedd said. She had only accepted him as her husband a month before and was new to the duties of a commander's wife, as well as the privileges and pleasures.

"What are you doing?" Goewin demanded as she entered through the longhouse gate and pursed her lips at Heledd.

"I am going to the *beudy*," Heledd said, "but I wanted to sit in the garden for a while."

"You are not going to the *beudy*." Goewin exclaimed. "How can you even think of such a thing. You should be indoors, lying down."

"Ach, if I let you have your way, I would have been lying in bed for the last eight months – as soon as you found out I was pregnant, you have been like an old woman."

"I blame your husband." Goewin snapped. "He should never have allowed you to work. Look at you. You are exhausted."

"Ach, I am not. I am very well. Tegwen Talog said, right from the beginning, I am built for breeding."

"What does that woman know about you? You are delicate. You should not be in this sun. If you cannot think of yourself, think of your child."

"How will sun hurt my child?" Heledd laughed, leaning back against the stone wall of the garden and caressing her *baban*. "He is sleeping in the warmth of it."

"You are just like your mother. No one could tell her anything."

"My mother had seven healthy, safely born, children. I will have as many and more."

"Only if you do as you are told," Goewin said, extending her hand to help Heledd rise from the bench. Heledd gazed at the woman's hand. When she clasped it, she pulled it toward her to lay it on her belly. "Yes, I know. The *baban* sleeps ... now. But he will wake soon enough to bring havoc. You need to rest when you are able."

"I am resting. And I need to walk. I get such cramps when I am idle, Goewin. It's worse than when Garmon keeps me awake at night with his restless turning to and fro."

"What cramps?" Tegwen asked, standing at the gate.

"This is your doing," Goewin replied. "Telling her she needs to walk."

"I do," Heledd said, insisting Branwedd help her to stand. "Let's go into the *buarth*. It's cooler there." She arched her back, placing her hands above her hips until she was outside the garden. While she walked toward the *pennaeth's* house, she felt a dragging sensation in her thighs and stopped for a moment to take another breath. She had been kept awake through the night, if not by Garmon's agitation, by slow, gentle waves coursing through her muscles. Now they were stronger, forcing her to stop and concentrate on them.

The *buarth* was not as cool as she had hoped. The bustle of the harvest preparations were already in full force. Because the spring had been wet and warm, the planting had been earlier and the harvest was only a few weeks away. The soldiers who were not training or patrolling, were repairing and building. Across the *buarth*, the shoemaker waved to her, beckoning her to look at the shoes she had finally found time for him to fit for her. Meini's daughter, Angharad, stood at the door of the apothecary, holding a bouquet of wild flowers. Meini, now carrying Geraint's firstborn, laid her hand on her little girl's head and waved. Heledd responded with a raised hand just as Mared rode through the gates of the *gaer*.

"You look like a huge, wine-soaked cloud," she laughed as she rode past, her own slender figure restored since the birth of her son, Rhydian, two months before.

"Don't let her upset you," Rhian told her, still nearly as round as she was when she was pregnant with her own child. "Some women are just meant to be blades of grass." She carried her seven-week old daughter wrapped close to her body in a linen shawl. "Ceinwen is the same, just like a twig. And Meleri. Thank goodness Camwy is like us," she said, glancing down at Heledd's expanse. She looked over her shoulder at the three women standing behind Heledd. "You'll be as glad to be relieved of this *baban* as I was, I'm sure," she whispered.

"Are you well?" Heledd asked, laying her hand on the top of the curly brown head of Nisien's daughter protruding from the cream-colored shawl.

"Tegwen told me I would soon forget," Rhian said. "You do, eventually."

"Hmmm," Heledd agreed, remembering the birth of Camwy's daughter, Medi. She was too close to her own time, both Tegwen and Goewin had told her, to be allowed to assist with either Rhian or Mared. "We don't want you giving birth at the same time," they had scolded, chasing her from the *hafod*. Heledd raised her hands and twisted her heavy braid off the back of her neck. "I will probably be roasted to a crisp before this one comes."

She continued toward Martyn the shoemaker's workshop, gratefully sitting under the canopy and allowing him to give her one final fitting before he declared the shoes were ready. He had used suede and dyed them with bark. She had to hold her leg up straight in front of her to see them and could only see they fit well. She had seen the quality of the suede and the fine stitching when she held them a few days past, before he had put the second layers of the soles and heels on. He fastened the buckle and invited her to stand in them. Heledd looked into his face for a moment, smiling slightly.

"I can't, Martyn," she said. "I'm having my *baban*...at the moment." The shoemaker leapt away from her as though he had been kicked and turned to the women near her. Heledd took a deep breath and called Bleddyn to her side. "Find your master," she murmured as she gave the staghound the only command she had ever needed.

When he mustered his command at dawn, Garmon had felt a sense of power and control he had seen the need of in past weeks. Within four hours, he had led his men far from the stifling confines of any inhabited area of the Bro-Dawel *ystad* to the very edge of land. He had divided the twenty recruits into four units, each with the task of finding the other three while remaining hidden themselves. The exercise was unfair for such inexperienced men but it gave him time to be alone and a way of assessing their potential. None of them were older than Geraint nor more than six months younger than Carwyn.

Garmon had been thinking about the need for a stronger army since his return from his second reconnaissance to Gwesyn and Talgarth at the end of spring. The dissatisfaction among the people on both *ystad* was dangerous, made even more dangerous by their lack of loyalty and discipline. Garmon now believed that one or two factions would rebel against Gwesyn that would spark desertion at Talgarth. Alienated warbands at harvest or during the winter would be a concern for the whole of the southern region, considering Hywel's treaty with Wessex. If Hywel called on him, Garmon was ready.

He rested his hands on the crown of the saddle and stared at the endless expanse of sea to the south. The cliff beneath him and the woods behind shielded him from observation. He straightened his back and closed his gloved hand on *Diawl's* reins, pressing his knee to the warhorse's shoulder to turn east again, toward the *gaer*. The sun had crested the sky and begun its afternoon journey behind him when he heard the staghounds baying in the green wood. With a broad smile, Garmon turned the warhorse to the north and set an easy gallop toward the hunting band.

Once within the quiet freshness of the woods, he slowed *Diawl* to a cantor, listening carefully for the thrash of hooves and the hounds' panting as they chased their quarry. He could hear the two hounds he had lent his stepfather baying further north. As he urged his horse to the chase in that direction, he heard the voices of three hounds, one in answer to the others. Garmon felt his heart clench. "*Uffern.*" He jerked the warhorse toward the *gaer*. When he crashed through the undergrowth out of the woods, he could see Heledd's staghound chasing his scent toward the sea. Garmon gave a sharp whistle and the hound whipped around to follow him home. *Diawl* was at full speed and the staghound fell behind, slowing to a trot, its mission completed. Even at full gallop, the warhorse could not reach the *gaer* in less than half an hour. He blocked his mind from what he could not know.

That Heledd had been alive when she sent the hound to find him was only a small solace. The dog would have taken an hour to get as far as he did, following Garmon's scent and whatever false trails had distracted him. He thought through the faces of the warriors who would be in the *gaer* to help her. His mind failed him for a moment when he imagined they had all taken the opportunity to escape the heat and drudgery to enjoy themselves in the early hunt. Who among them, besides himself, would leave her alone, unprotected? What enemy had come?

He was on the ground and running into the *gaer* before *Diawl* had come to the gates – open gates. Aled and Geraint were running through the *buarth* to meet him. A boy had caught *Diawl's* reins and led the winded animal toward the stables.

"Between myself and God, I thought you wouldn't make it," Aled called, turning back toward the longhouse. Geraint stopped long enough to take a few breaths and followed again on Garmon's heels. Outside his house, stewards, warriors and the shoemaker stood in silent groups. When they saw Garmon running toward them they stepped aside. Aled threw open the door of the house, shouting, "He's here."

When Garmon burst into the room, he came to a sudden halt, staring at the sea of women's faces turned toward him. He pushed through the crowd. Their silence cut into his flesh as though he had run onto a battlefield. The door of his bedroom flew open and he pushed through it, past Meini and Ceinwen, the only faces he recognized.

"Praise be to God," Goewin whispered, coming toward him with her hands outstretched. "She's been calling for you for hours."

"I never thought I would be happy to see *your* face," Mared commented, getting up from kneeling by the bed. "This has been unbearable."

"Don't ask me how," Tegwen told him in a low voice, laying her hand on Garmon's shoulder, "but she has been determined to hold on until you arrived." Camwy and Meleri stepped away from the bed to let him closer. Garmon closed his eyes a moment and swallowed hard before taking their places, bending one knee to the floor. Heledd's eyes were closed, the lids stained dark purple. Her cheeks were blotched and her lips were pale.

"Heledd," he murmured, taking her hand and pressing her fingers to his lips.

"I thought you'd never come," she whispered, opening her eyes. "Where have you been?"

"I'm here now," he answered. "I won't leave you again."

"What were you thinking? You must have known I would need you," she croaked, laying her free hand on his wrist.

"I'm here now," he replied, bowing his head slightly.

"Your son is impatient to be born and you have been enjoying a ride in the woods," Heledd complained. "Help me to sit." Garmon glanced at Tegwen, a doubtful frown on his forehead. "What are you looking at her for? Help me up. It's the least you can do since you've made me wait all these hours."

"Step back, Garmon," Goewin told him once Heledd was on her feet. "We can manage without you now."

"No, stay with me," Heledd pouted, grabbing his hand.

"Heledd, it's better if he goes," Tegwen said.

"I'm not having this *baban* alone," Heledd declared, pulling herself into Garmon's arms. "Just hold me," she whispered, turning her back to him and crouching by the bed with a cry from a place deep within her most primitive being. Goewin wiped the sweat from her foster child's brow and Tegwen knelt ready with linen toweling in her arms. Meini patted Garmon's shoulder as she gave Heledd a sip of water.

"You're all right," Mared murmured, holding Heledd's left hand while Ceinwen held the right and Garmon crouched behind her with his arms enfolding her and his child. "Your *baban* is almost here, Heledd. You're all right now."

Heledd threw her head back against Garmon's shoulder, looking up at him. "Thank you," she sighed, kissed her husband's granite-like jaw and bore down with all her might to push her son into the world.

Garmon's face was still ghost-like when he stepped into the

twilight of the midsummer evening to the silent faces surrounding his door. The women in the house were already at work. Aled was the first to approach his foster brother. Geraint stood nearby, peering into the house to catch a glimpse of his own wife.

"Garmon," Aled asked under his breath, "are you all right? What's happened?"

Garmon turned to look at his closest friend, the trace of a smile forming and disappearing at the corner of his mouth. "A boy," he said. "So small. They wouldn't let me hold him."

"Don't listen to him," Mared said, pushing past and running into Rheinallt's arms. "She's had the most enormous, strapping big brute of a boy I've ever seen," she told her husband. "And now she's hungry. Wait until you see him. He's the image of my stepmother, you know. I would not have believed it."

Before she finished giving the news, a cheer rose from the crowd of watchers and the bonfire built quietly in the *buarth*, in the hope Garmon's firstborn would arrive safely, was ablaze. Jugs of ale and mead appeared from every *hafod*.

"Heledd wants to call him Owein," Mared continued, "after his grandmother and Tawel after our river. Garmon, poor soul, has not offered any opinion. I don't think he knows what day it is anymore. You're fortunate," she told her husband, "I didn't do the same thing to you. I like this idea, now I've thought about it."

"No," Rheinallt said, looking at Garmon's bloodless face. "Never in all God's creation."

"Coward," Mared laughed, hugging him around the chest.

Owein Tawel *mab* Garmon *wyr* Ieuan Bannawg *llyswyr* Huw screeched his anger at the way he had been treated and turned his head to his mother's breast as soon as the midwives had bathed and wrapped him in linen swaddling. Unimpressed by their admiration, he closed his eyes and was asleep as soon as his mother lowered her eyes to gaze at him.

"Grandson or granddaughter?" Huw demanded as he entered his stepson's house and was shushed by twenty different female voices. "A simple answer is enough," he bellowed, opening the bedroom door with more care. "I'm told he looks like my wife," Huw murmured as he bent over the head of his third grandchild.

"You tell me," Heledd said, smiling into the *pennaeth's* beaming face. Huw nodded, scratching a tear from the corner of his eye. "Have you seen Garmon? Is he all right?"

"He'll recover. The first one is always a shock," Huw replied, sitting on the edge of the bed and taking the *baban* into his arms. "Are you certain about this name you've given him?"

"Don't you like it?"

"Garmon is already boasting. Aled has threatened to drown him."

"That's only just," Heledd replied, caressing the top of Owein's head.

"He has Creiddwen's eyes," Huw said. "And his father's. Her hair was this color, like Carwyn. Set this little one between his father and his uncle and all the world will see my wife in them."

o o o o o

# GLOSSARY

In most instances, the following words are used so their meaning is explained within the context of the story. I have taken a few liberties with the plural, adjective and possessive forms of some words. Welsh follows the Latin & other Romance languages noun/adjective (as in *vin rouge / vino rosso / gwin coch*) rather than the Teutonic adjective/noun (red wine) but to do that in a book written in English would be a step too far. I wanted to use some Welsh to give some flavor of the language Heledd and her friends speak.

Welsh also uses a similar form of expressing ownership: the object is dominant and the owner is subordinate: her cloak is *ei chlogyn hi*. Heledd's cloak is *clogyn Heledd*. For the purposes of this story, I have used the English possessive construction of adding 'apostrophe s'. I simplified the mutations that occur in specific juxtapositions of words starting with certain letters, such as in *ei chlogyn hi*: *ei* designates (in this instance) female when followed by *hi*. If followed by '*e*' then the mutation is male and is *ei glogyn e*. These mutations are the aspirate and soft mutations, respectively. There is also the nasal mutation.

You can hear how these words are pronounced on many online Welsh language sites. The emphasis is almost always on the next to last syllable, as in most Romance languages.

Welsh vowels are the same as in Italian, open and full - one of the reasons why Welsh is called the language of heaven. Welsh also has more vowels than English, not just "and sometimes Y and W": AEIOUYW.

Annwn: underworld (AHN-noon)

Annwyl: dear (AHN-nooeel)

Baban: infant (BAH-bahn)

Bardd: poet (BAHRTH – DD is always pronounced as the 'th' in 'with')

Boneddiges/Bonheddig: lady / gentleman (bohn-eTH-I-ges/bohn-ETH-ig)

*Buarth*: farm yard (BEE-ahrth – th is always as in 'thin'

Beudy: milking parlor/shed (BAY-dee)

Caer: fort (CEYER)

Calan Gaeaf: beginning of winter, All Hallows' Eve (CAHL-ahn GEYE-ahv)

Carthen: blanket (CAHR-then)

Diawl: devil (DEE-awl)

Gwraig: wife (GOOR-eyeg)

Gwyddbwyll: a board game, similar to Chess (GWITH-booell – 'LL' is aspirated - this is a tricky letter! Tongue at the roof of your mouth, blow an L sound without annunciating.)

Hafod(ydd): small house(s) (HAHV-od/hahv-OD-iTH)

Llys: court (LLEES)

Mab: son (MAHB)

Meddyg: medic (METH-ig)

Menyw: woman (MEHN-you)

Merch: daughter, girl (MEHRCH – CH is hard as in 'loch')

Pennaeth: chieftain/leader (PEHN- neyeth

Porth: entry way to house or castle (POHRTH)

Trwsus: trousers/leggings (TROO-sis)

Uffern: hell (EE-ffehrn)

Uwd: porridge (EE-ood)

Ystad: estate of land (UH-stahd)

o o o o o

Thank you for reading *Traitor's Daughter*, the story of Heledd and Garmon. If you have enjoyed this book, you may enjoy the planned sequel, *Vengeance's Son*:

*Raised on a hunger for vengeance, Meilor Gwesyn's grandson plans to abduct Anwen Garmon – the daughter of his mother's despised cousin, Heledd, but Anwen has her own plans for Gwesyn Gwern.*

*Vengeance's Son*, Fall 2014

You may also enjoy the other novels I have written set in 9th and 10th Century Wales. These include the series, *Pendyffryn: The Conquerors*:

*Invasion, Book 1*, November 2012
*Salvation, Book 2*, January 2013
*Betrayal, Book 3*, March 2013
*Revival, Book 4*, June 2013
*Reconciliation, Book 5*, January 2014

Reader's Comments about *Traitor's Daughter*

"I like the premise of the story and the setting a lot. It's not an era that's been done a lot, so that's a good thing. I like how manipulative Alys is…. And now you have left me hanging, you temptress!"—Lizzie W.

"Well researched and written. …I loved your characters."—Judy C.

"I enjoyed reading this awesome book."—Denise P.

"I loved Garmon. I think about Heledd and Garmon all the time."—Celeste A.

"...I thought this book was awesome. The story has depth and I liked being swept back in time. The plot is great. ...I find myself thinking about this story days later."—Tifferz Book Reviews, May 2012

For *Invasion*:

"Your writing and craftsmanship are absolutely lovely. This is a wonderful story and I was very engaged in it. ...It is wonderful and epic."—Christa D.

o o o o o

# ABOUT THE AUTHOR

Lily Dewaruile is the pen name of an American author who lived in Cymru/Wales for thirty years, an immigrant to this Celtic country who fell in love with the language and the history as well as *un Cymro arbennig* (one special Welshman). While she and her Cymro were raising three fine young men, Lily continued her writing about her adopted country, set in one of her favorite periods in its history, the 9th and 10th Centuries.

Her novels reflect her deep admiration for the people whose strength and commitment to their way of life and culture, endure and overpower those who come to conquer. Though none of her characters, nor the events of these novels, are real, they reflect the spirit and essence of Cymru.

If you would like to share your thoughts about *Traitor's Daughter* or *Pendyffryn: The Conquerors*, please contact Lily:
http://facebook.com/LilyDewaruile
http://lilydewaruile.wordpress.com
http://goodreads.com
or visit my website, http://lilydewaruile.com
or Twitter: @LilyDewaruile.

Diolch yn fawr,

*Lily Dewaruile*